UP TO NO GHOUL

HarperAlley is an imprint of HarperCollins Publishers.

Up to No Ghoul
Text copyright © 2022 by Cullen Bunn
Illustrations copyright © 2022 by Cat Farris
All rights reserved. Manufactured in Italy.
Library of Congress Control Number: 2021950886
ISBN 978-0-06-289613-1 — ISBN 978-0-06-289612-4 (pbk.)

The artist used Clip Studio Paint, ink, watercolor, and mixed
media paper to create the illustrations for this book.
Typography by Rick Farley
22 23 24 25 26 RTLO 10 9 8 7 6 5 4 3 2 1
First Edition

UP TO NO GHOUL

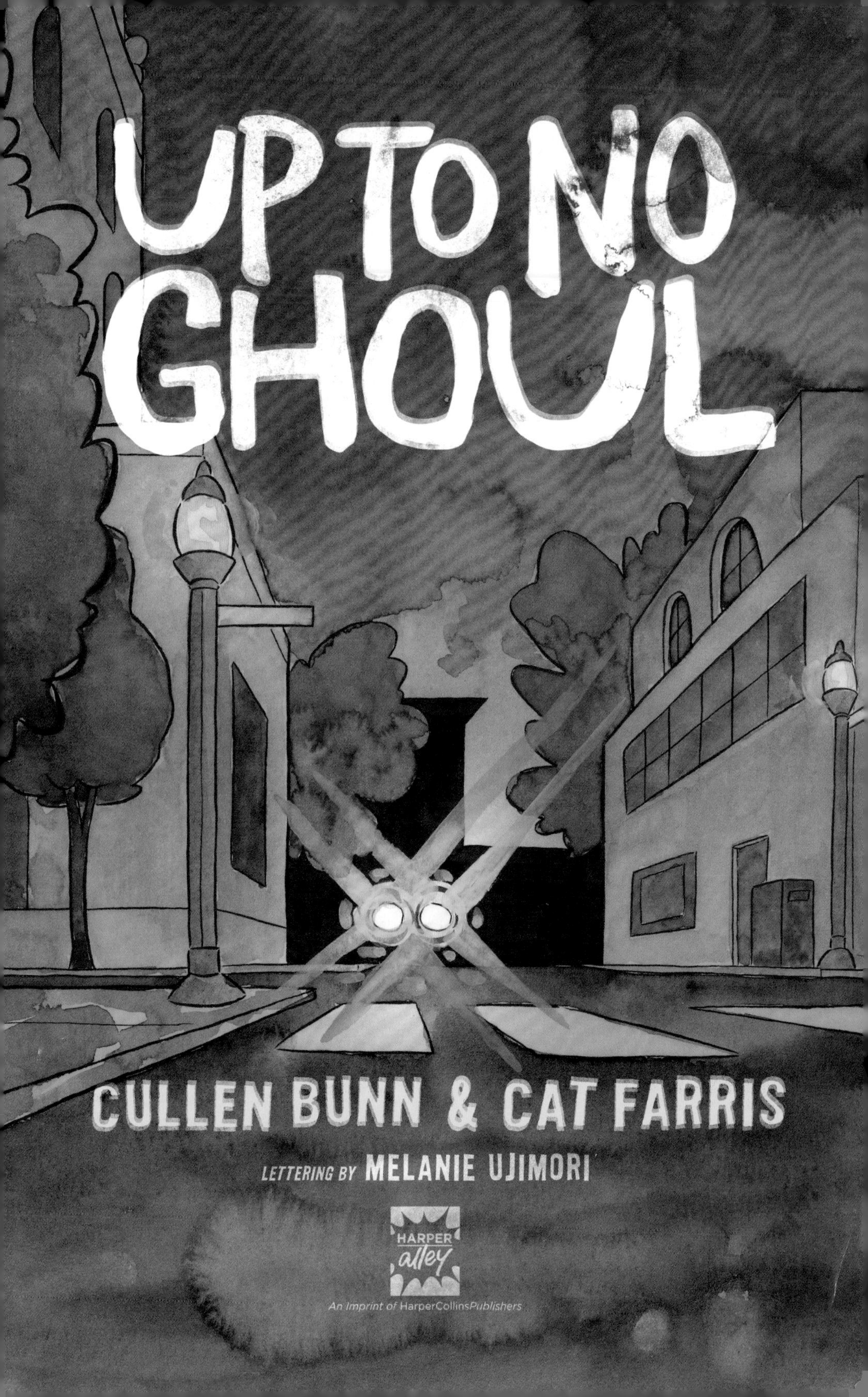

CULLEN BUNN & CAT FARRIS

LETTERING BY MELANIE UJIMORI

HARPER alley
An Imprint of HarperCollinsPublishers

For Anton, who might love ghouls even more than me.

—C.B.

For Jesse Hamm; thank you for being a friend.

—C.F.

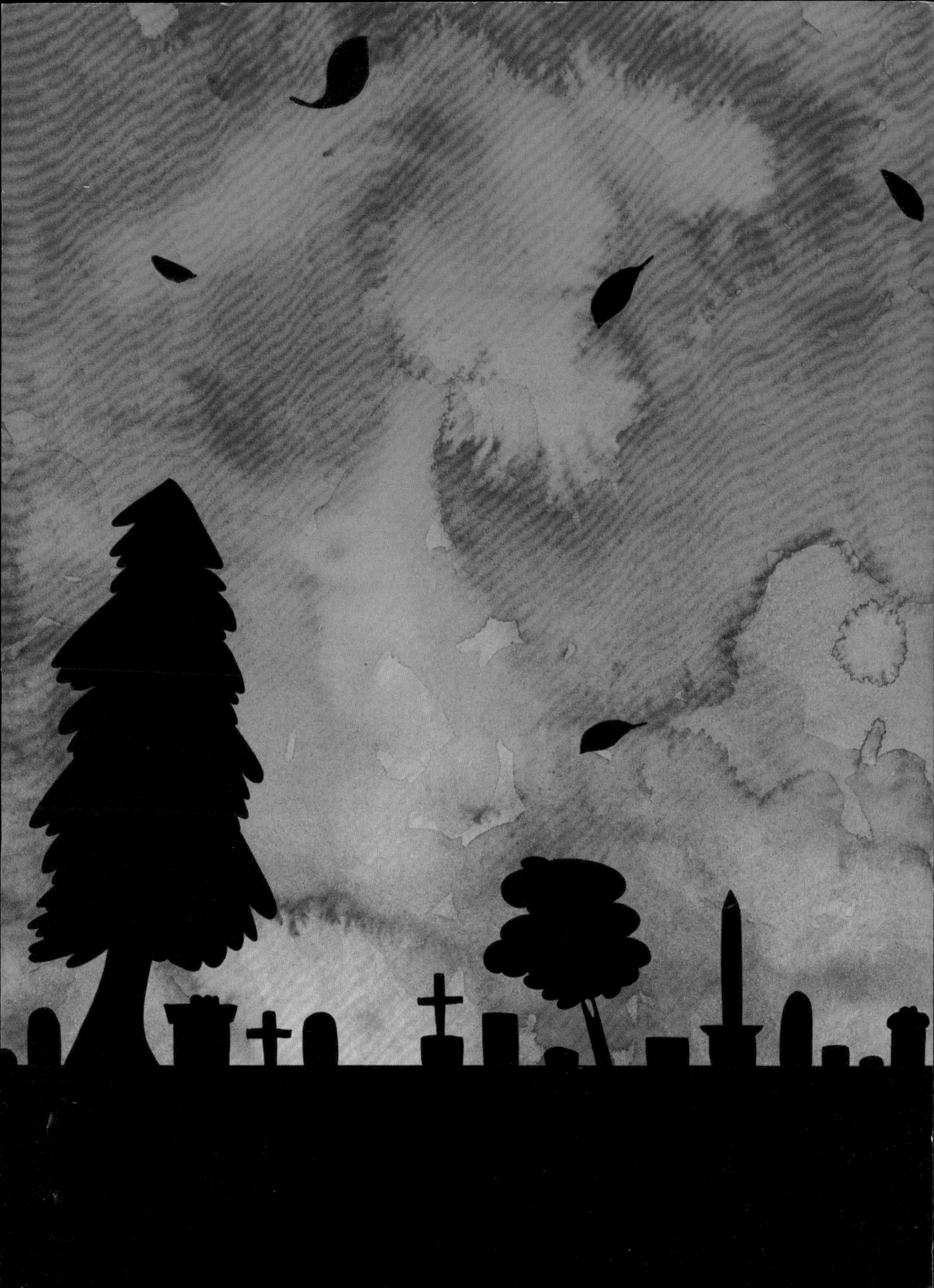

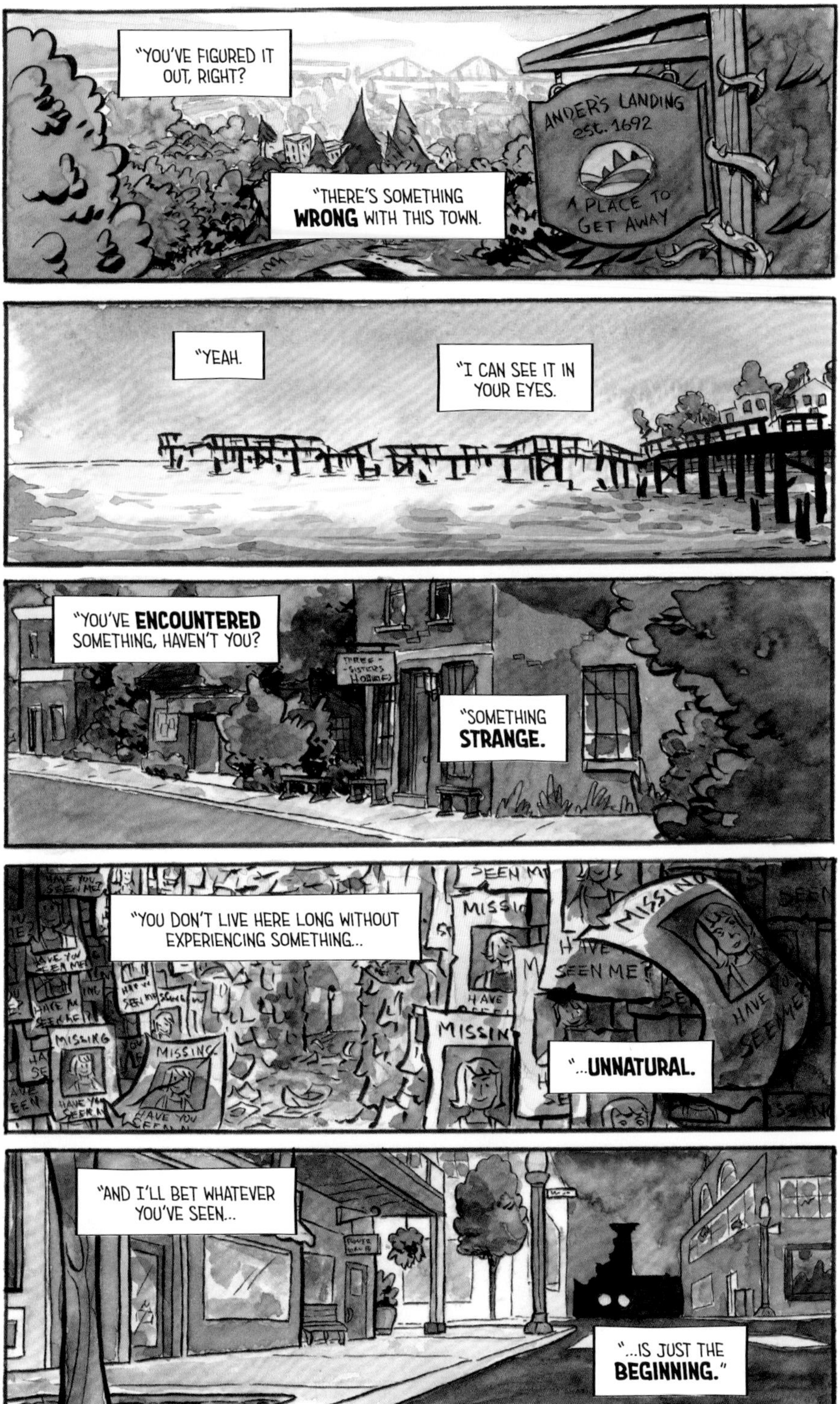

"YOU'VE FIGURED IT OUT, RIGHT?
ANDER'S LANDING
est. 1692
A PLACE TO GET AWAY
"THERE'S SOMETHING **WRONG** WITH THIS TOWN.
"YEAH.
"I CAN SEE IT IN YOUR EYES.
"YOU'VE **ENCOUNTERED** SOMETHING, HAVEN'T YOU?
"SOMETHING **STRANGE.**
"YOU DON'T LIVE HERE LONG WITHOUT EXPERIENCING SOMETHING...
MISSING
HAVE YOU SEEN ME?
"...**UNNATURAL.**
"AND I'LL BET WHATEVER YOU'VE SEEN...
"...IS JUST THE **BEGINNING.**"

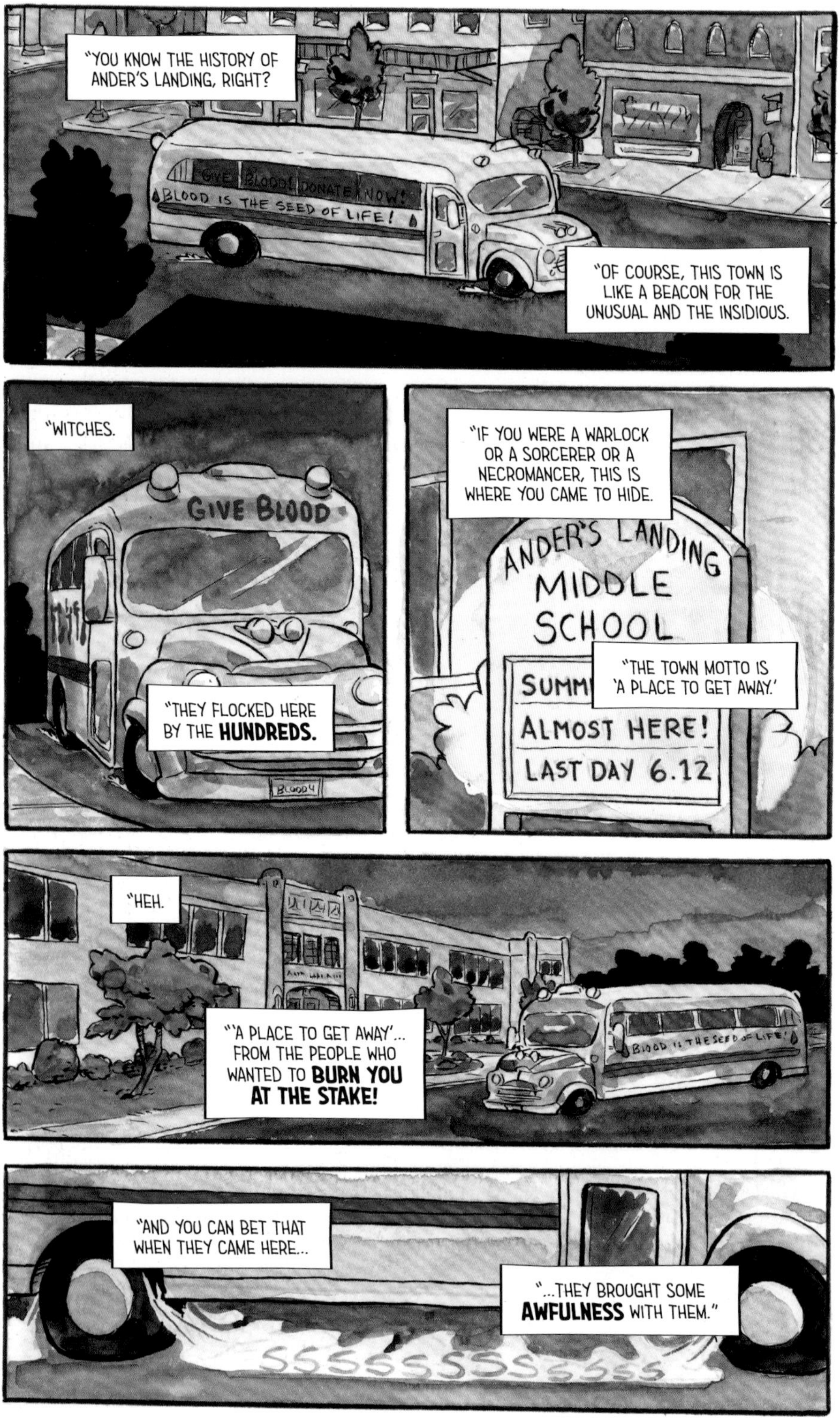
"YOU KNOW THE HISTORY OF ANDER'S LANDING, RIGHT?
GIVE BLOOD! DONATE NOW!
BLOOD IS THE SEED OF LIFE!
"OF COURSE, THIS TOWN IS LIKE A BEACON FOR THE UNUSUAL AND THE INSIDIOUS.
"WITCHES.
GIVE BLOOD
"THEY FLOCKED HERE BY THE **HUNDREDS.**
BLOOD4
"IF YOU WERE A WARLOCK OR A SORCERER OR A NECROMANCER, THIS IS WHERE YOU CAME TO HIDE.
ANDER'S LANDING MIDDLE SCHOOL
SUMM
ALMOST HERE!
LAST DAY 6.12
"THE TOWN MOTTO IS 'A PLACE TO GET AWAY.'
"HEH.
"'A PLACE TO GET AWAY'... FROM THE PEOPLE WHO WANTED TO **BURN YOU AT THE STAKE!**
BLOOD IS THE SEED OF LIFE!
"AND YOU CAN BET THAT WHEN THEY CAME HERE...
"...THEY BROUGHT SOME **AWFULNESS** WITH THEM."
SSSSSSSSSSSSSS

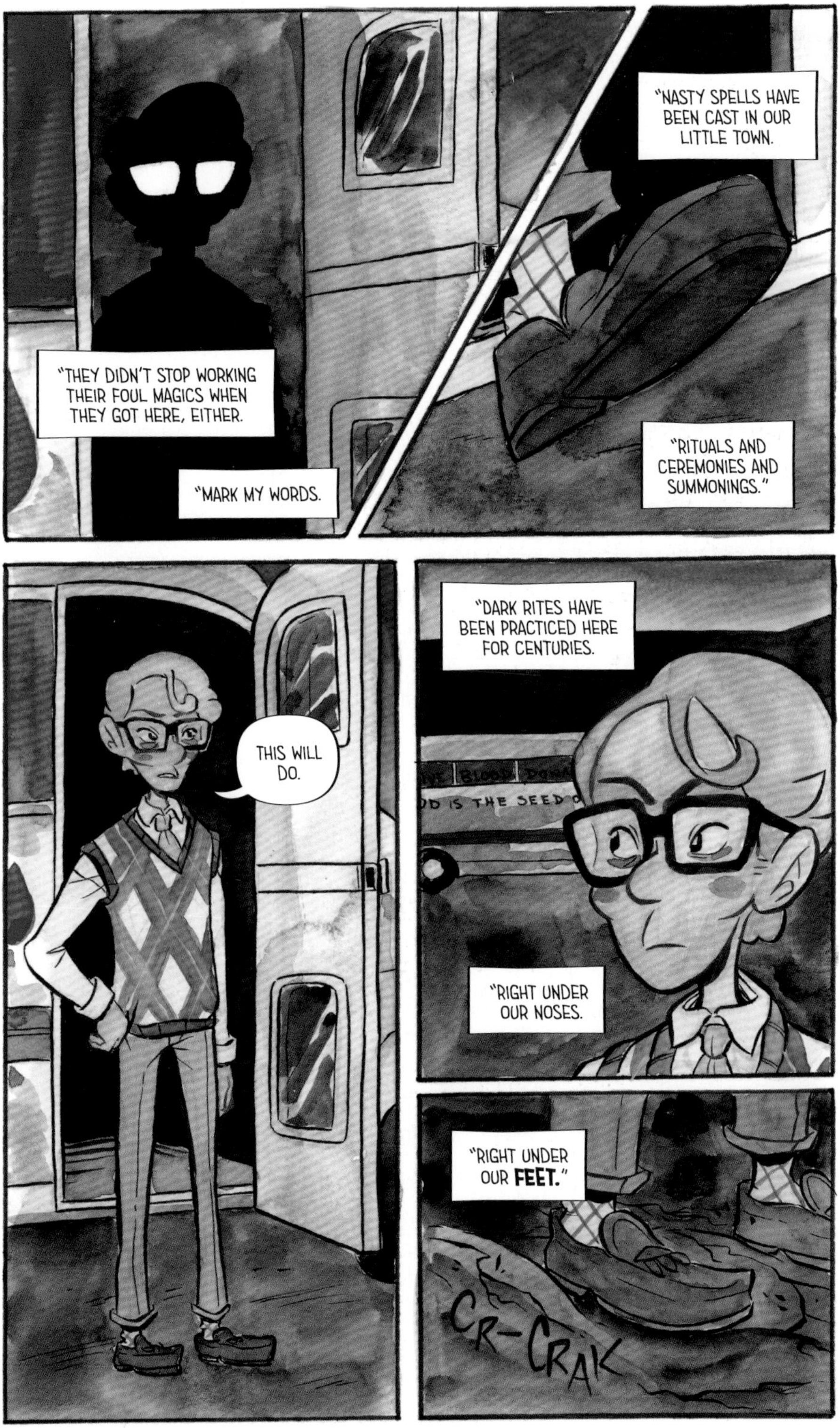
"THEY DIDN'T STOP WORKING THEIR FOUL MAGICS WHEN THEY GOT HERE, EITHER.
"MARK MY WORDS.
"NASTY SPELLS HAVE BEEN CAST IN OUR LITTLE TOWN.
"RITUALS AND CEREMONIES AND SUMMONINGS."
THIS WILL DO.
"DARK RITES HAVE BEEN PRACTICED HERE FOR CENTURIES.
"RIGHT UNDER OUR NOSES.
"RIGHT UNDER OUR **FEET.**"
CR-CRAK

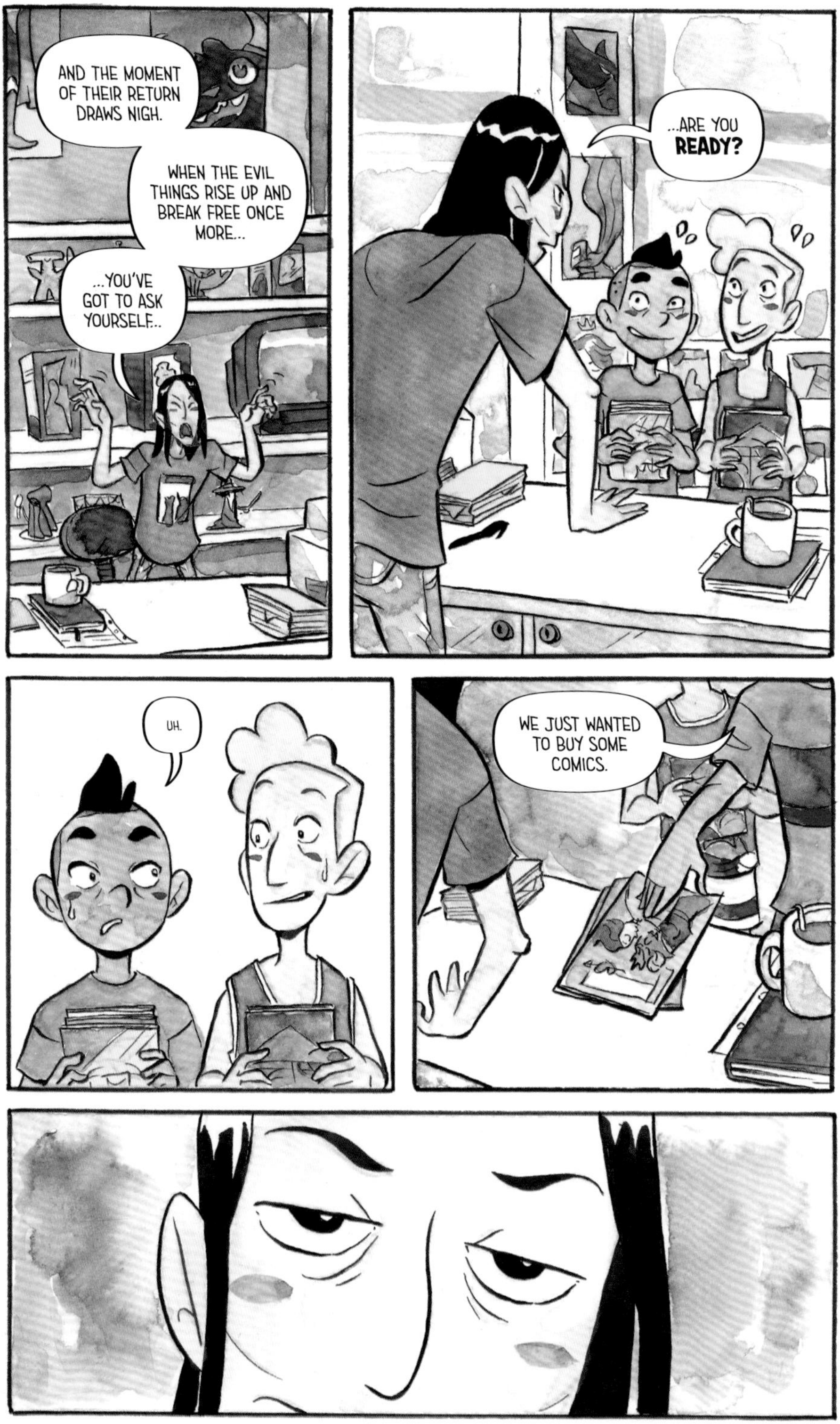
AND THE MOMENT OF THEIR RETURN DRAWS NIGH.
WHEN THE EVIL THINGS RISE UP AND BREAK FREE ONCE MORE...
...YOU'VE GOT TO ASK YOURSELF...
...ARE YOU **READY?**
UH.
WE JUST WANTED TO BUY SOME COMICS.

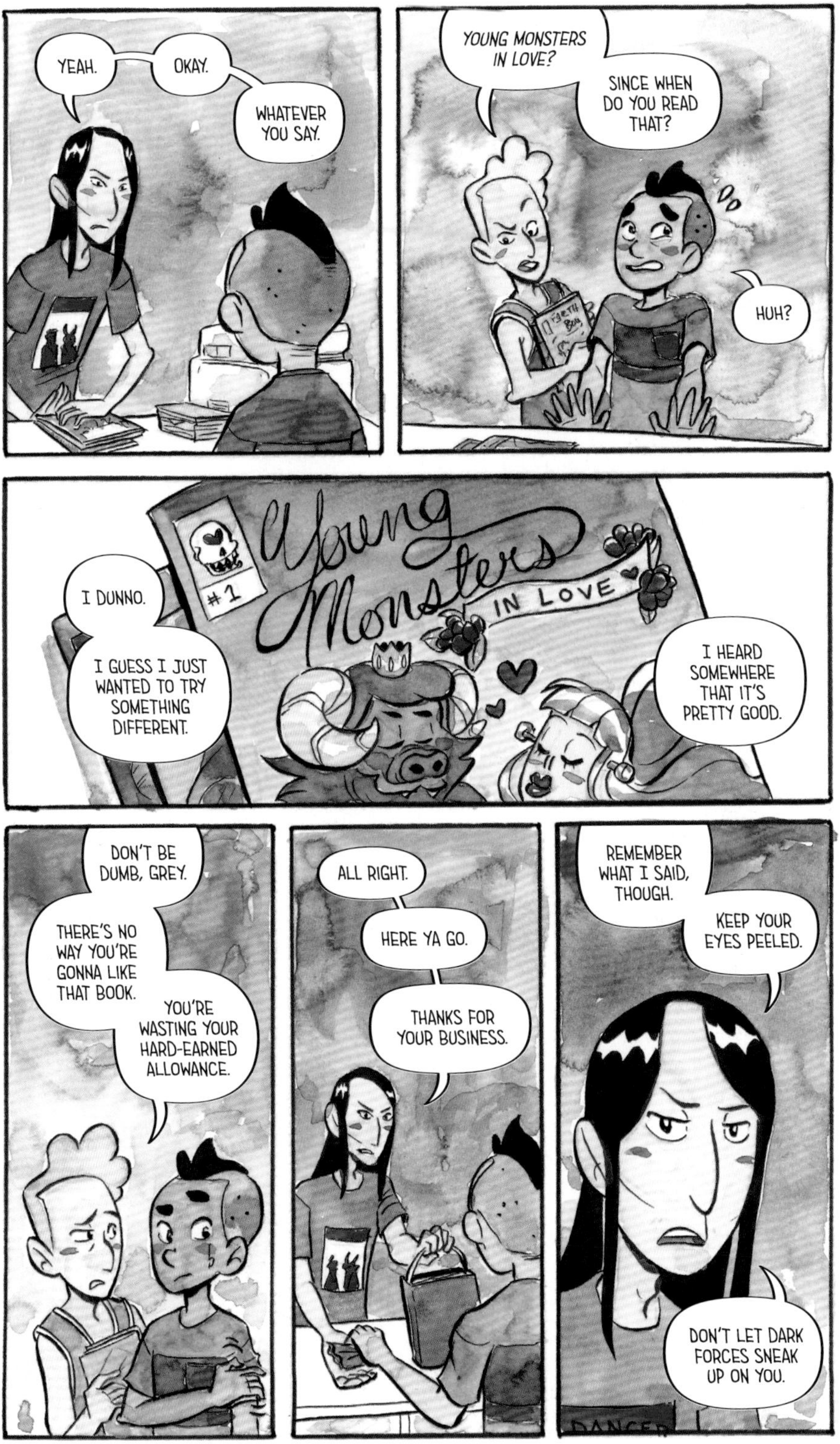
YEAH.
OKAY.
WHATEVER YOU SAY.
YOUNG MONSTERS IN LOVE?
SINCE WHEN DO YOU READ THAT?
HUH?
Young Monsters IN LOVE
#1
I DUNNO.
I GUESS I JUST WANTED TO TRY SOMETHING DIFFERENT.
I HEARD SOMEWHERE THAT IT'S PRETTY GOOD.
DON'T BE DUMB, GREY.
THERE'S NO WAY YOU'RE GONNA LIKE THAT BOOK.
YOU'RE WASTING YOUR HARD-EARNED ALLOWANCE.
ALL RIGHT.
HERE YA GO.
THANKS FOR YOUR BUSINESS.
REMEMBER WHAT I SAID, THOUGH.
KEEP YOUR EYES PEELED.
DON'T LET DARK FORCES SNEAK UP ON YOU.

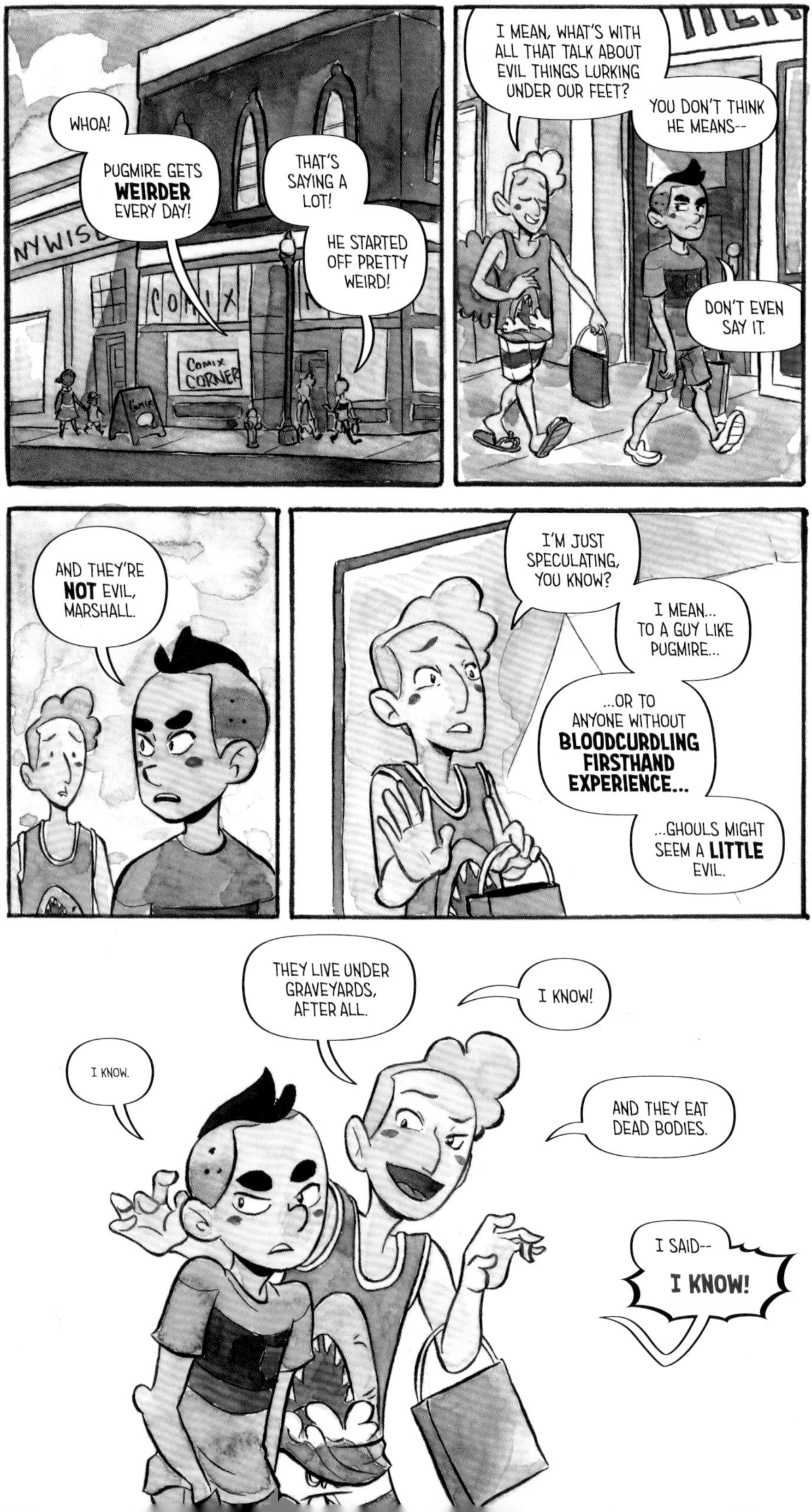
WHOA!
PUGMIRE GETS **WEIRDER** EVERY DAY!
THAT'S SAYING A LOT!
HE STARTED OFF PRETTY WEIRD!
COMIX
Comix CORNER
I MEAN, WHAT'S WITH ALL THAT TALK ABOUT EVIL THINGS LURKING UNDER OUR FEET?
YOU DON'T THINK HE MEANS--
DON'T EVEN SAY IT.
AND THEY'RE **NOT** EVIL, MARSHALL.
I'M JUST SPECULATING, YOU KNOW?
I MEAN... TO A GUY LIKE PUGMIRE...
...OR TO ANYONE WITHOUT **BLOODCURDLING FIRSTHAND EXPERIENCE...**
...GHOULS MIGHT SEEM A **LITTLE** EVIL.
THEY LIVE UNDER GRAVEYARDS, AFTER ALL.
I KNOW!
I KNOW.
AND THEY EAT DEAD BODIES.
I SAID--
I KNOW!

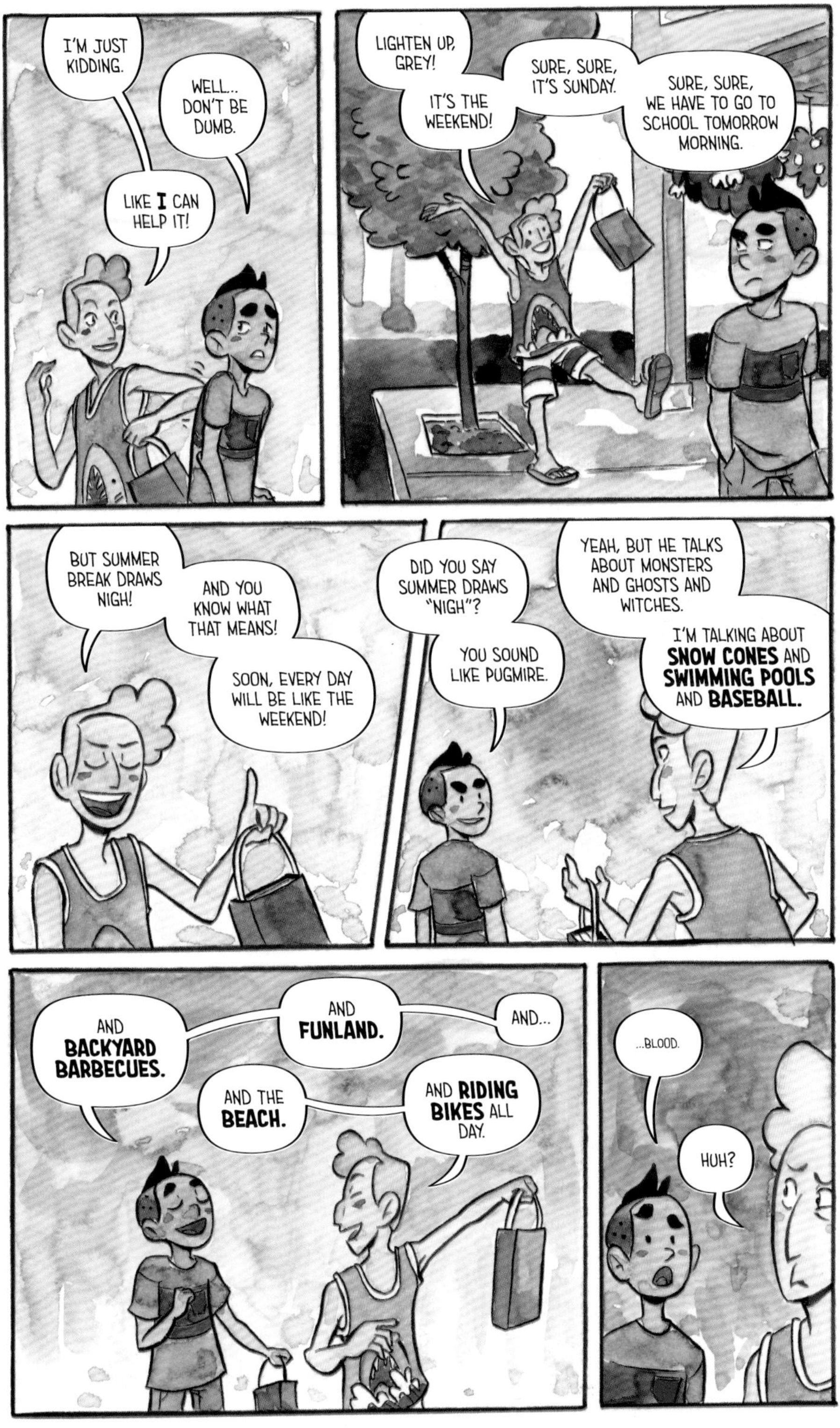
I'M JUST KIDDING.
WELL... DON'T BE DUMB.
LIKE **I** CAN HELP IT!
LIGHTEN UP, GREY!
IT'S THE WEEKEND!
SURE, SURE, IT'S SUNDAY.
SURE, SURE, WE HAVE TO GO TO SCHOOL TOMORROW MORNING.
BUT SUMMER BREAK DRAWS NIGH!
AND YOU KNOW WHAT THAT MEANS!
SOON, EVERY DAY WILL BE LIKE THE WEEKEND!
DID YOU SAY SUMMER DRAWS "NIGH"?
YOU SOUND LIKE PUGMIRE.
YEAH, BUT HE TALKS ABOUT MONSTERS AND GHOSTS AND WITCHES.
I'M TALKING ABOUT **SNOW CONES** AND **SWIMMING POOLS** AND **BASEBALL.**
AND **BACKYARD BARBECUES.**
AND **FUNLAND.**
AND...
AND THE **BEACH.**
AND **RIDING BIKES** ALL DAY.
...BLOOD.
HUH?

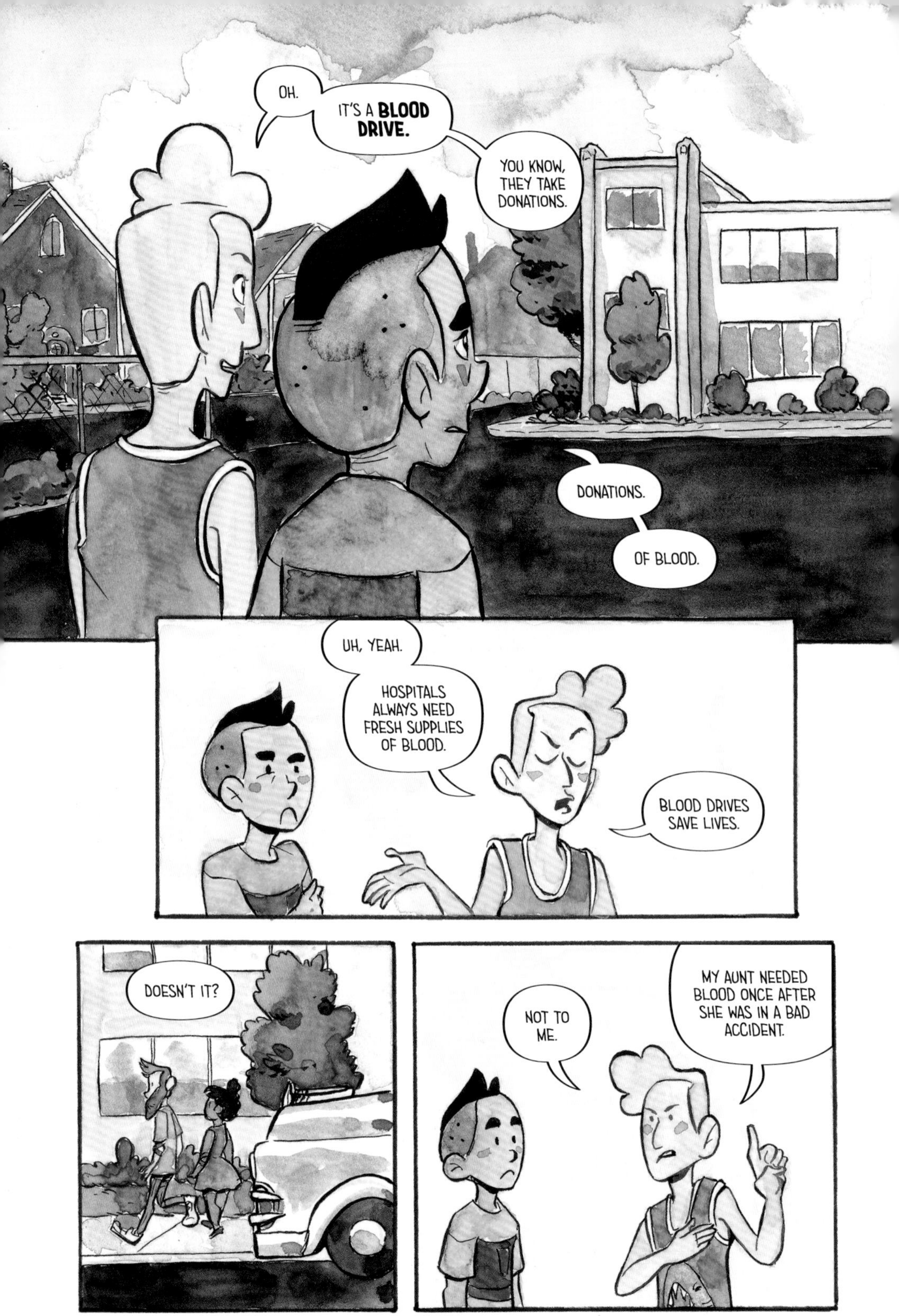
OH.
IT'S A **BLOOD DRIVE.**
YOU KNOW, THEY TAKE DONATIONS.
DONATIONS.
OF BLOOD.
UH, YEAH.
HOSPITALS ALWAYS NEED FRESH SUPPLIES OF BLOOD.
BLOOD DRIVES SAVE LIVES.
DOESN'T IT?
NOT TO ME.
MY AUNT NEEDED BLOOD ONCE AFTER SHE WAS IN A BAD ACCIDENT.

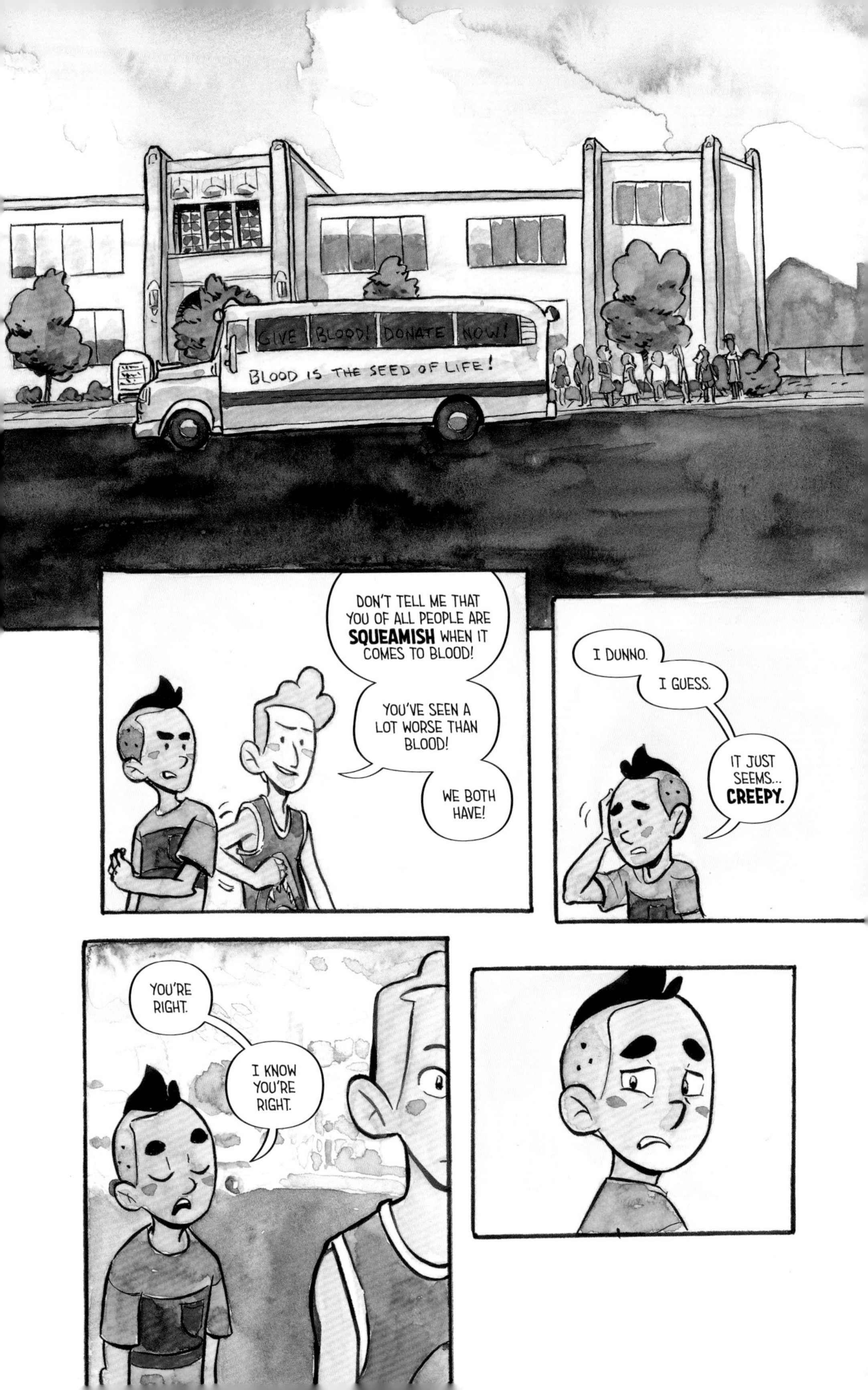
GIVE BLOOD! DONATE NOW!
BLOOD IS THE SEED OF LIFE!
DON'T TELL ME THAT YOU OF ALL PEOPLE ARE **SQUEAMISH** WHEN IT COMES TO BLOOD!
YOU'VE SEEN A LOT WORSE THAN BLOOD!
WE BOTH HAVE!
I DUNNO.
I GUESS.
IT JUST SEEMS... **CREEPY.**
YOU'RE RIGHT.
I KNOW YOU'RE RIGHT.

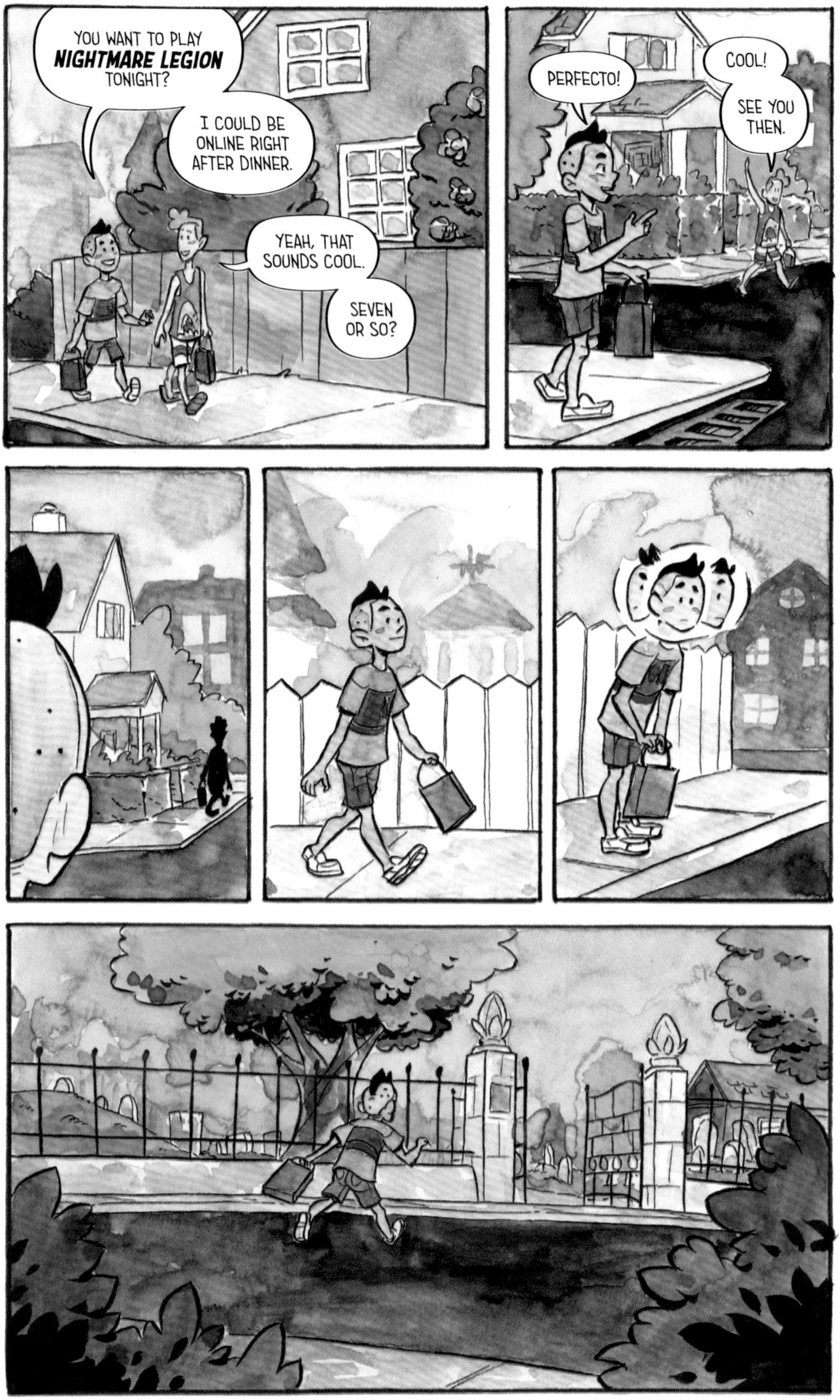
YOU WANT TO PLAY NIGHTMARE LEGION TONIGHT?
I COULD BE ONLINE RIGHT AFTER DINNER.
YEAH, THAT SOUNDS COOL.
SEVEN OR SO?
PERFECTO!
COOL!
SEE YOU THEN.

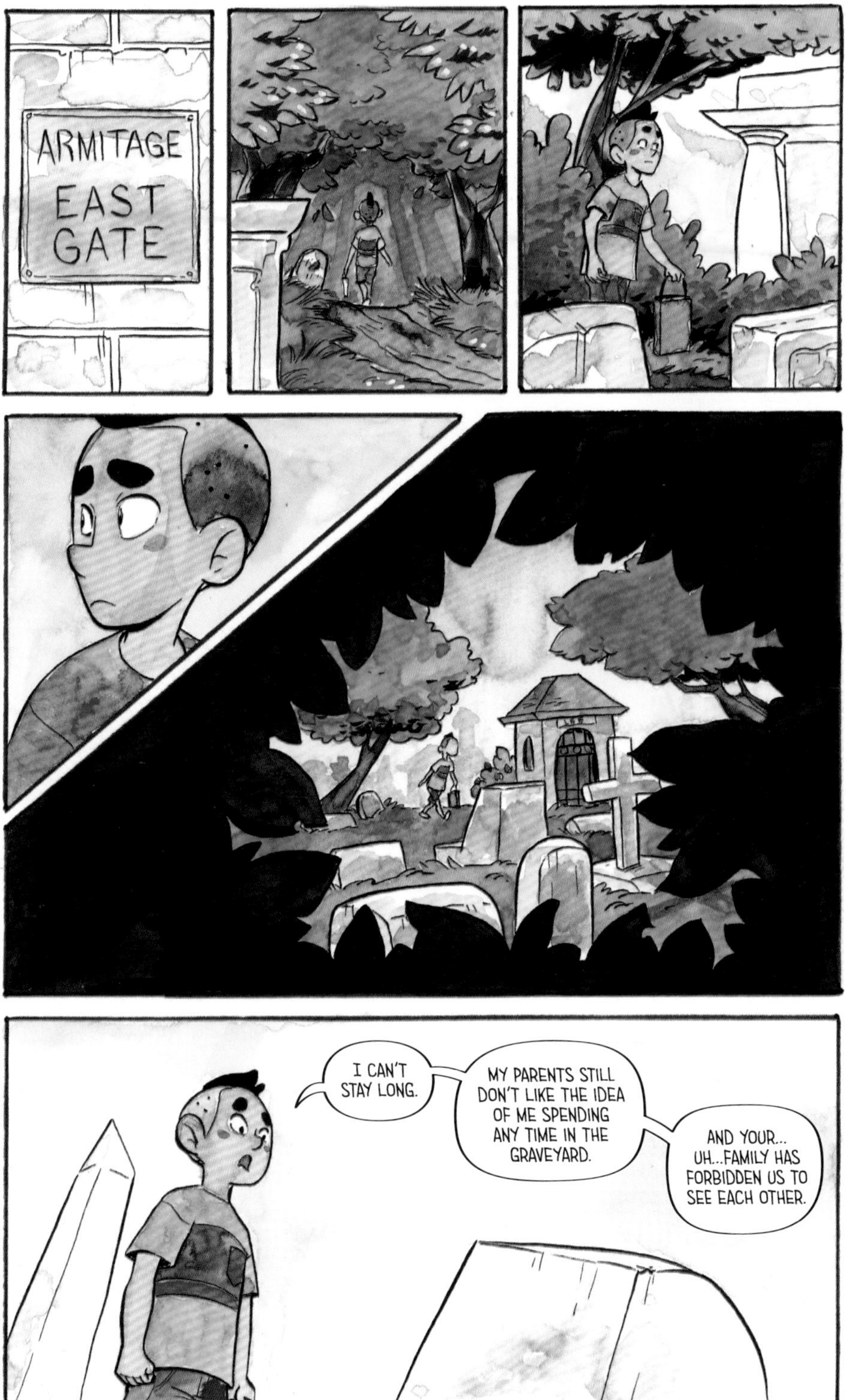
ARMITAGE
EAST GATE
I CAN'T STAY LONG.
MY PARENTS STILL DON'T LIKE THE IDEA OF ME SPENDING ANY TIME IN THE GRAVEYARD.
AND YOUR... UH...FAMILY HAS FORBIDDEN US TO SEE EACH OTHER.

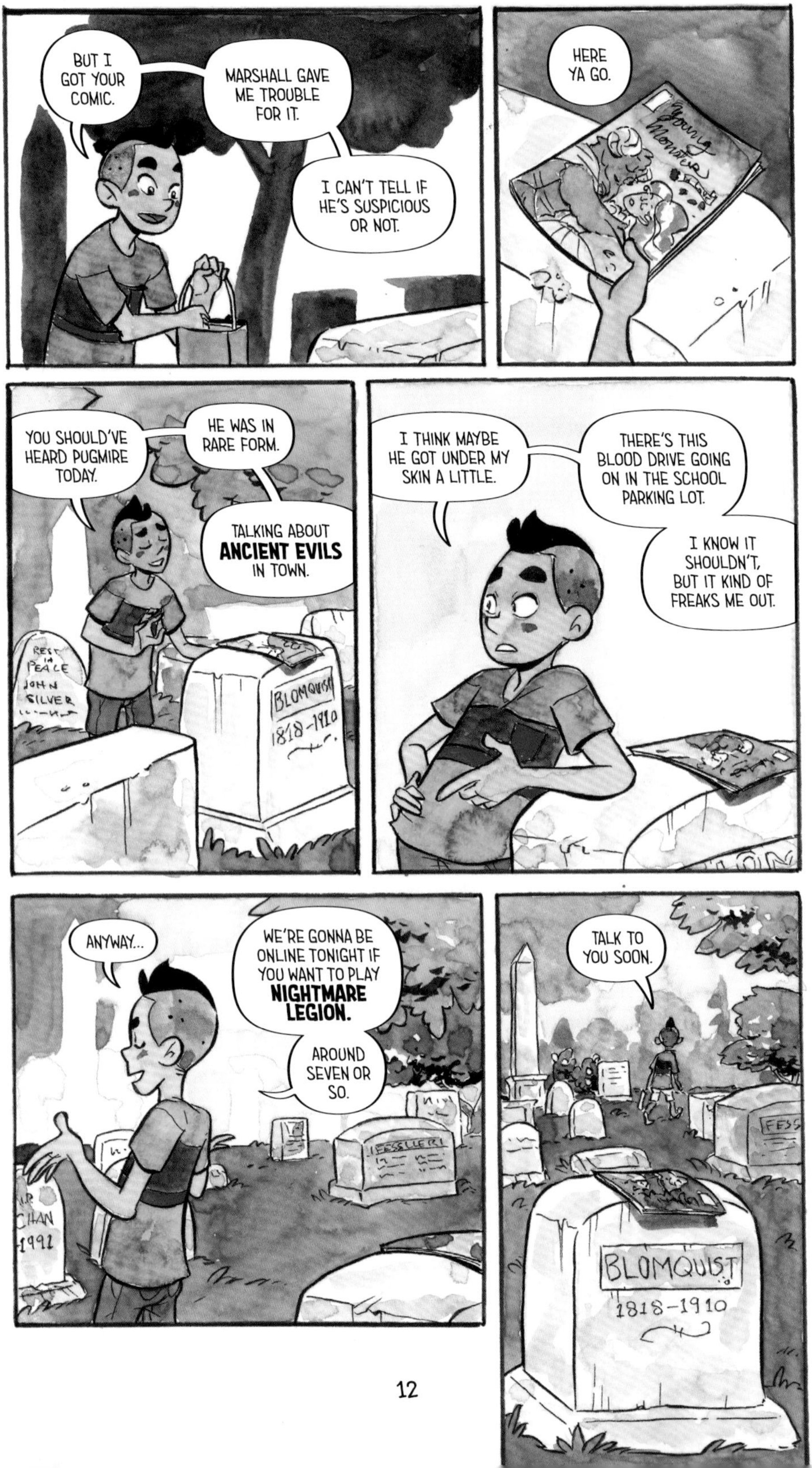
BUT I GOT YOUR COMIC.
MARSHALL GAVE ME TROUBLE FOR IT.
I CAN'T TELL IF HE'S SUSPICIOUS OR NOT.
HERE YA GO.
YOU SHOULD'VE HEARD PUGMIRE TODAY.
HE WAS IN RARE FORM.
TALKING ABOUT **ANCIENT EVILS** IN TOWN.
REST IN PEACE JOHN SILVER
BLOMQUIST 1818-1910
I THINK MAYBE HE GOT UNDER MY SKIN A LITTLE.
THERE'S THIS BLOOD DRIVE GOING ON IN THE SCHOOL PARKING LOT.
I KNOW IT SHOULDN'T, BUT IT KIND OF FREAKS ME OUT.
ANYWAY...
WE'RE GONNA BE ONLINE TONIGHT IF YOU WANT TO PLAY **NIGHTMARE LEGION.**
AROUND SEVEN OR SO.
FESSLER
CHAN 1991
TALK TO YOU SOON.
BLOMQUIST
1818-1910

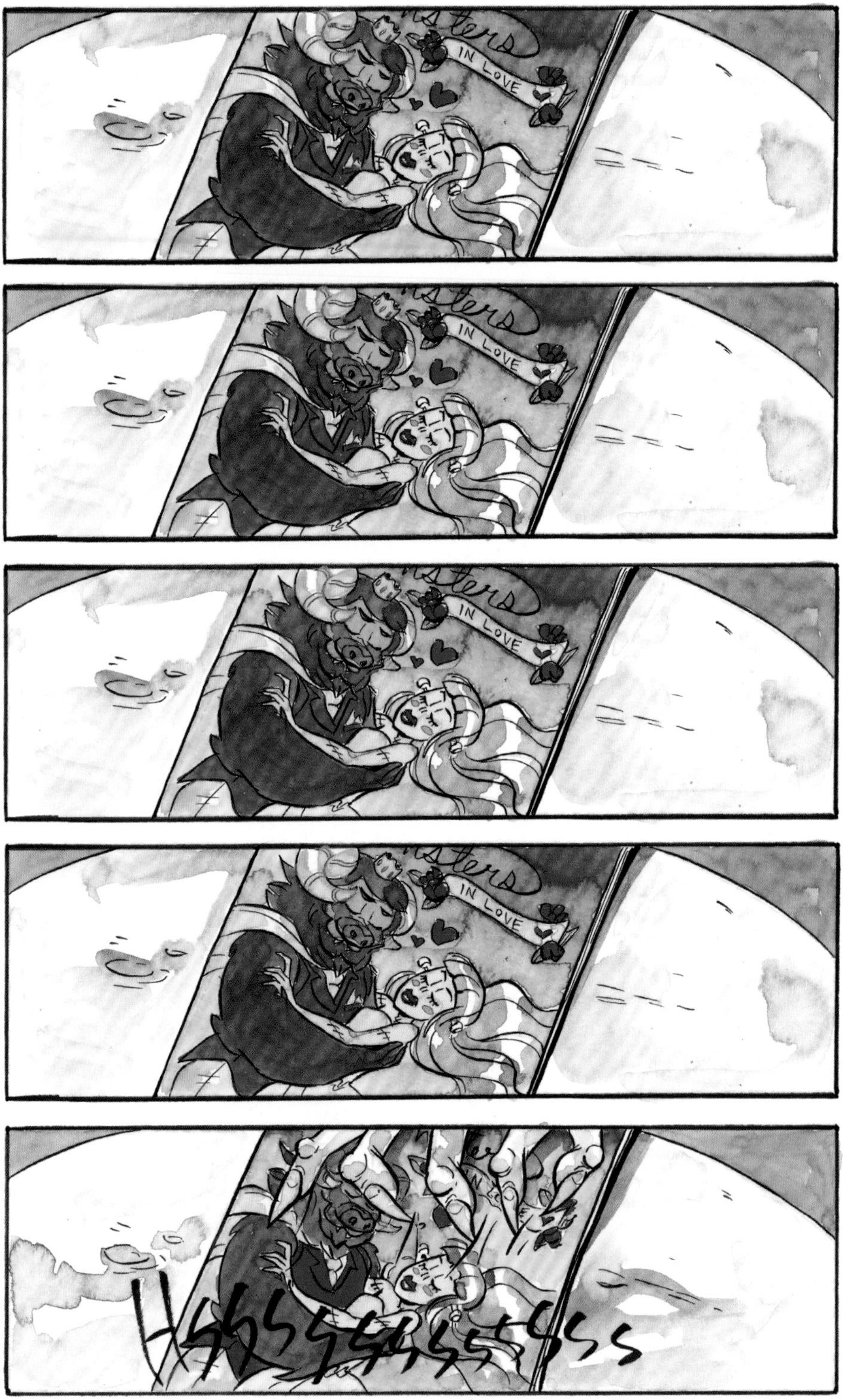
IN LOVE
IN LOVE
IN LOVE
IN LOVE
Hssssssssssss

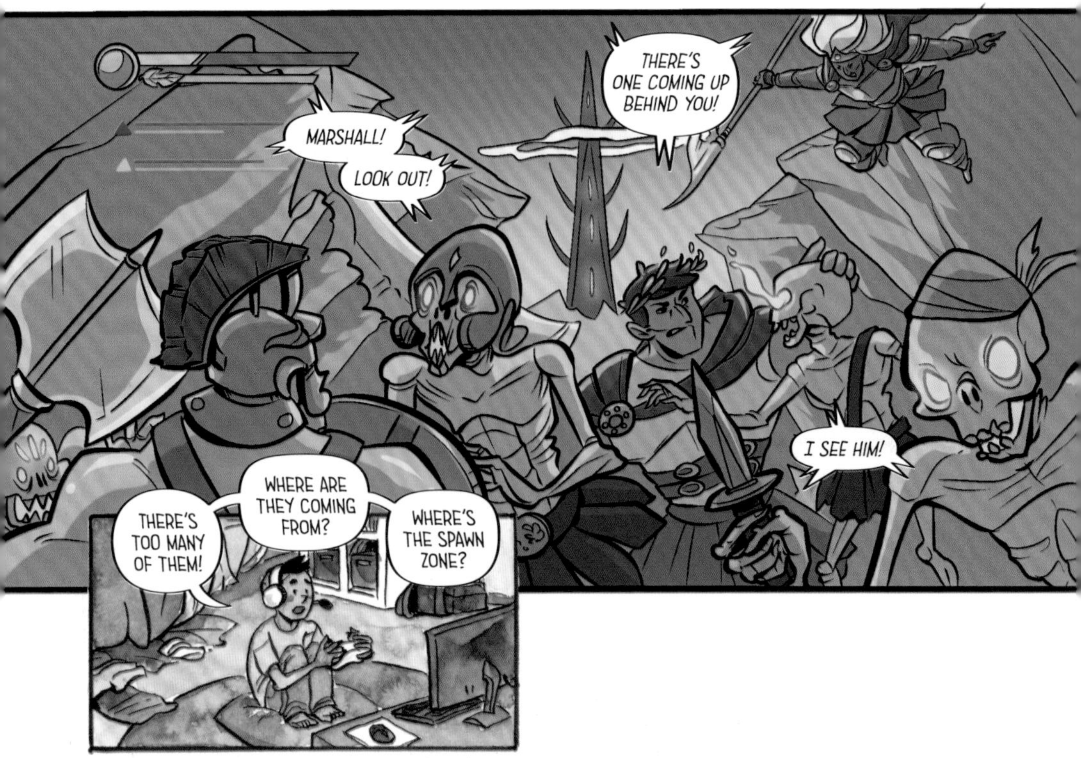
MARSHALL!
LOOK OUT!
THERE'S ONE COMING UP BEHIND YOU!
I SEE HIM!
THERE'S TOO MANY OF THEM!
WHERE ARE THEY COMING FROM?
WHERE'S THE SPAWN ZONE?

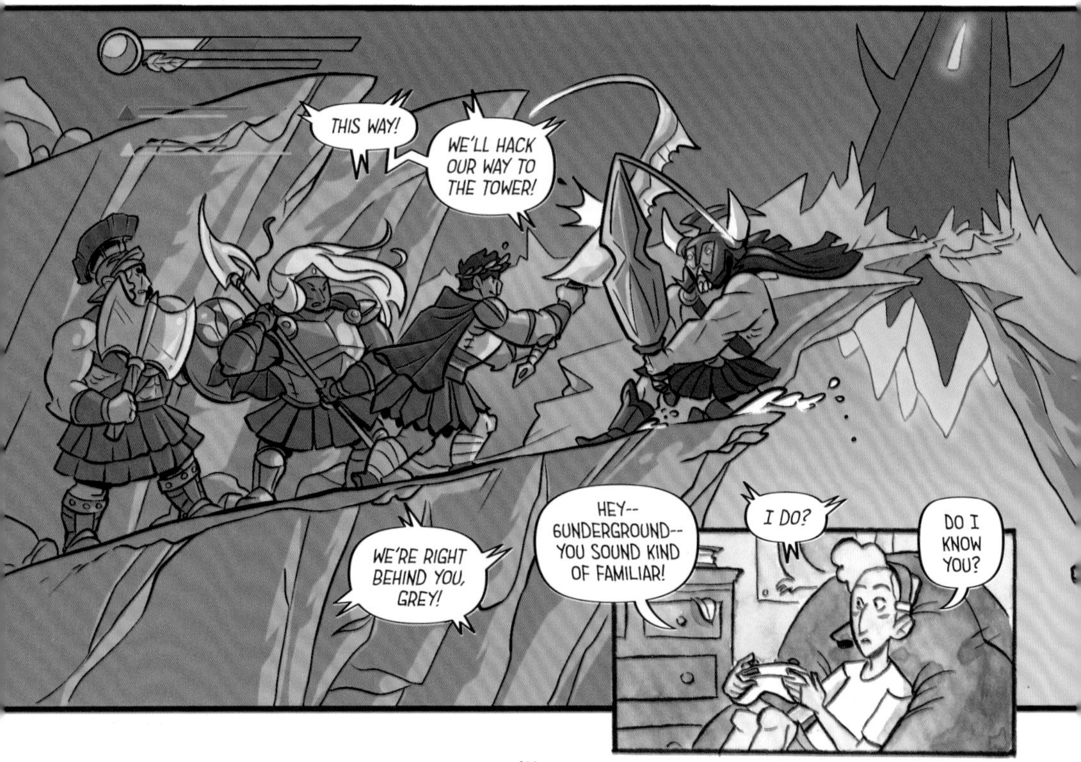
THIS WAY!
WE'LL HACK OUR WAY TO THE TOWER!
WE'RE RIGHT BEHIND YOU, GREY!
HEY-- 6UNDERGROUND-- YOU SOUND KIND OF FAMILIAR!
I DO?
DO I KNOW YOU?

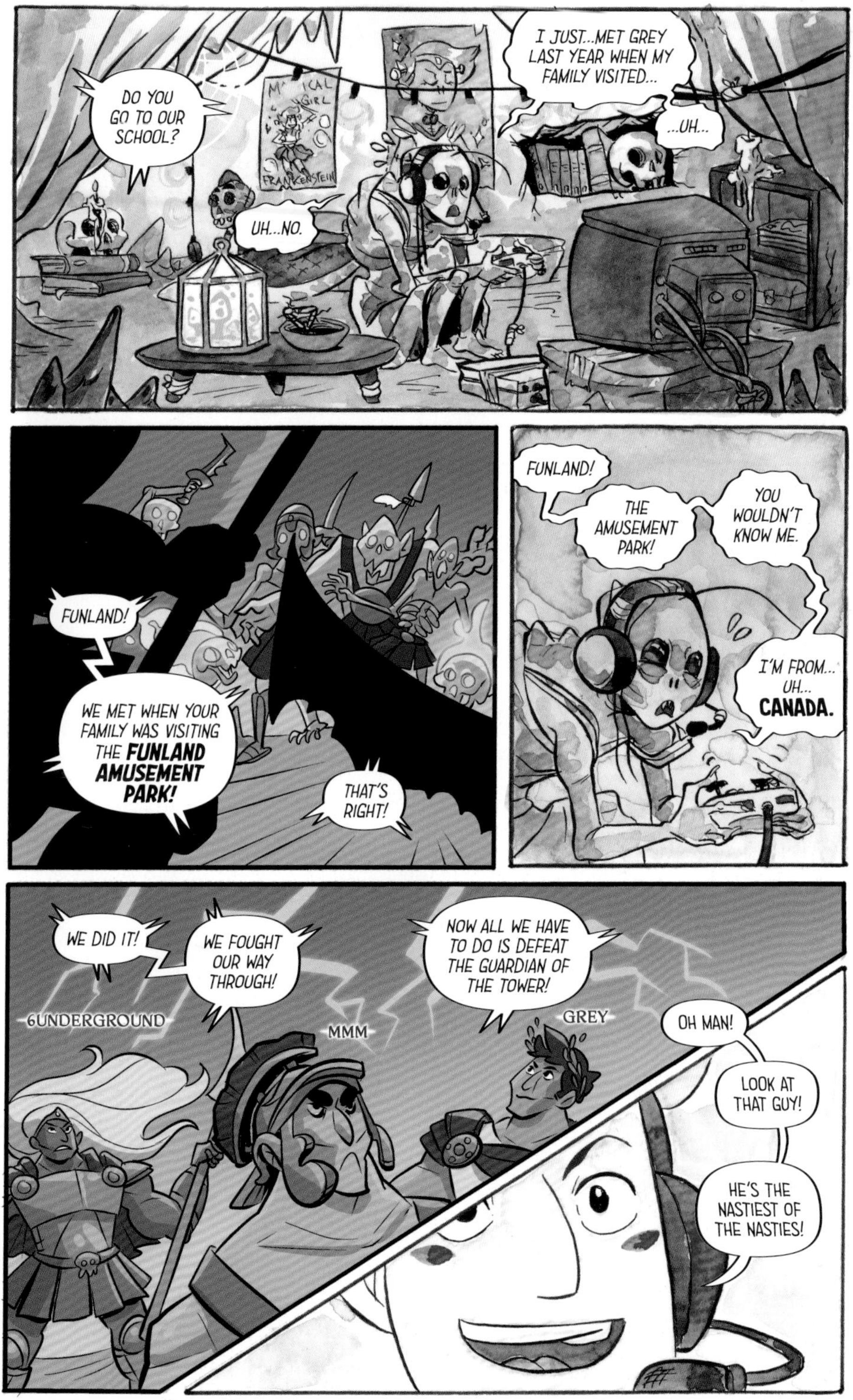
DO YOU GO TO OUR SCHOOL?
UH...NO.
I JUST...MET GREY LAST YEAR WHEN MY FAMILY VISITED...
...UH...
MAGICAL GIRL FRANKENSTEIN
FUNLAND!
WE MET WHEN YOUR FAMILY WAS VISITING THE **FUNLAND AMUSEMENT PARK!**
THAT'S RIGHT!
FUNLAND!
THE AMUSEMENT PARK!
YOU WOULDN'T KNOW ME.
I'M FROM... UH... **CANADA.**
WE DID IT!
WE FOUGHT OUR WAY THROUGH!
NOW ALL WE HAVE TO DO IS DEFEAT THE GUARDIAN OF THE TOWER!
6UNDERGROUND
MMM
GREY
OH MAN!
LOOK AT THAT GUY!
HE'S THE NASTIEST OF THE NASTIES!

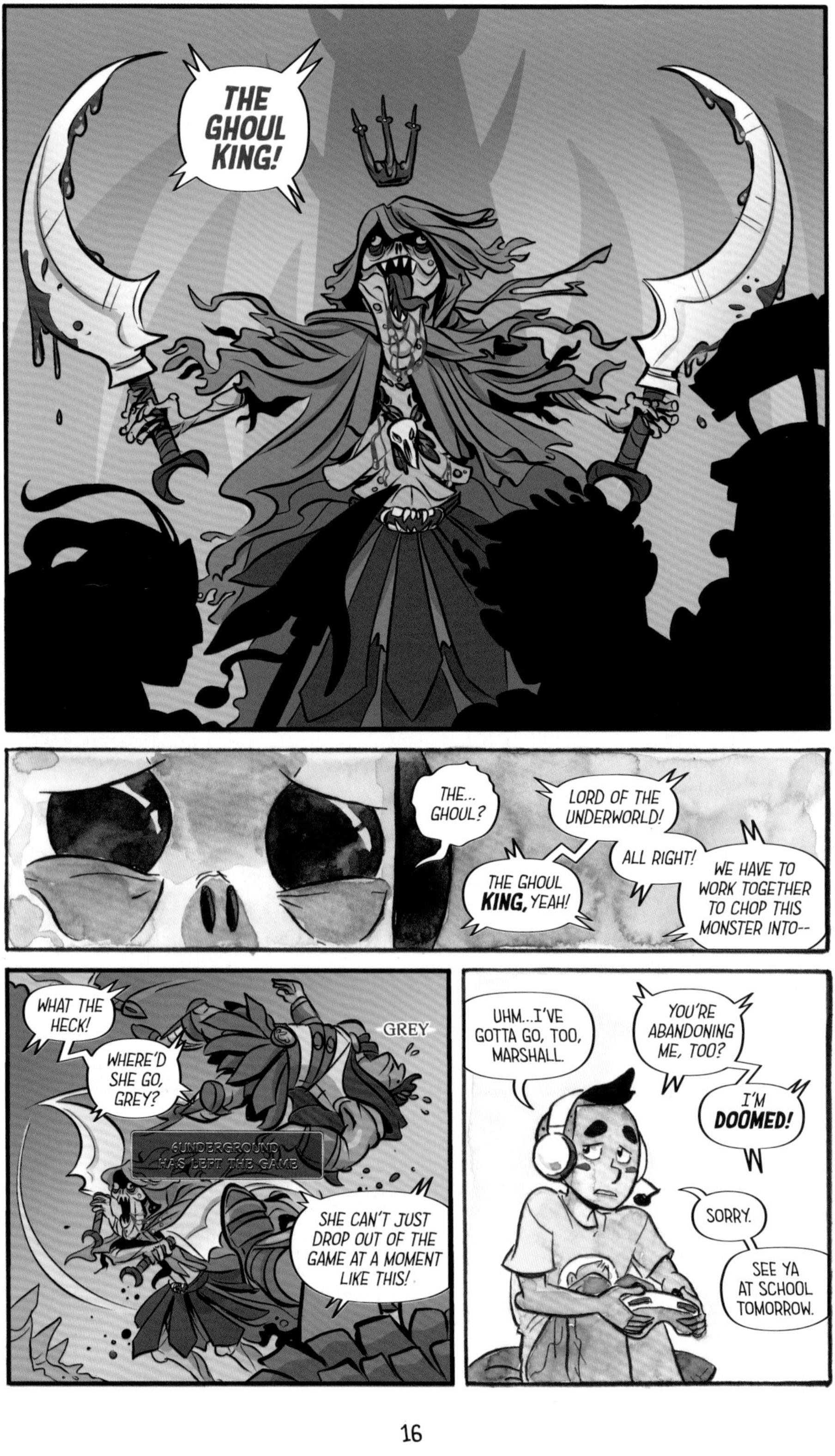
THE GHOUL KING!
THE... GHOUL?
LORD OF THE UNDERWORLD!
THE GHOUL KING, YEAH!
ALL RIGHT!
WE HAVE TO WORK TOGETHER TO CHOP THIS MONSTER INTO--
WHAT THE HECK!
GREY
WHERE'D SHE GO, GREY?
6UNDERGROUND HAS LEFT THE GAME
SHE CAN'T JUST DROP OUT OF THE GAME AT A MOMENT LIKE THIS!
UHM...I'VE GOTTA GO, TOO, MARSHALL.
YOU'RE ABANDONING ME, TOO?
I'M DOOMED!
SORRY.
SEE YA AT SCHOOL TOMORROW.

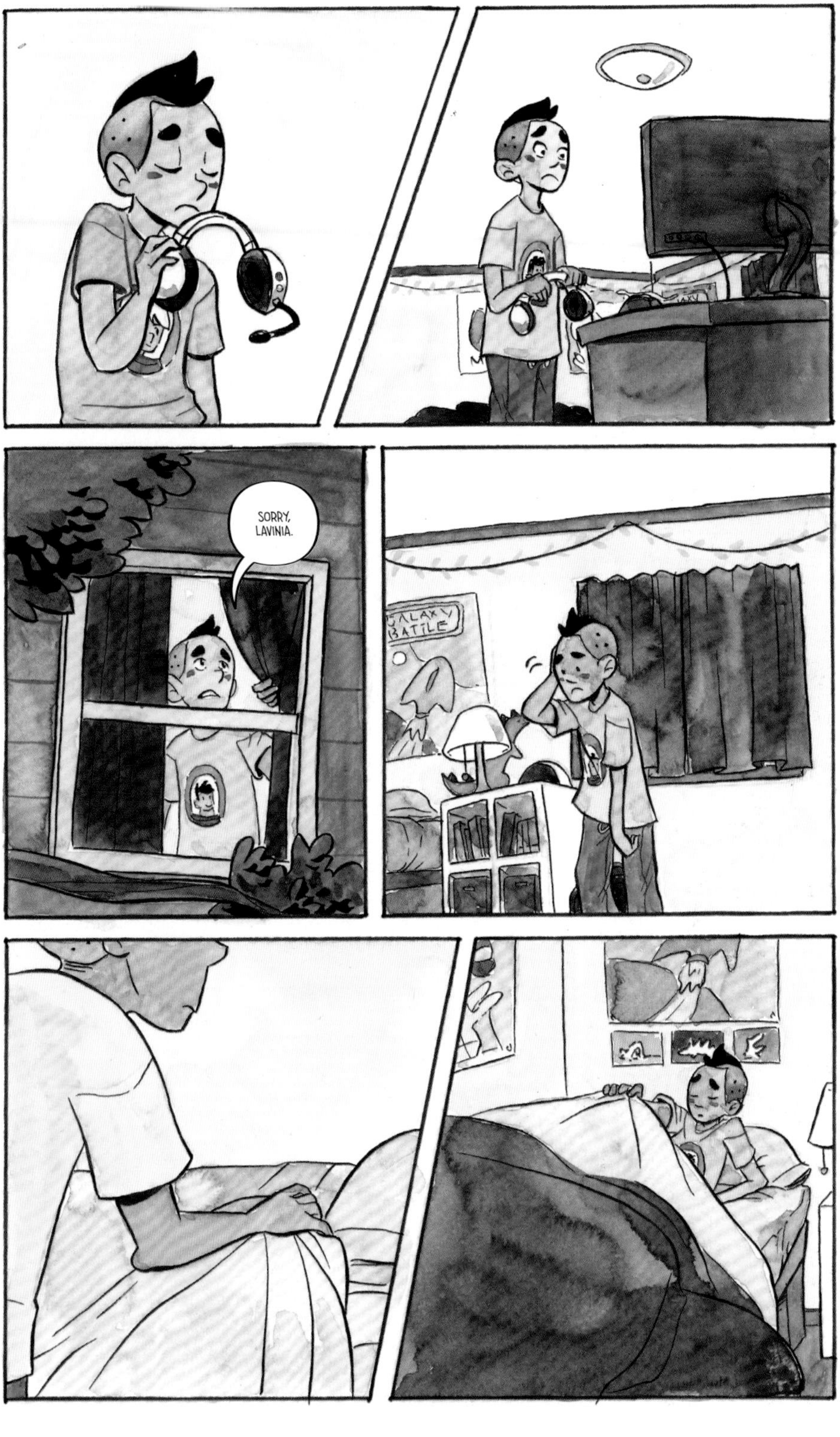
SORRY, LAVINIA.
GALAXY BATTLE

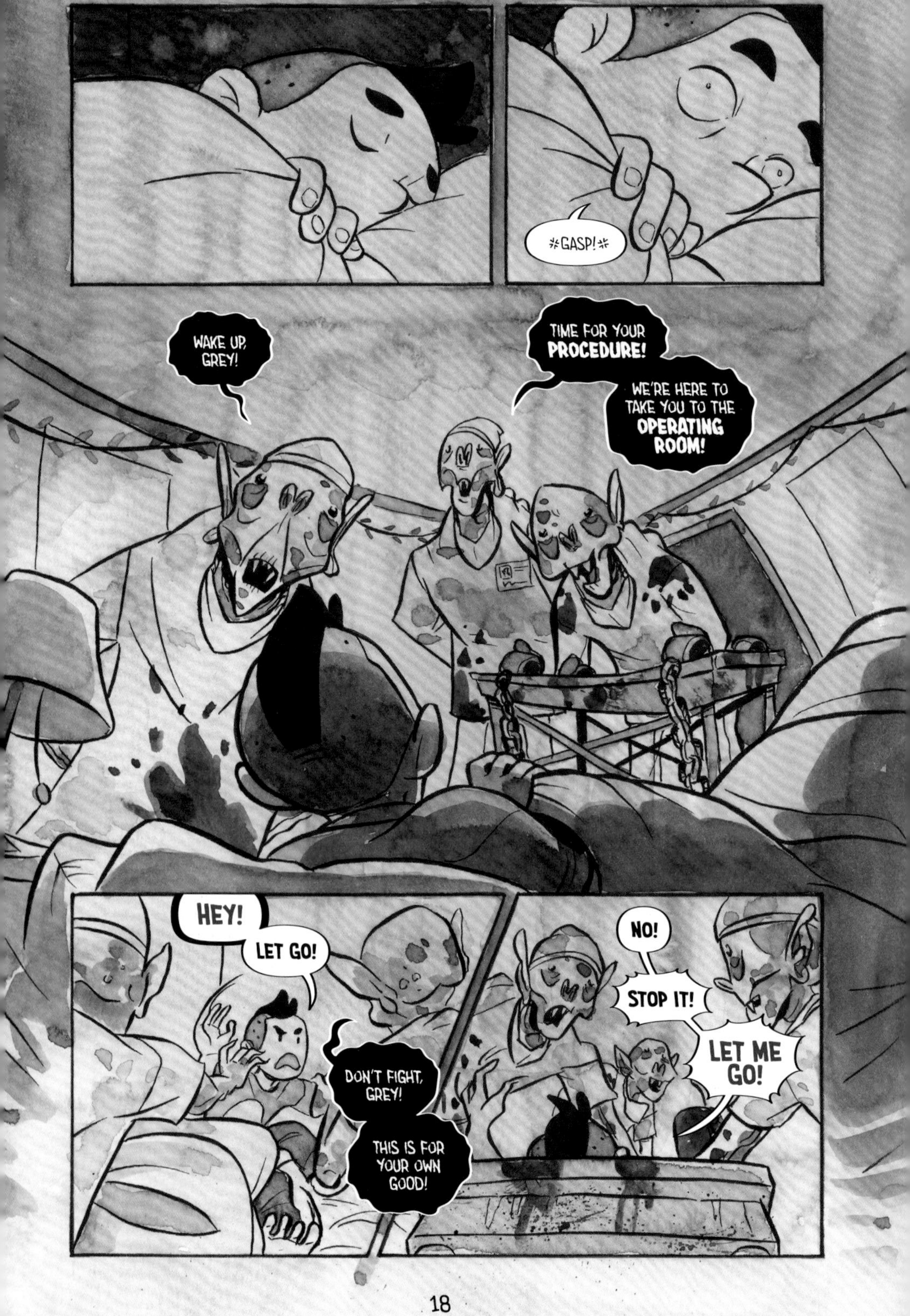

GASP!
WAKE UP, GREY!
TIME FOR YOUR PROCEDURE!
WE'RE HERE TO TAKE YOU TO THE OPERATING ROOM!
HEY!
LET GO!
DON'T FIGHT, GREY!
THIS IS FOR YOUR OWN GOOD!
NO!
STOP IT!
LET ME GO!

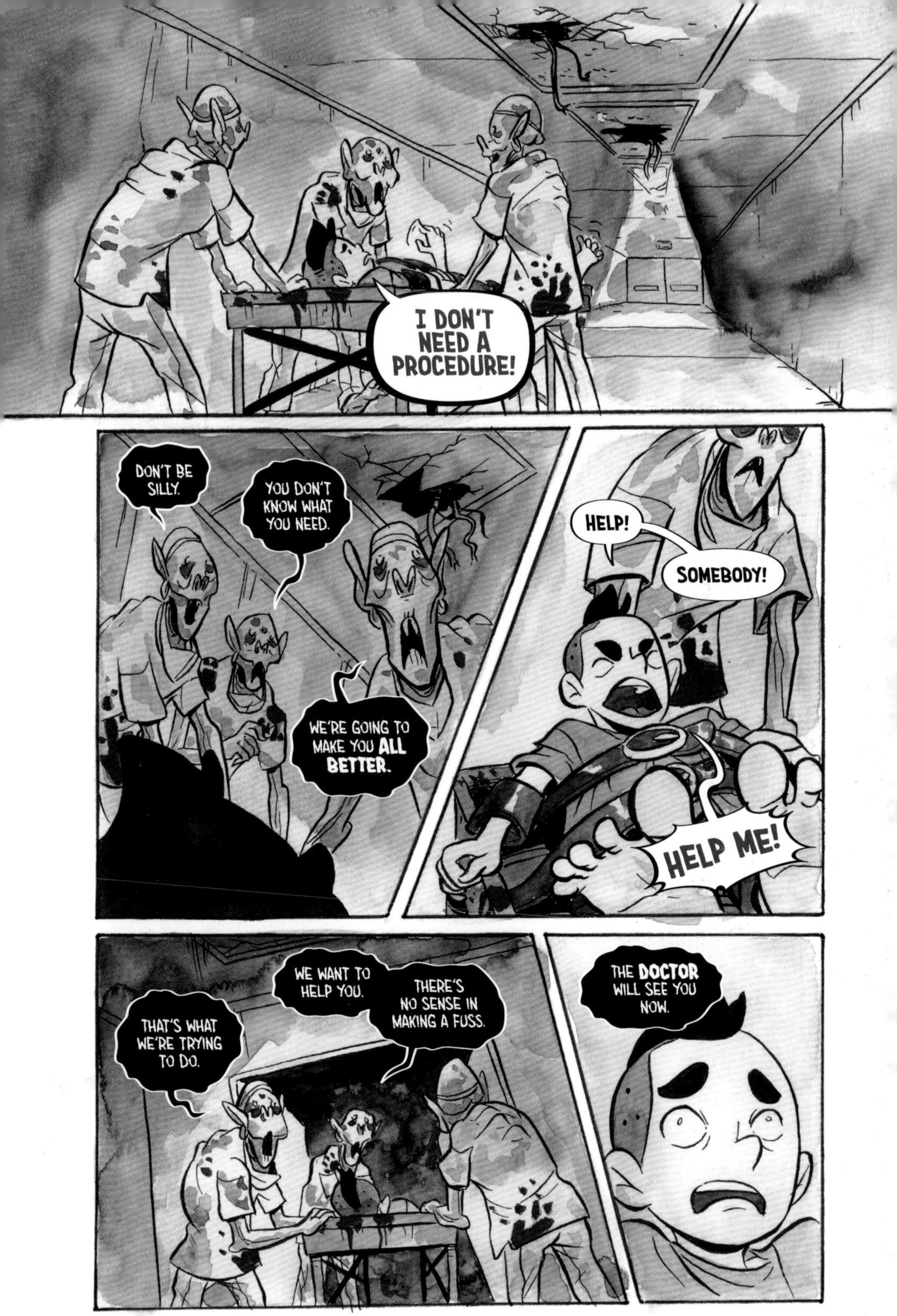
I DON'T NEED A PROCEDURE!
DON'T BE SILLY.
YOU DON'T KNOW WHAT YOU NEED.
WE'RE GOING TO MAKE YOU ALL BETTER.
HELP!
SOMEBODY!
HELP ME!
THAT'S WHAT WE'RE TRYING TO DO.
WE WANT TO HELP YOU.
THERE'S NO SENSE IN MAKING A FUSS.
THE DOCTOR WILL SEE YOU NOW.

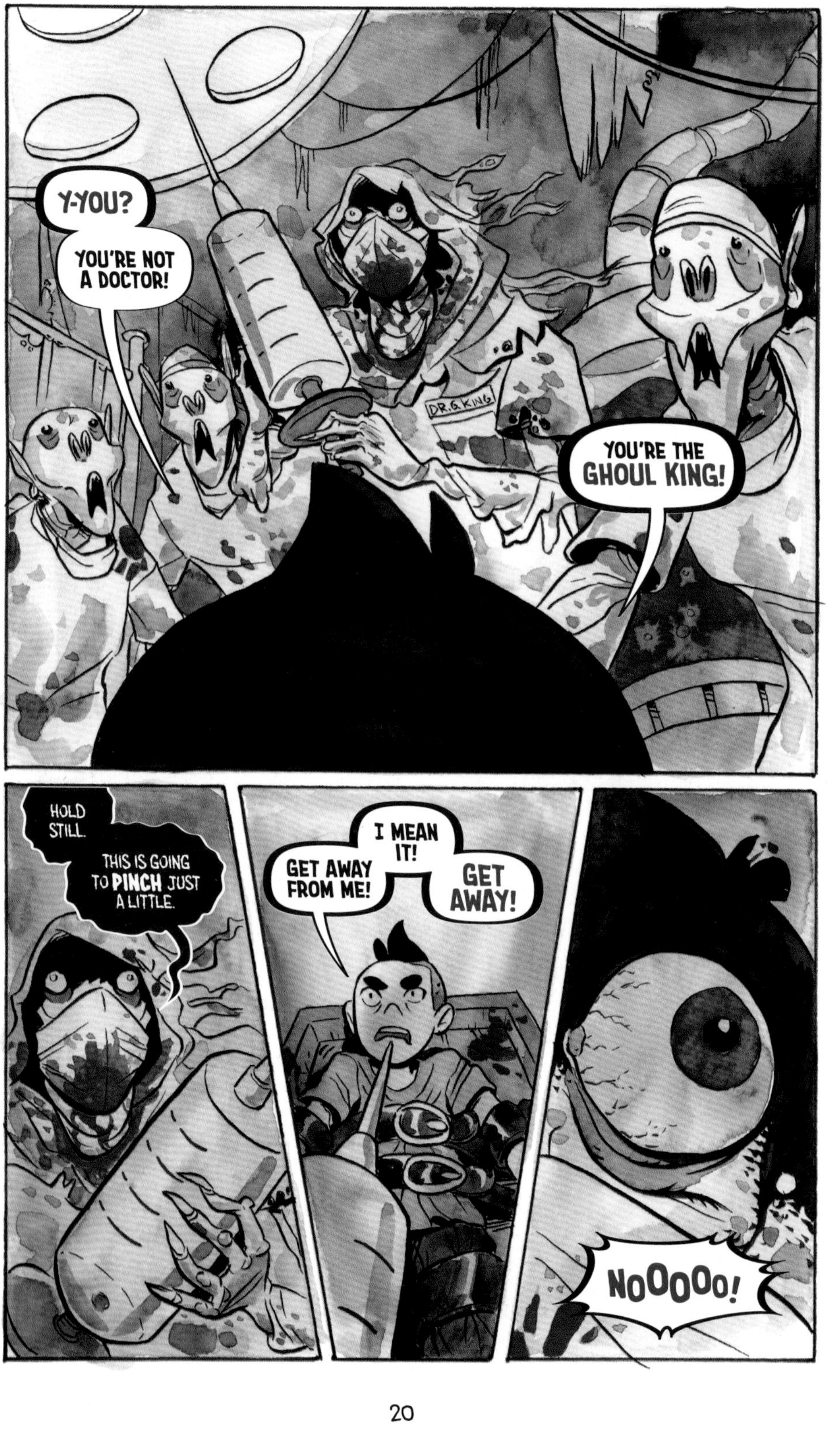
Y-YOU?
YOU'RE NOT A DOCTOR!
DR. G. KING
YOU'RE THE GHOUL KING!
HOLD STILL.
THIS IS GOING TO PINCH JUST A LITTLE.
GET AWAY FROM ME!
I MEAN IT!
GET AWAY!
NOOOOO!

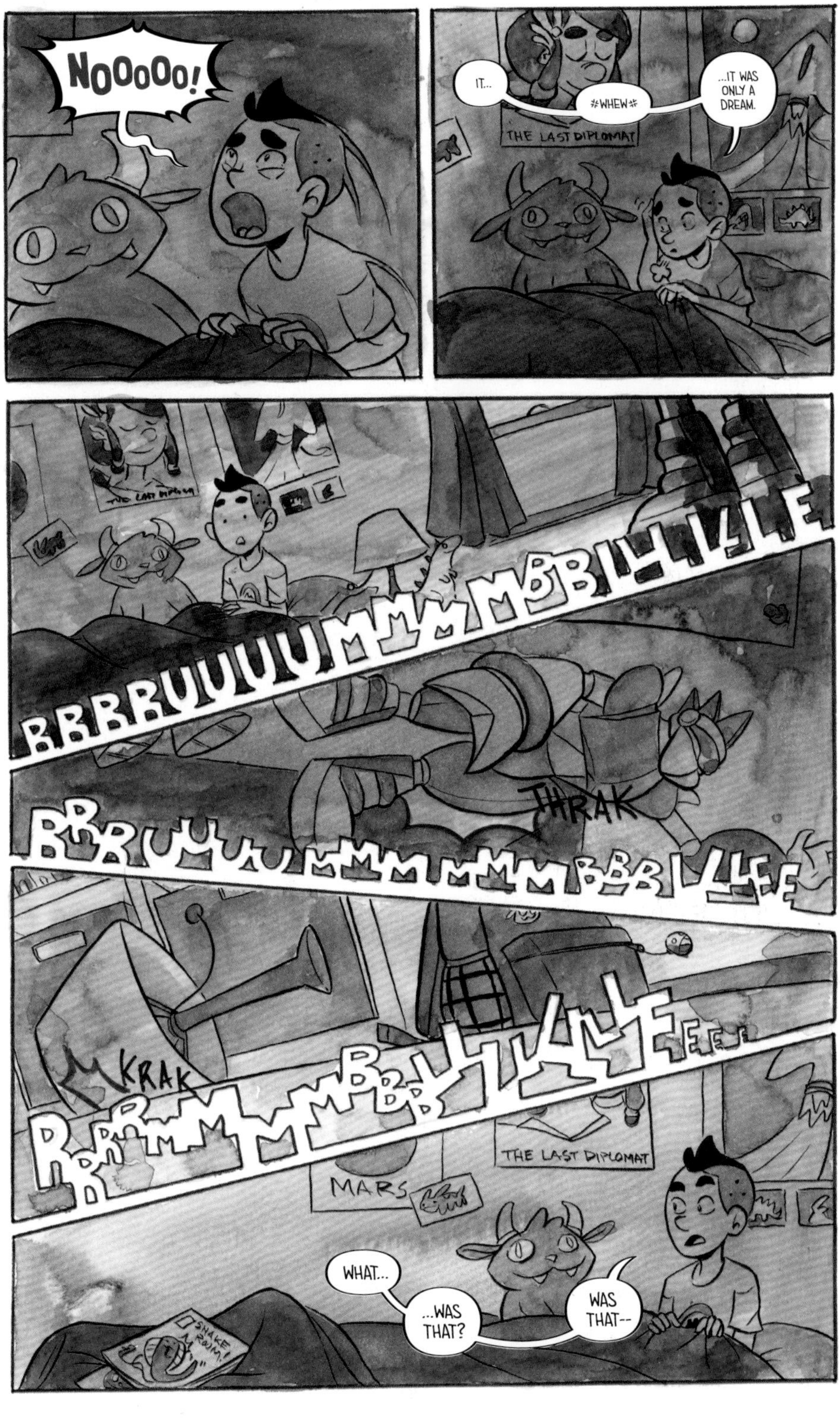
NOOOOO!
THE LAST DIPLOMAT
IT...
WHEW
...IT WAS ONLY A DREAM.
BRRRUUUUMMMMMMBBLLLLE
THRAK
BRRRUUUMMMMMMMMBBBLLLEE
KRAK
RRRRRMMMMMBBBBLLLEEEE
THE LAST DIPLOMAT
MARS
WHAT...
...WAS THAT?
WAS THAT--

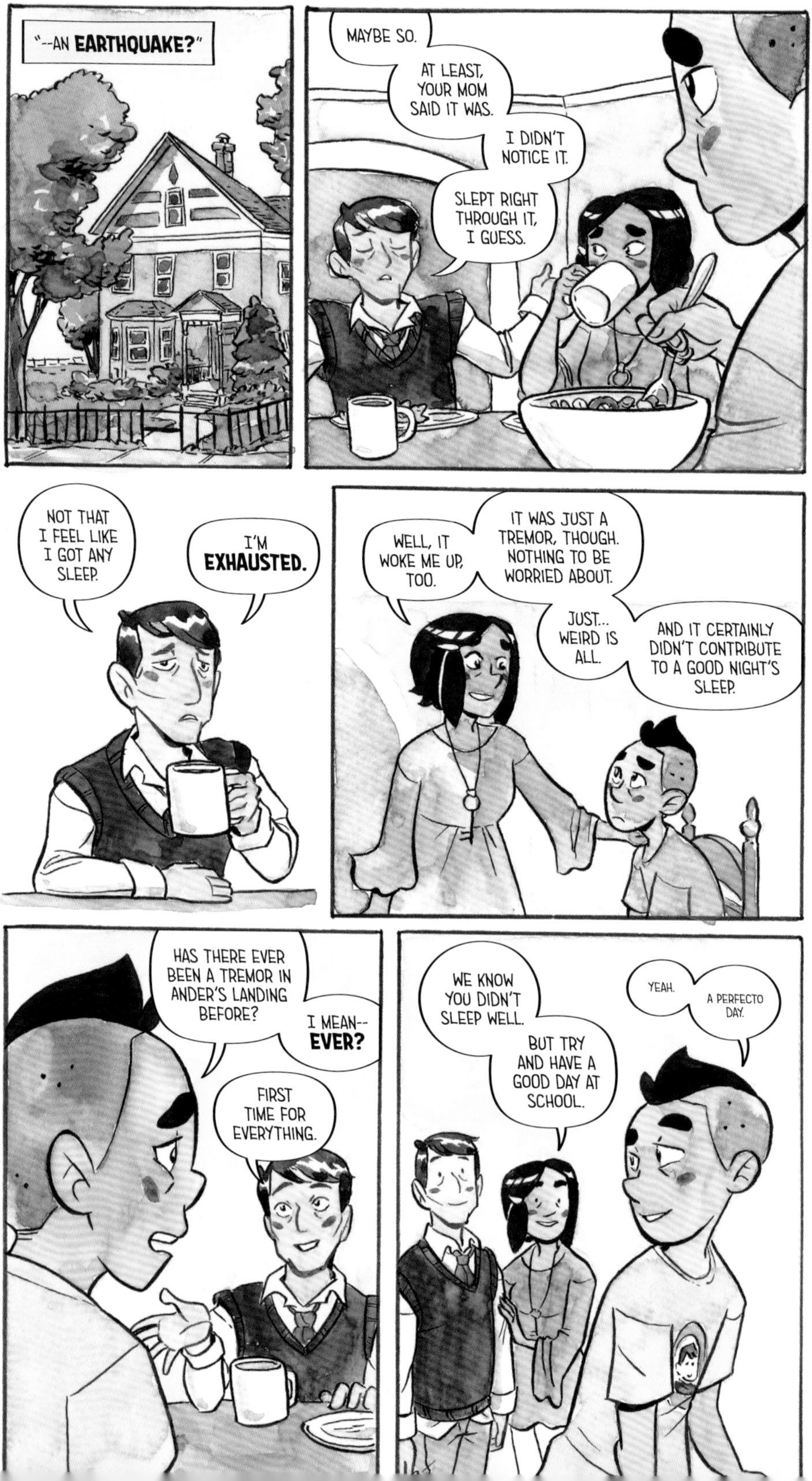
"--AN **EARTHQUAKE?**"
MAYBE SO.
AT LEAST, YOUR MOM SAID IT WAS.
I DIDN'T NOTICE IT.
SLEPT RIGHT THROUGH IT, I GUESS.
NOT THAT I FEEL LIKE I GOT ANY SLEEP.
I'M **EXHAUSTED.**
WELL, IT WOKE ME UP, TOO.
IT WAS JUST A TREMOR, THOUGH. NOTHING TO BE WORRIED ABOUT.
JUST... WEIRD IS ALL.
AND IT CERTAINLY DIDN'T CONTRIBUTE TO A GOOD NIGHT'S SLEEP.
HAS THERE EVER BEEN A TREMOR IN ANDER'S LANDING BEFORE?
I MEAN-- **EVER?**
FIRST TIME FOR EVERYTHING.
WE KNOW YOU DIDN'T SLEEP WELL.
BUT TRY AND HAVE A GOOD DAY AT SCHOOL.
YEAH.
A PERFECTO DAY.

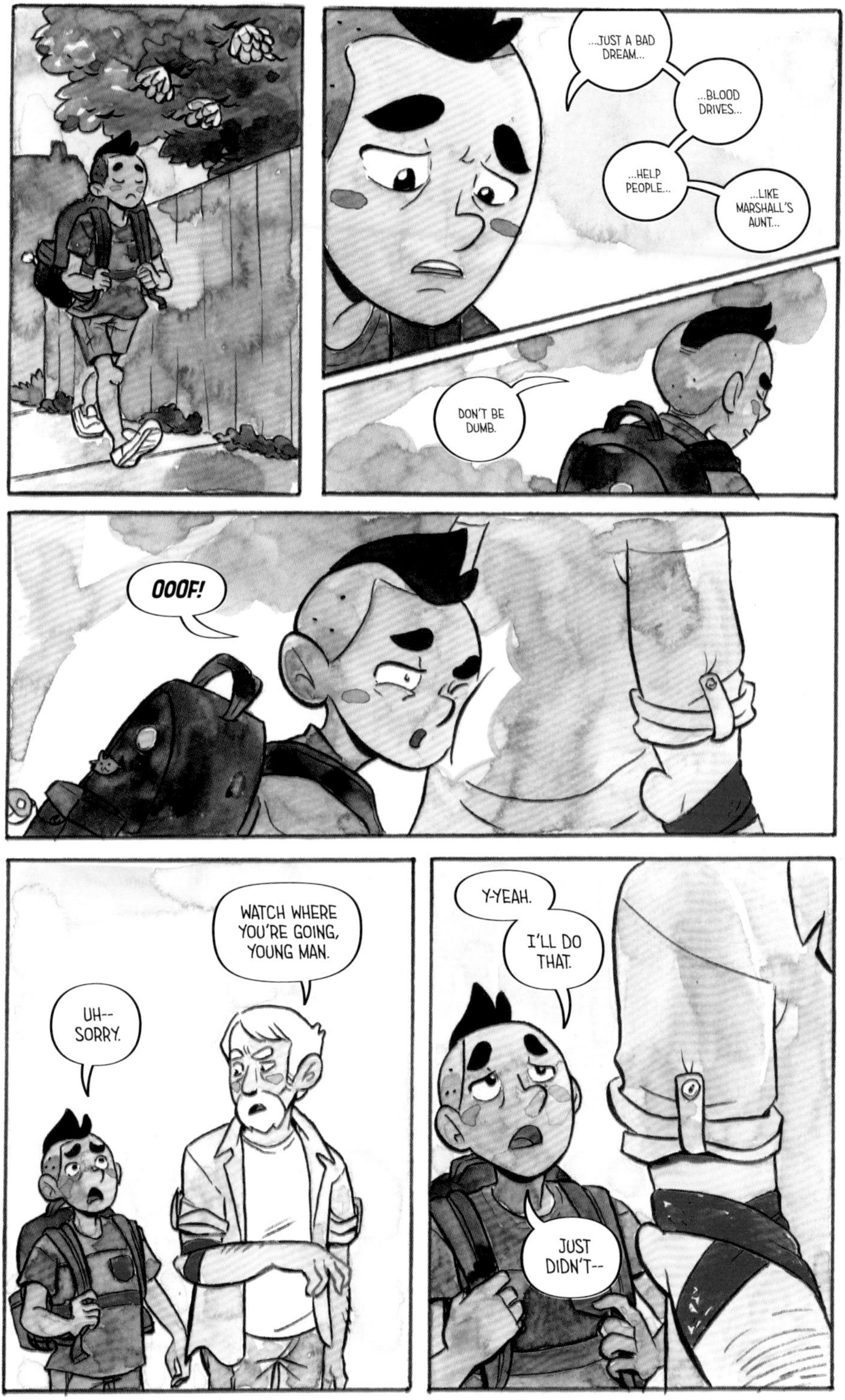
...JUST A BAD DREAM...
...BLOOD DRIVES...
...HELP PEOPLE...
...LIKE MARSHALL'S AUNT...
DON'T BE DUMB.
OOOF!
WATCH WHERE YOU'RE GOING, YOUNG MAN.
UH-- SORRY.
Y-YEAH.
I'LL DO THAT.
JUST DIDN'T--

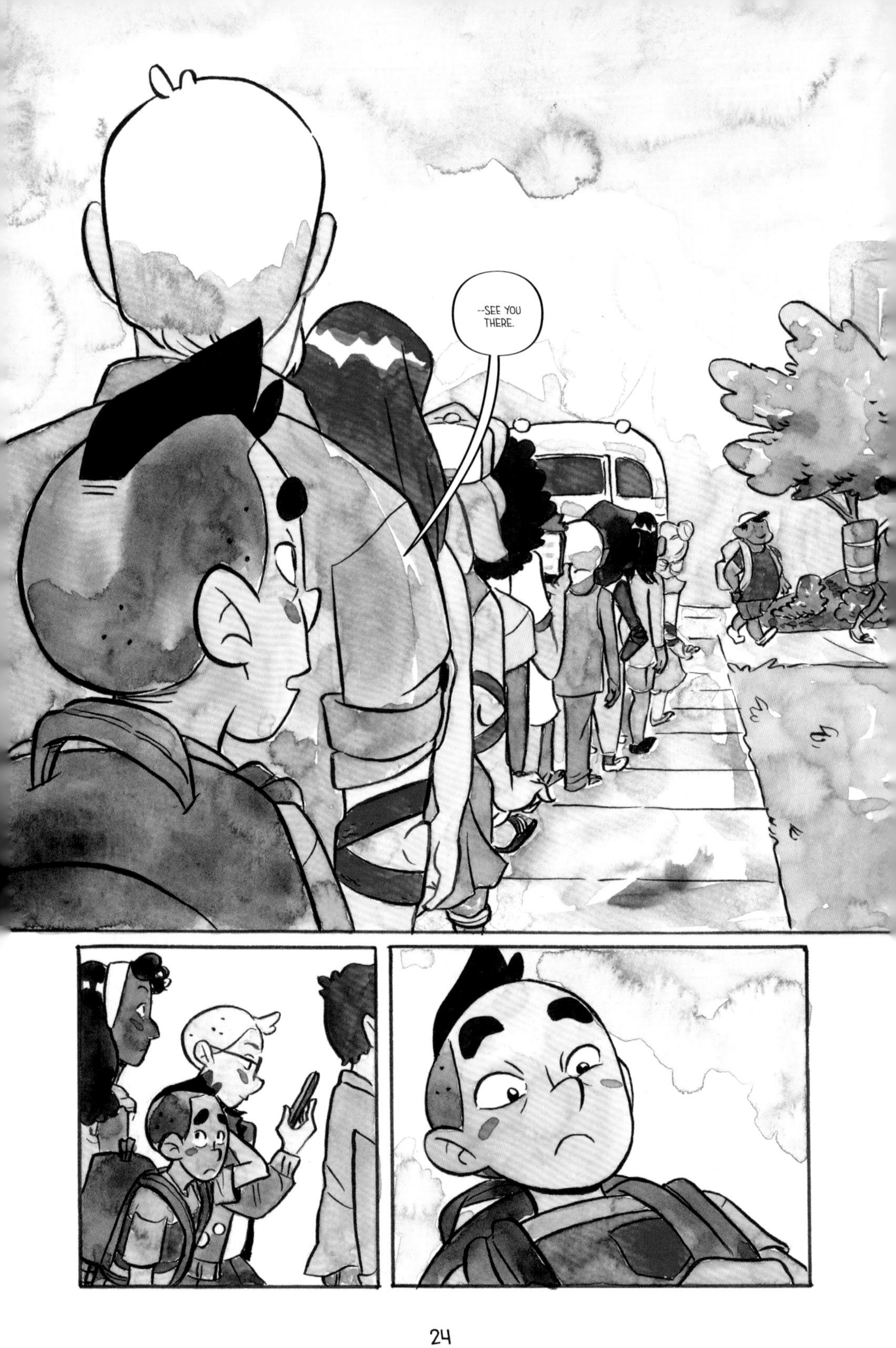
--SEE YOU THERE.

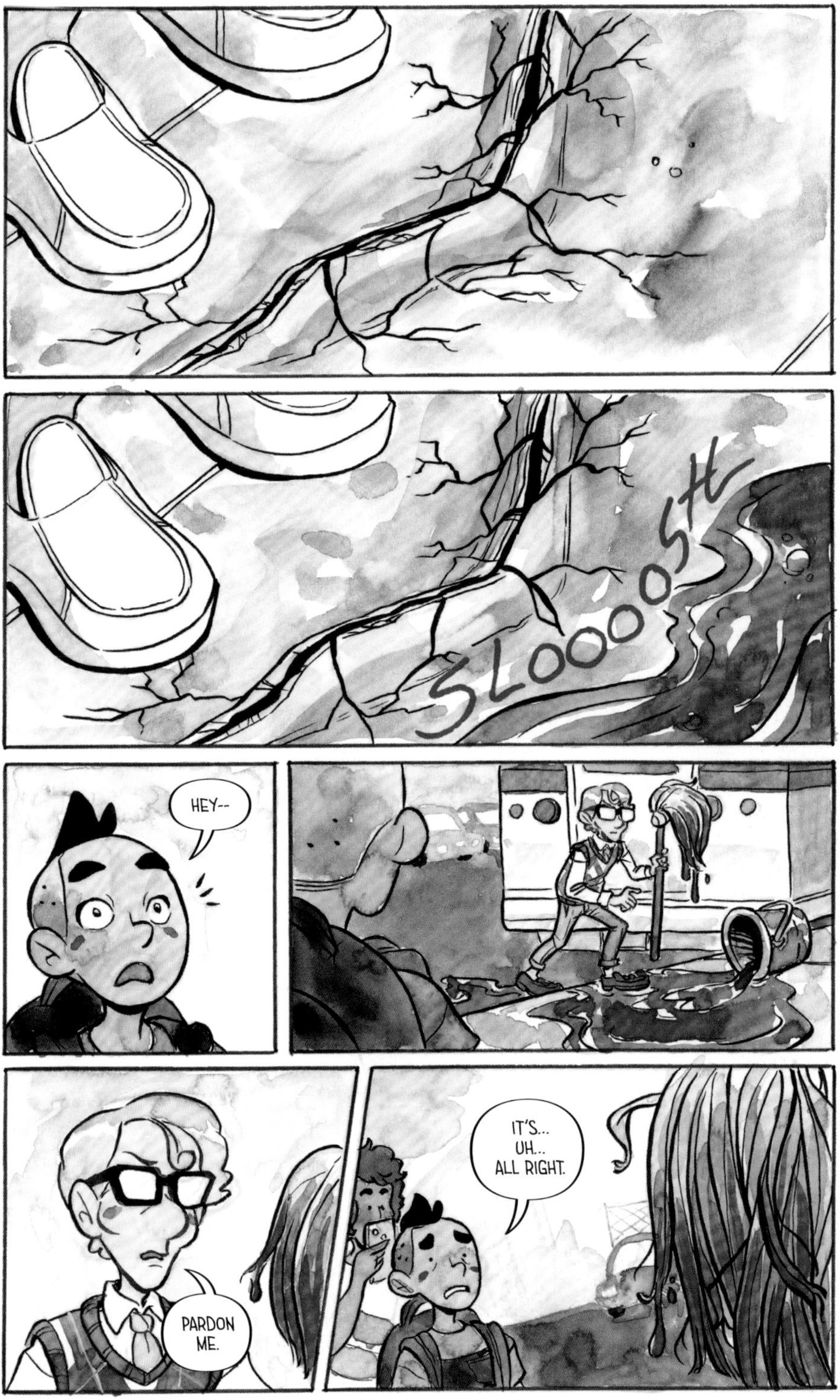
SLOOOOSH
HEY--
PARDON ME.
IT'S... UH... ALL RIGHT.

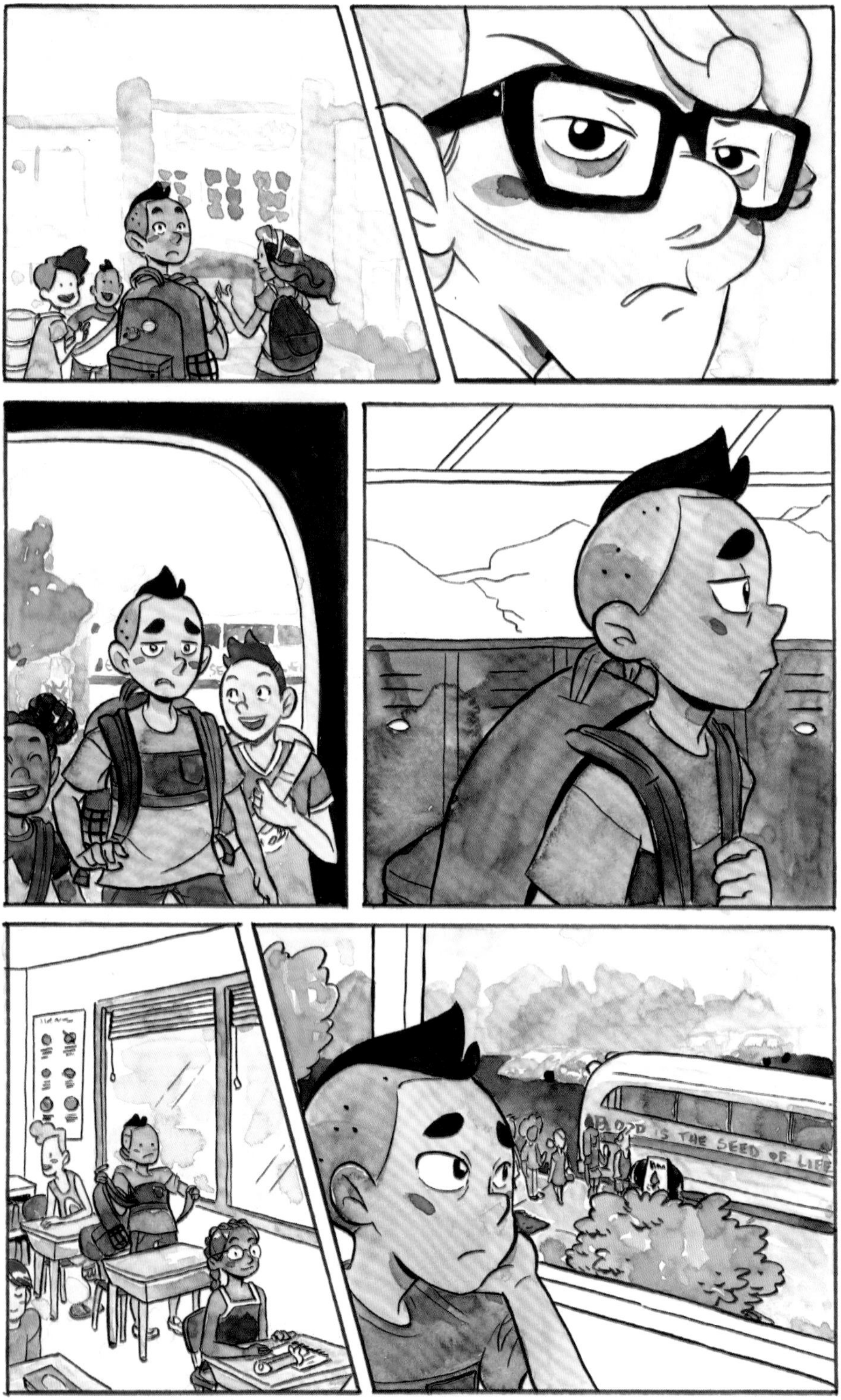
IS THE SEED OF LIFE

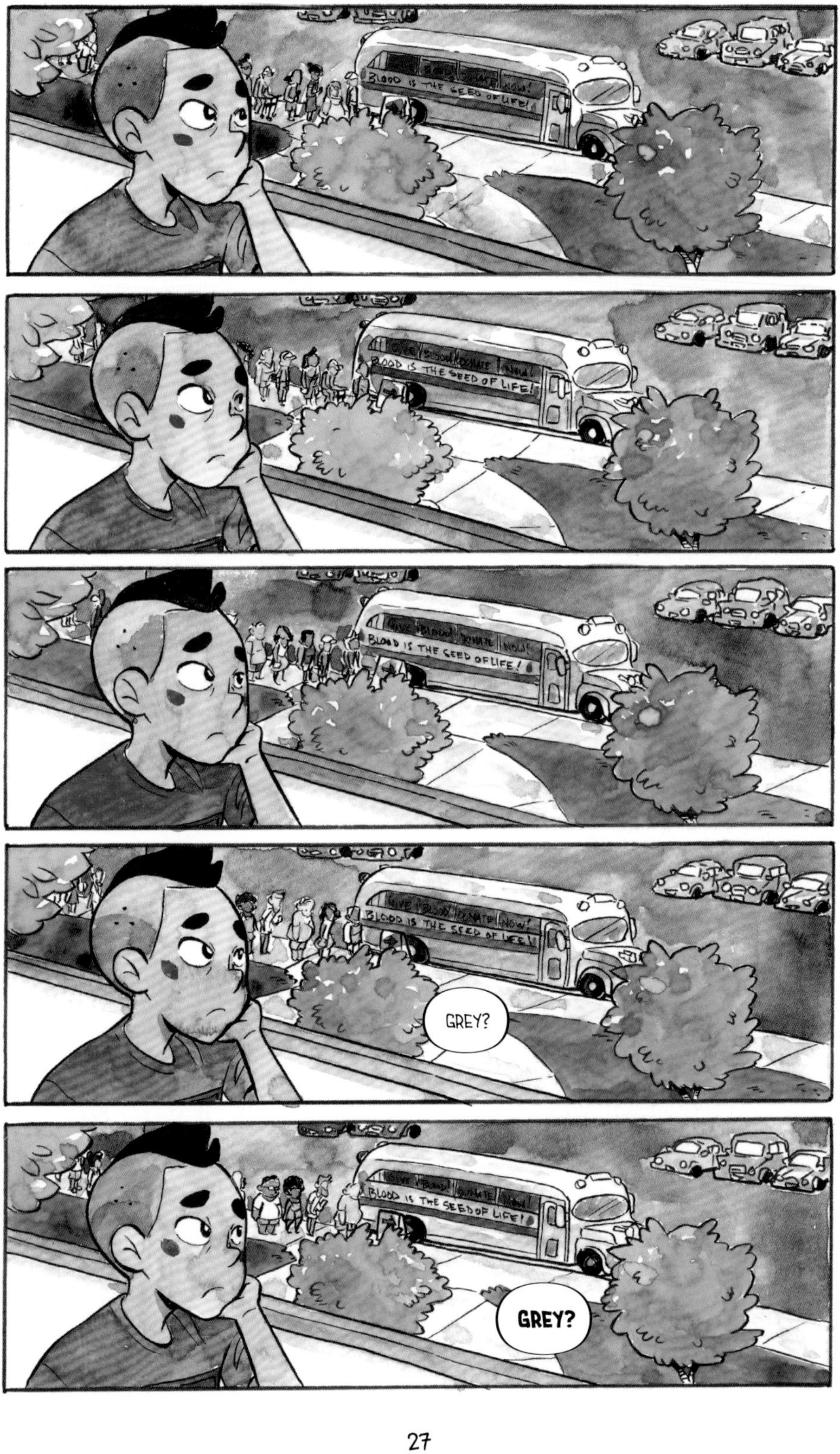
GIVE BLOOD DONATE NOW!
BLOOD IS THE SEED OF LIFE!
GREY?
GREY?

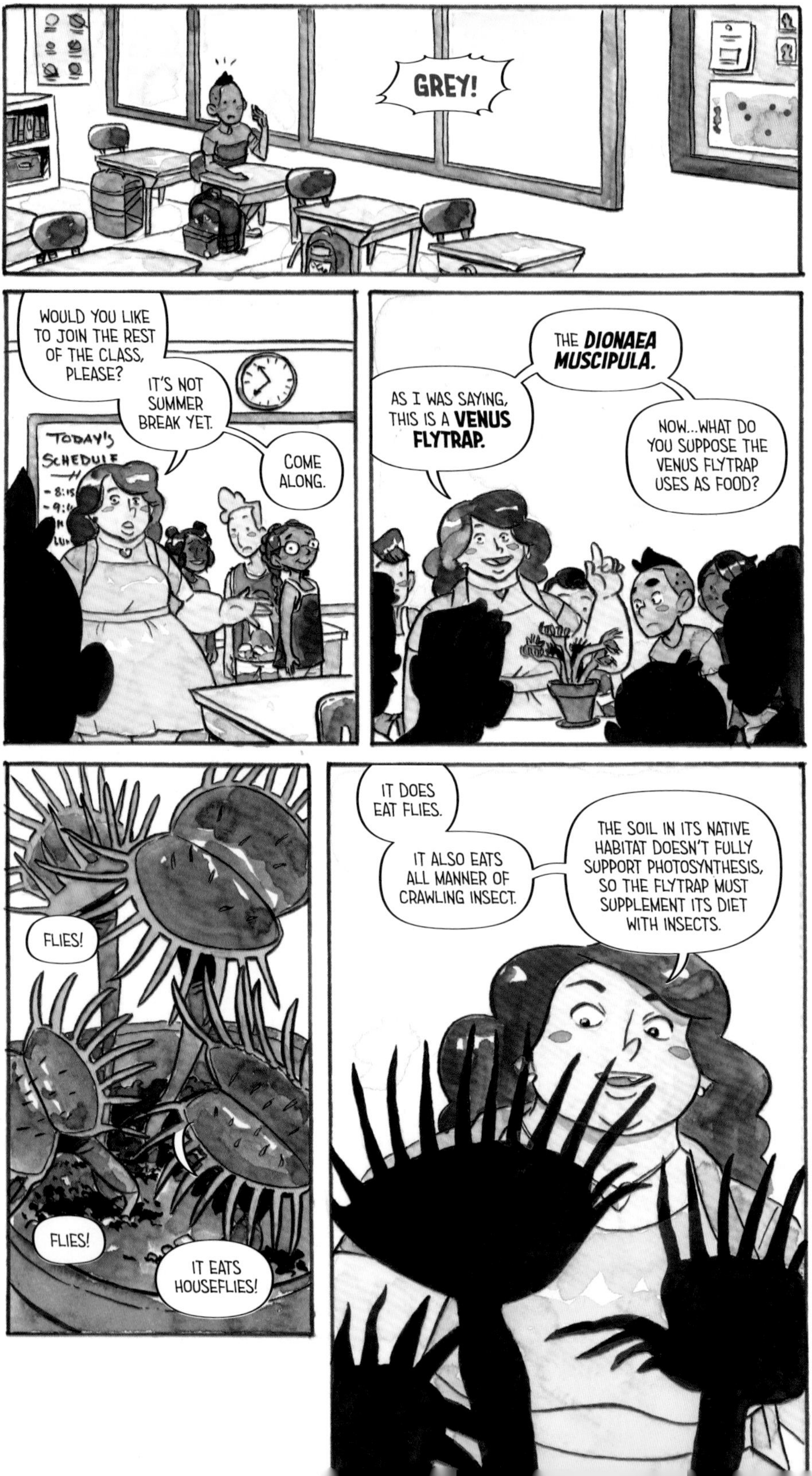
GREY!
WOULD YOU LIKE TO JOIN THE REST OF THE CLASS, PLEASE?
IT'S NOT SUMMER BREAK YET.
COME ALONG.
TODAY'S SCHEDULE
AS I WAS SAYING, THIS IS A VENUS FLYTRAP.
THE DIONAEA MUSCIPULA.
NOW...WHAT DO YOU SUPPOSE THE VENUS FLYTRAP USES AS FOOD?
FLIES!
FLIES!
IT EATS HOUSEFLIES!
IT DOES EAT FLIES.
IT ALSO EATS ALL MANNER OF CRAWLING INSECT.
THE SOIL IN ITS NATIVE HABITAT DOESN'T FULLY SUPPORT PHOTOSYNTHESIS, SO THE FLYTRAP MUST SUPPLEMENT ITS DIET WITH INSECTS.

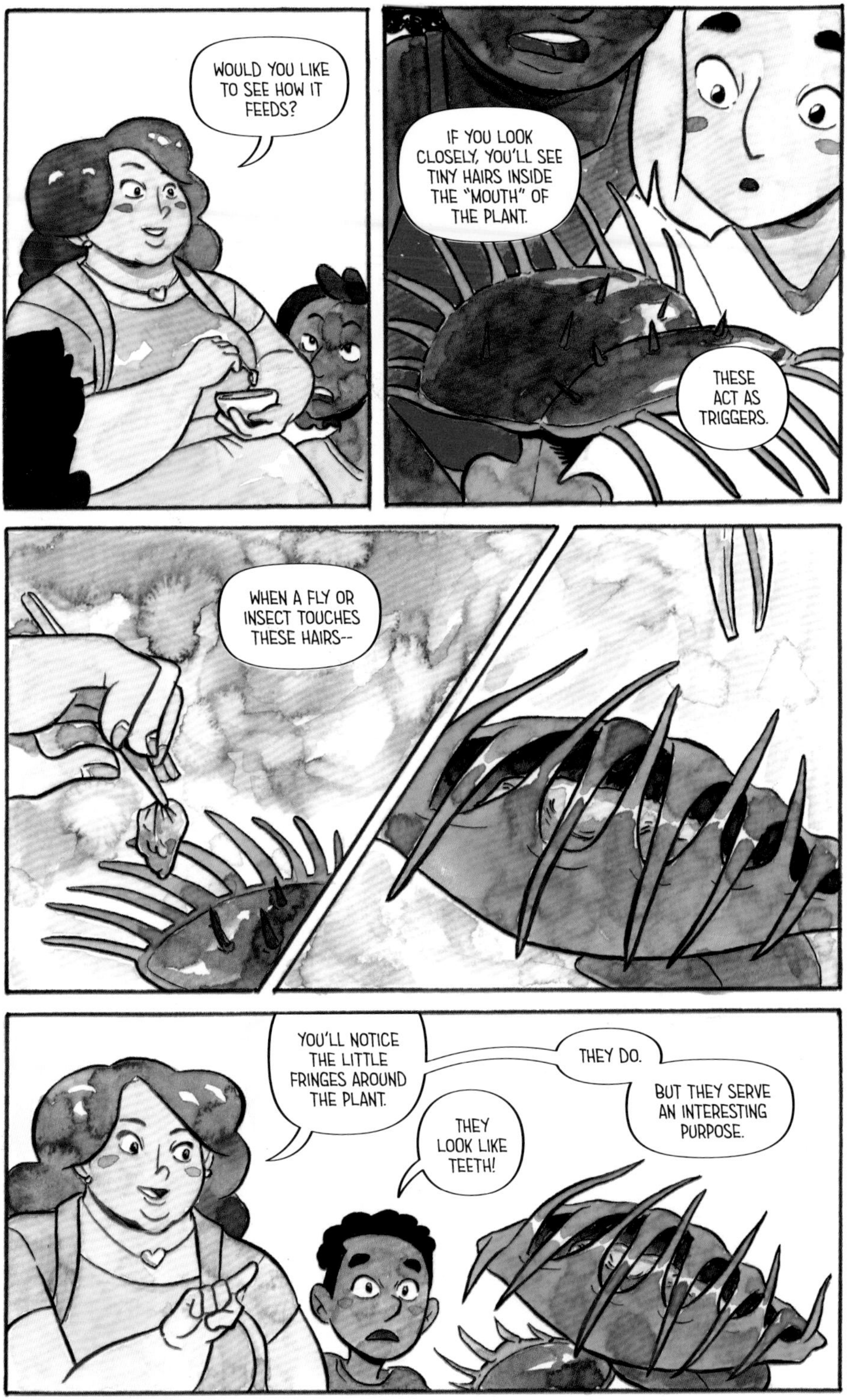
WOULD YOU LIKE TO SEE HOW IT FEEDS?
IF YOU LOOK CLOSELY, YOU'LL SEE TINY HAIRS INSIDE THE "MOUTH" OF THE PLANT.
THESE ACT AS TRIGGERS.
WHEN A FLY OR INSECT TOUCHES THESE HAIRS--
YOU'LL NOTICE THE LITTLE FRINGES AROUND THE PLANT.
THEY LOOK LIKE TEETH!
THEY DO.
BUT THEY SERVE AN INTERESTING PURPOSE.

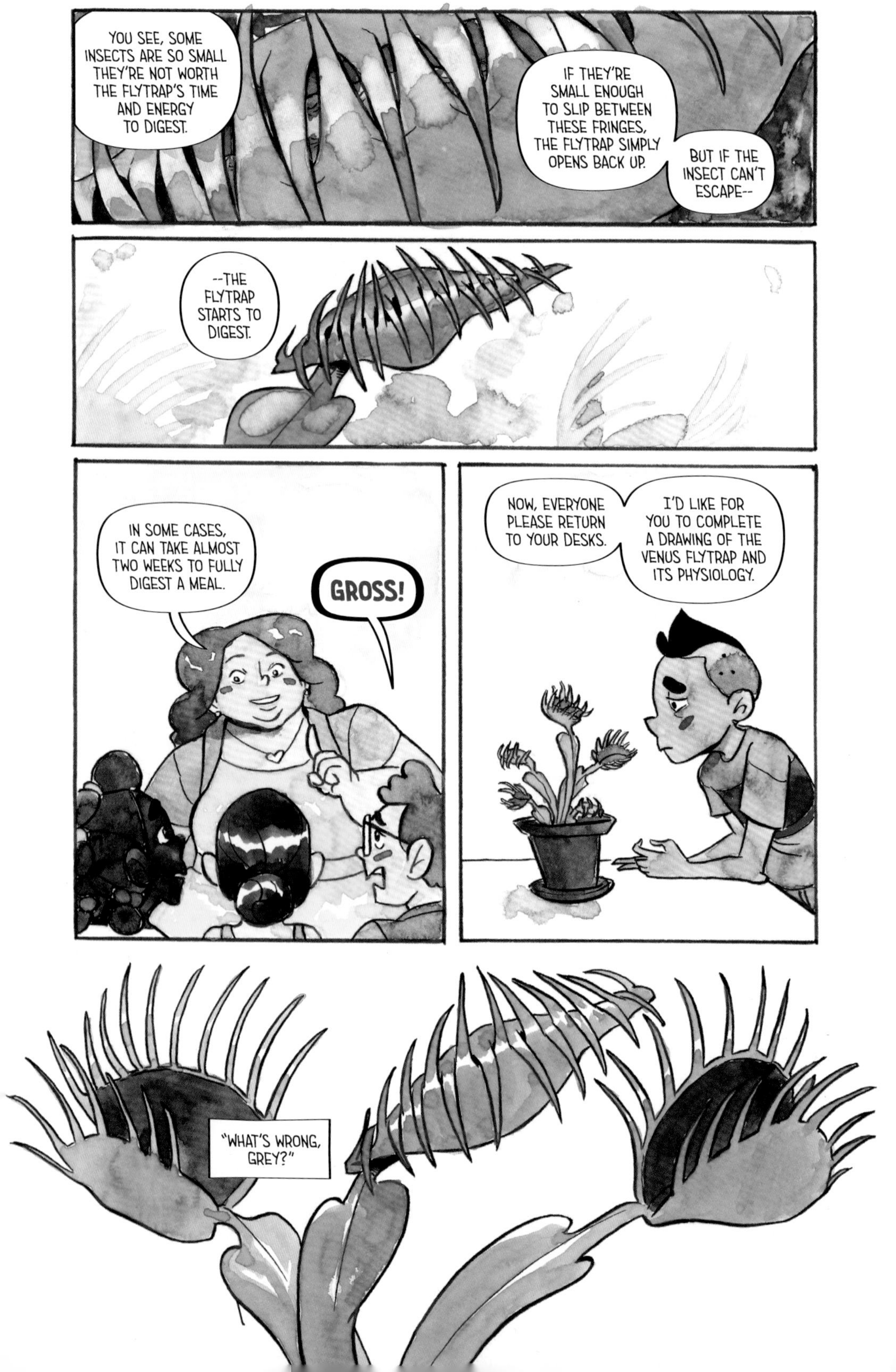
YOU SEE, SOME INSECTS ARE SO SMALL THEY'RE NOT WORTH THE FLYTRAP'S TIME AND ENERGY TO DIGEST.
IF THEY'RE SMALL ENOUGH TO SLIP BETWEEN THESE FRINGES, THE FLYTRAP SIMPLY OPENS BACK UP.
BUT IF THE INSECT CAN'T ESCAPE--
--THE FLYTRAP STARTS TO DIGEST.
IN SOME CASES, IT CAN TAKE ALMOST TWO WEEKS TO FULLY DIGEST A MEAL.
GROSS!
NOW, EVERYONE PLEASE RETURN TO YOUR DESKS.
I'D LIKE FOR YOU TO COMPLETE A DRAWING OF THE VENUS FLYTRAP AND ITS PHYSIOLOGY.
"WHAT'S WRONG, GREY?"

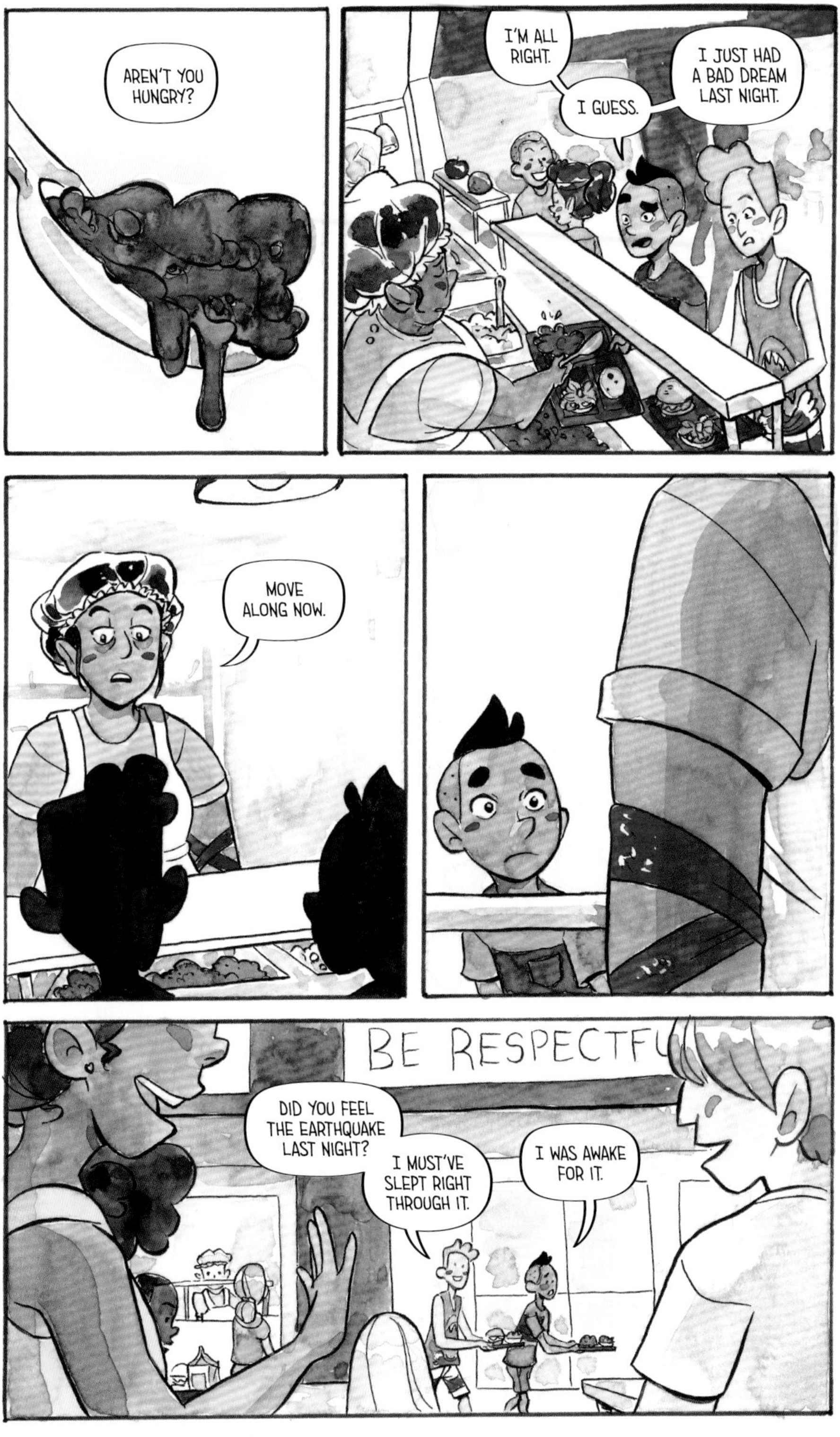
AREN'T YOU HUNGRY?
I'M ALL RIGHT.
I GUESS.
I JUST HAD A BAD DREAM LAST NIGHT.
MOVE ALONG NOW.
BE RESPECTFU
DID YOU FEEL THE EARTHQUAKE LAST NIGHT?
I MUST'VE SLEPT RIGHT THROUGH IT.
I WAS AWAKE FOR IT.

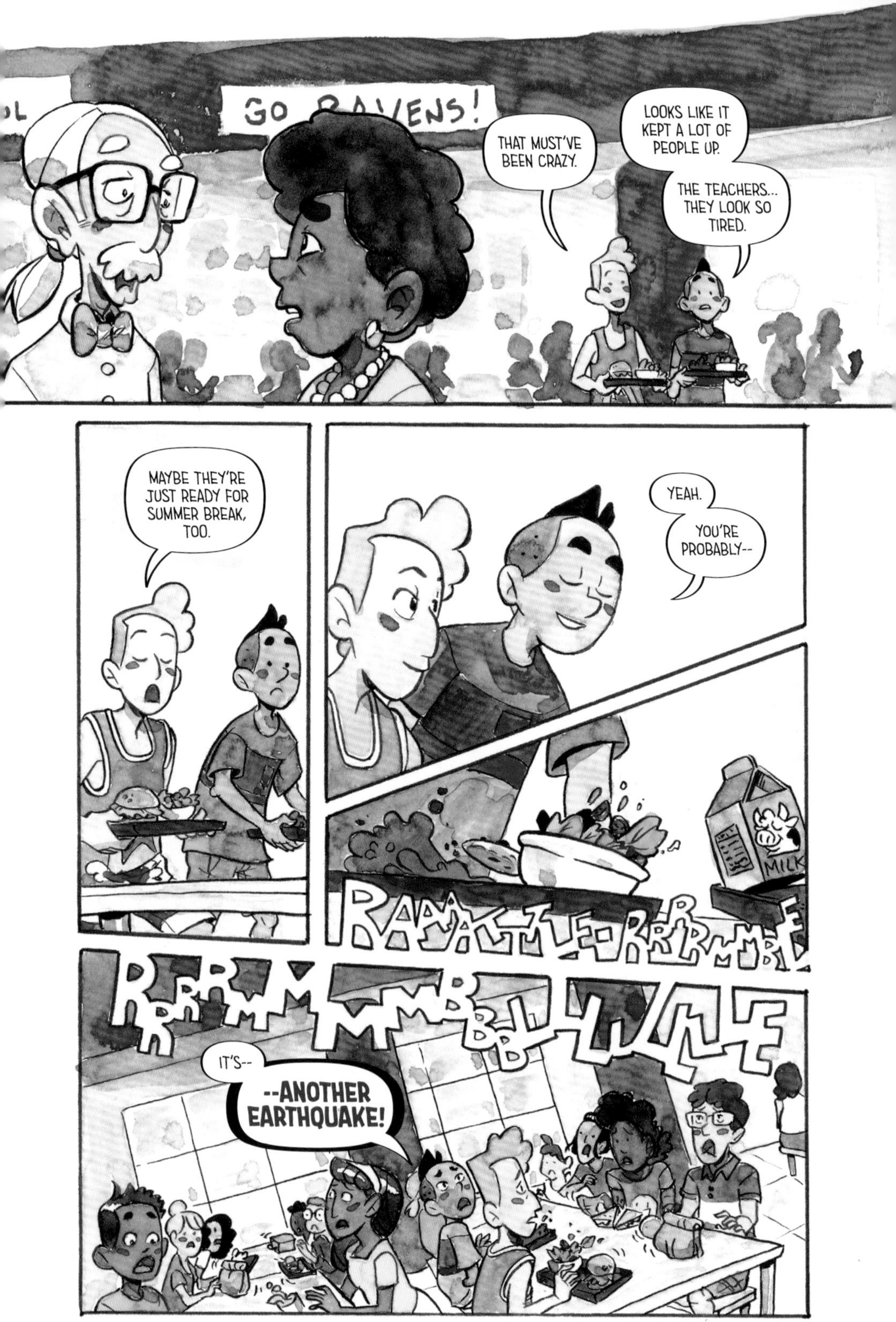
GO RAVENS!
THAT MUST'VE BEEN CRAZY.
LOOKS LIKE IT KEPT A LOT OF PEOPLE UP.
THE TEACHERS... THEY LOOK SO TIRED.
MAYBE THEY'RE JUST READY FOR SUMMER BREAK, TOO.
YEAH.
YOU'RE PROBABLY--
MILK
IT'S--
--ANOTHER EARTHQUAKE!

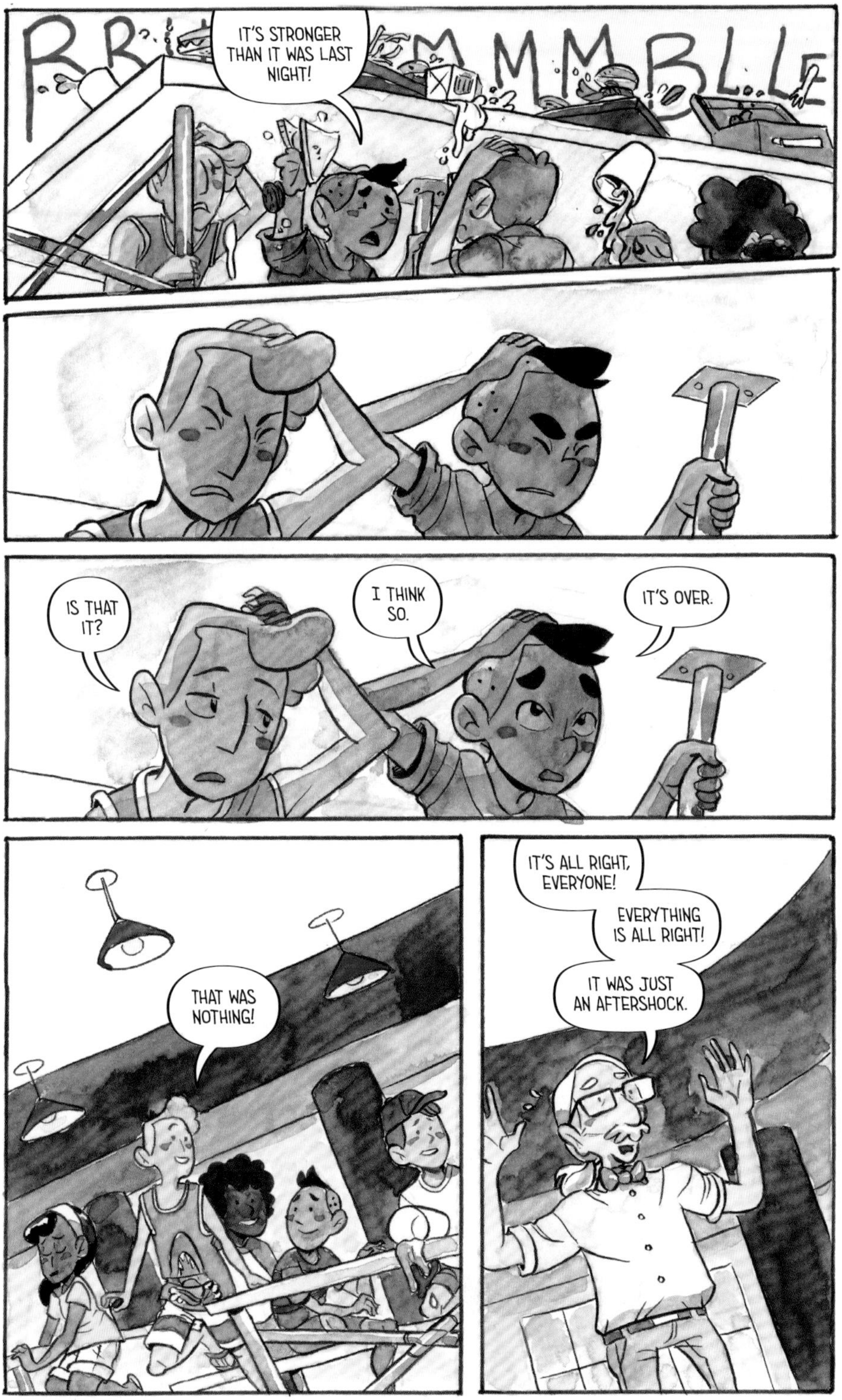
RR MMMBLLE
IT'S STRONGER THAN IT WAS LAST NIGHT!
IS THAT IT?
I THINK SO.
IT'S OVER.
THAT WAS NOTHING!
IT'S ALL RIGHT, EVERYONE!
EVERYTHING IS ALL RIGHT!
IT WAS JUST AN AFTERSHOCK.

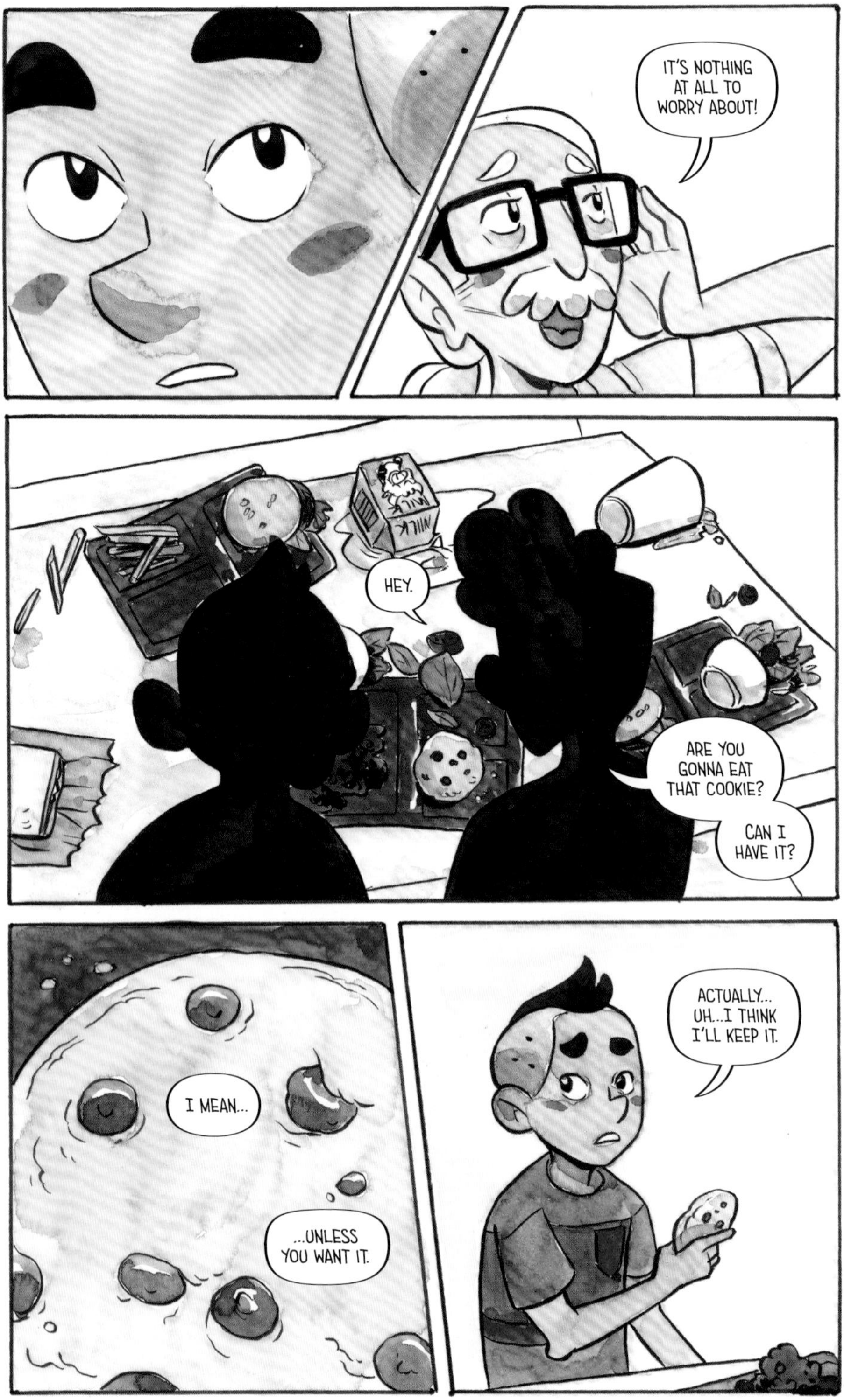
IT'S NOTHING AT ALL TO WORRY ABOUT!
HEY.
ARE YOU GONNA EAT THAT COOKIE?
CAN I HAVE IT?
I MEAN...
...UNLESS YOU WANT IT.
ACTUALLY... UH...I THINK I'LL KEEP IT.

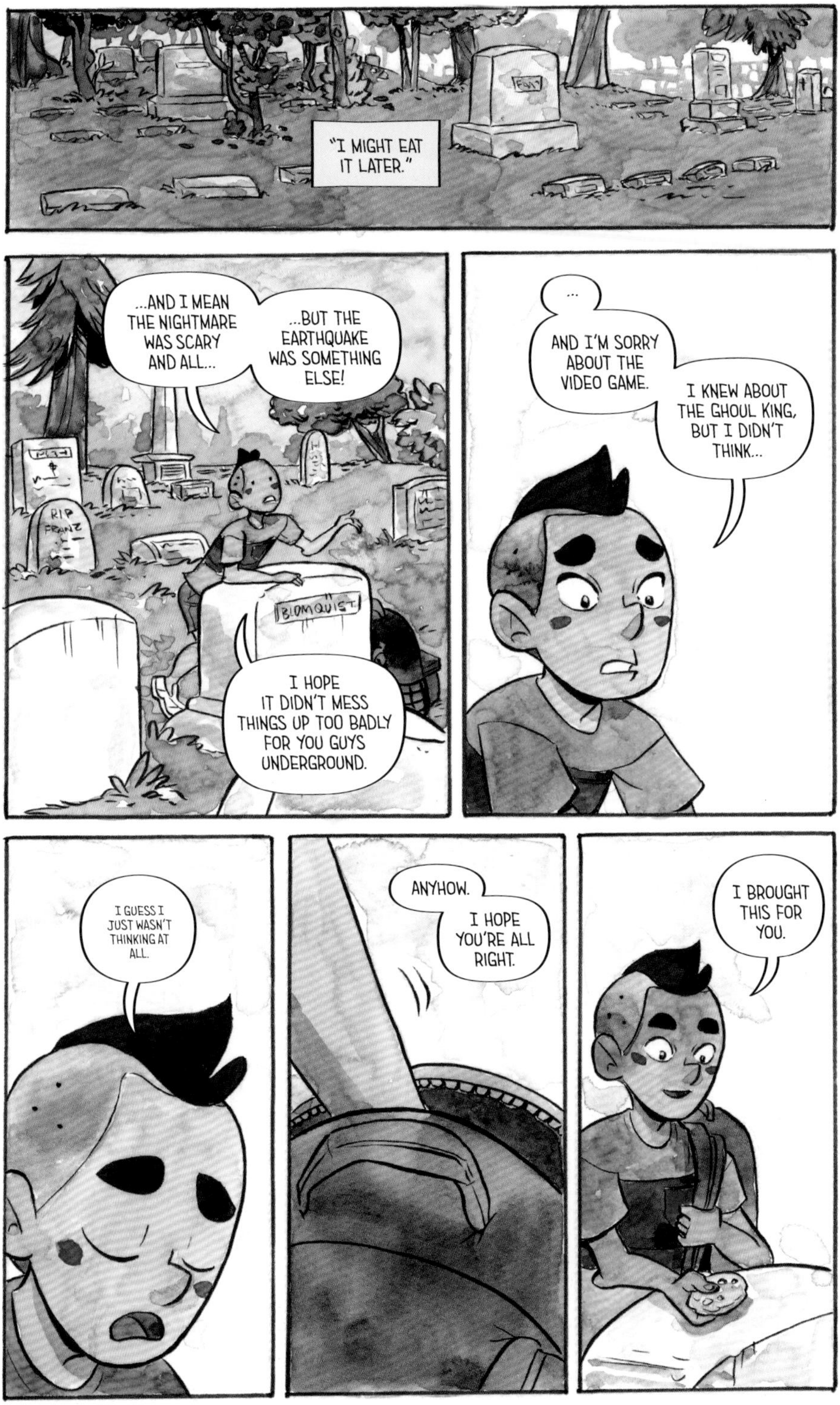
"I MIGHT EAT IT LATER."
...AND I MEAN THE NIGHTMARE WAS SCARY AND ALL...
...BUT THE EARTHQUAKE WAS SOMETHING ELSE!
BLOMQUIST
RIP FRANZ
I HOPE IT DIDN'T MESS THINGS UP TOO BADLY FOR YOU GUYS UNDERGROUND.
...
AND I'M SORRY ABOUT THE VIDEO GAME.
I KNEW ABOUT THE GHOUL KING, BUT I DIDN'T THINK...
I GUESS I JUST WASN'T THINKING AT ALL.
ANYHOW.
I HOPE YOU'RE ALL RIGHT.
I BROUGHT THIS FOR YOU.

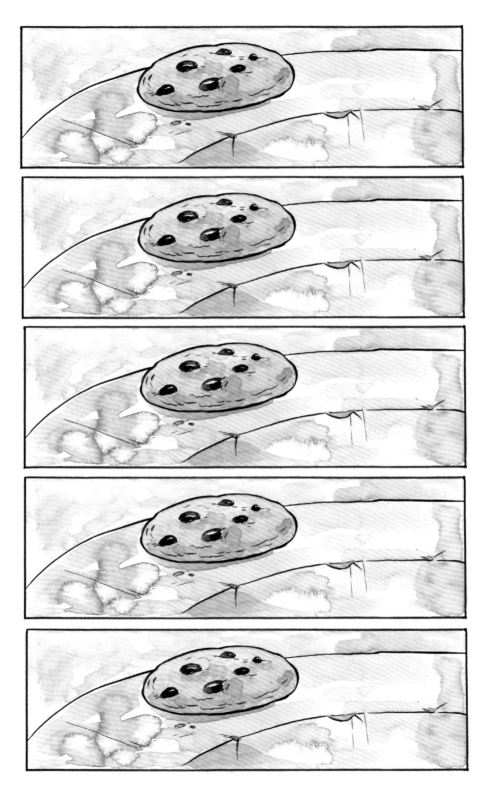

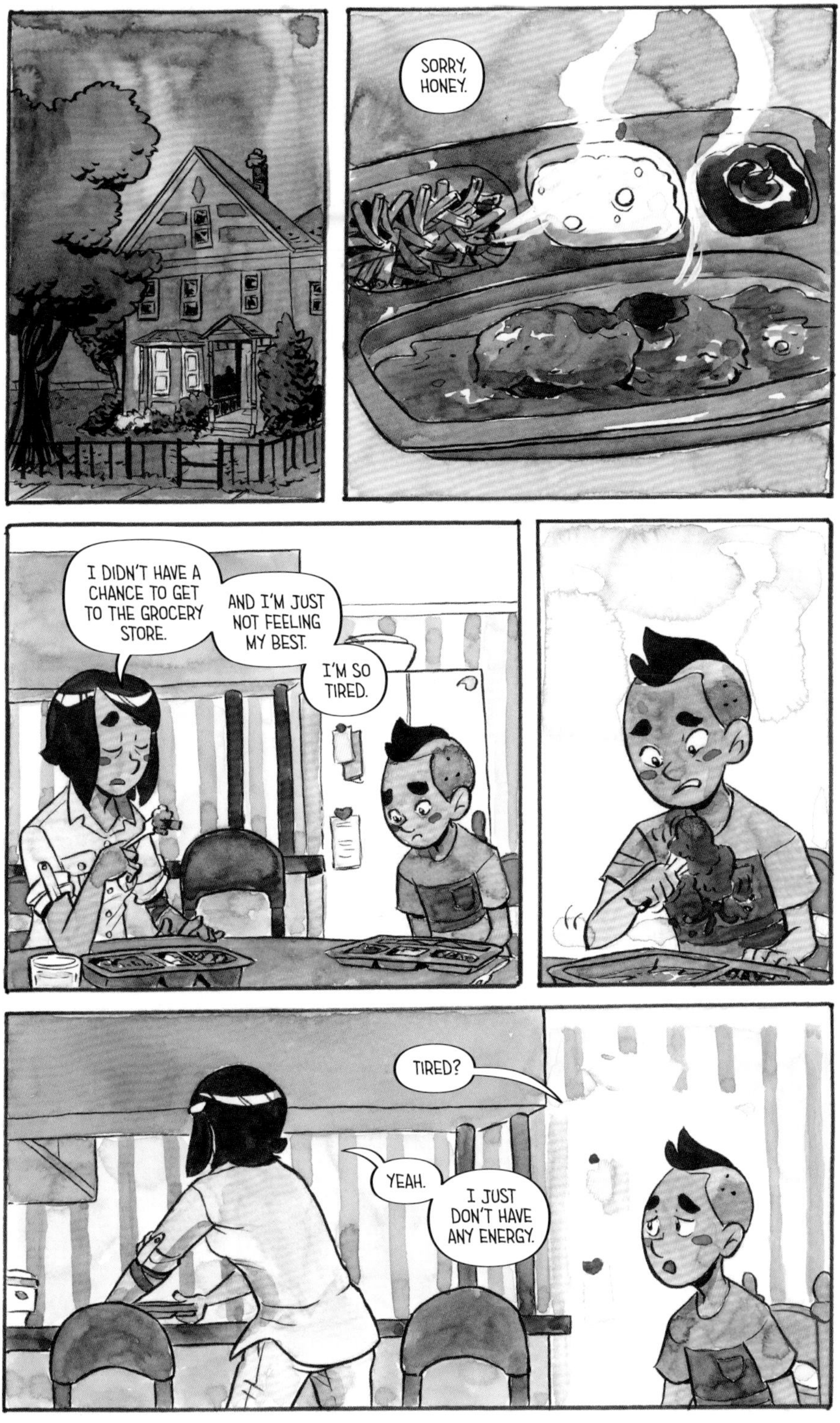
SORRY, HONEY.
I DIDN'T HAVE A CHANCE TO GET TO THE GROCERY STORE.
AND I'M JUST NOT FEELING MY BEST.
I'M SO TIRED.
TIRED?
YEAH.
I JUST DON'T HAVE ANY ENERGY.

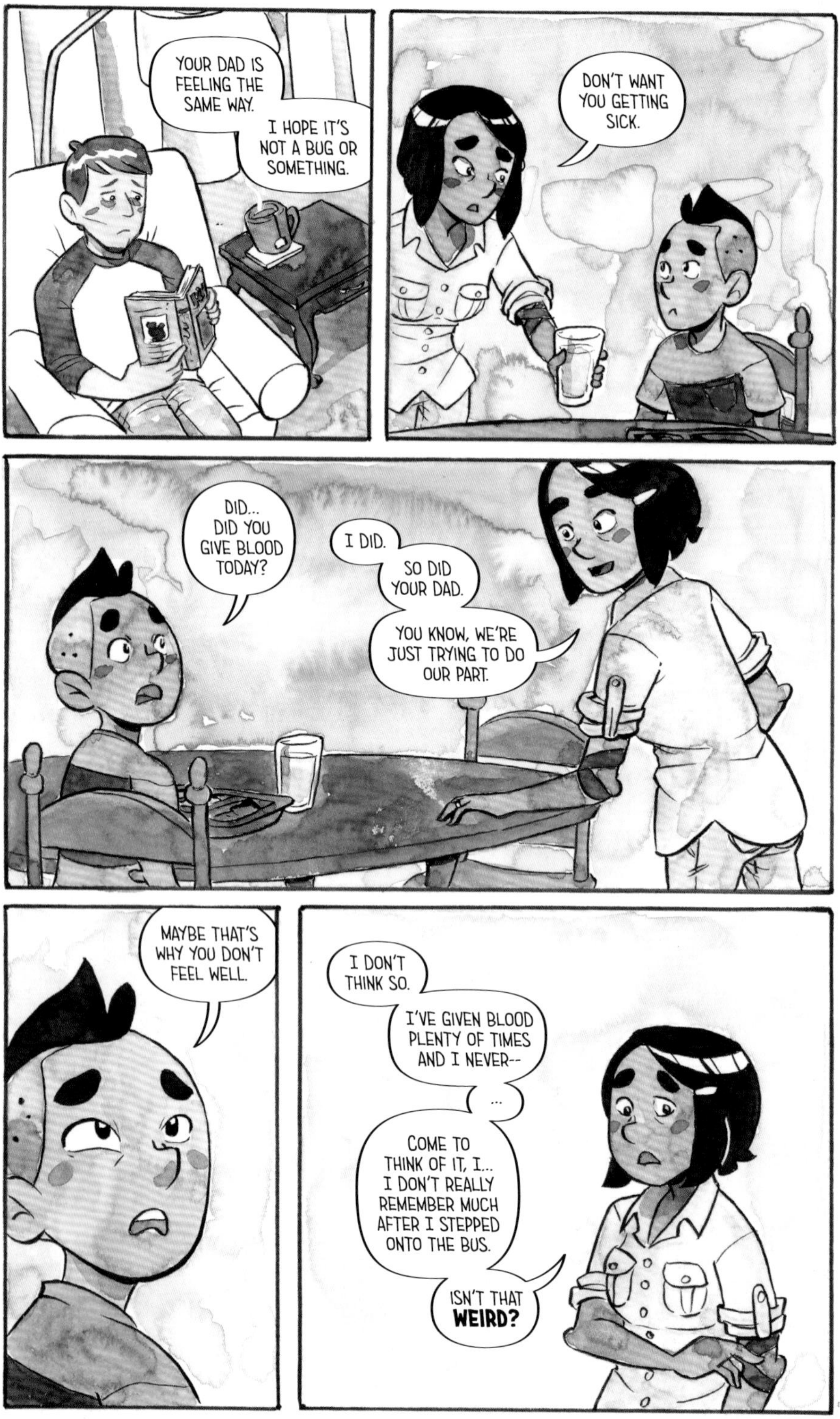
YOUR DAD IS FEELING THE SAME WAY.
I HOPE IT'S NOT A BUG OR SOMETHING.
DON'T WANT YOU GETTING SICK.
DID... DID YOU GIVE BLOOD TODAY?
I DID.
SO DID YOUR DAD.
YOU KNOW, WE'RE JUST TRYING TO DO OUR PART.
MAYBE THAT'S WHY YOU DON'T FEEL WELL.
I DON'T THINK SO.
I'VE GIVEN BLOOD PLENTY OF TIMES AND I NEVER--
...
COME TO THINK OF IT, I... I DON'T REALLY REMEMBER MUCH AFTER I STEPPED ONTO THE BUS.
ISN'T THAT **WEIRD?**

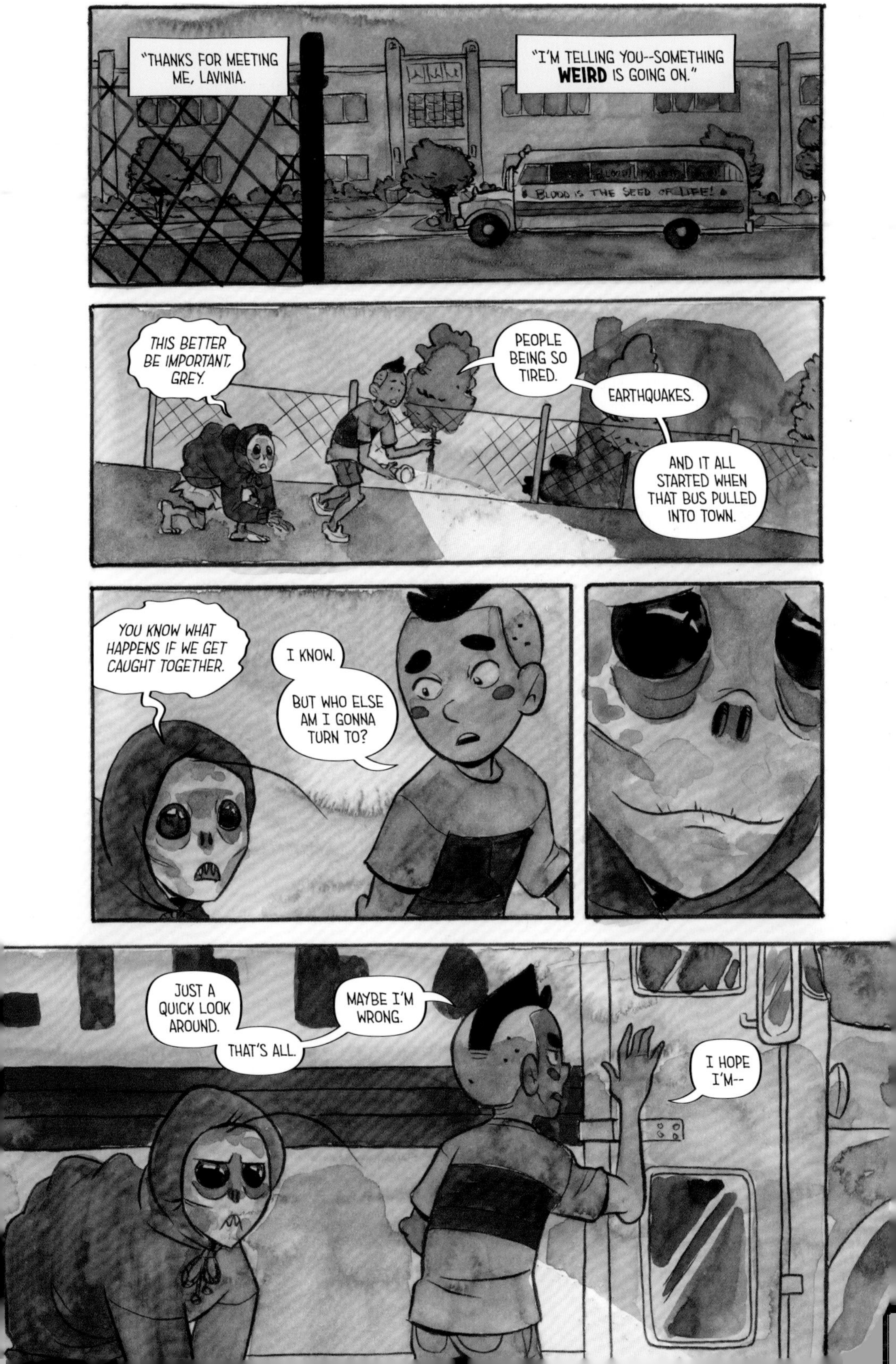

"THANKS FOR MEETING ME, LAVINIA.
"I'M TELLING YOU--SOMETHING **WEIRD** IS GOING ON."
BLOOD IS THE SEED OF LIFE!
THIS BETTER BE IMPORTANT, GREY.
PEOPLE BEING SO TIRED.
EARTHQUAKES.
AND IT ALL STARTED WHEN THAT BUS PULLED INTO TOWN.
YOU KNOW WHAT HAPPENS IF WE GET CAUGHT TOGETHER.
I KNOW.
BUT WHO ELSE AM I GONNA TURN TO?
JUST A QUICK LOOK AROUND.
THAT'S ALL.
MAYBE I'M WRONG.
I HOPE I'M--

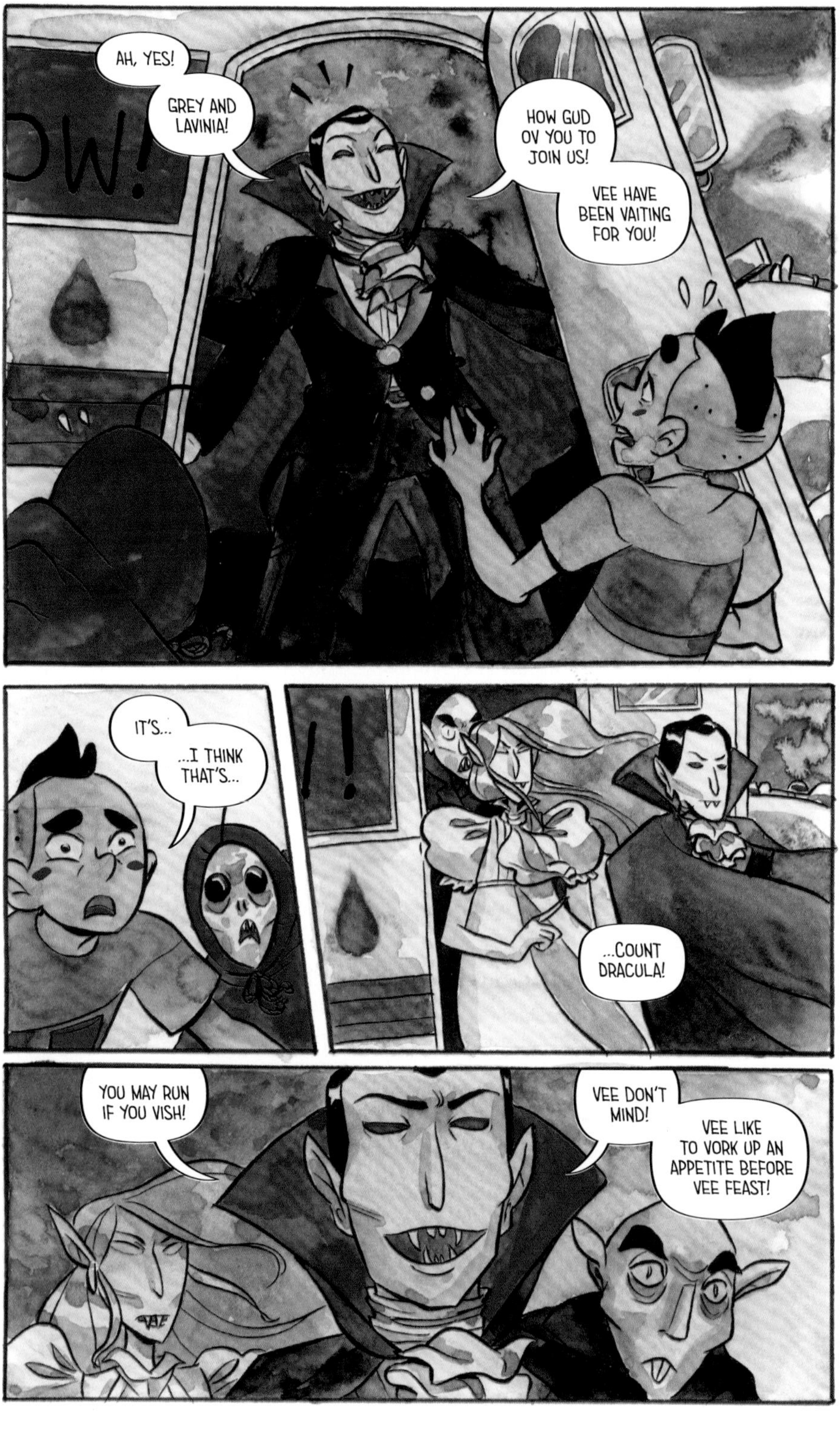
AH, YES!
GREY AND LAVINIA!
HOW GUD OV YOU TO JOIN US!
VEE HAVE BEEN VAITING FOR YOU!
IT'S...
...I THINK THAT'S...
!
...COUNT DRACULA!
YOU MAY RUN IF YOU VISH!
VEE DON'T MIND!
VEE LIKE TO VORK UP AN APPETITE BEFORE VEE FEAST!

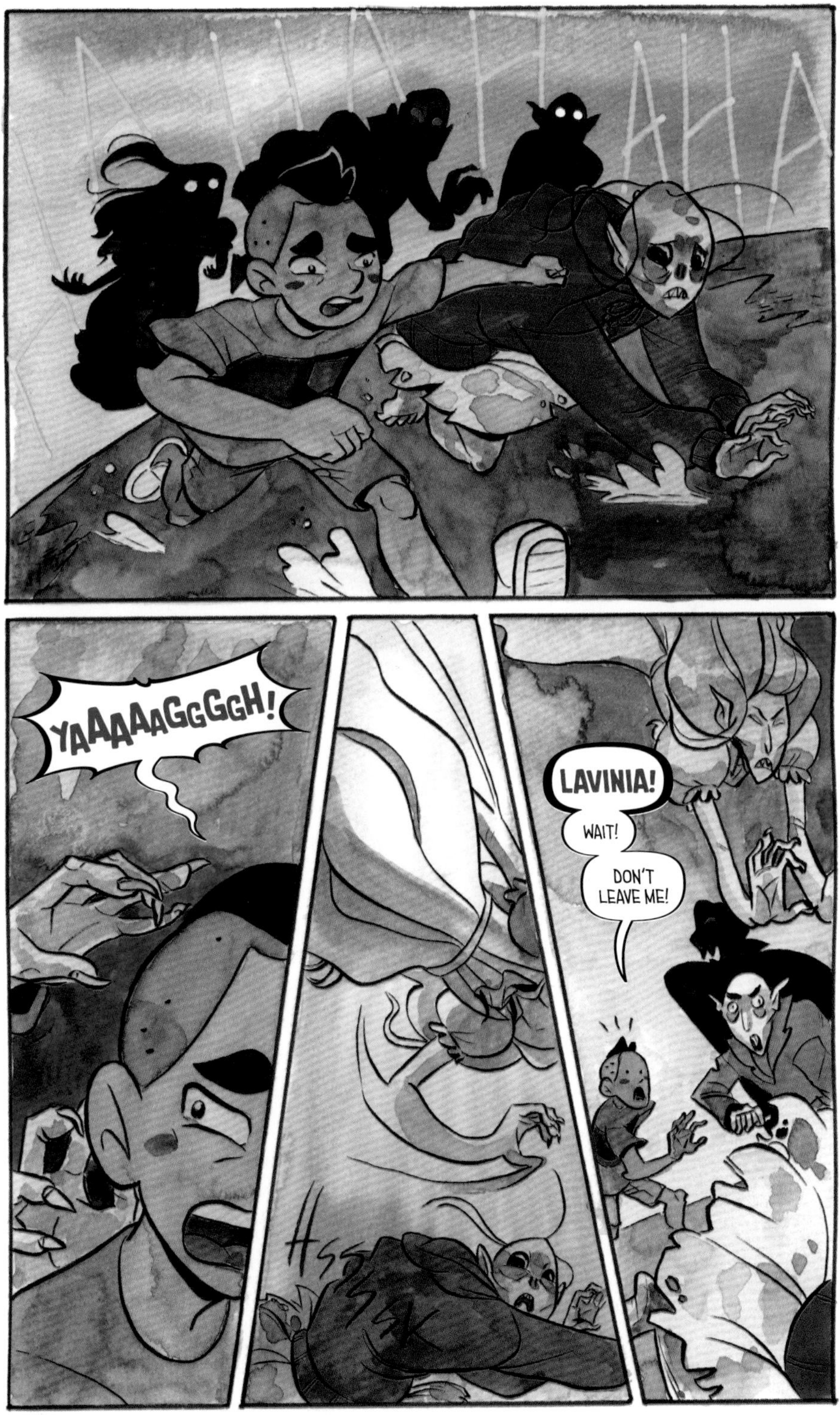
YAAAAAGGGGH!
LAVINIA!
WAIT!
DON'T LEAVE ME!

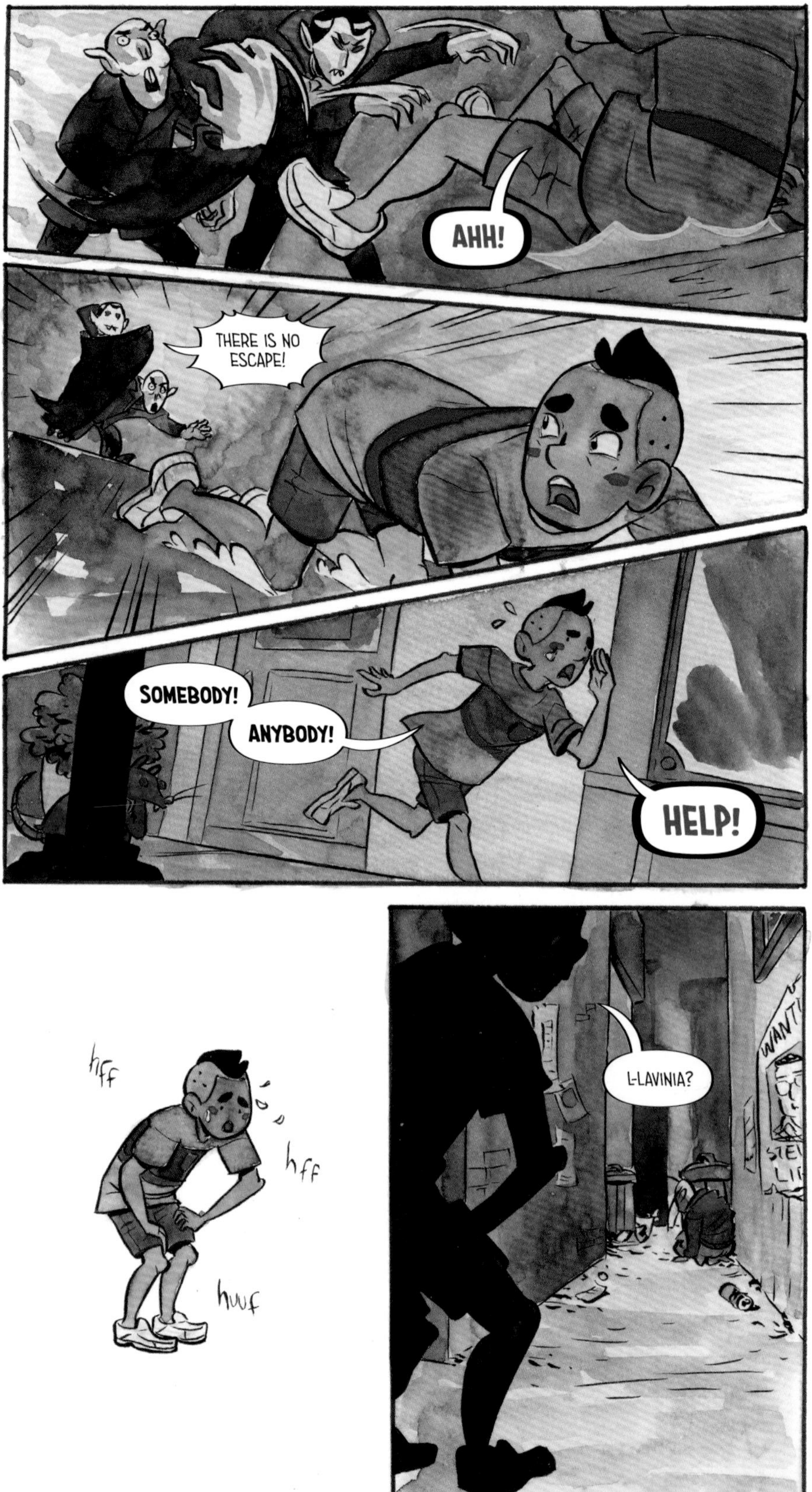
AHH!
THERE IS NO ESCAPE!
SOMEBODY!
ANYBODY!
HELP!
hff
hff
huuf
L-LAVINIA?

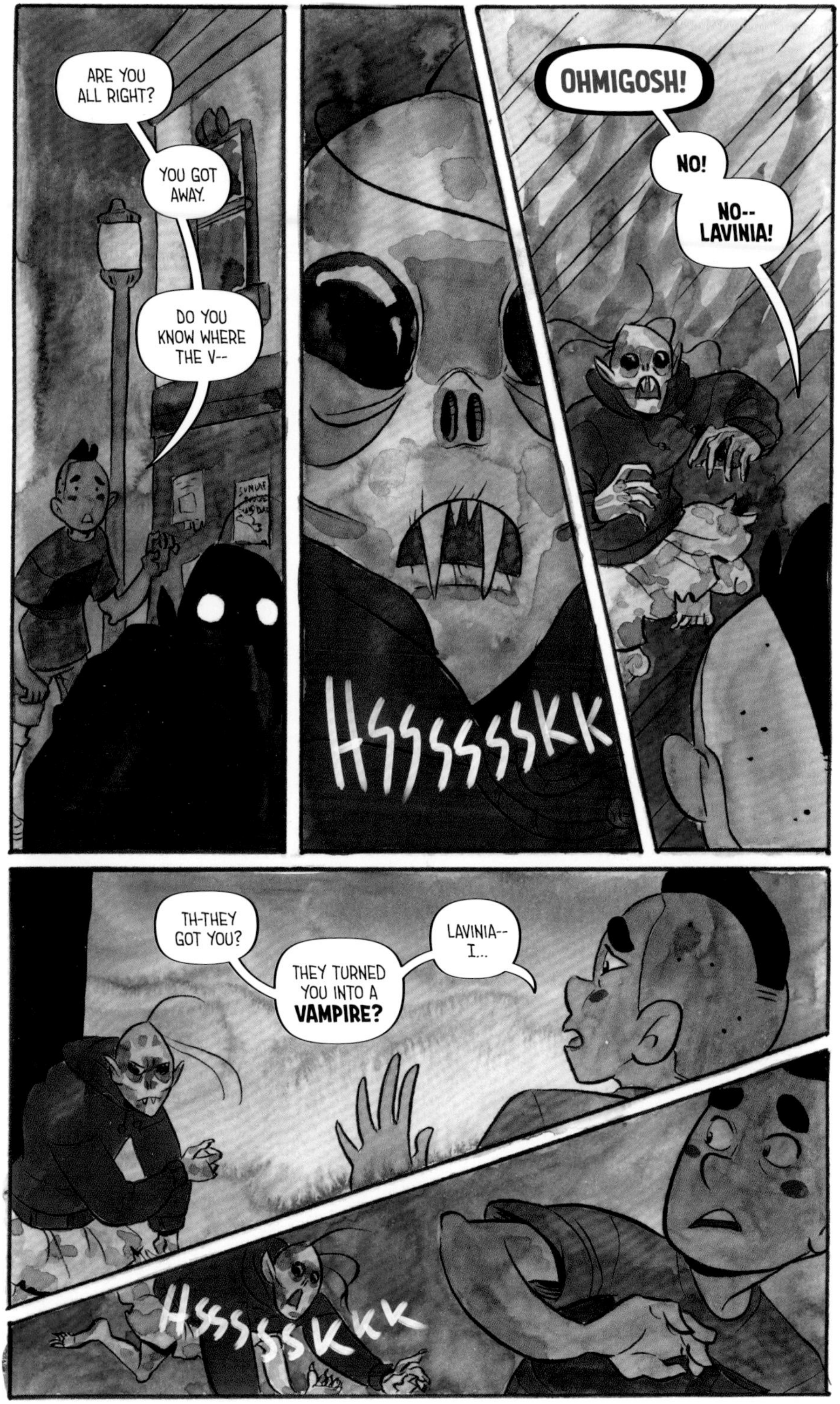
ARE YOU ALL RIGHT?
YOU GOT AWAY.
DO YOU KNOW WHERE THE V--
HSSSSSSSKK
OHMIGOSH!
NO!
NO-- LAVINIA!
TH-THEY GOT YOU?
THEY TURNED YOU INTO A **VAMPIRE?**
LAVINIA-- I...
HSSSSSKKK

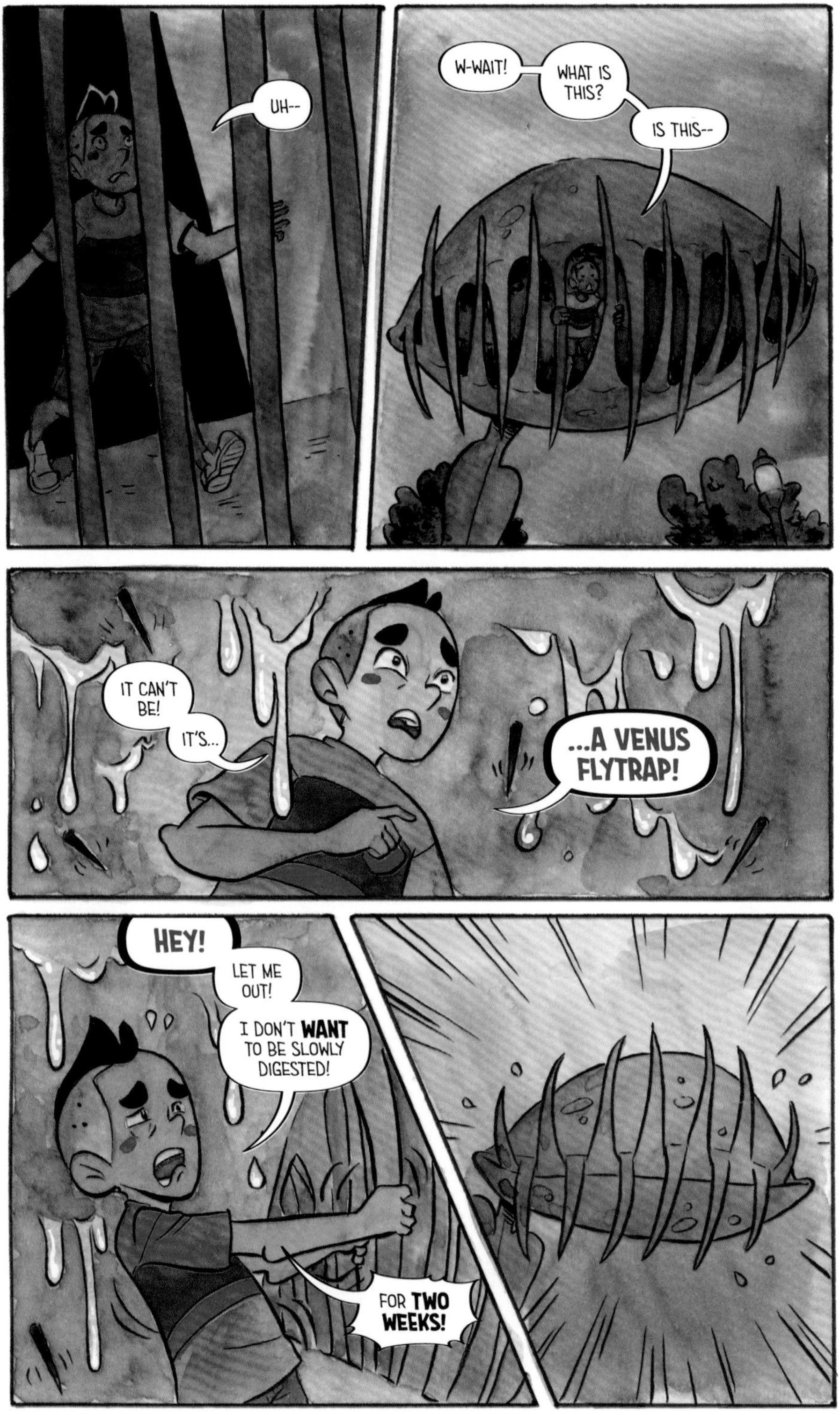

UH--
W-WAIT!
WHAT IS THIS?
IS THIS--
IT CAN'T BE!
IT'S...
...A VENUS FLYTRAP!
HEY!
LET ME OUT!
I DON'T **WANT** TO BE SLOWLY DIGESTED!
FOR **TWO WEEKS!**

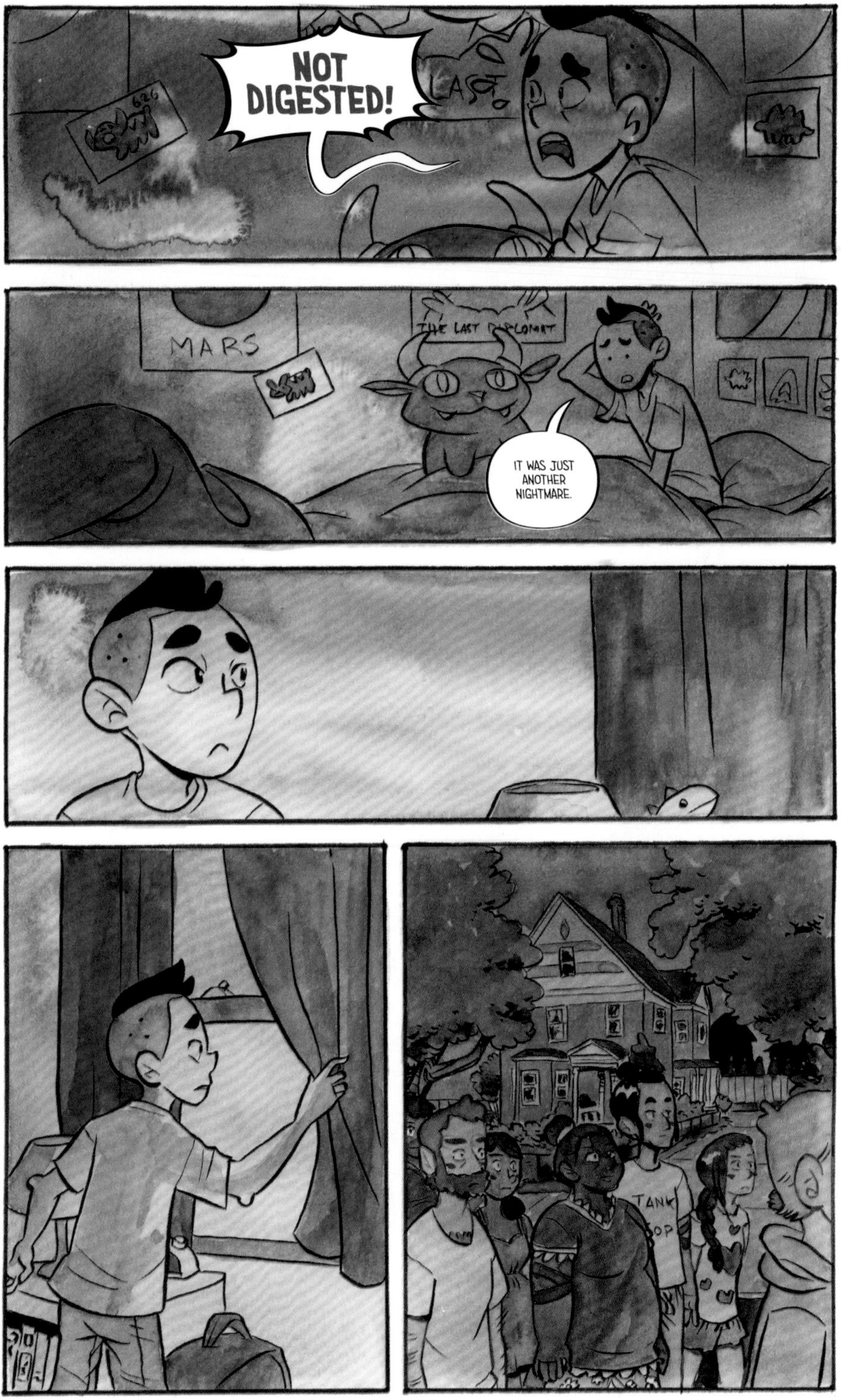
NOT DIGESTED!
IT WAS JUST ANOTHER NIGHTMARE.

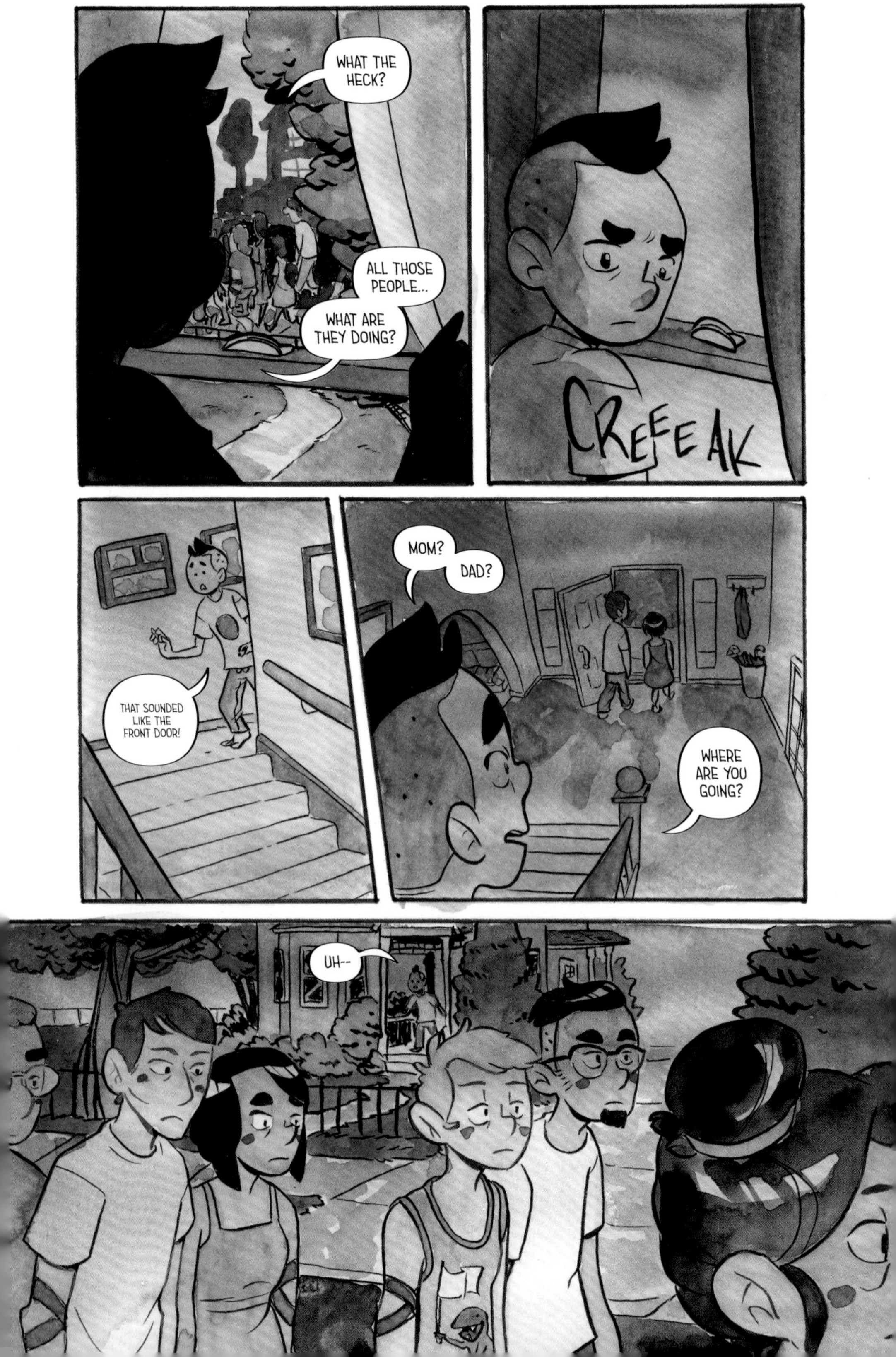
WHAT THE HECK?
ALL THOSE PEOPLE...
WHAT ARE THEY DOING?
CREEEAK
THAT SOUNDED LIKE THE FRONT DOOR!
MOM?
DAD?
WHERE ARE YOU GOING?
UH--

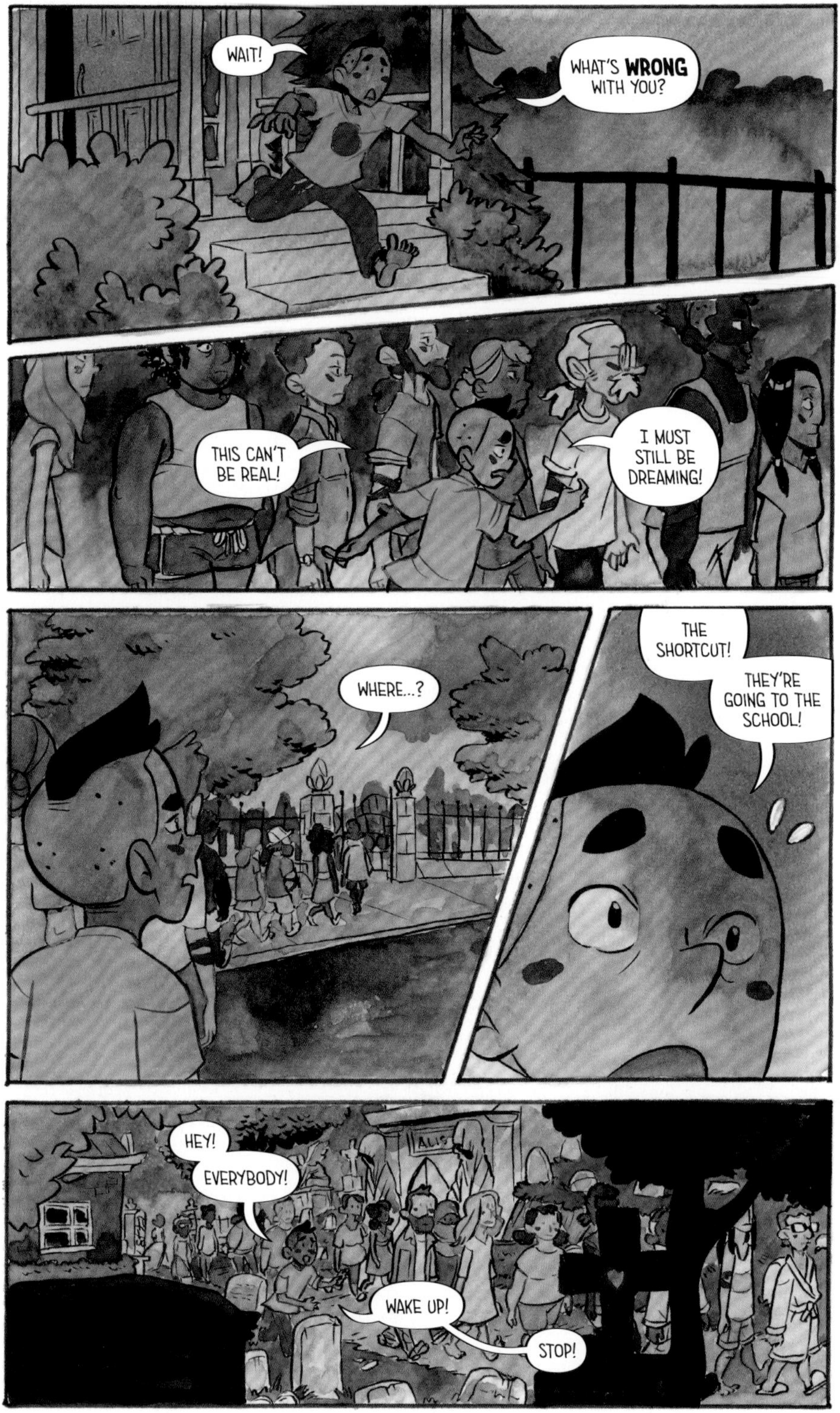
WAIT!
WHAT'S **WRONG** WITH YOU?
THIS CAN'T BE REAL!
I MUST STILL BE DREAMING!
WHERE...?
THE SHORTCUT!
THEY'RE GOING TO THE SCHOOL!
HEY!
EVERYBODY!
WAKE UP!
STOP!

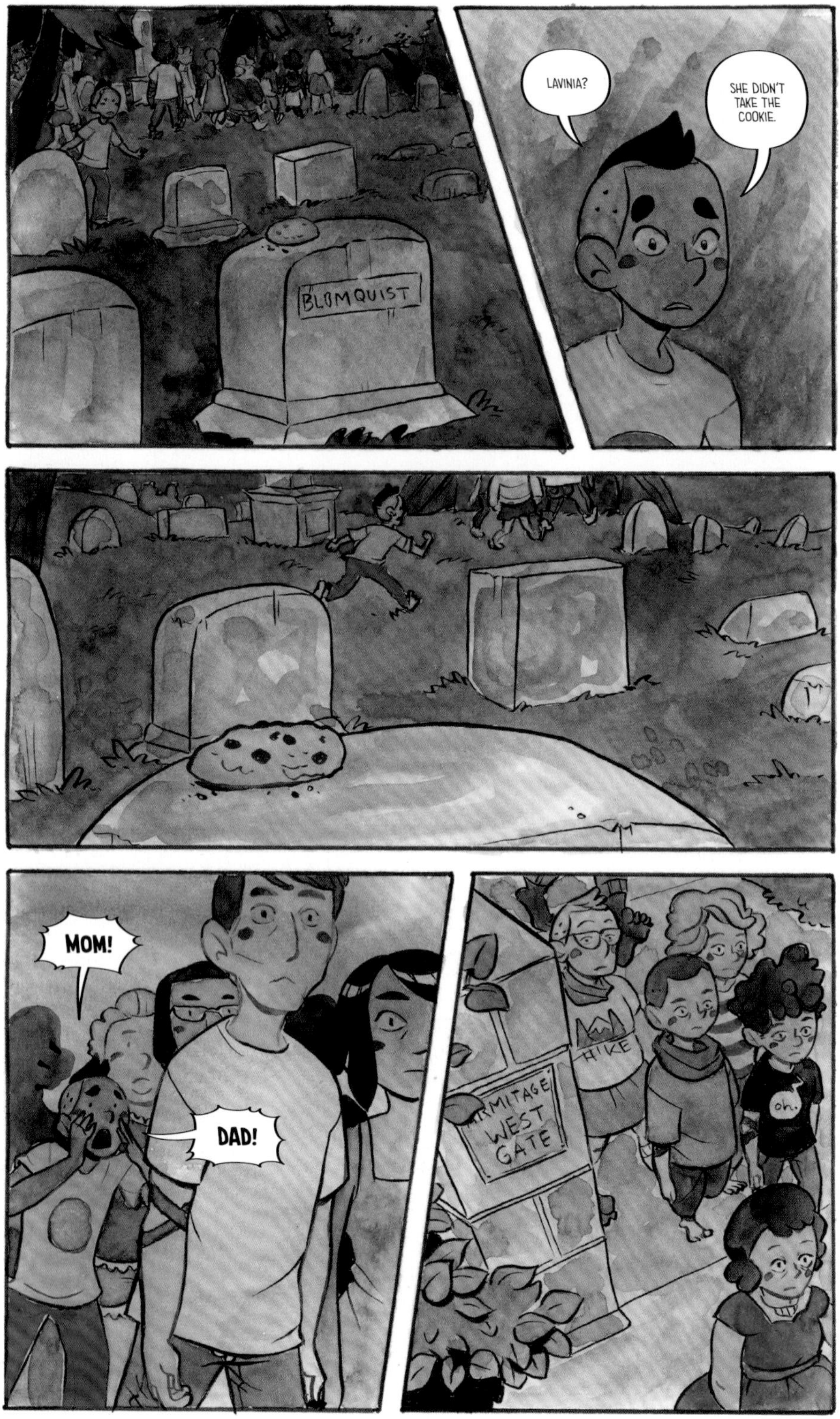
BLOMQUIST
LAVINIA?
SHE DIDN'T TAKE THE COOKIE.
MOM!
DAD!
HIKE
oh.
ARMITAGE WEST GATE

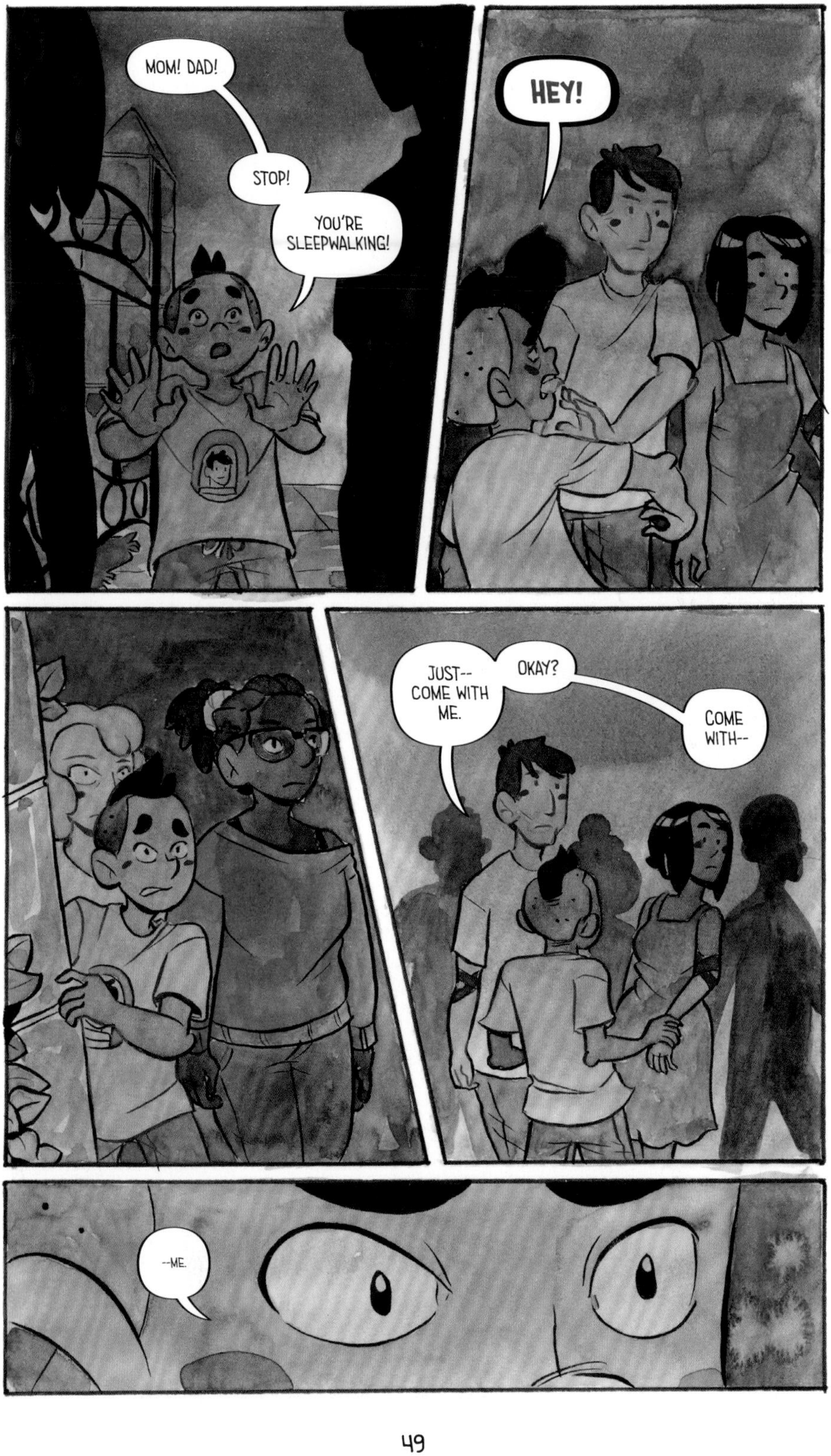
MOM! DAD!
STOP!
YOU'RE SLEEPWALKING!
HEY!
JUST-- COME WITH ME.
OKAY?
COME WITH--
--ME.

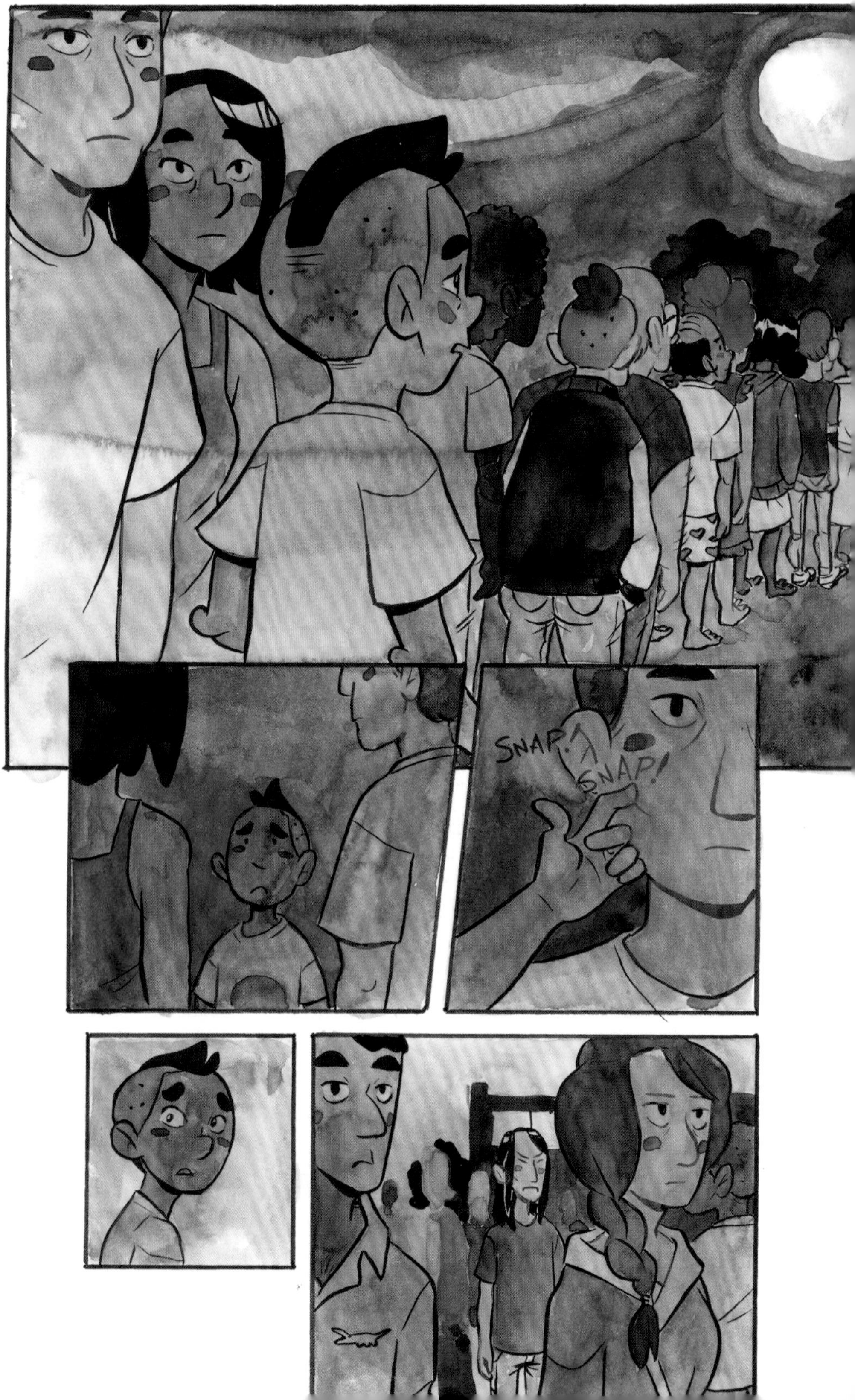
SNAP!
SNAP!

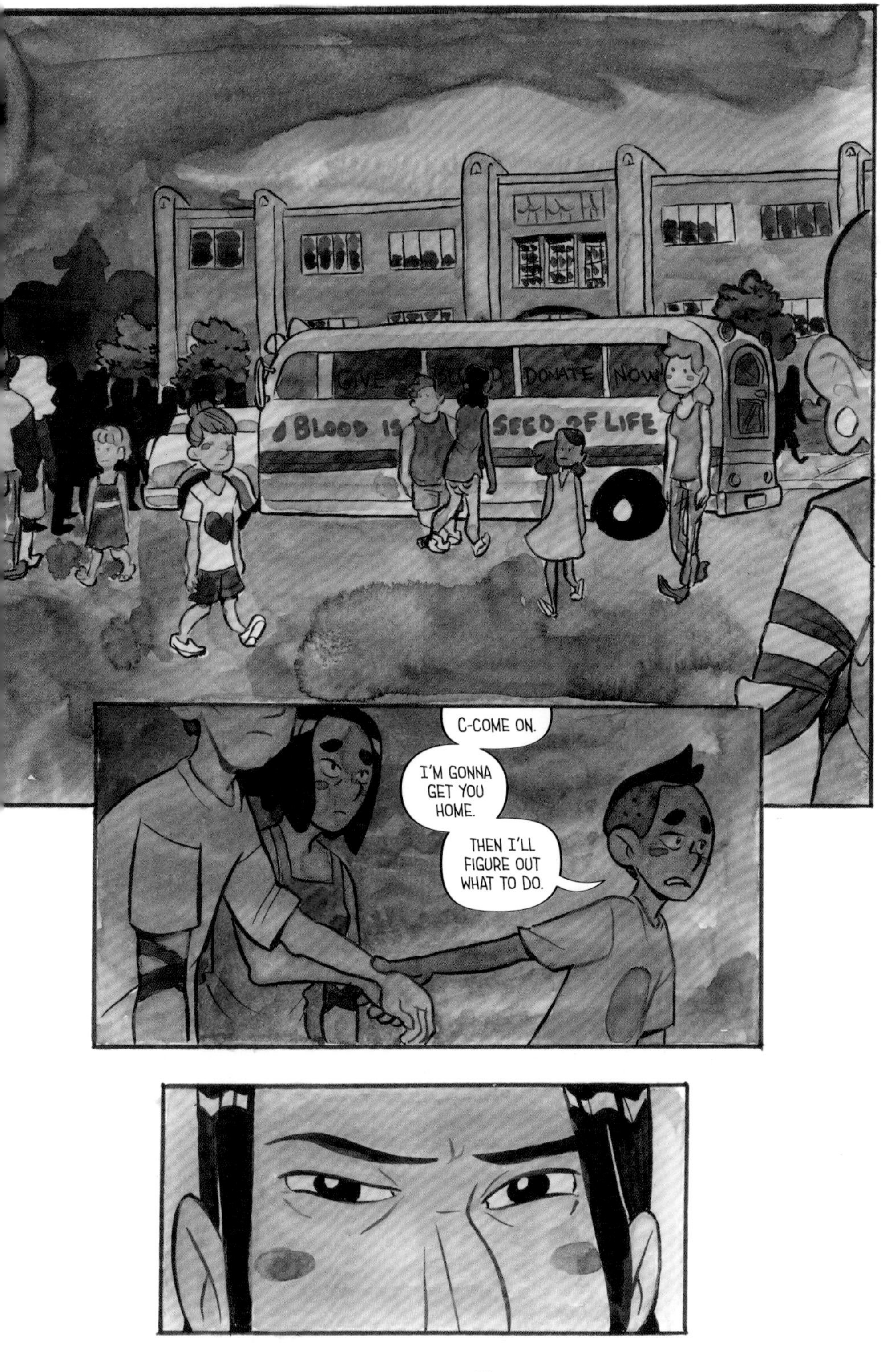
GIVE
DONATE NOW
BLOOD IS
SEED OF LIFE
C-COME ON.
I'M GONNA GET YOU HOME.
THEN I'LL FIGURE OUT WHAT TO DO.

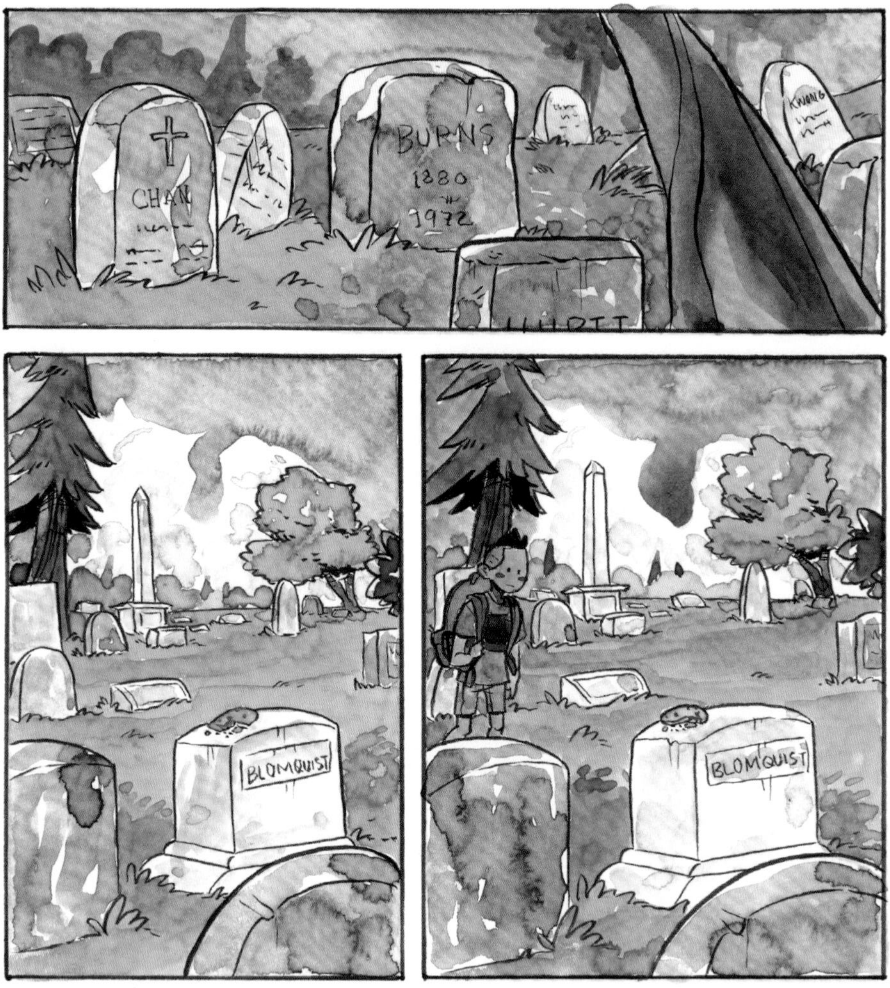
CHAN
BURNS
1880
1972
KWONG
BLOMQUIST
BLOMQUIST
LAVINIA?

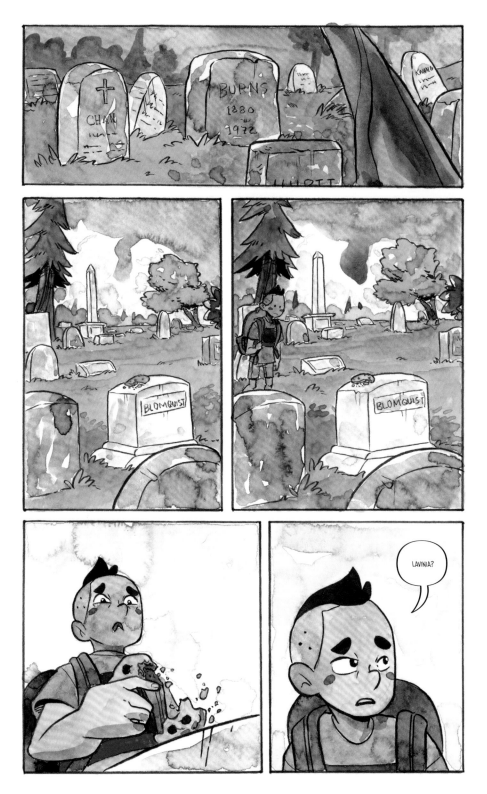

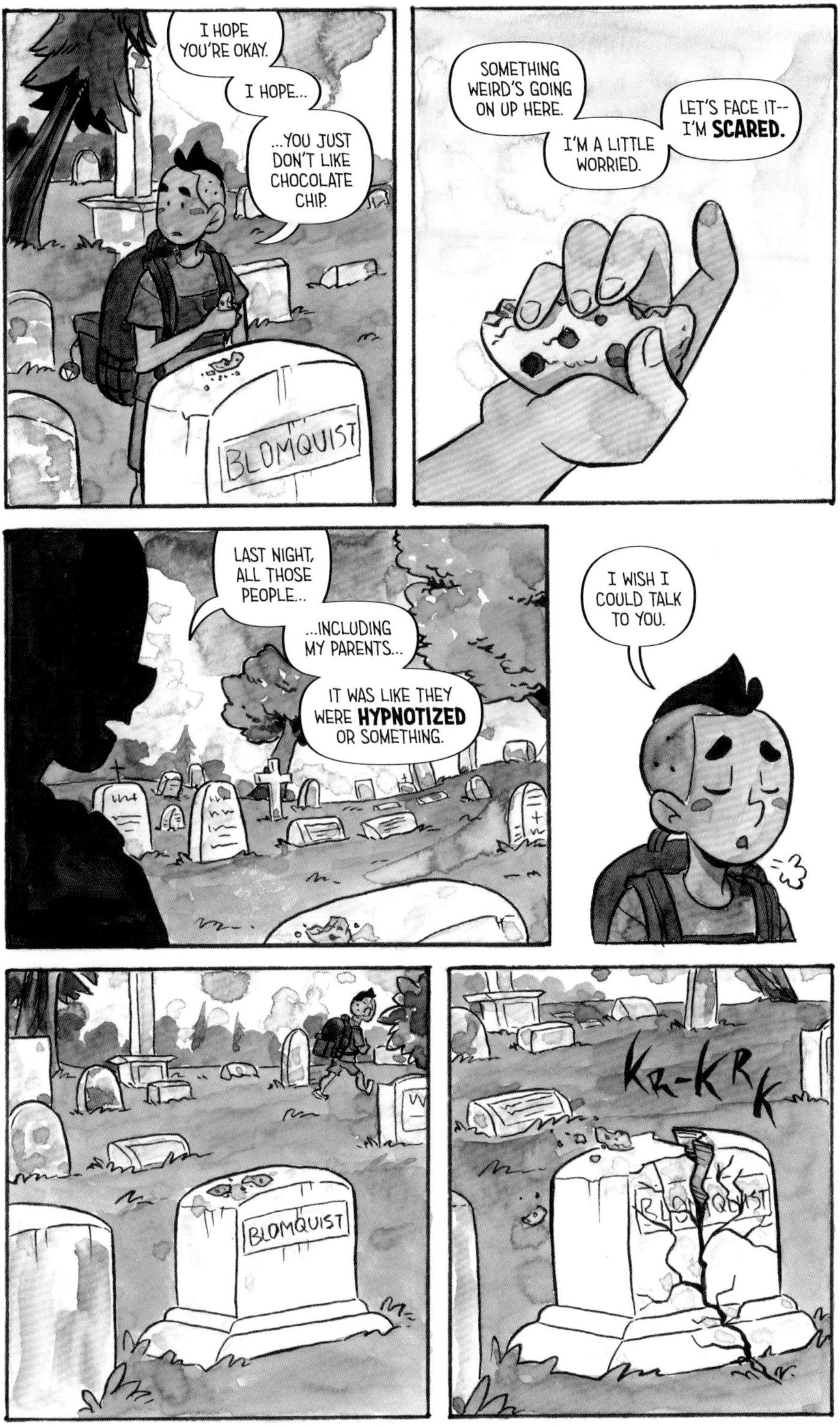

I HOPE YOU'RE OKAY.
I HOPE...
...YOU JUST DON'T LIKE CHOCOLATE CHIP.
BLOMQUIST
SOMETHING WEIRD'S GOING ON UP HERE.
I'M A LITTLE WORRIED.
LET'S FACE IT-- I'M **SCARED.**
LAST NIGHT, ALL THOSE PEOPLE...
...INCLUDING MY PARENTS...
IT WAS LIKE THEY WERE **HYPNOTIZED** OR SOMETHING.
I WISH I COULD TALK TO YOU.
BLOMQUIST
KR-KRK
BLOMQUIST

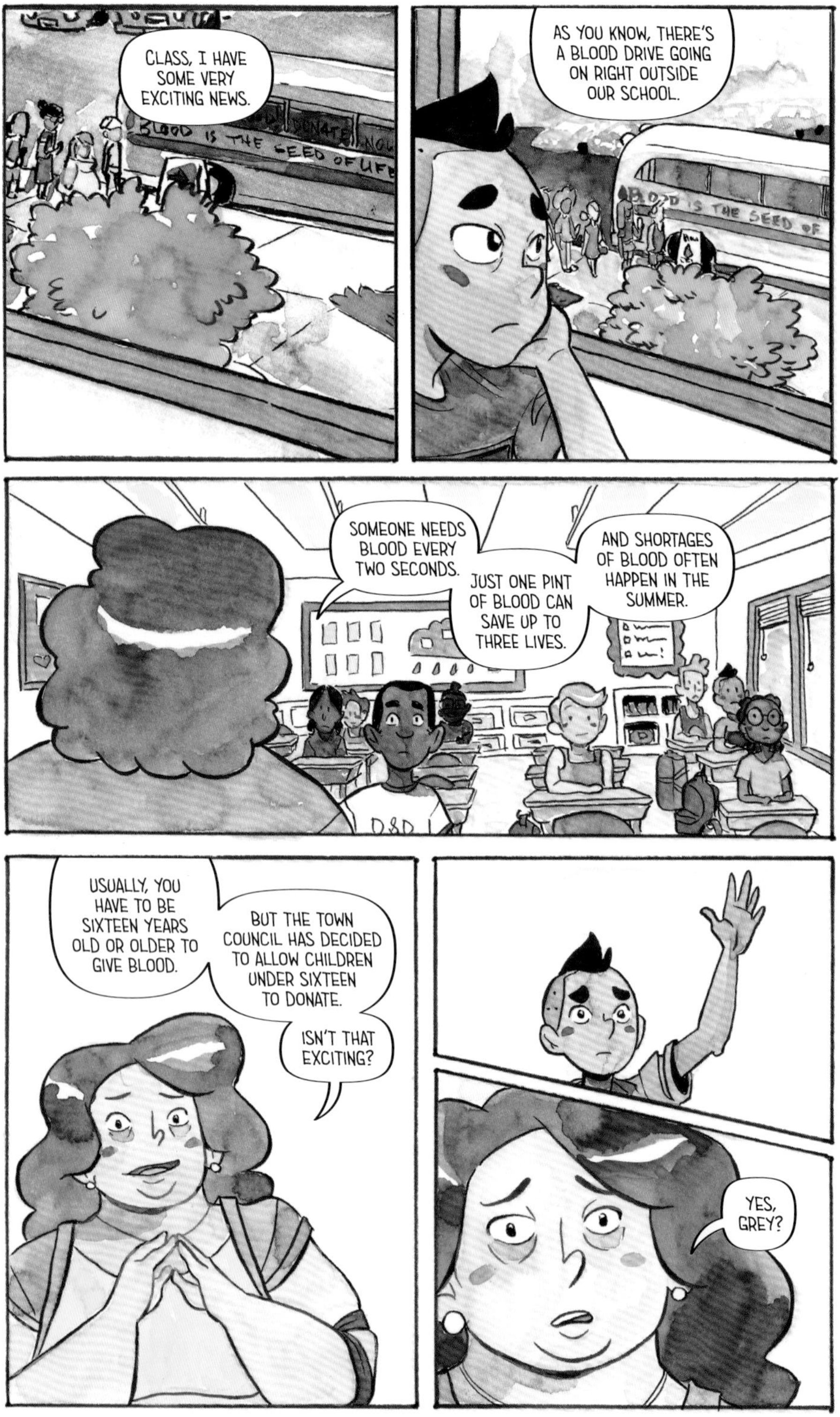
CLASS, I HAVE SOME VERY EXCITING NEWS.
AS YOU KNOW, THERE'S A BLOOD DRIVE GOING ON RIGHT OUTSIDE OUR SCHOOL.
BLOOD IS THE SEED OF LIFE
DONATE NOW
SOMEONE NEEDS BLOOD EVERY TWO SECONDS.
JUST ONE PINT OF BLOOD CAN SAVE UP TO THREE LIVES.
AND SHORTAGES OF BLOOD OFTEN HAPPEN IN THE SUMMER.
USUALLY, YOU HAVE TO BE SIXTEEN YEARS OLD OR OLDER TO GIVE BLOOD.
BUT THE TOWN COUNCIL HAS DECIDED TO ALLOW CHILDREN UNDER SIXTEEN TO DONATE.
ISN'T THAT EXCITING?
YES, GREY?

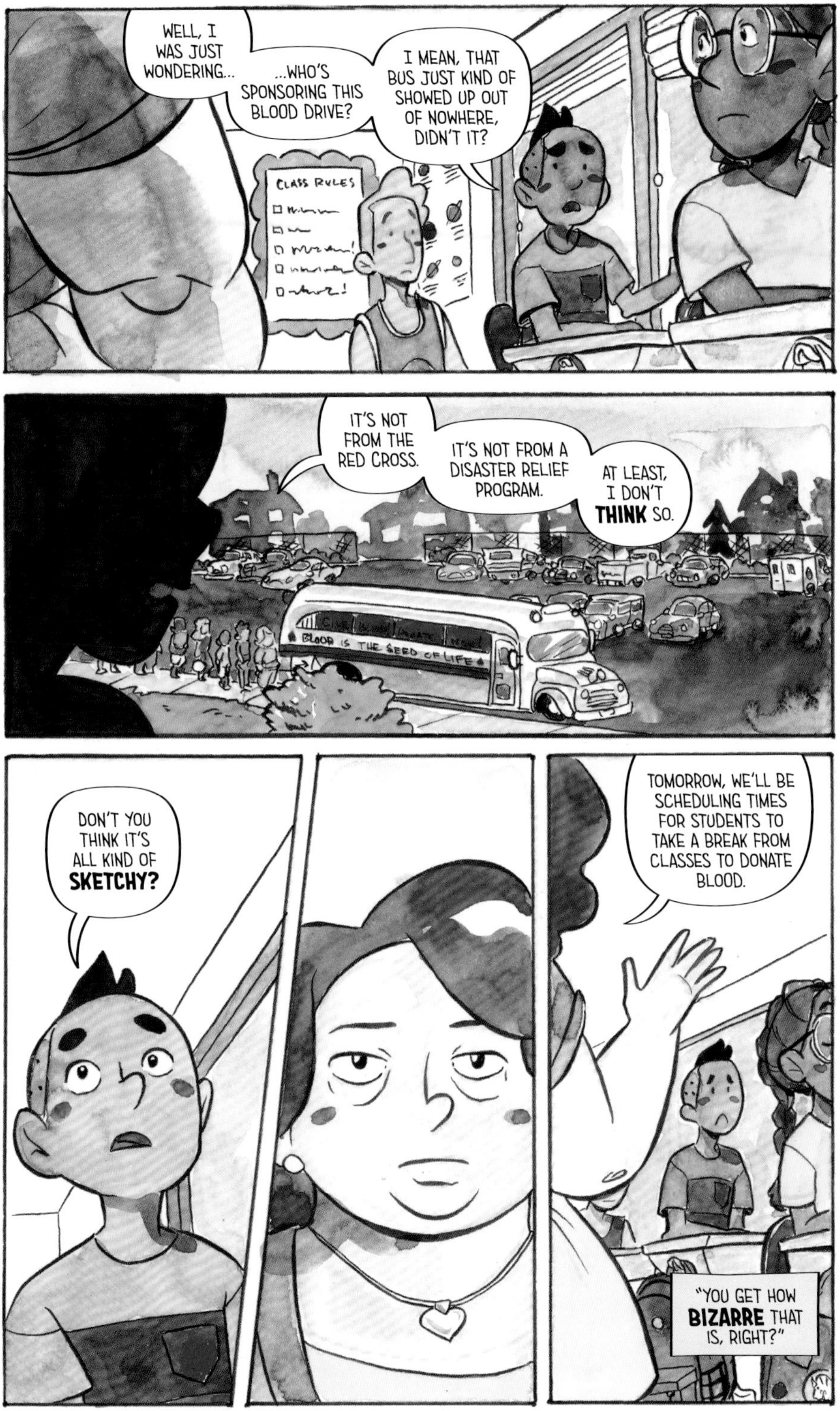
WELL, I WAS JUST WONDERING...
...WHO'S SPONSORING THIS BLOOD DRIVE?
I MEAN, THAT BUS JUST KIND OF SHOWED UP OUT OF NOWHERE, DIDN'T IT?
CLASS RULES
IT'S NOT FROM THE RED CROSS.
IT'S NOT FROM A DISASTER RELIEF PROGRAM.
AT LEAST, I DON'T **THINK** SO.
BLOOD IS THE SEED OF LIFE
DON'T YOU THINK IT'S ALL KIND OF **SKETCHY?**
TOMORROW, WE'LL BE SCHEDULING TIMES FOR STUDENTS TO TAKE A BREAK FROM CLASSES TO DONATE BLOOD.
"YOU GET HOW **BIZARRE** THAT IS, RIGHT?"

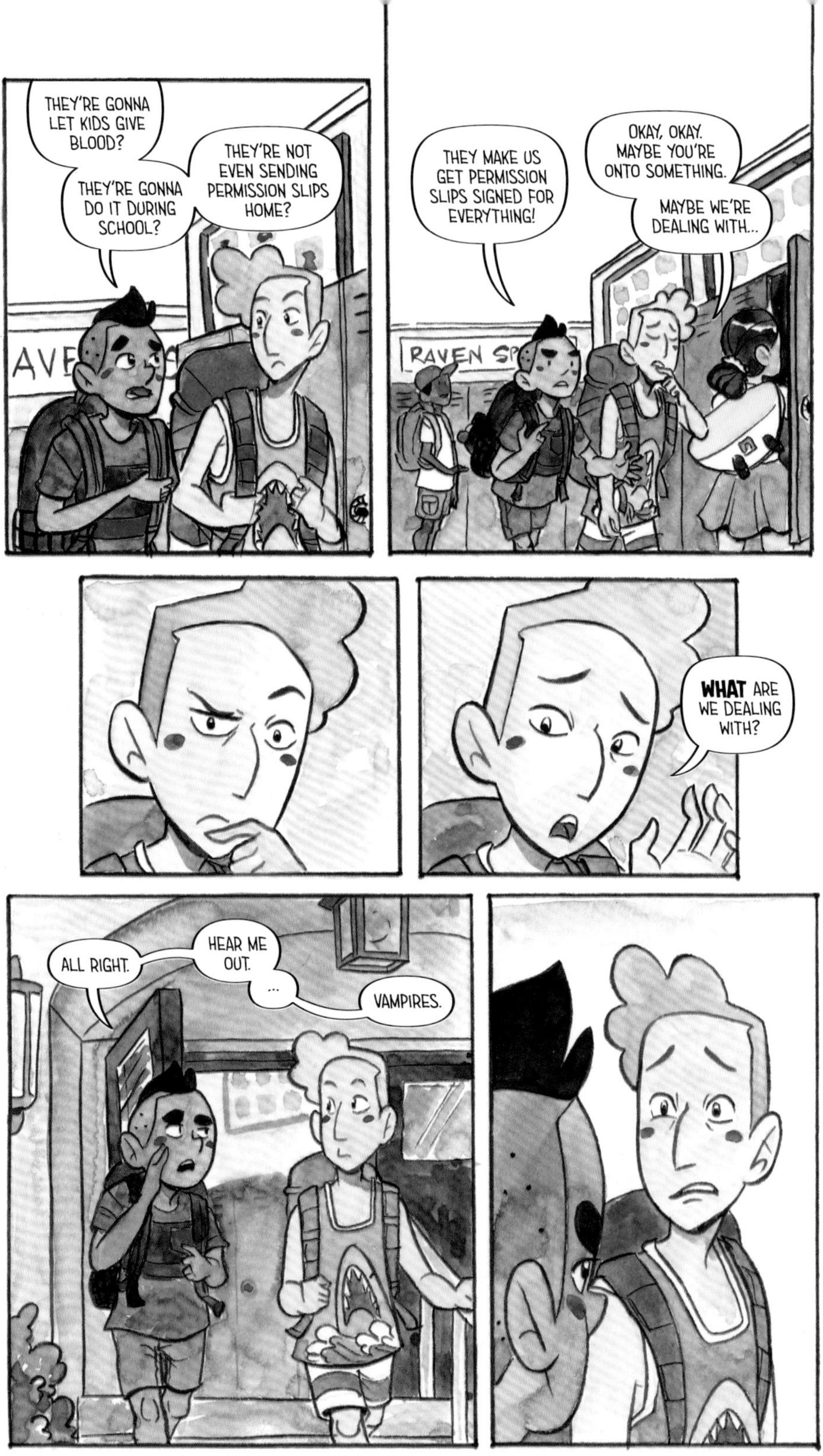
THEY'RE GONNA LET KIDS GIVE BLOOD?
THEY'RE GONNA DO IT DURING SCHOOL?
THEY'RE NOT EVEN SENDING PERMISSION SLIPS HOME?
AVE
THEY MAKE US GET PERMISSION SLIPS SIGNED FOR EVERYTHING!
OKAY, OKAY. MAYBE YOU'RE ONTO SOMETHING.
MAYBE WE'RE DEALING WITH...
RAVEN SP
WHAT ARE WE DEALING WITH?
ALL RIGHT.
HEAR ME OUT.
...
VAMPIRES.

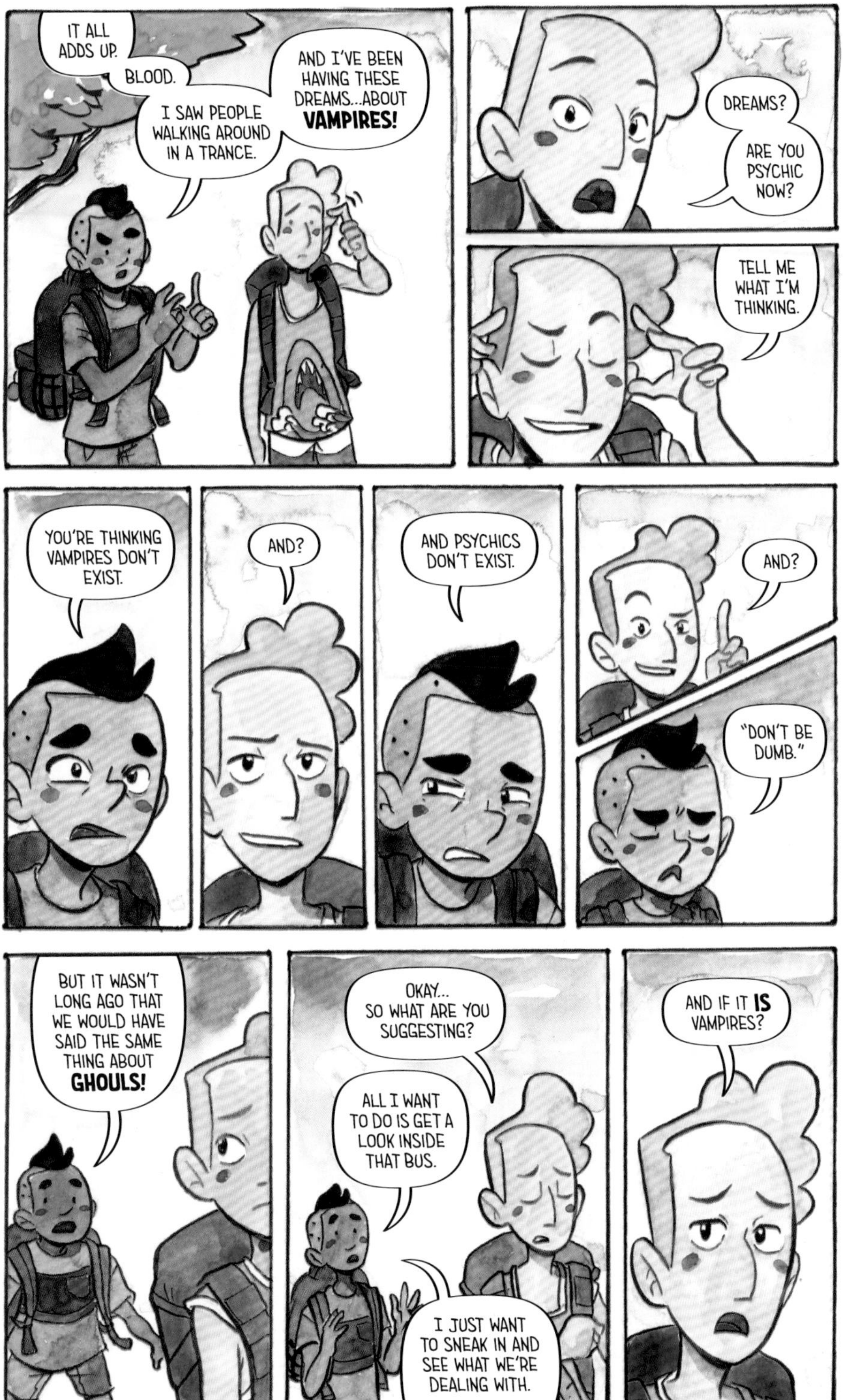

IT ALL ADDS UP.
BLOOD.
I SAW PEOPLE WALKING AROUND IN A TRANCE.
AND I'VE BEEN HAVING THESE DREAMS...ABOUT **VAMPIRES!**
DREAMS?
ARE YOU PSYCHIC NOW?
TELL ME WHAT I'M THINKING.
YOU'RE THINKING VAMPIRES DON'T EXIST.
AND?
AND PSYCHICS DON'T EXIST.
AND?
"DON'T BE DUMB."
BUT IT WASN'T LONG AGO THAT WE WOULD HAVE SAID THE SAME THING ABOUT **GHOULS!**
OKAY... SO WHAT ARE YOU SUGGESTING?
ALL I WANT TO DO IS GET A LOOK INSIDE THAT BUS.
I JUST WANT TO SNEAK IN AND SEE WHAT WE'RE DEALING WITH.
AND IF IT **IS** VAMPIRES?

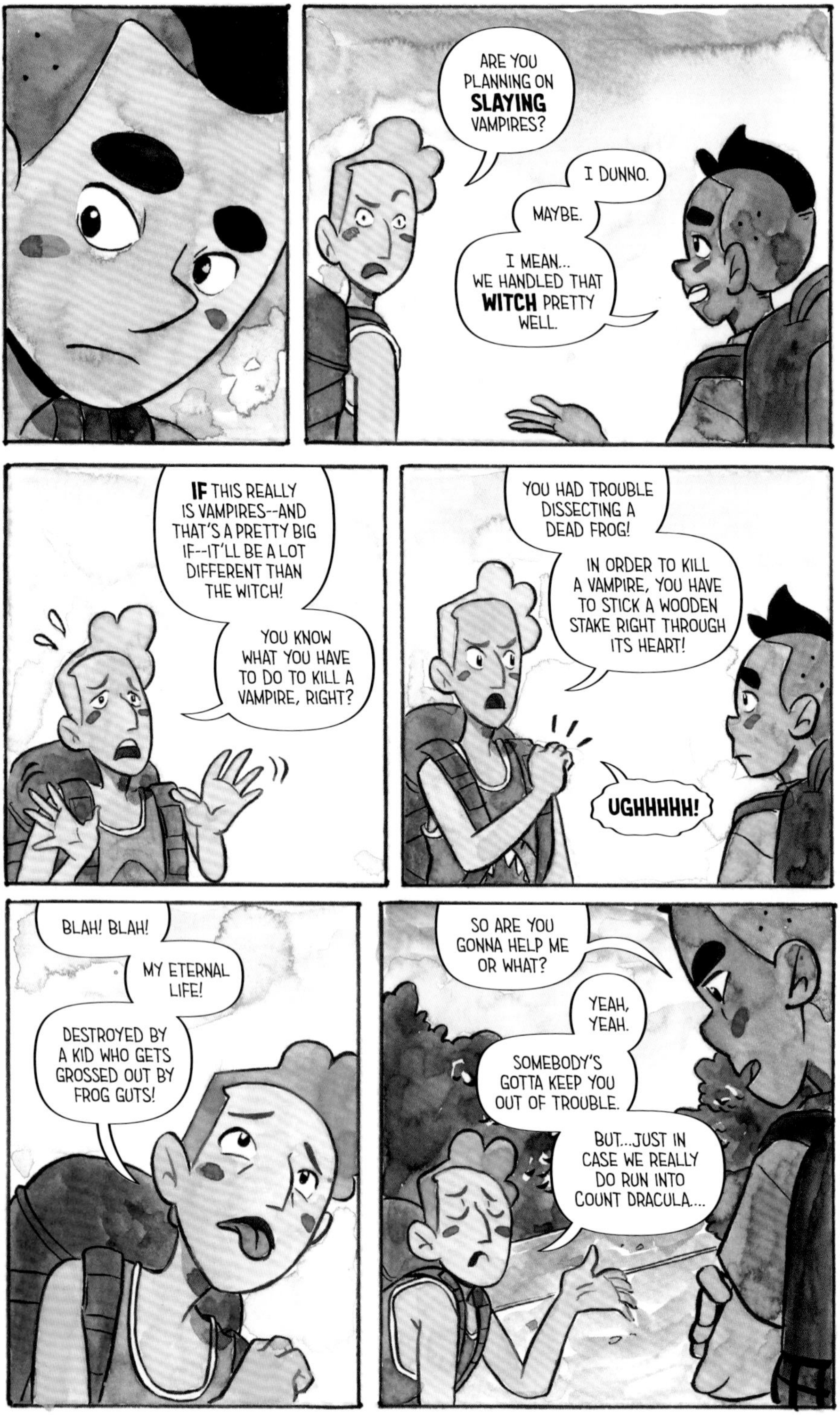
ARE YOU PLANNING ON **SLAYING** VAMPIRES?
I DUNNO.
MAYBE.
I MEAN... WE HANDLED THAT **WITCH** PRETTY WELL.
IF THIS REALLY IS VAMPIRES--AND THAT'S A PRETTY BIG IF--IT'LL BE A LOT DIFFERENT THAN THE WITCH!
YOU KNOW WHAT YOU HAVE TO DO TO KILL A VAMPIRE, RIGHT?
YOU HAD TROUBLE DISSECTING A DEAD FROG!
IN ORDER TO KILL A VAMPIRE, YOU HAVE TO STICK A WOODEN STAKE RIGHT THROUGH ITS HEART!
UGHHHHH!
BLAH! BLAH!
MY ETERNAL LIFE!
DESTROYED BY A KID WHO GETS GROSSED OUT BY FROG GUTS!
SO ARE YOU GONNA HELP ME OR WHAT?
YEAH, YEAH.
SOMEBODY'S GOTTA KEEP YOU OUT OF TROUBLE.
BUT...JUST IN CASE WE REALLY DO RUN INTO COUNT DRACULA....

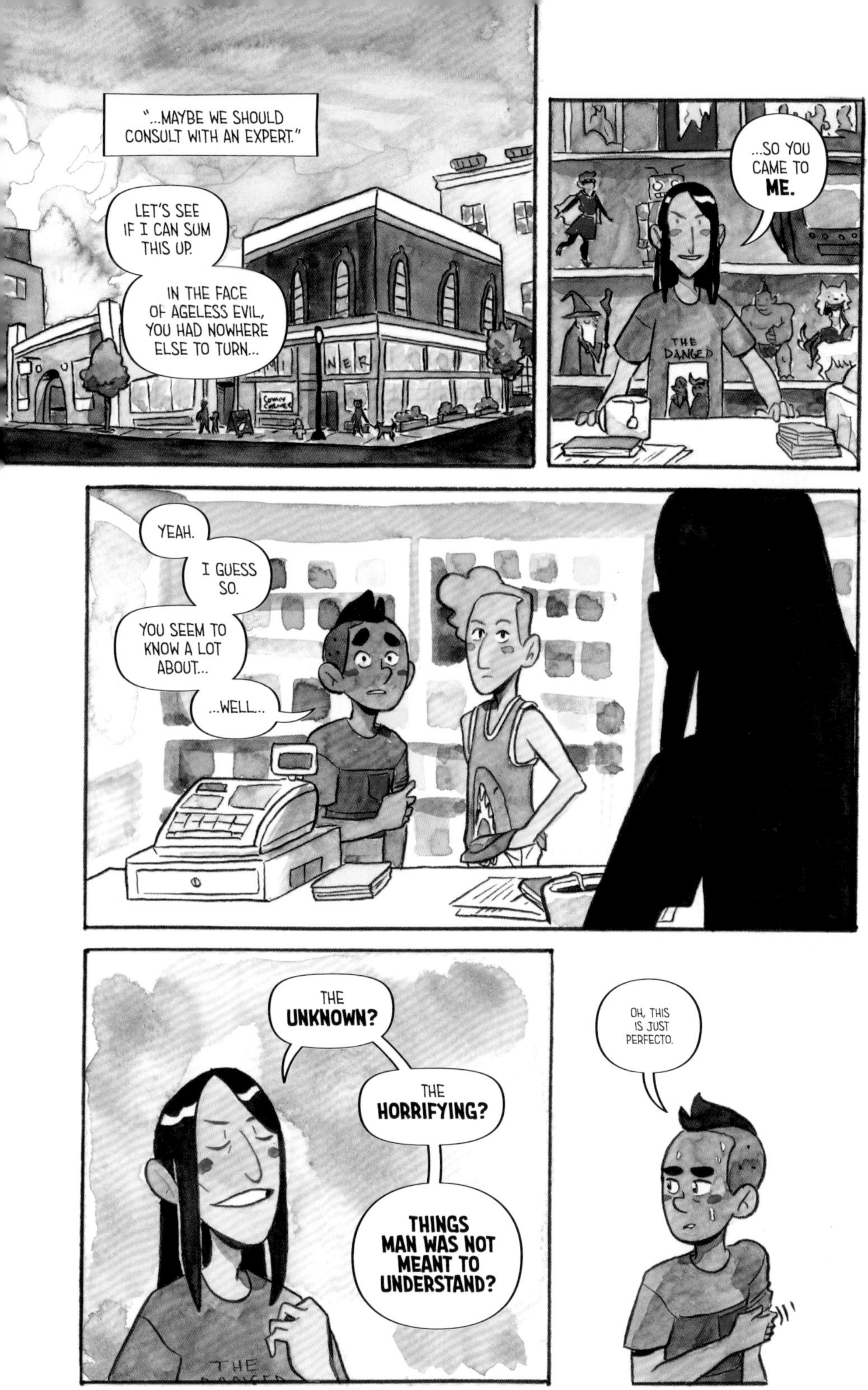
"...MAYBE WE SHOULD CONSULT WITH AN EXPERT."
LET'S SEE IF I CAN SUM THIS UP.
IN THE FACE OF AGELESS EVIL, YOU HAD NOWHERE ELSE TO TURN...
...SO YOU CAME TO **ME.**
THE DANGED
YEAH.
I GUESS SO.
YOU SEEM TO KNOW A LOT ABOUT...
...WELL...
THE **UNKNOWN?**
THE **HORRIFYING?**
THINGS MAN WAS NOT MEANT TO UNDERSTAND?
OH, THIS IS JUST PERFECTO.
THE

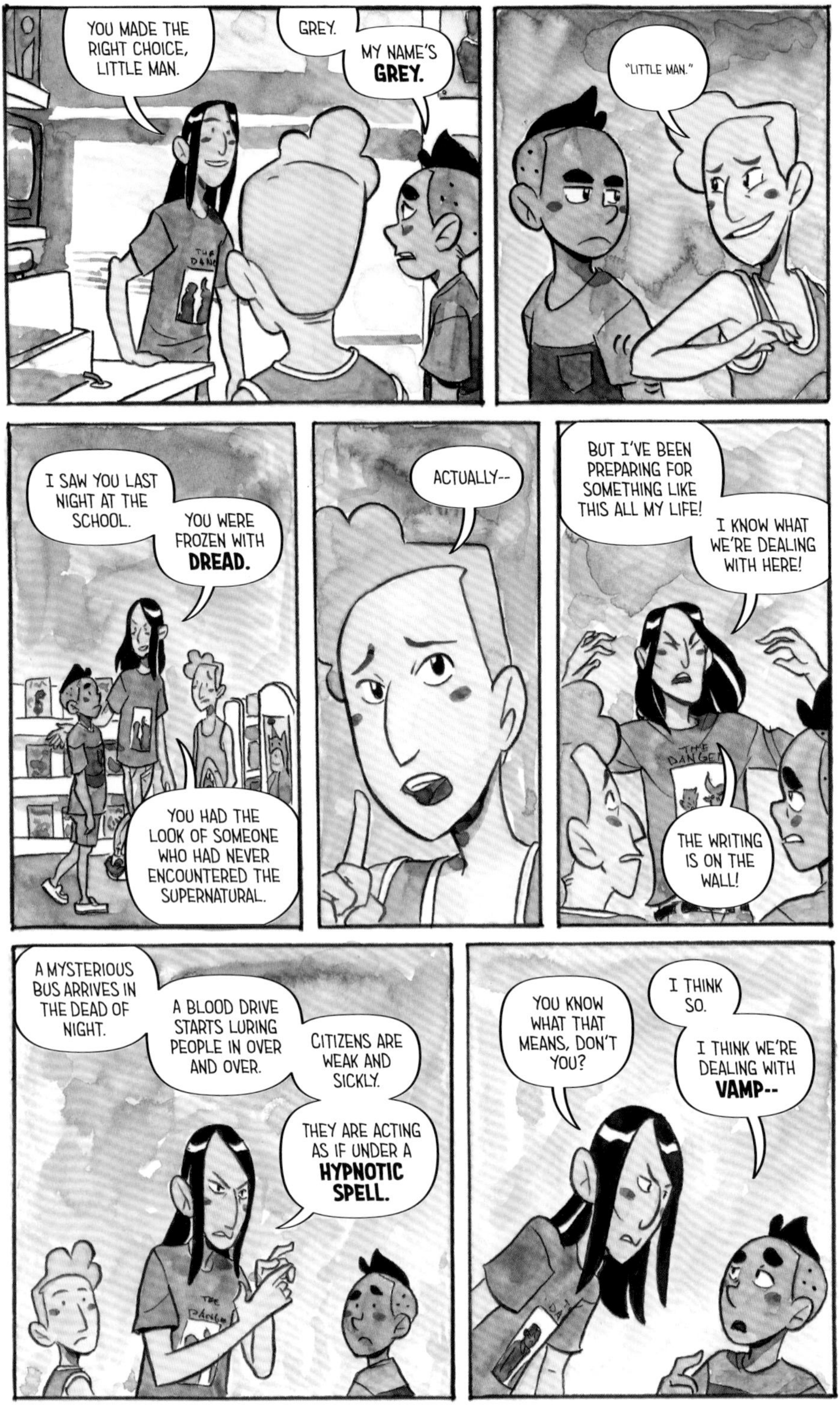
YOU MADE THE RIGHT CHOICE, LITTLE MAN.
GREY.
MY NAME'S GREY.
"LITTLE MAN."
I SAW YOU LAST NIGHT AT THE SCHOOL.
YOU WERE FROZEN WITH DREAD.
YOU HAD THE LOOK OF SOMEONE WHO HAD NEVER ENCOUNTERED THE SUPERNATURAL.
ACTUALLY--
BUT I'VE BEEN PREPARING FOR SOMETHING LIKE THIS ALL MY LIFE!
I KNOW WHAT WE'RE DEALING WITH HERE!
THE WRITING IS ON THE WALL!
A MYSTERIOUS BUS ARRIVES IN THE DEAD OF NIGHT.
A BLOOD DRIVE STARTS LURING PEOPLE IN OVER AND OVER.
CITIZENS ARE WEAK AND SICKLY.
THEY ARE ACTING AS IF UNDER A HYPNOTIC SPELL.
YOU KNOW WHAT THAT MEANS, DON'T YOU?
I THINK SO.
I THINK WE'RE DEALING WITH VAMP--

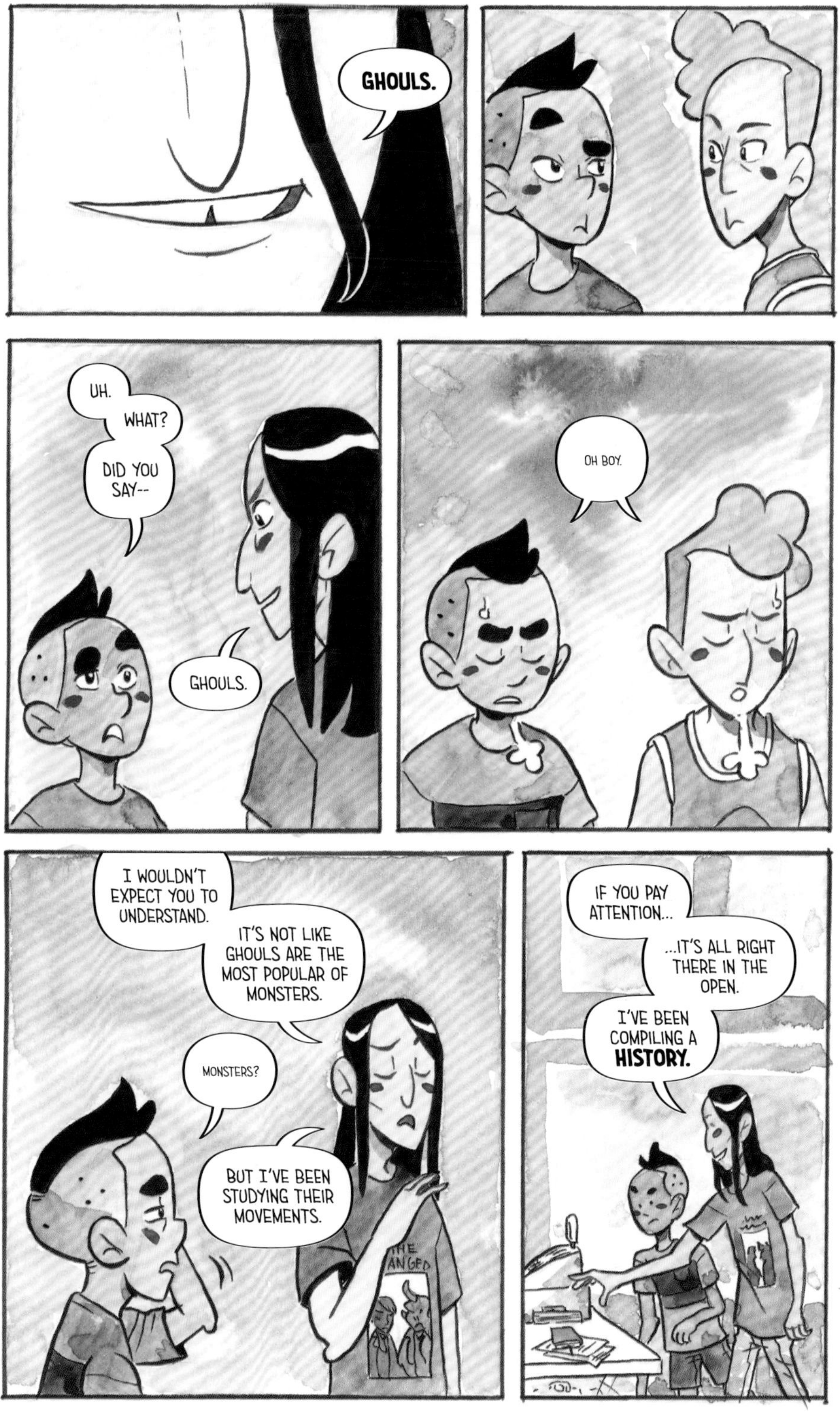
GHOULS.
UH.
WHAT?
DID YOU SAY--
GHOULS.
OH BOY.
I WOULDN'T EXPECT YOU TO UNDERSTAND.
IT'S NOT LIKE GHOULS ARE THE MOST POPULAR OF MONSTERS.
MONSTERS?
BUT I'VE BEEN STUDYING THEIR MOVEMENTS.
IF YOU PAY ATTENTION...
...IT'S ALL RIGHT THERE IN THE OPEN.
I'VE BEEN COMPILING A **HISTORY.**

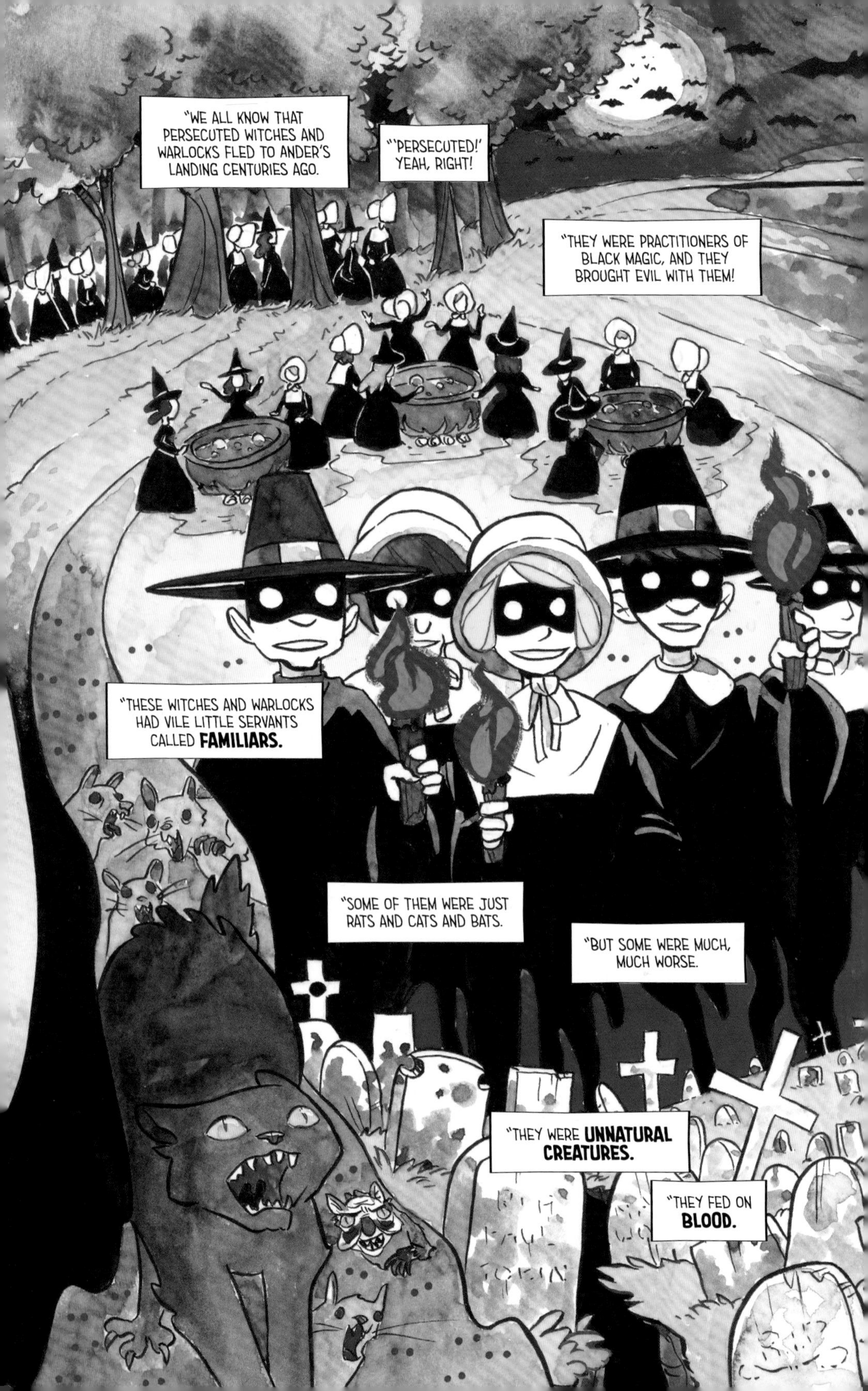
"WE ALL KNOW THAT PERSECUTED WITCHES AND WARLOCKS FLED TO ANDER'S LANDING CENTURIES AGO.
"'PERSECUTED!' YEAH, RIGHT!
"THEY WERE PRACTITIONERS OF BLACK MAGIC, AND THEY BROUGHT EVIL WITH THEM!
"THESE WITCHES AND WARLOCKS HAD VILE LITTLE SERVANTS CALLED **FAMILIARS.**
"SOME OF THEM WERE JUST RATS AND CATS AND BATS.
"BUT SOME WERE MUCH, MUCH WORSE.
"THEY WERE **UNNATURAL CREATURES.**
"THEY FED ON **BLOOD.**

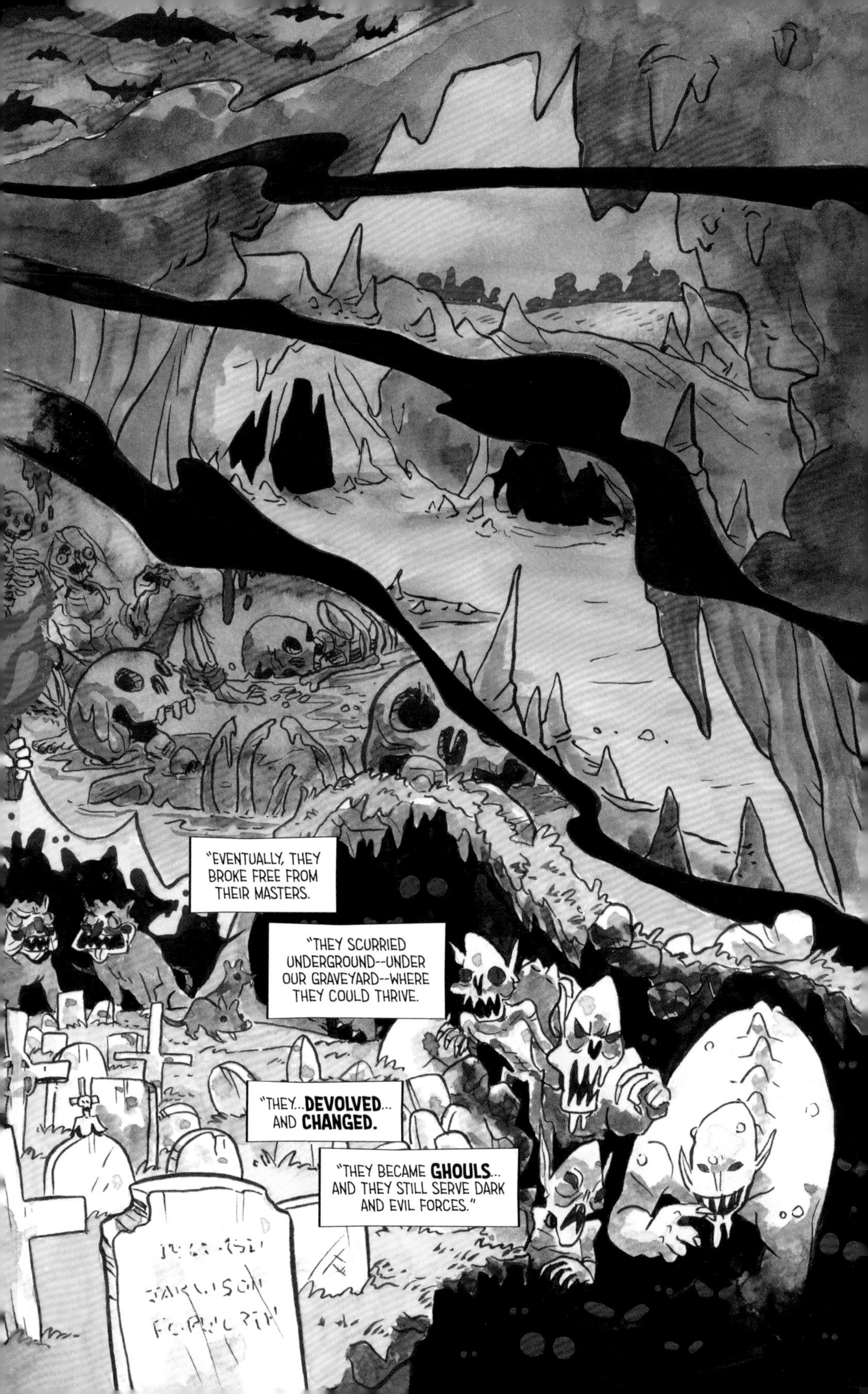
"EVENTUALLY, THEY BROKE FREE FROM THEIR MASTERS.
"THEY SCURRIED UNDERGROUND--UNDER OUR GRAVEYARD--WHERE THEY COULD THRIVE.
"THEY...DEVOLVED... AND CHANGED.
"THEY BECAME GHOULS... AND THEY STILL SERVE DARK AND EVIL FORCES."

65

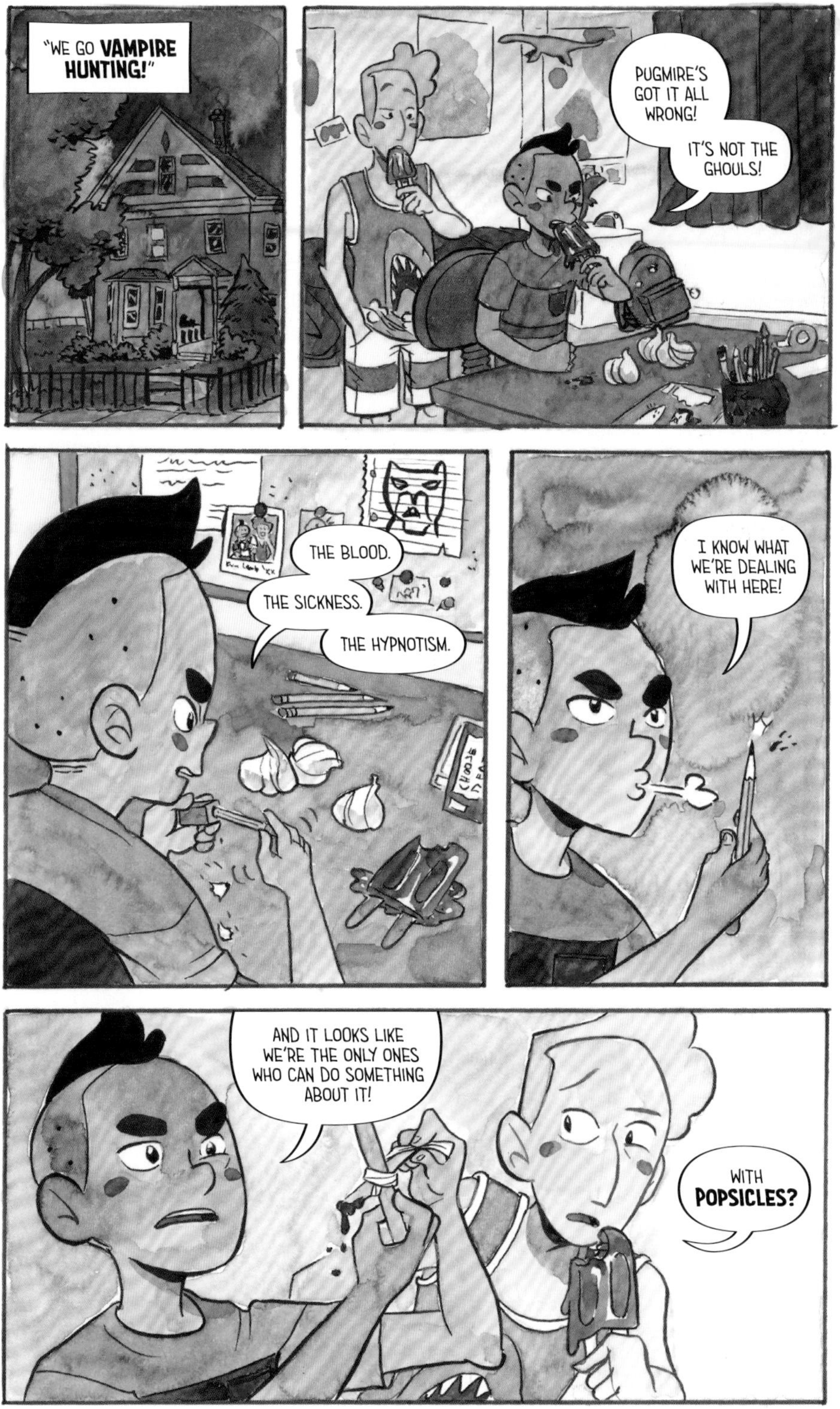
"WE GO **VAMPIRE HUNTING!**"
PUGMIRE'S GOT IT ALL WRONG!
IT'S NOT THE GHOULS!
THE BLOOD.
THE SICKNESS.
THE HYPNOTISM.
I KNOW WHAT WE'RE DEALING WITH HERE!
AND IT LOOKS LIKE WE'RE THE ONLY ONES WHO CAN DO SOMETHING ABOUT IT!
WITH **POPSICLES?**

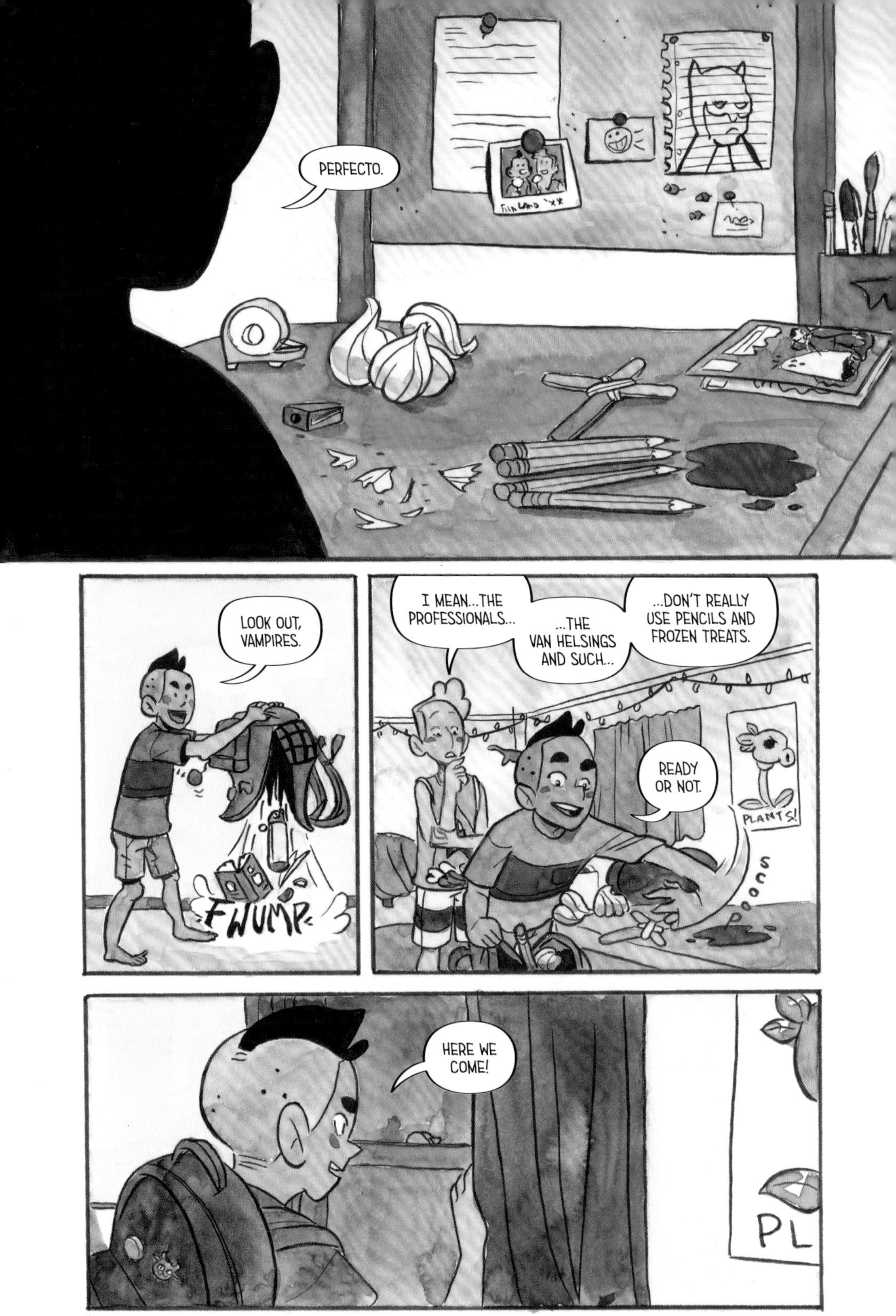
PERFECTO.
LOOK OUT, VAMPIRES.
FWUMP
I MEAN...THE PROFESSIONALS...
...THE VAN HELSINGS AND SUCH...
...DON'T REALLY USE PENCILS AND FROZEN TREATS.
READY OR NOT.
PLANTS!
SCOOOO
HERE WE COME!
PL

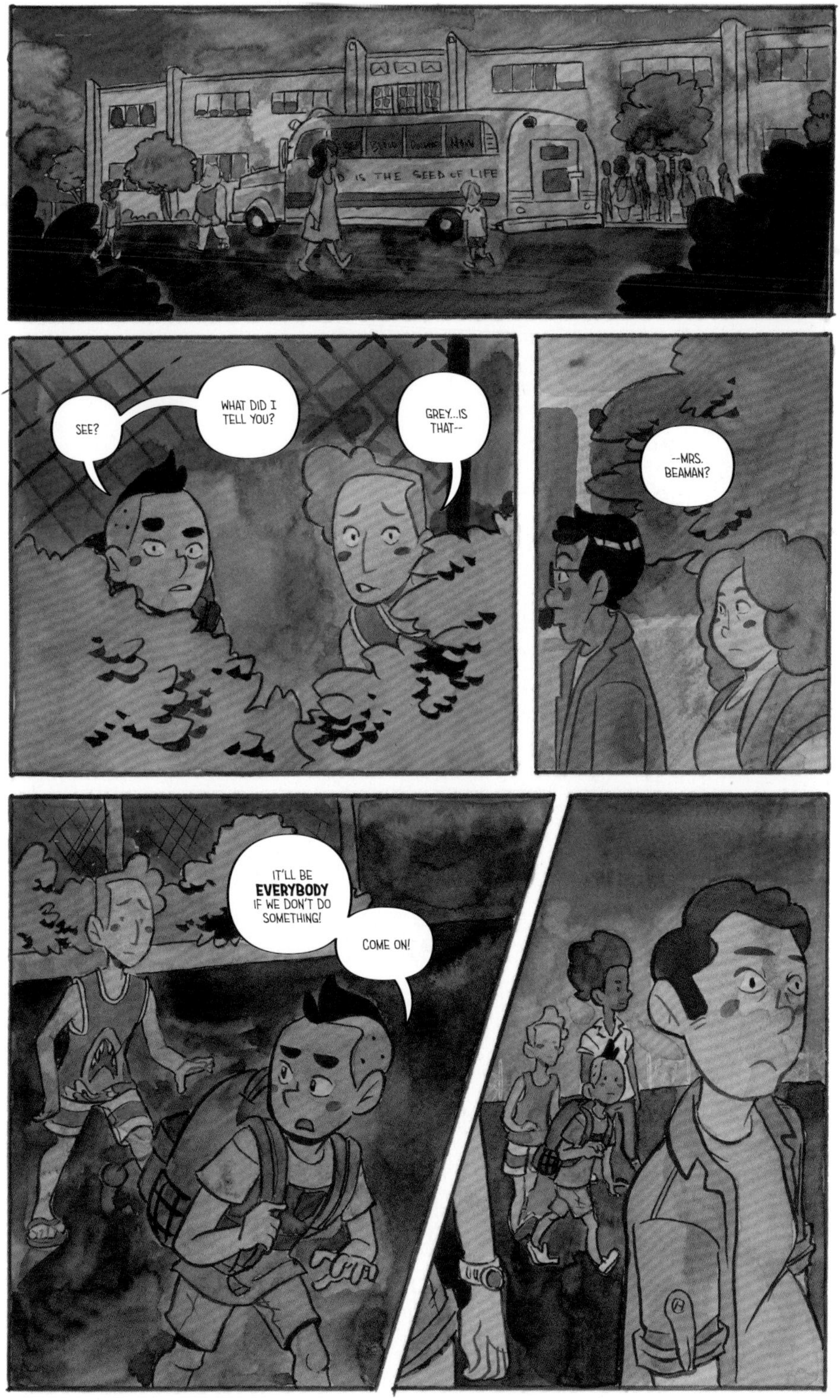
SEE?
WHAT DID I TELL YOU?
GREY...IS THAT--
--MRS. BEAMAN?
IT'LL BE **EVERYBODY** IF WE DON'T DO SOMETHING!
COME ON!

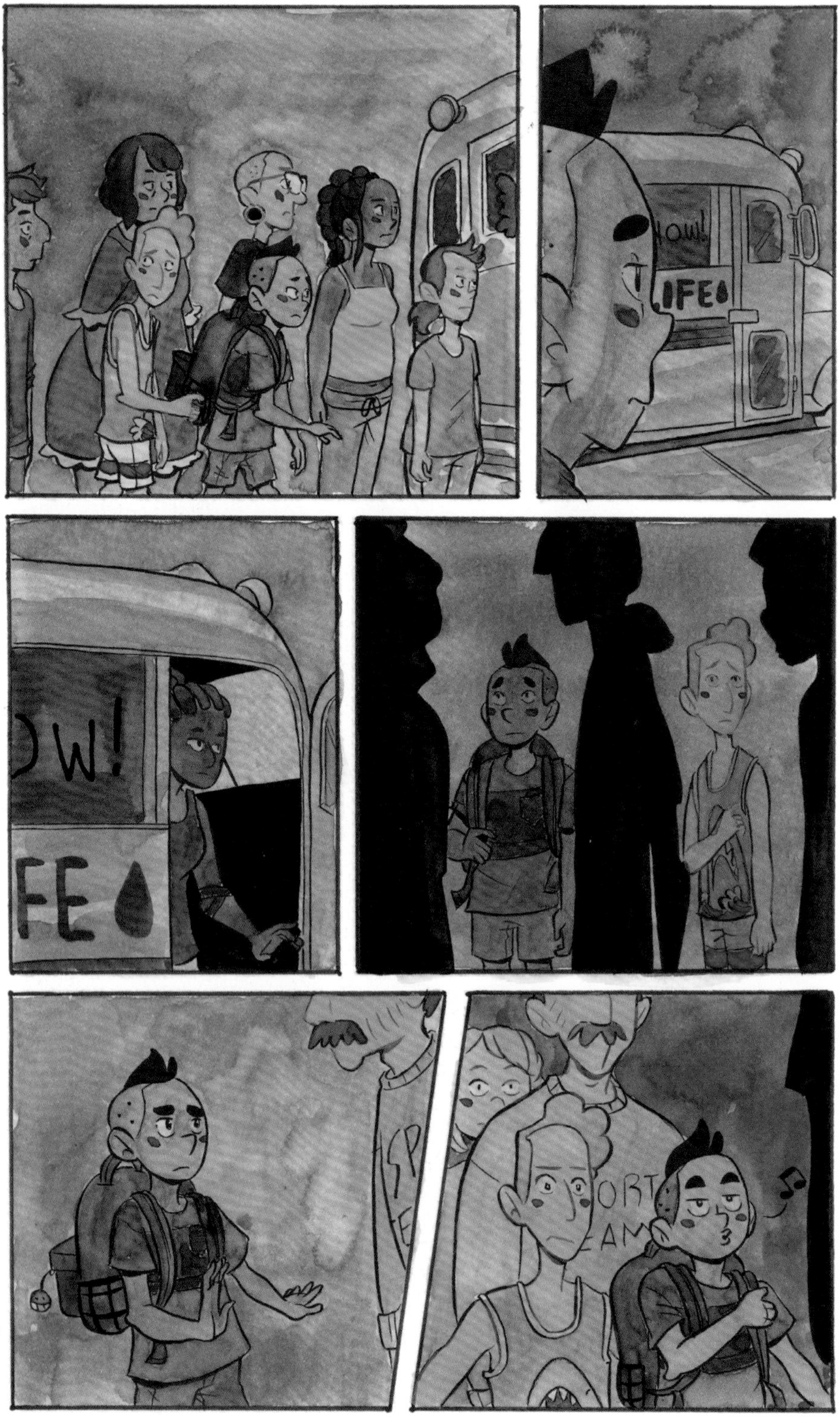

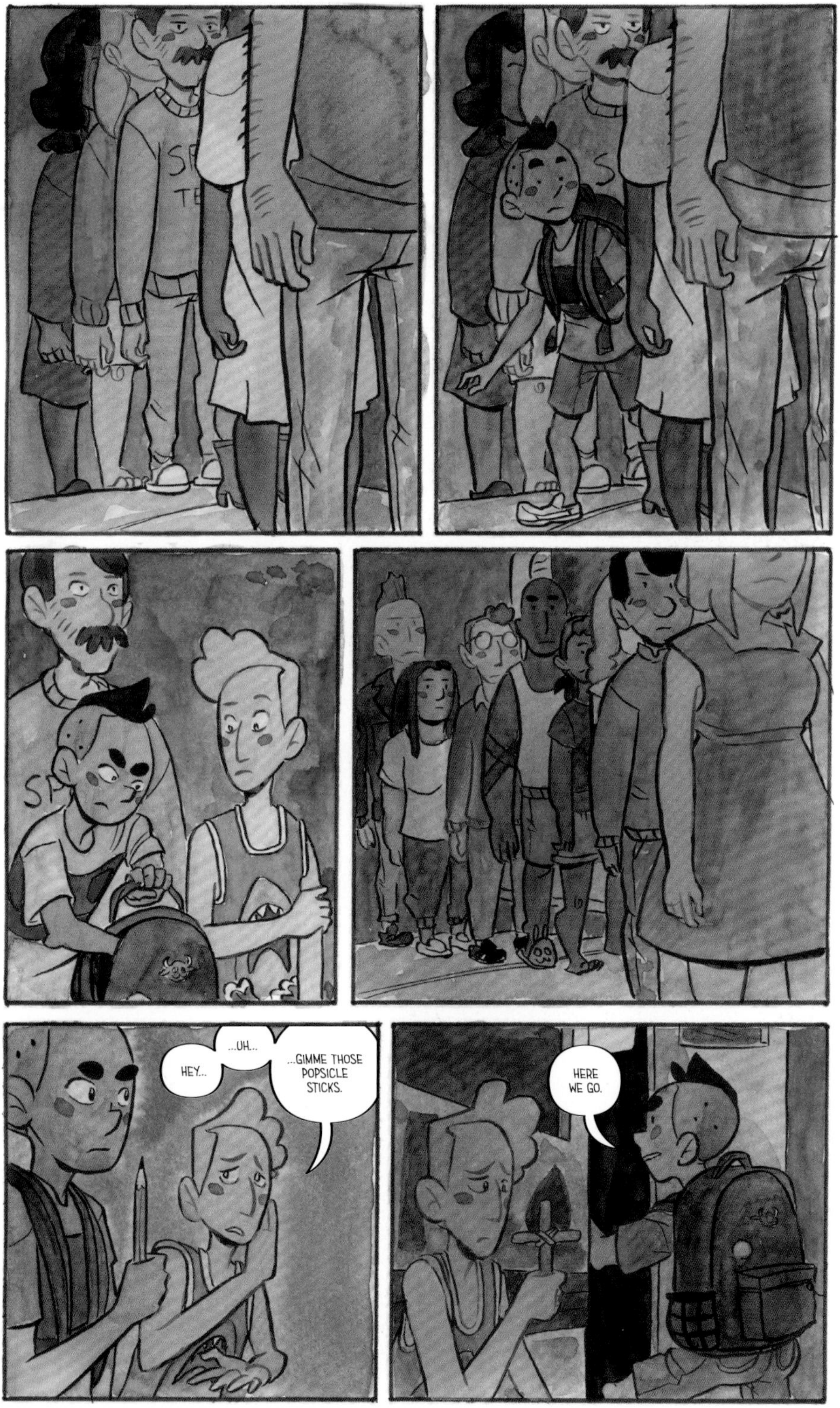
HEY...
...UH...
...GIMME THOSE POPSICLE STICKS.
HERE WE GO.

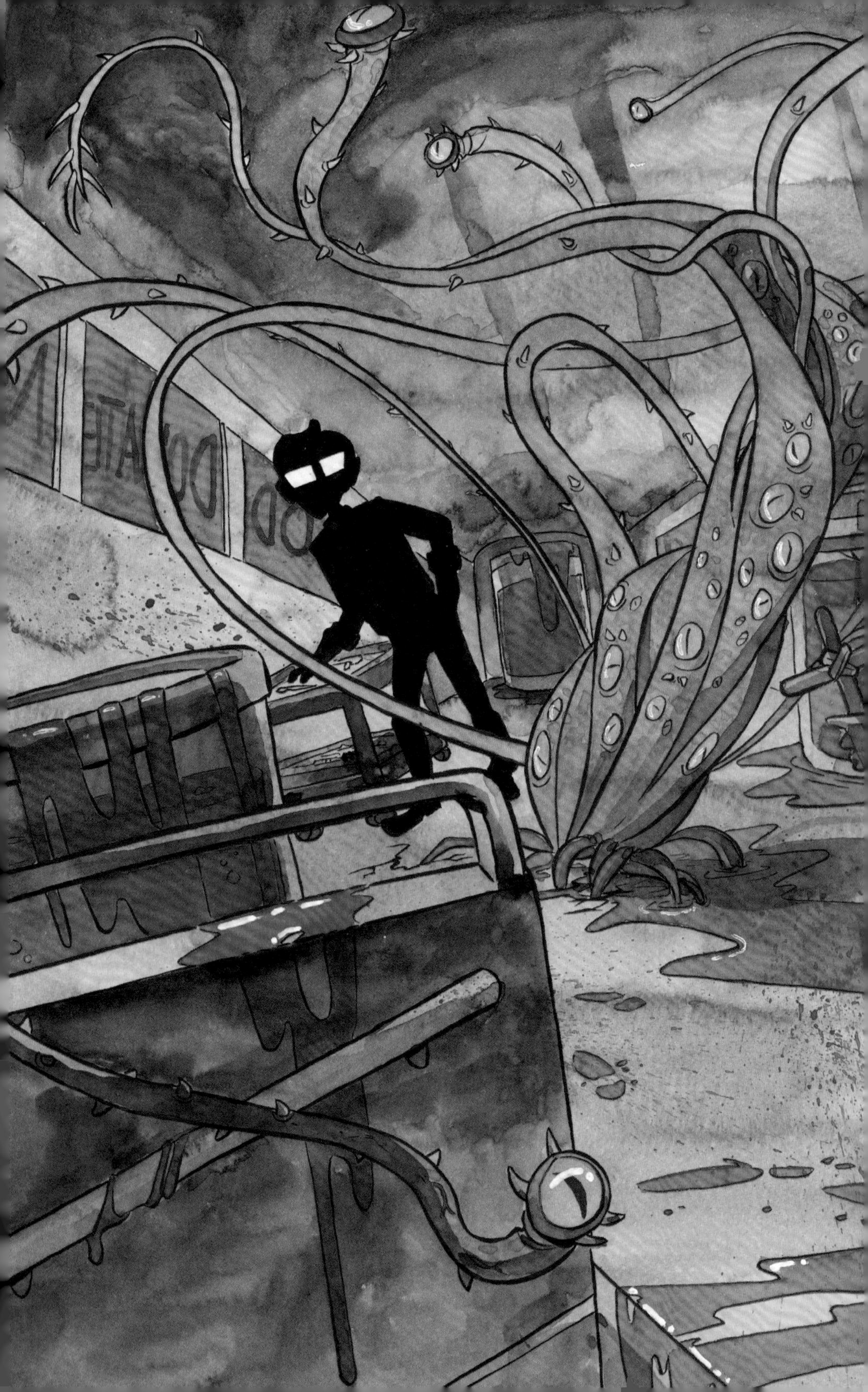

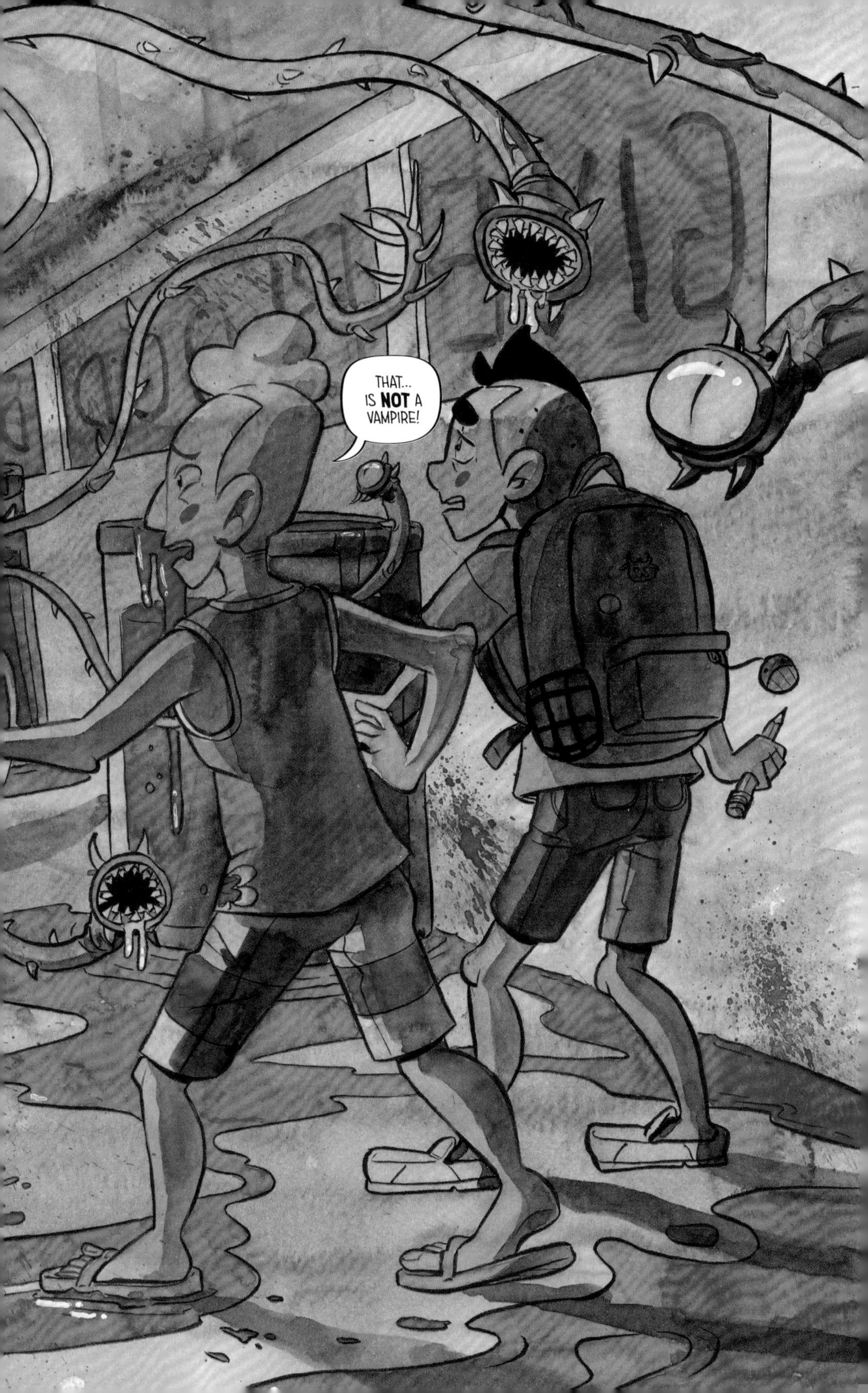
THAT... IS **NOT** A VAMPIRE!

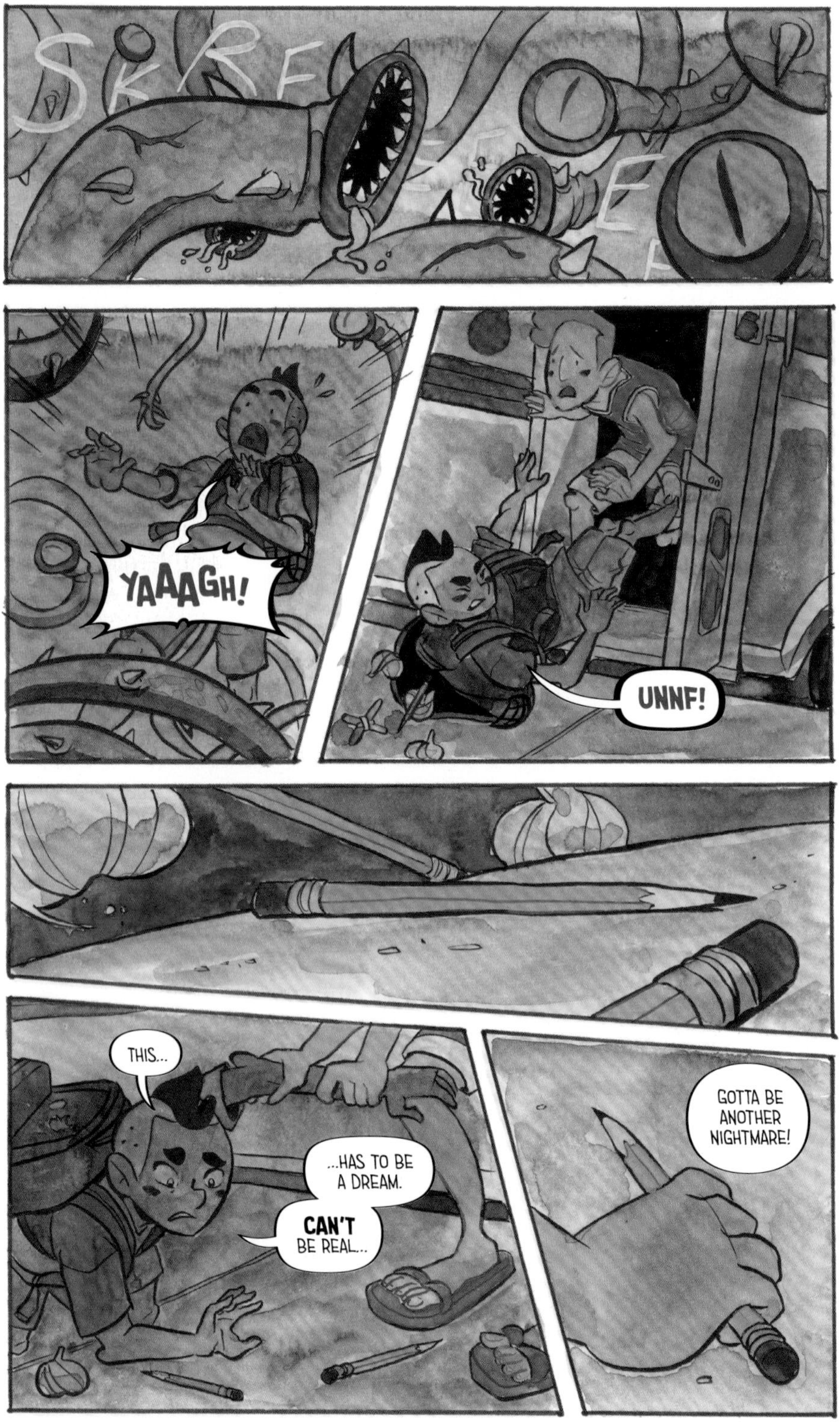
SKREEEE
YAAAGH!
UNNF!
THIS...
...HAS TO BE A DREAM.
CAN'T BE REAL...
GOTTA BE ANOTHER NIGHTMARE!

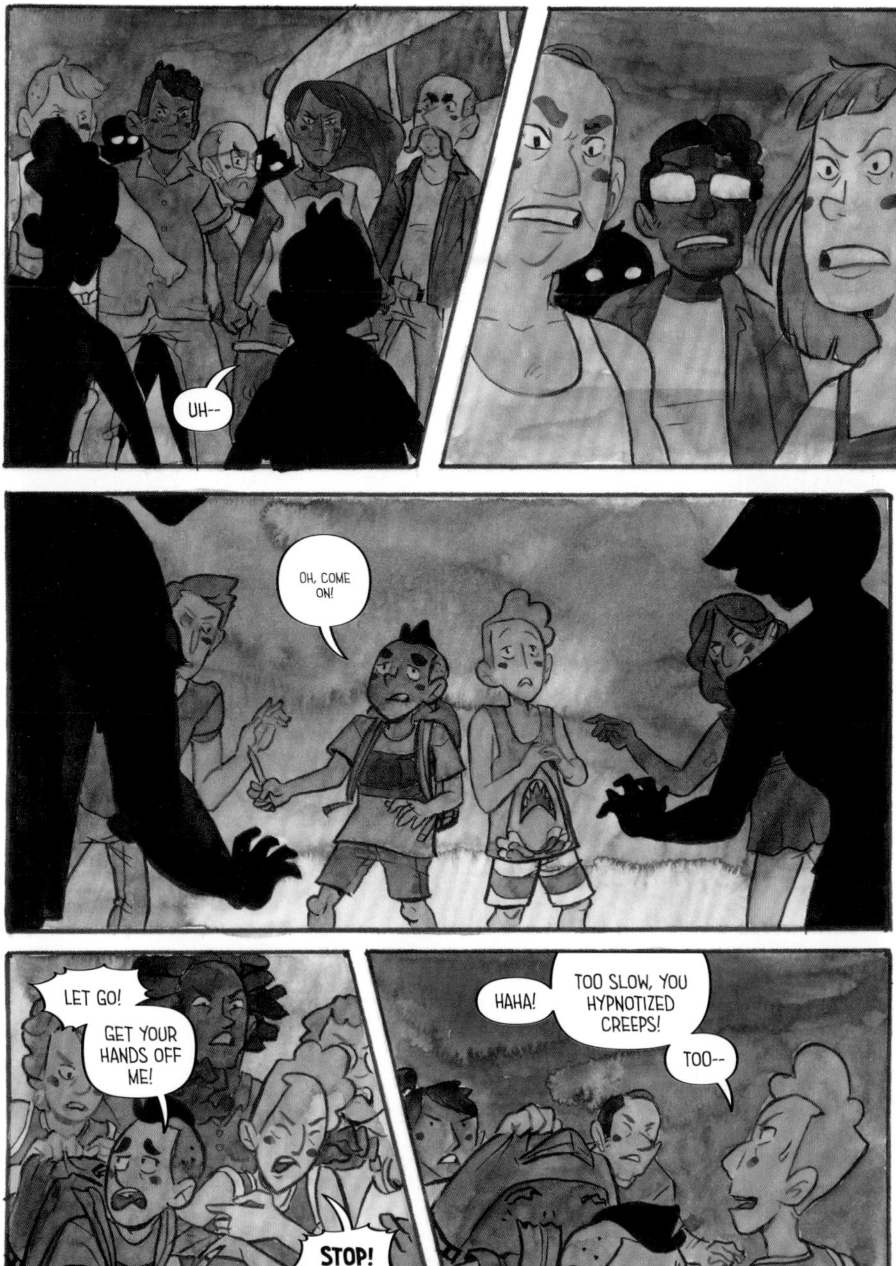
UH--
OH, COME ON!
LET GO!
GET YOUR HANDS OFF ME!
STOP!
HAHA!
TOO SLOW, YOU HYPNOTIZED CREEPS!
TOO--

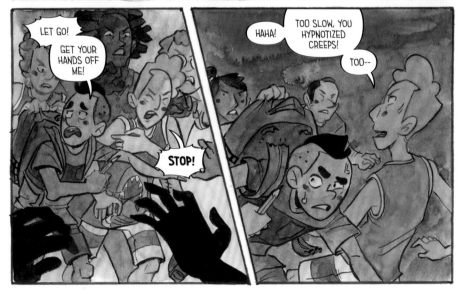

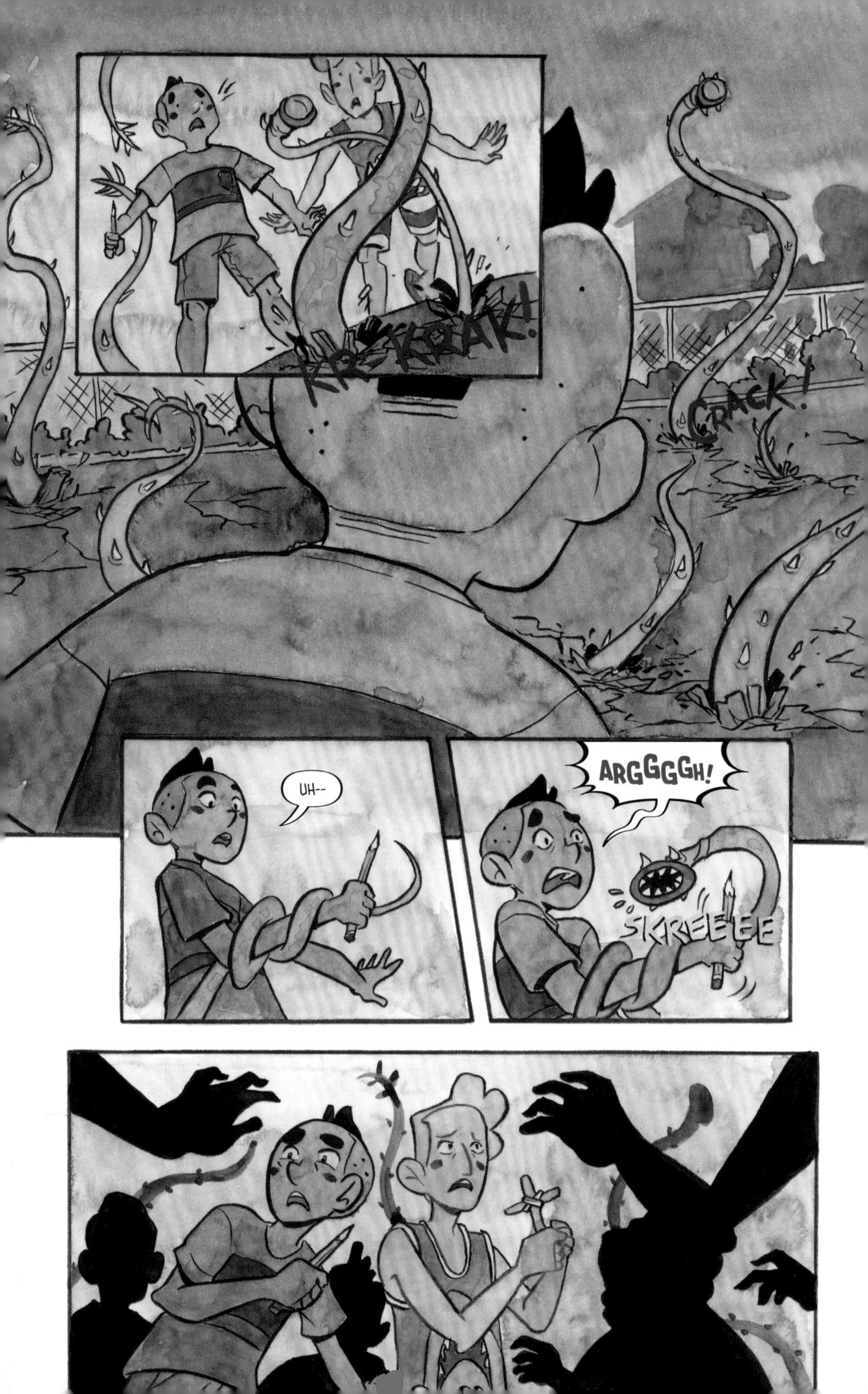
KR-KRAK!
CRACK!
UH--
ARGGGGH!
SKREEEEE

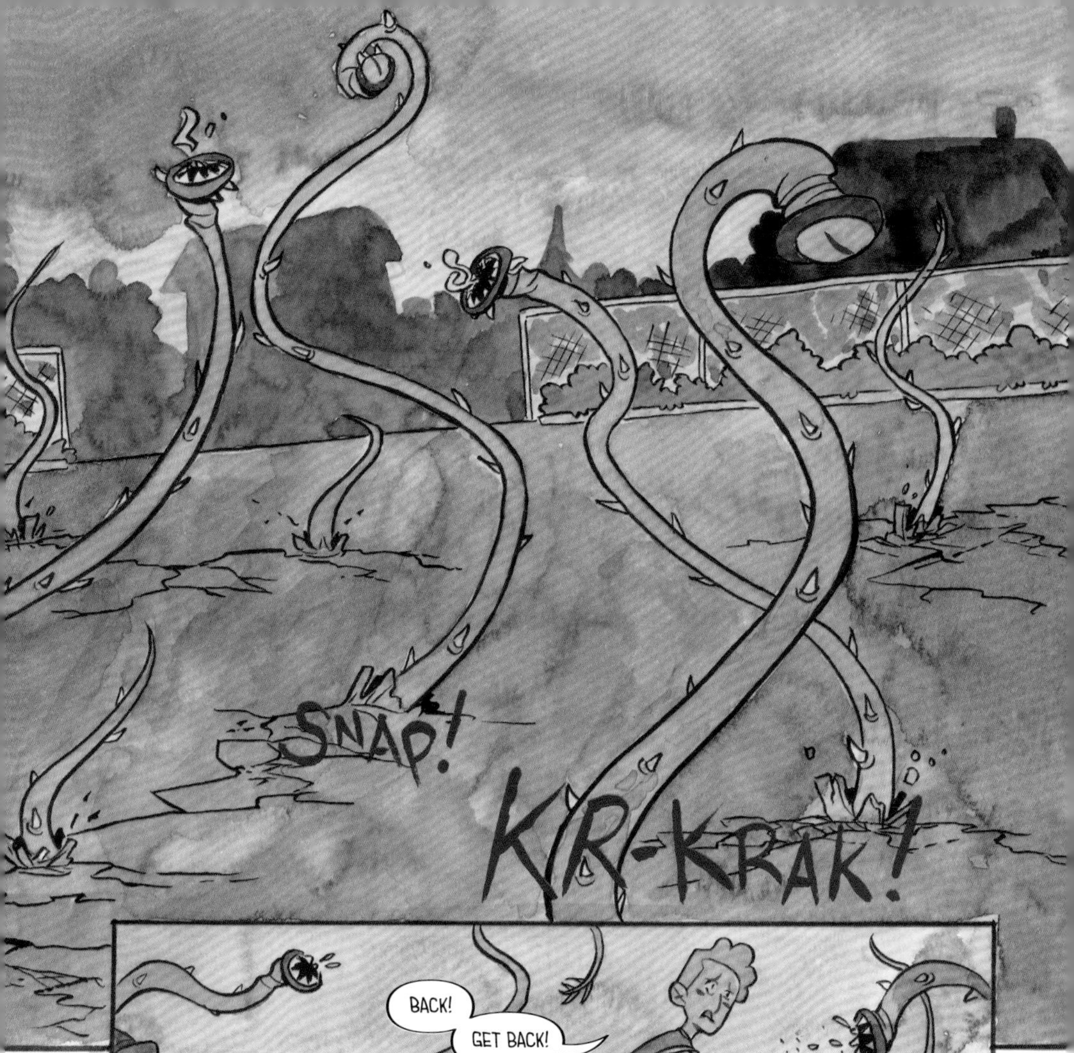
SNAP!
KR-KRAK!

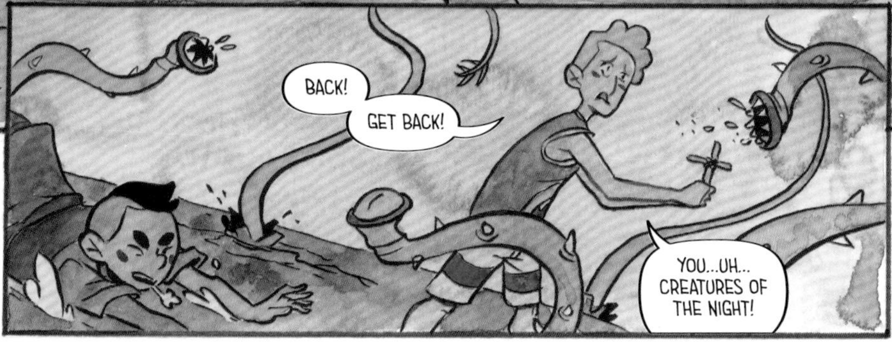
BACK!
GET BACK!
YOU...UH... CREATURES OF THE NIGHT!

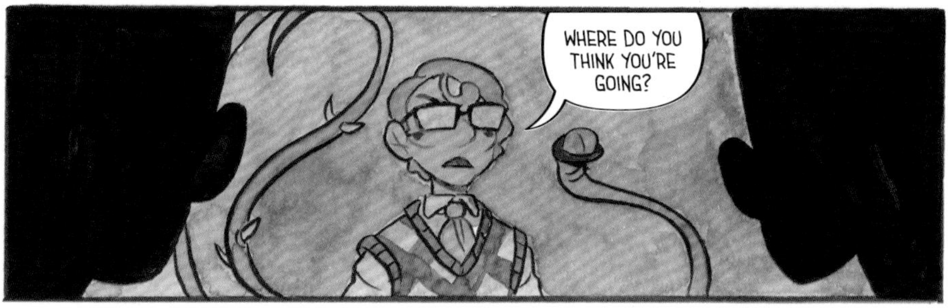
WHERE DO YOU THINK YOU'RE GOING?

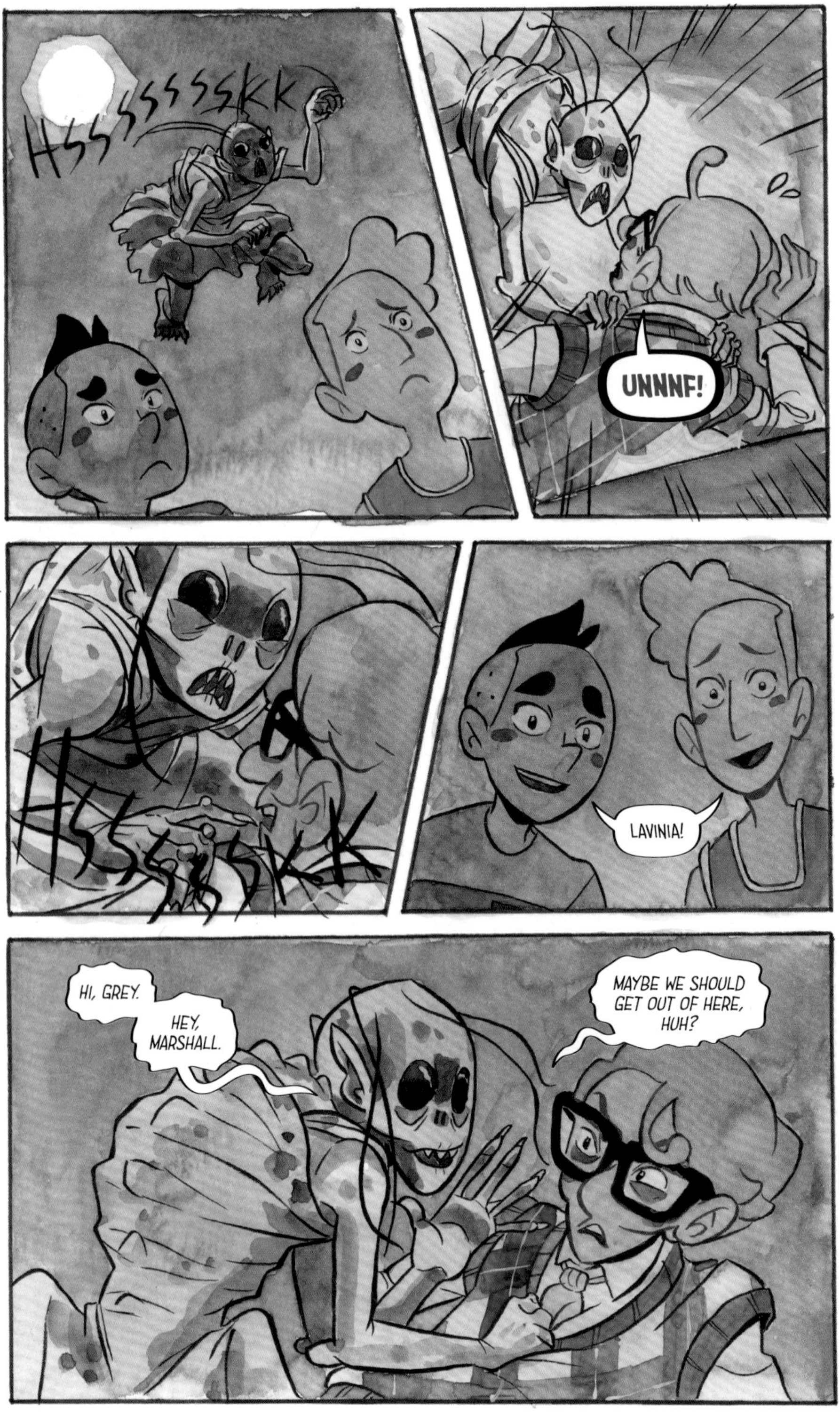
HSSSSSSSKK
UNNNF!
HSSSSSSKK
LAVINIA!
HI, GREY.
HEY, MARSHALL.
MAYBE WE SHOULD GET OUT OF HERE, HUH?

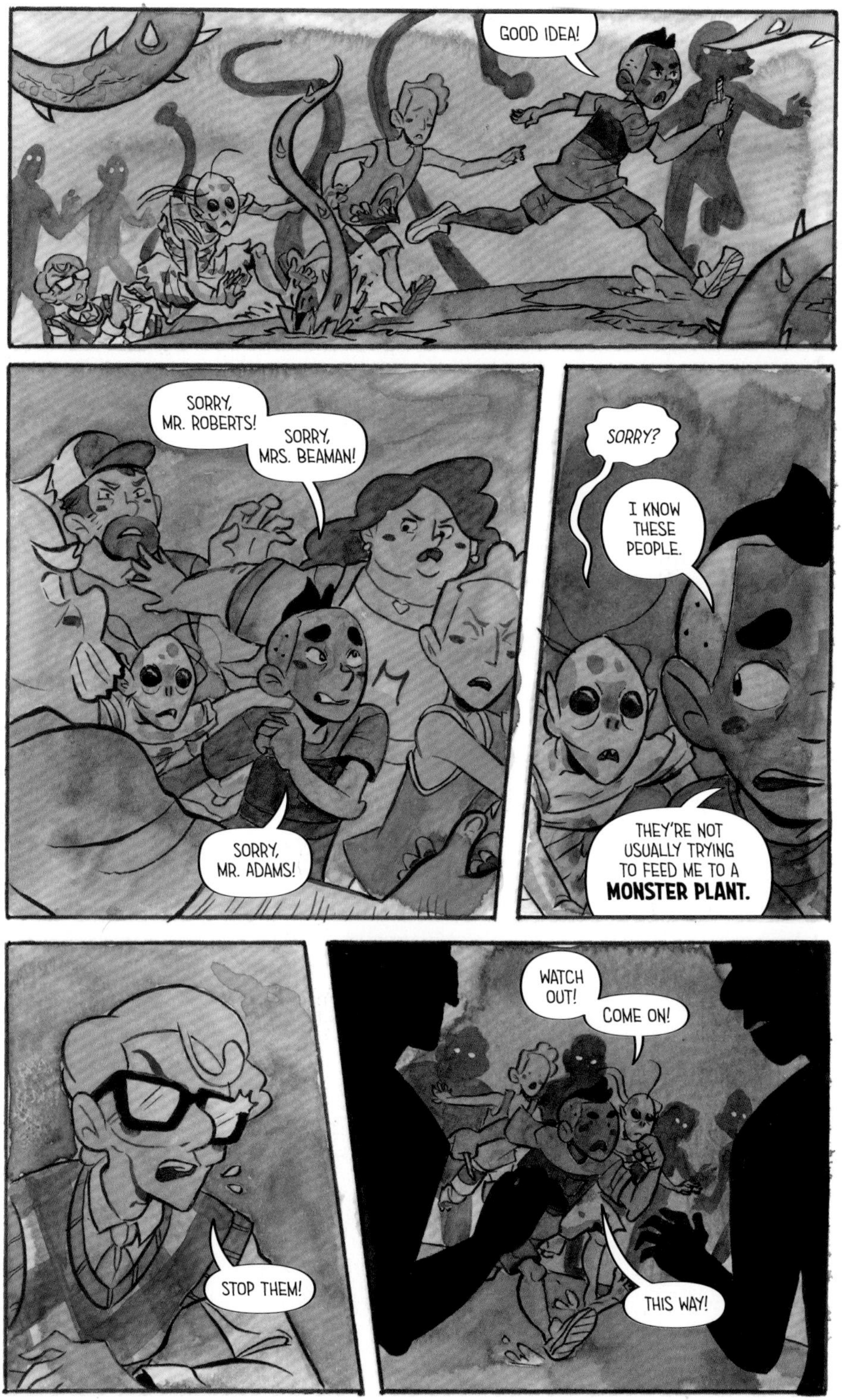
GOOD IDEA!
SORRY, MR. ROBERTS!
SORRY, MRS. BEAMAN!
SORRY, MR. ADAMS!
SORRY?
I KNOW THESE PEOPLE.
THEY'RE NOT USUALLY TRYING TO FEED ME TO A **MONSTER PLANT.**
STOP THEM!
WATCH OUT!
COME ON!
THIS WAY!

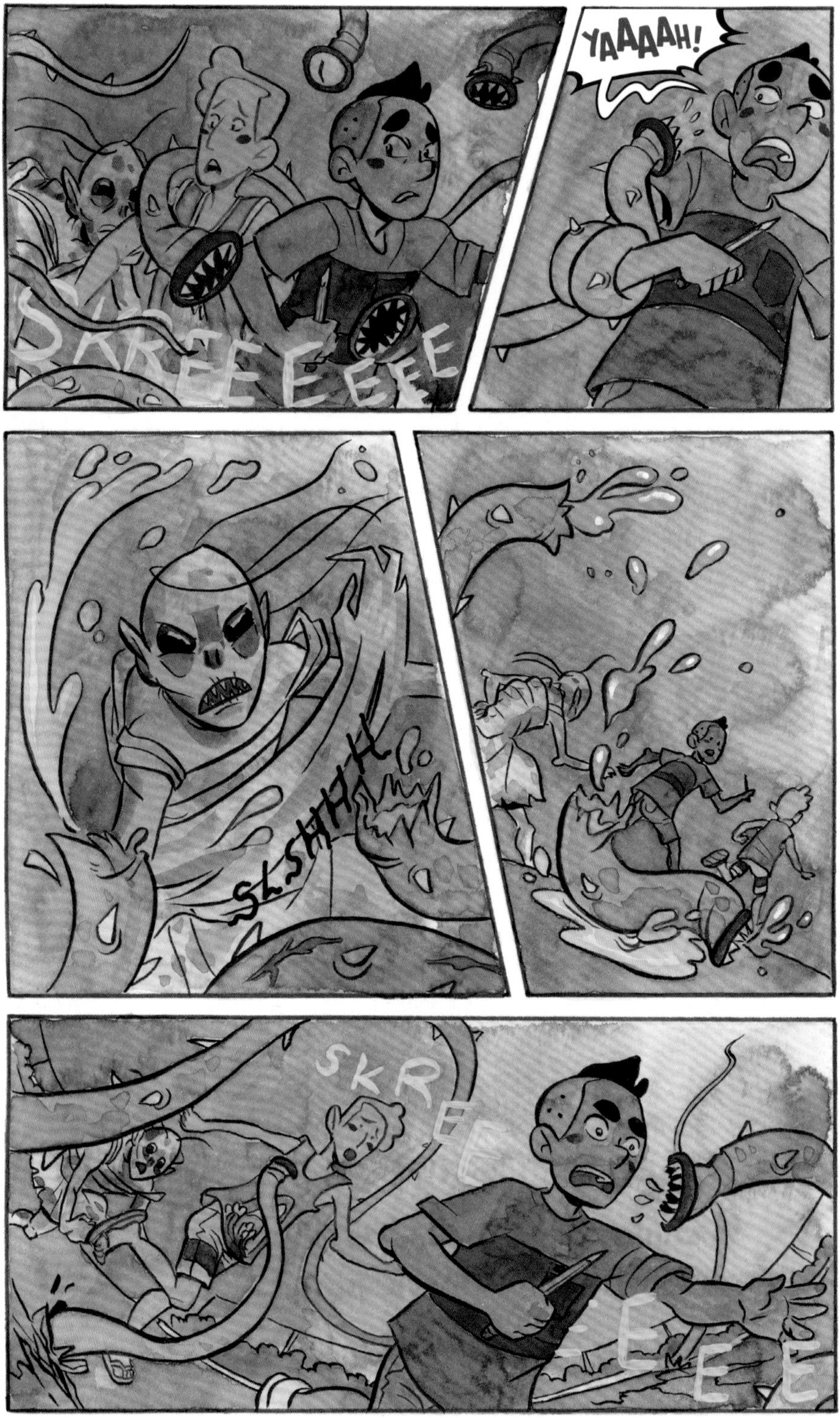
SKREEEEEEE
YAAAAH!
SLSHHH
SKREEEEEE

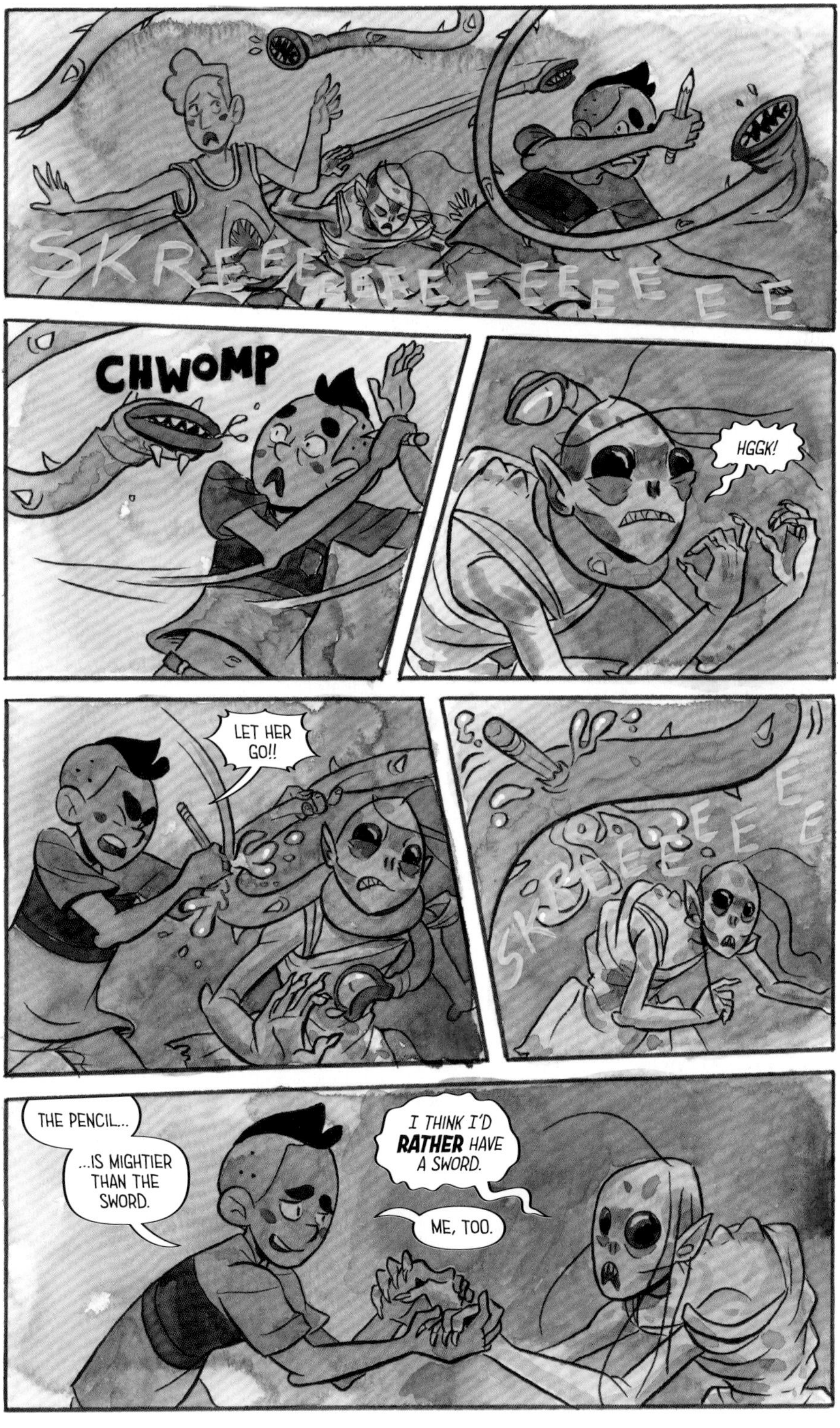
SKREEEEEEEEEEEEEE
CHWOMP
HGGK!
LET HER GO!!
SKREEEEEEEEE
THE PENCIL...
...IS MIGHTIER THAN THE SWORD.
I THINK I'D **RATHER** HAVE A SWORD.
ME, TOO.

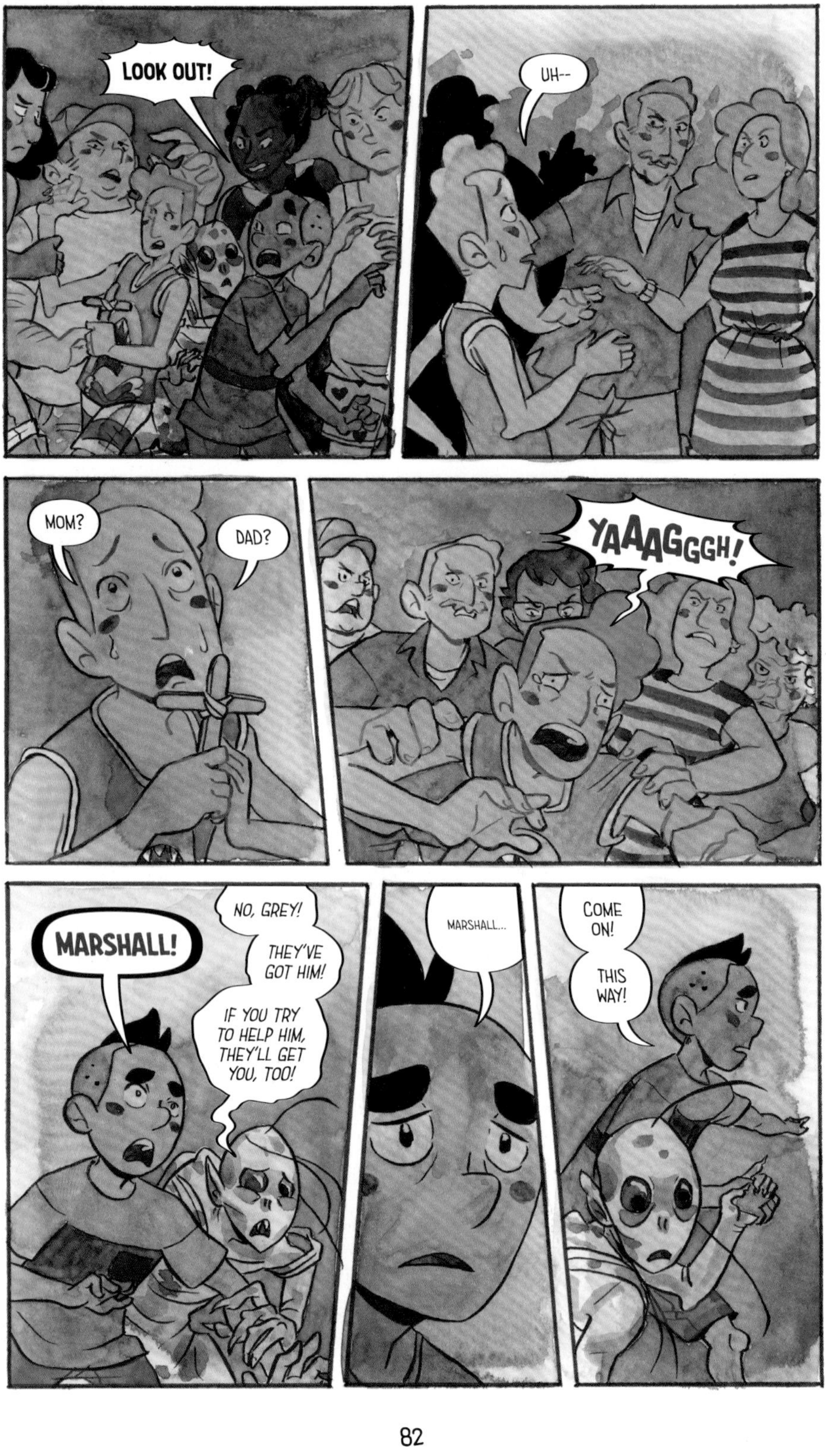
LOOK OUT!
UH--
MOM?
DAD?
YAAAGGGH!
MARSHALL!
NO, GREY!
THEY'VE GOT HIM!
IF YOU TRY TO HELP HIM, THEY'LL GET YOU, TOO!
MARSHALL...
COME ON!
THIS WAY!

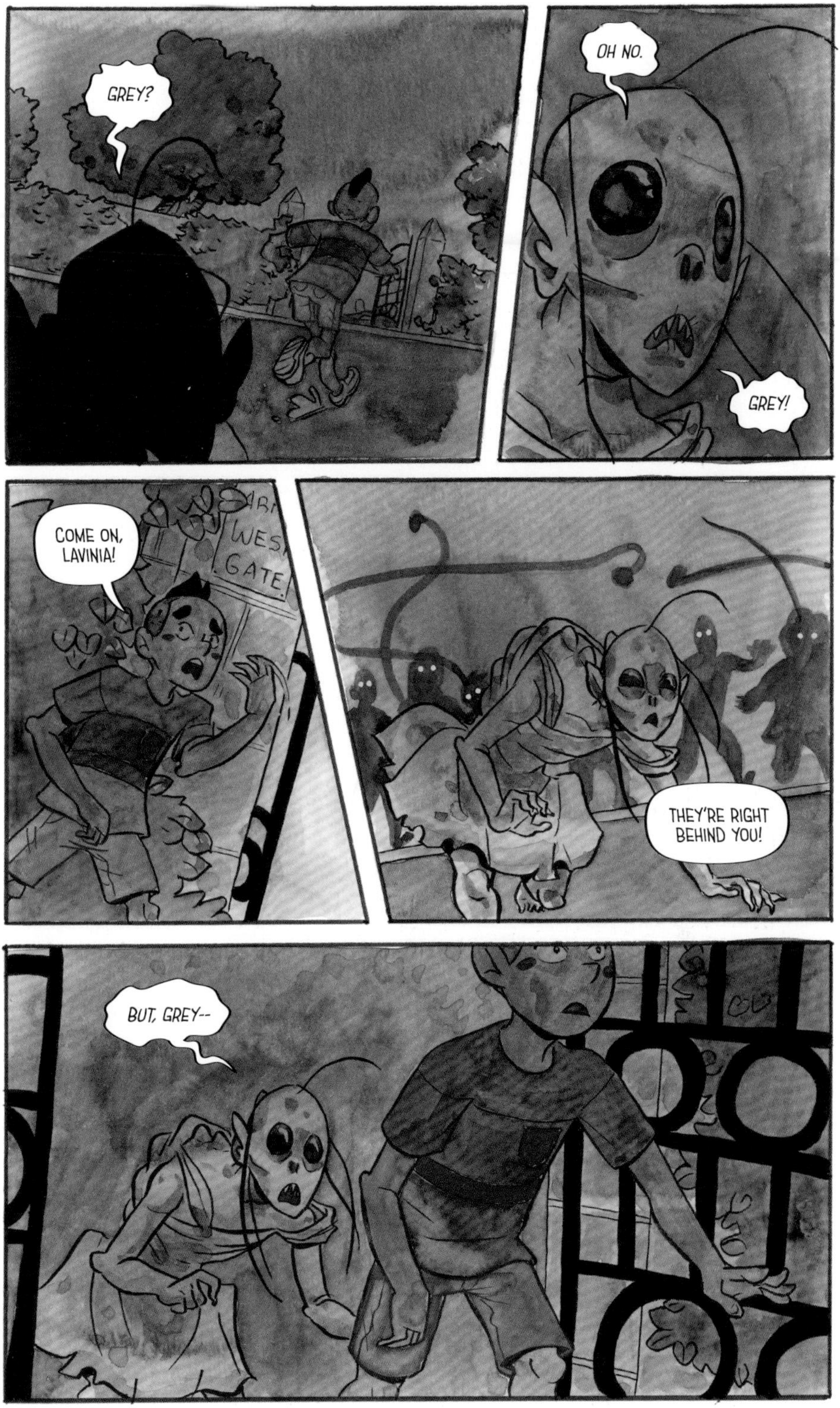
GREY?
OH NO.
GREY!
COME ON, LAVINIA!
THEY'RE RIGHT BEHIND YOU!
BUT, GREY--

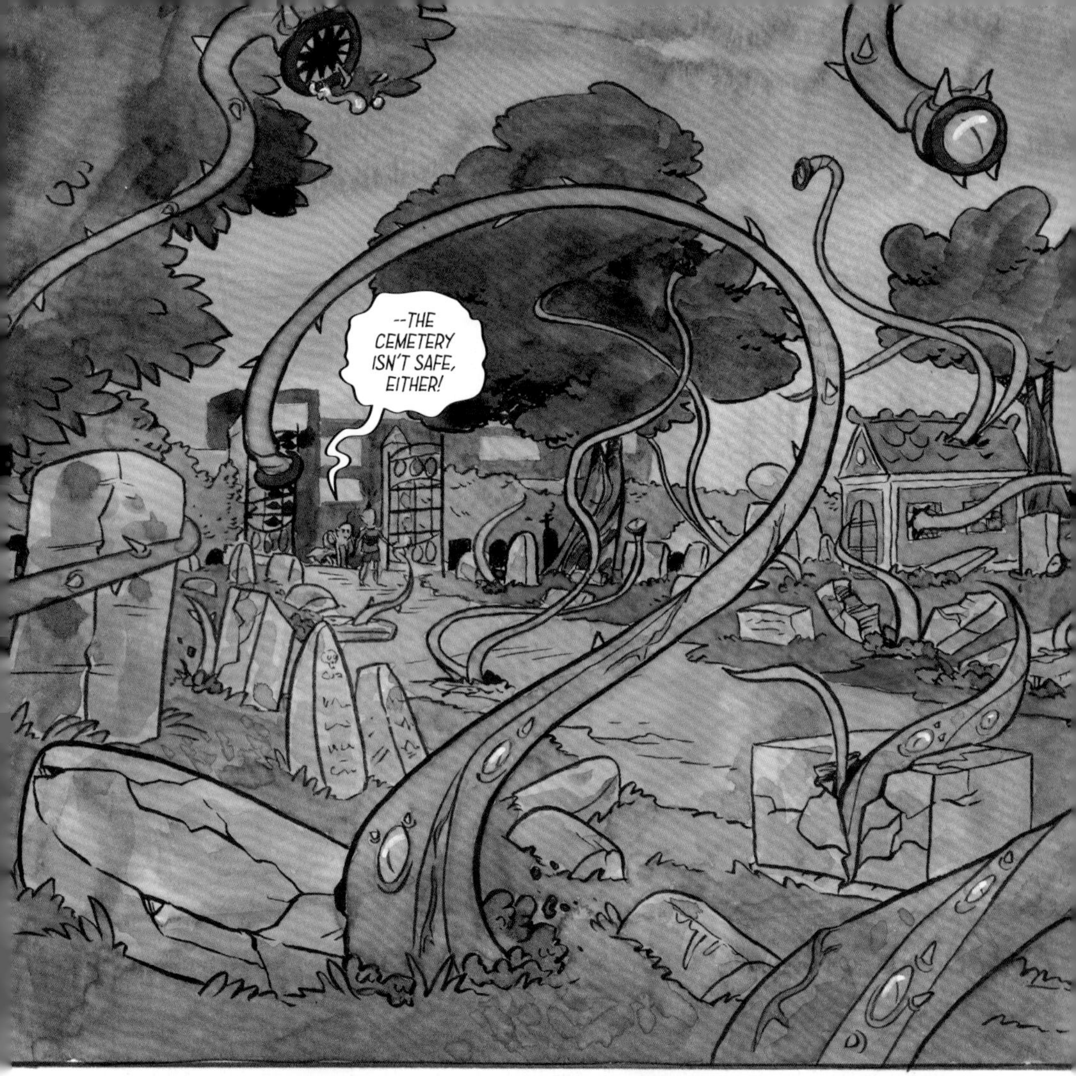
--THE CEMETERY ISN'T SAFE, EITHER!

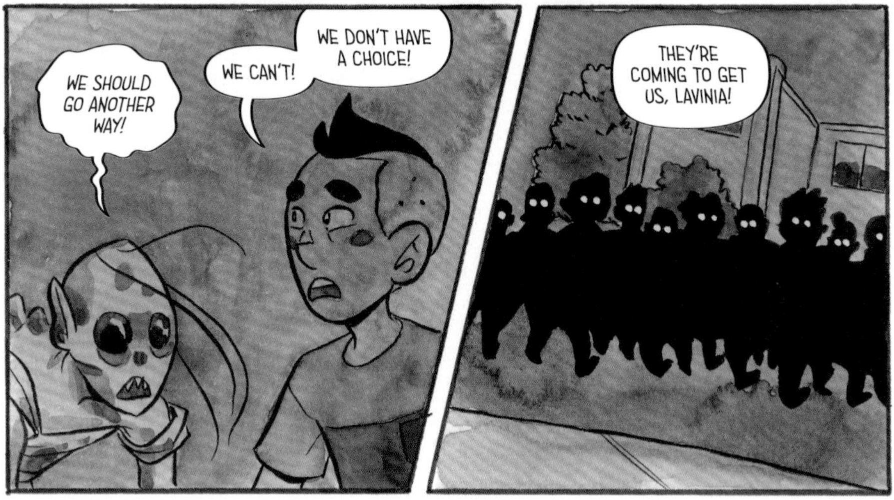
WE SHOULD GO ANOTHER WAY!
WE CAN'T!
WE DON'T HAVE A CHOICE!
THEY'RE COMING TO GET US, LAVINIA!

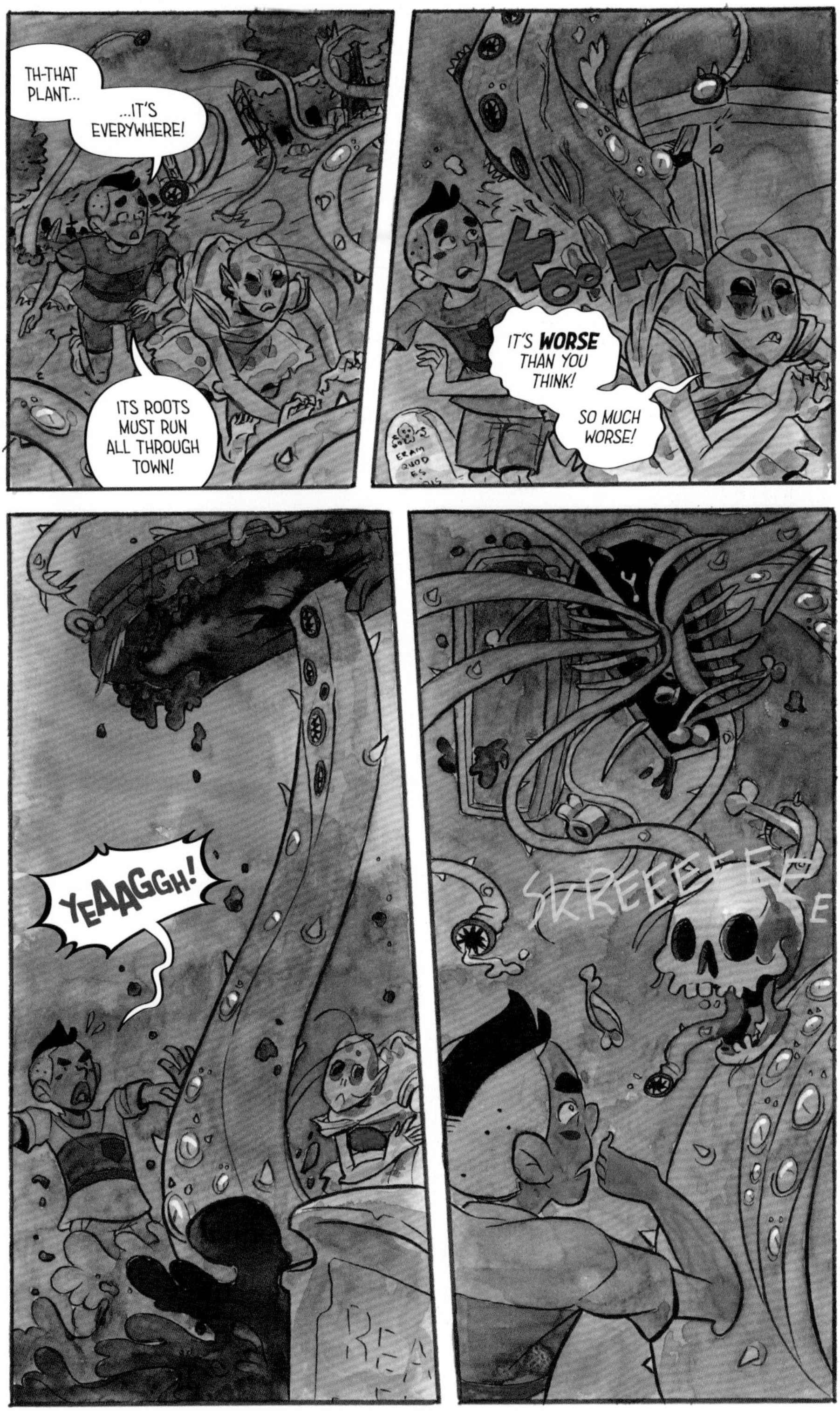
TH-THAT PLANT...
...IT'S EVERYWHERE!
ITS ROOTS MUST RUN ALL THROUGH TOWN!
KOOM
ERAM QUOD ES
IT'S **WORSE** THAN YOU THINK!
SO MUCH WORSE!
YEAAGGH!
SKREEEEEEE

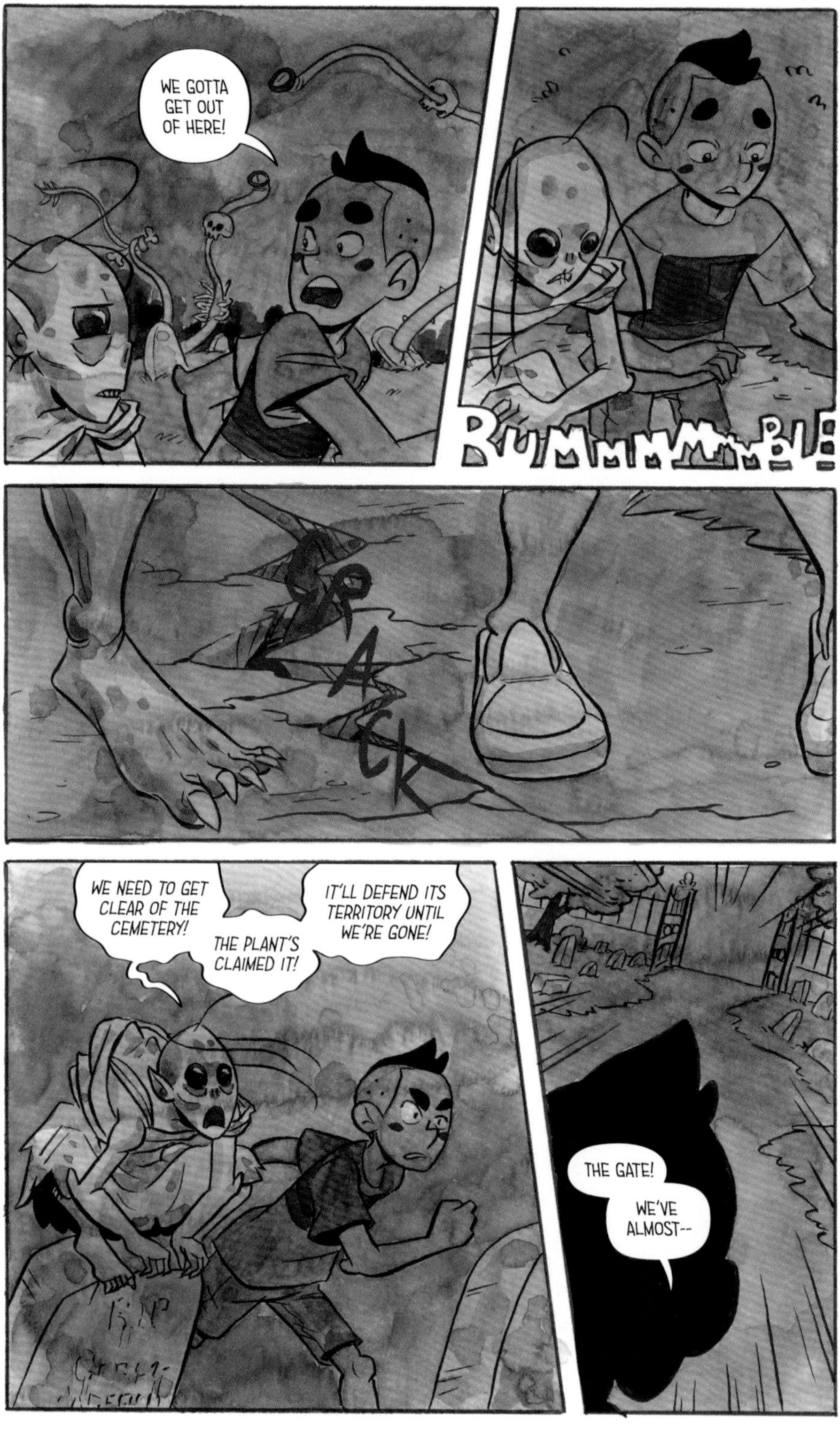
WE GOTTA GET OUT OF HERE!
RUMMMMMMBLE!
CRACK
WE NEED TO GET CLEAR OF THE CEMETERY!
THE PLANT'S CLAIMED IT!
IT'LL DEFEND ITS TERRITORY UNTIL WE'RE GONE!
THE GATE!
WE'VE ALMOST--

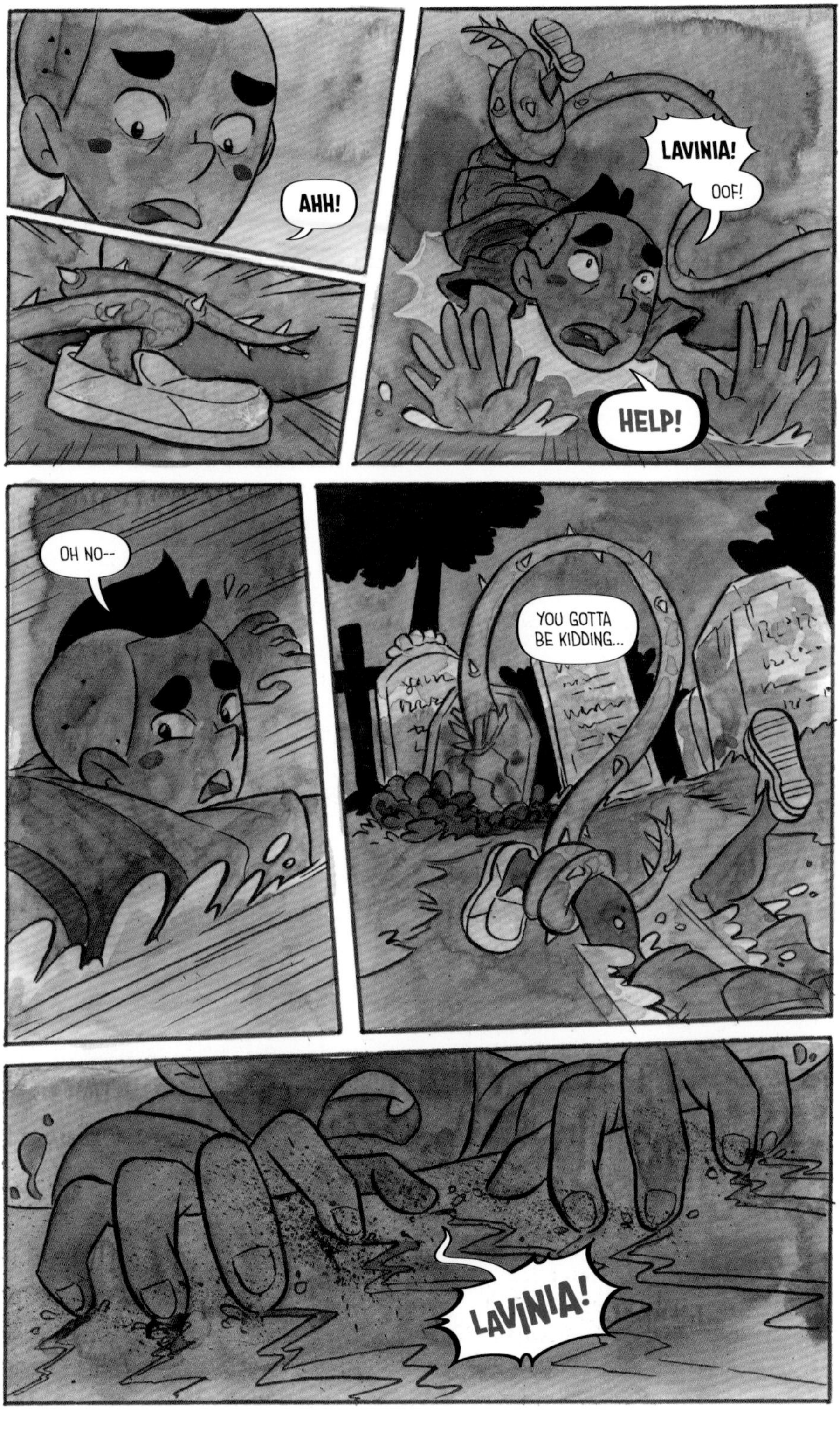
AHH!
LAVINIA!
OOF!
HELP!
OH NO--
YOU GOTTA BE KIDDING...
LAVINIA!

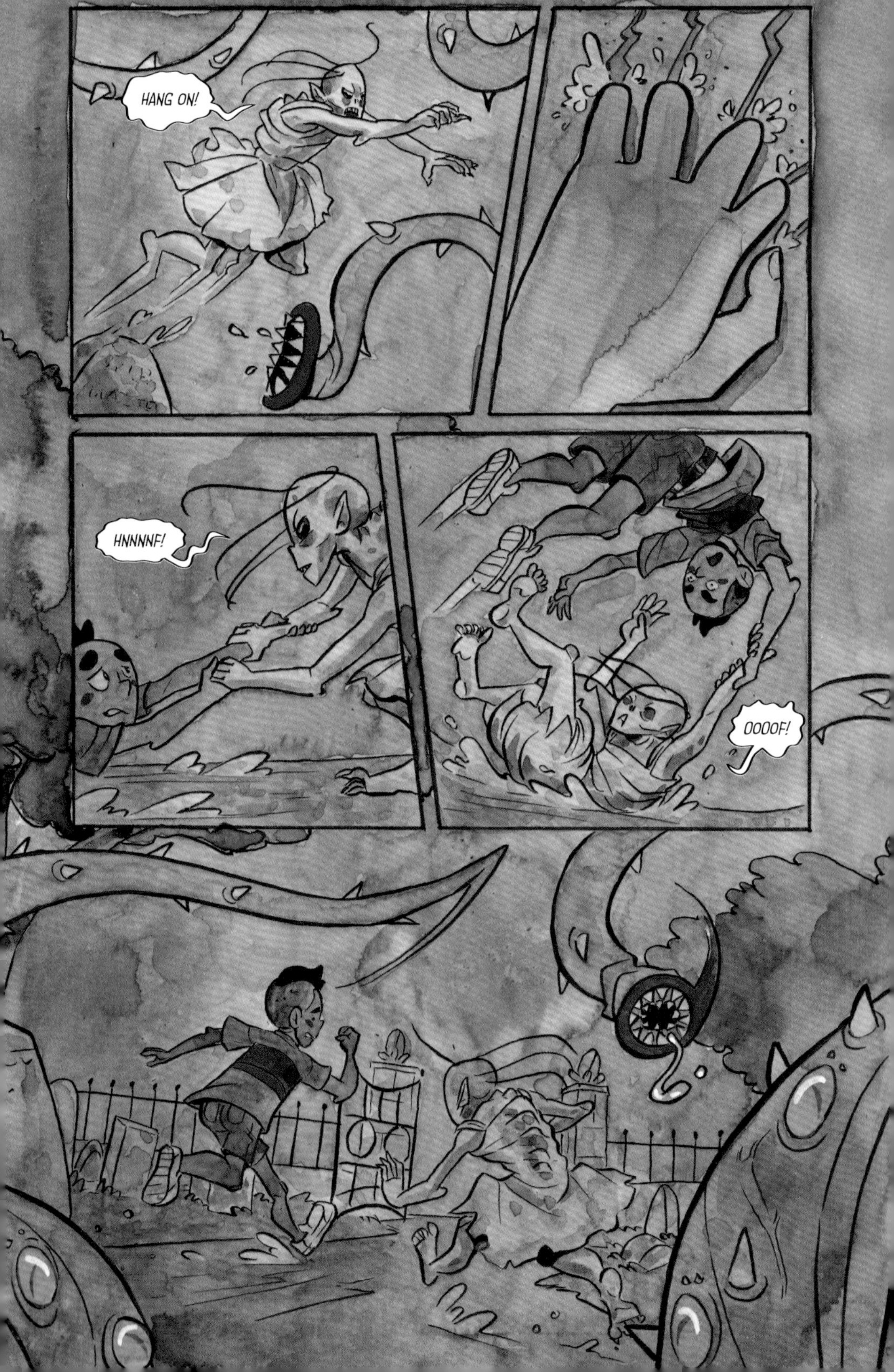
HANG ON!
HNNNNF!
OOOOF!

89

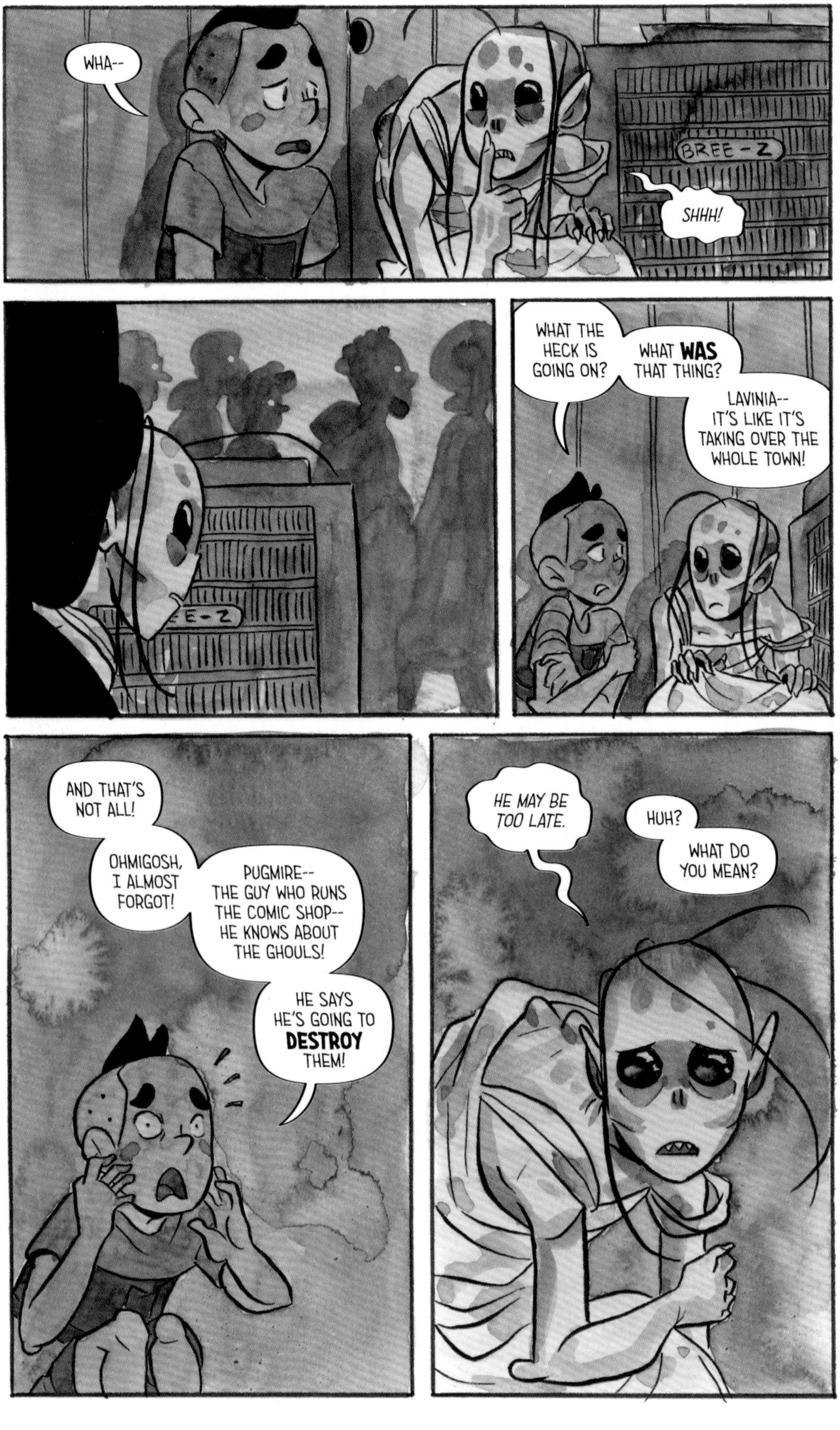
WHA--
SHHH!
BREE-Z
EE-Z
WHAT THE HECK IS GOING ON?
WHAT **WAS** THAT THING?
LAVINIA-- IT'S LIKE IT'S TAKING OVER THE WHOLE TOWN!
AND THAT'S NOT ALL!
OHMIGOSH, I ALMOST FORGOT!
PUGMIRE-- THE GUY WHO RUNS THE COMIC SHOP-- HE KNOWS ABOUT THE GHOULS!
HE SAYS HE'S GOING TO **DESTROY** THEM!
HE MAY BE TOO LATE.
HUH?
WHAT DO YOU MEAN?

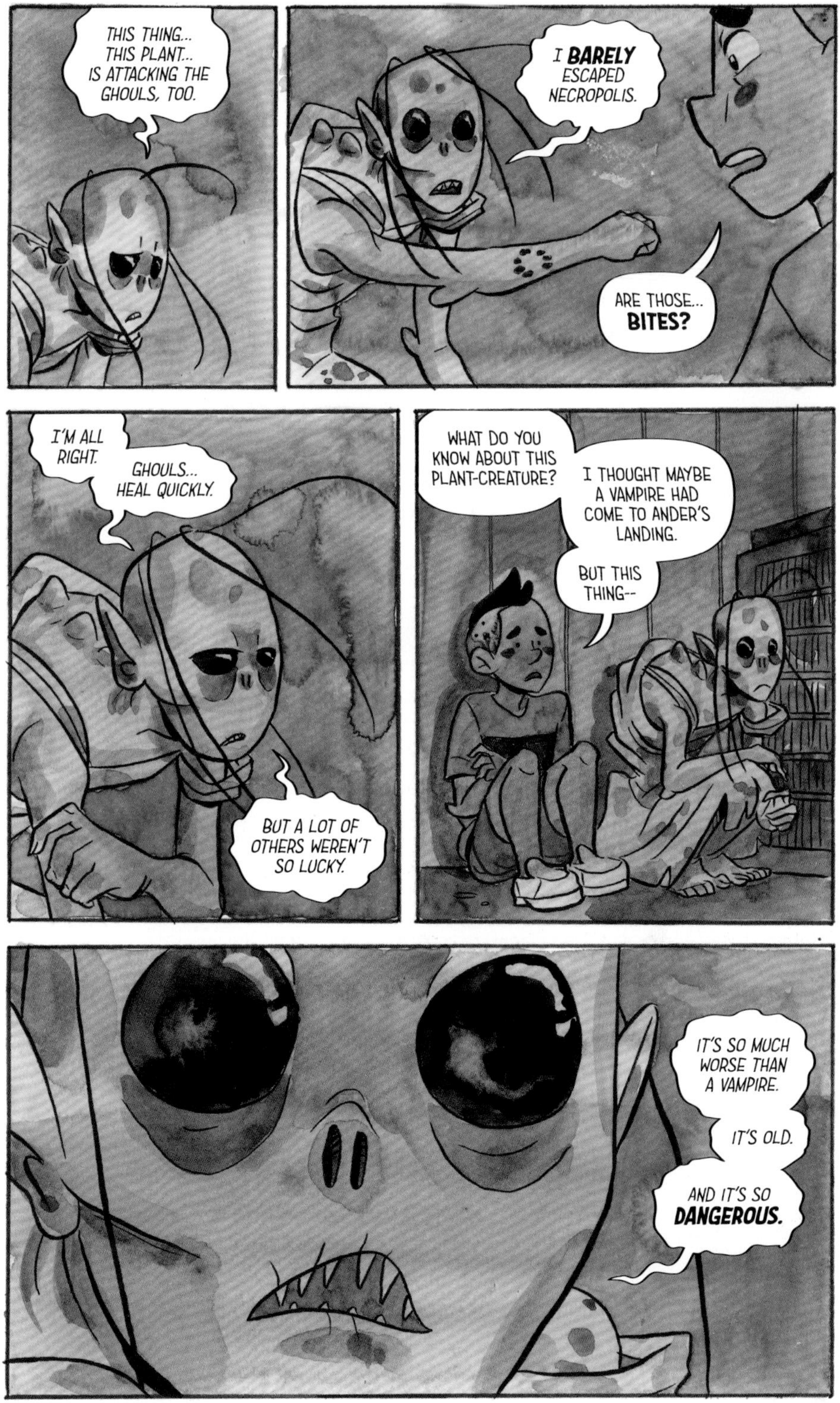
THIS THING... THIS PLANT... IS ATTACKING THE GHOULS, TOO.
I **BARELY** ESCAPED NECROPOLIS.
ARE THOSE... **BITES?**
I'M ALL RIGHT.
GHOULS... HEAL QUICKLY.
BUT A LOT OF OTHERS WEREN'T SO LUCKY.
WHAT DO YOU KNOW ABOUT THIS PLANT-CREATURE?
I THOUGHT MAYBE A VAMPIRE HAD COME TO ANDER'S LANDING.
BUT THIS THING--
IT'S SO MUCH WORSE THAN A VAMPIRE.
IT'S OLD.
AND IT'S SO **DANGEROUS.**

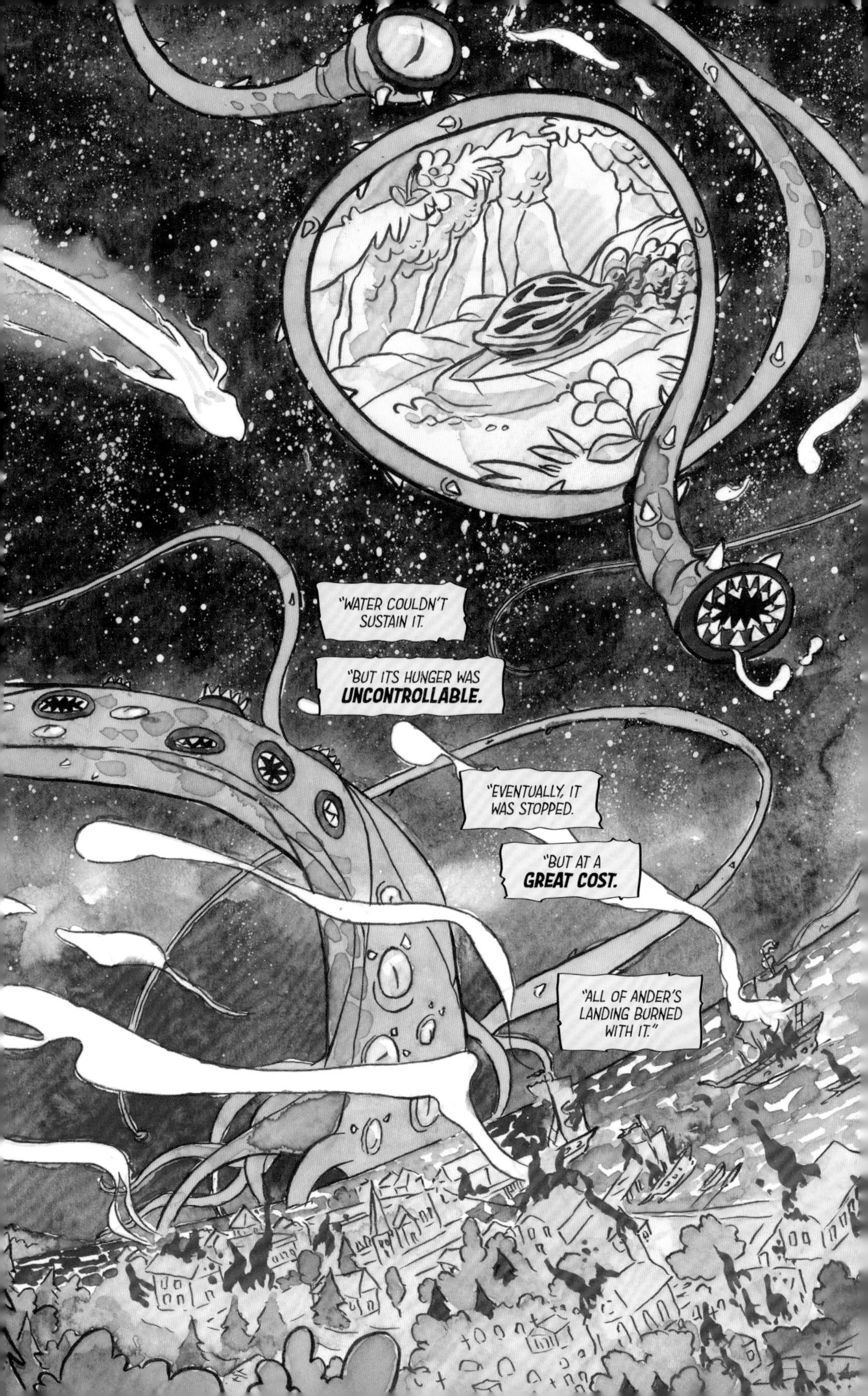
"WATER COULDN'T SUSTAIN IT.
"BUT ITS HUNGER WAS **UNCONTROLLABLE.**
"EVENTUALLY, IT WAS STOPPED.
"BUT AT A **GREAT COST.**
"ALL OF ANDER'S LANDING BURNED WITH IT."

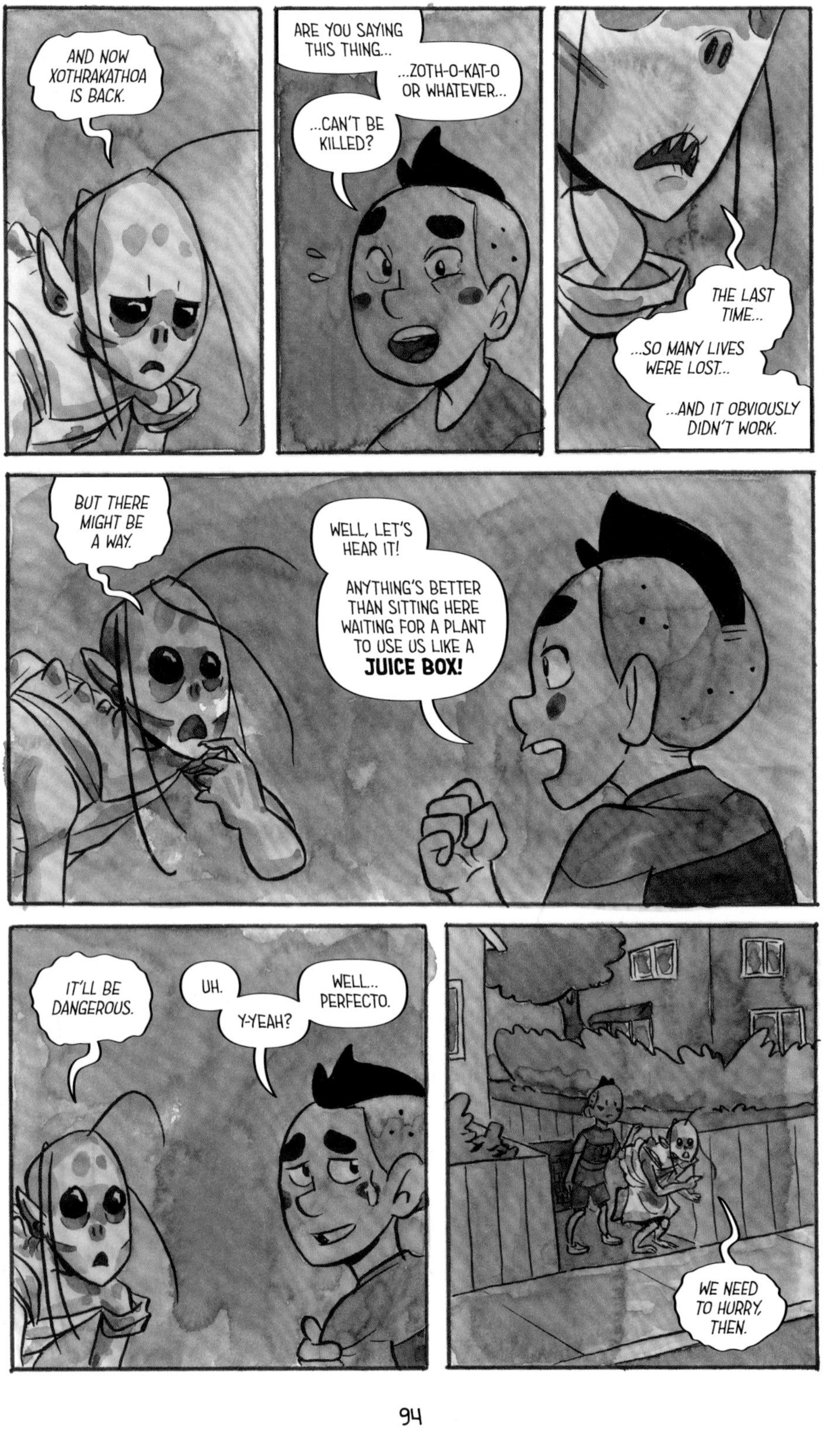
AND NOW XOTHRAKATHOA IS BACK.
ARE YOU SAYING THIS THING...
...ZOTH-O-KAT-O OR WHATEVER...
...CAN'T BE KILLED?
THE LAST TIME...
...SO MANY LIVES WERE LOST...
...AND IT OBVIOUSLY DIDN'T WORK.
BUT THERE MIGHT BE A WAY.
WELL, LET'S HEAR IT!
ANYTHING'S BETTER THAN SITTING HERE WAITING FOR A PLANT TO USE US LIKE A **JUICE BOX!**
IT'LL BE DANGEROUS.
UH.
Y-YEAH?
WELL... PERFECTO.
WE NEED TO HURRY, THEN.

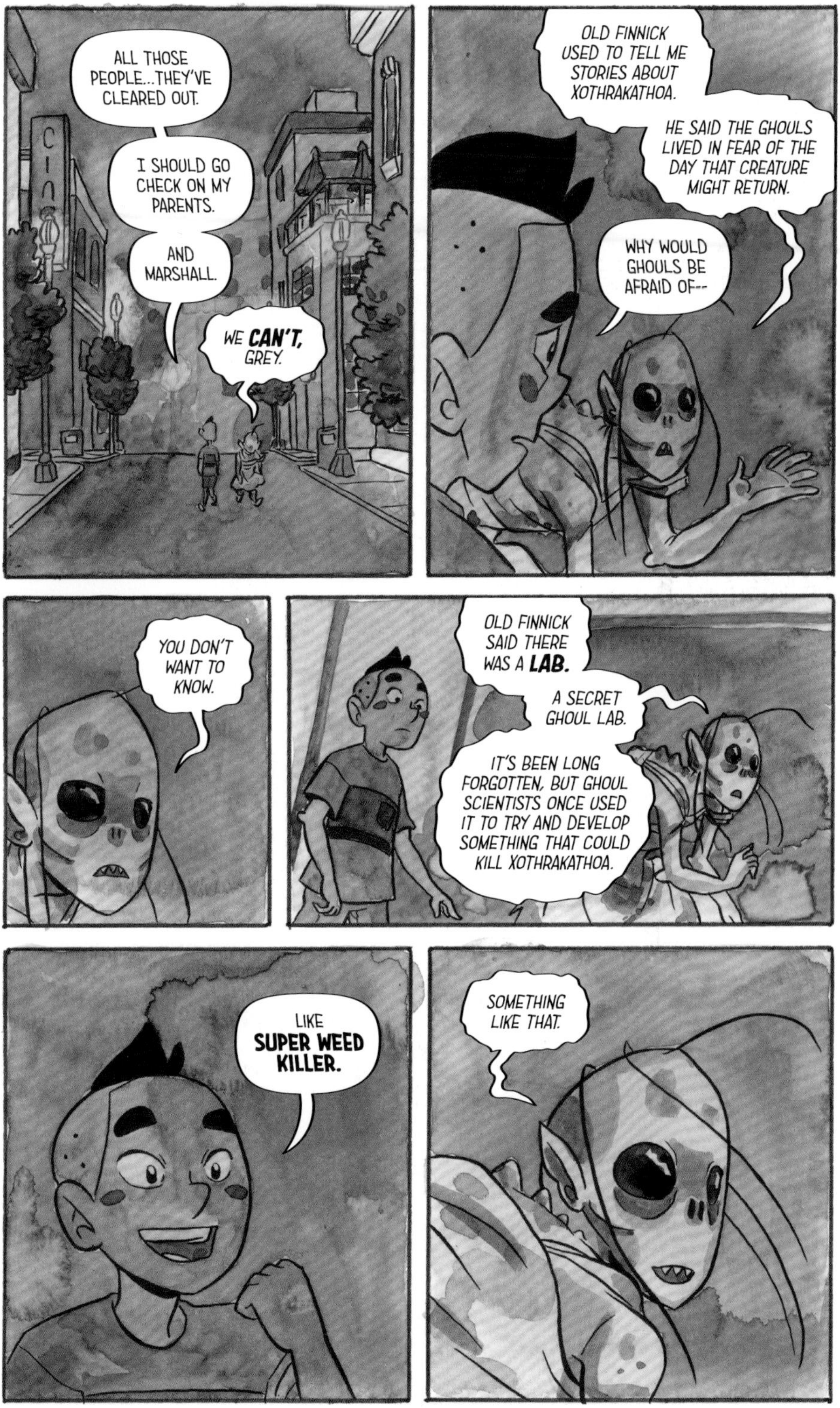
ALL THOSE PEOPLE...THEY'VE CLEARED OUT.
I SHOULD GO CHECK ON MY PARENTS.
AND MARSHALL.
WE **CAN'T,** GREY.
OLD FINNICK USED TO TELL ME STORIES ABOUT XOTHRAKATHOA.
HE SAID THE GHOULS LIVED IN FEAR OF THE DAY THAT CREATURE MIGHT RETURN.
WHY WOULD GHOULS BE AFRAID OF--
YOU DON'T WANT TO KNOW.
OLD FINNICK SAID THERE WAS A **LAB.**
A SECRET GHOUL LAB.
IT'S BEEN LONG FORGOTTEN, BUT GHOUL SCIENTISTS ONCE USED IT TO TRY AND DEVELOP SOMETHING THAT COULD KILL XOTHRAKATHOA.
LIKE **SUPER WEED KILLER.**
SOMETHING LIKE THAT.

96

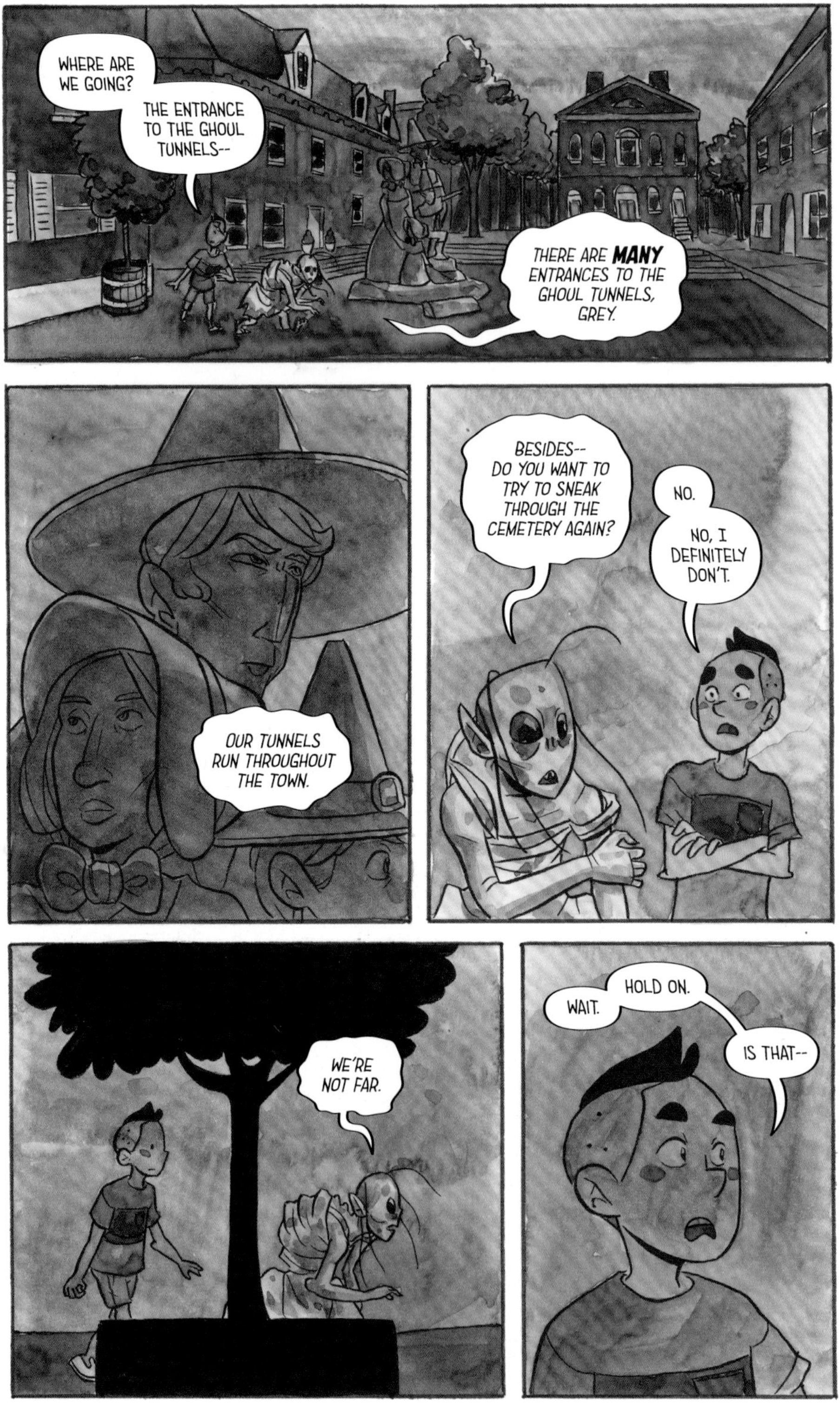
WHERE ARE WE GOING?
THE ENTRANCE TO THE GHOUL TUNNELS--
THERE ARE **MANY** ENTRANCES TO THE GHOUL TUNNELS, GREY.
OUR TUNNELS RUN THROUGHOUT THE TOWN.
BESIDES-- DO YOU WANT TO TRY TO SNEAK THROUGH THE CEMETERY AGAIN?
NO.
NO, I DEFINITELY DON'T.
WE'RE NOT FAR.
WAIT.
HOLD ON.
IS THAT--

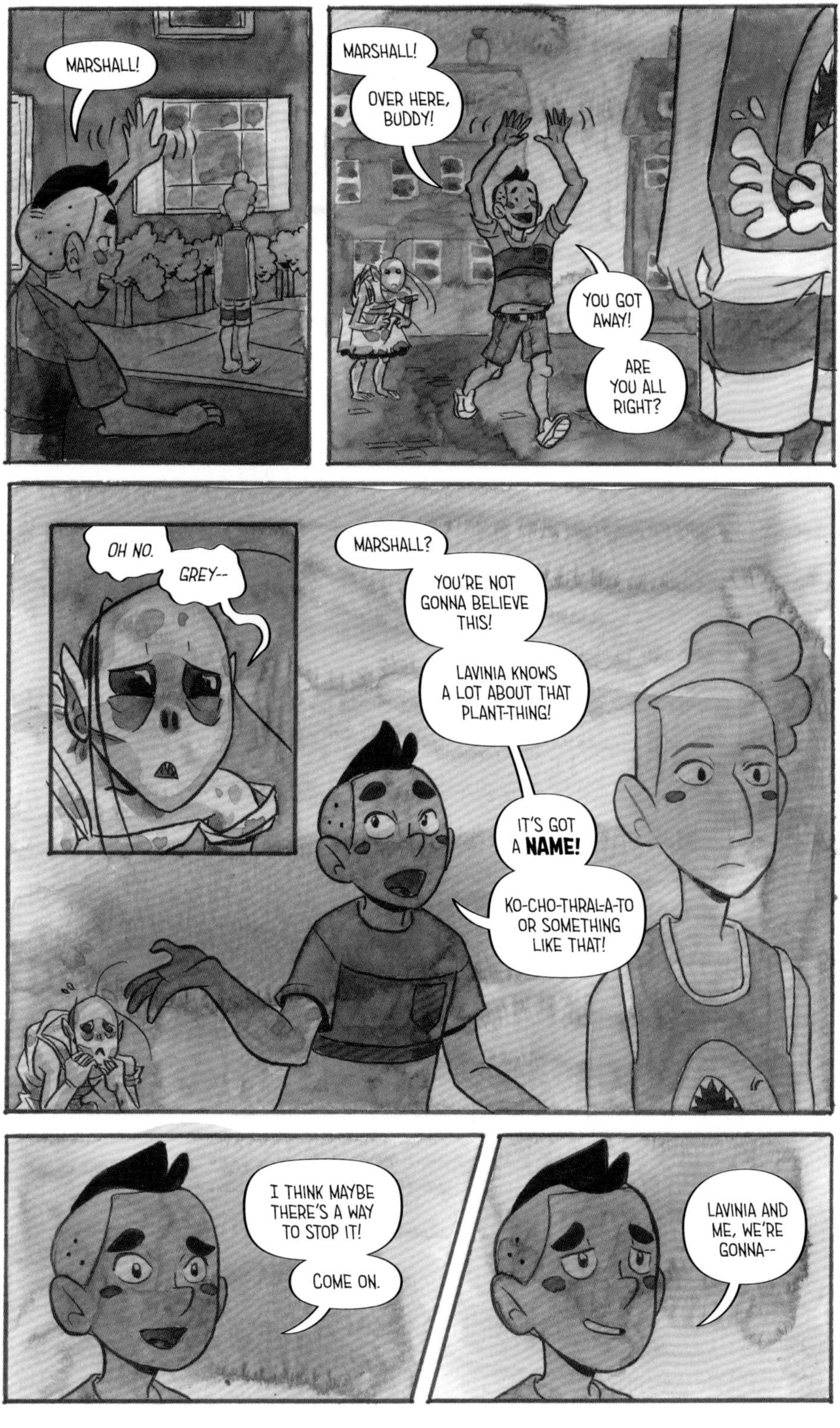
MARSHALL!
MARSHALL!
OVER HERE, BUDDY!
YOU GOT AWAY!
ARE YOU ALL RIGHT?
OH NO.
GREY--
MARSHALL?
YOU'RE NOT GONNA BELIEVE THIS!
LAVINIA KNOWS A LOT ABOUT THAT PLANT-THING!
IT'S GOT A **NAME!**
KO-CHO-THRAL-A-TO OR SOMETHING LIKE THAT!
I THINK MAYBE THERE'S A WAY TO STOP IT!
COME ON.
LAVINIA AND ME, WE'RE GONNA--

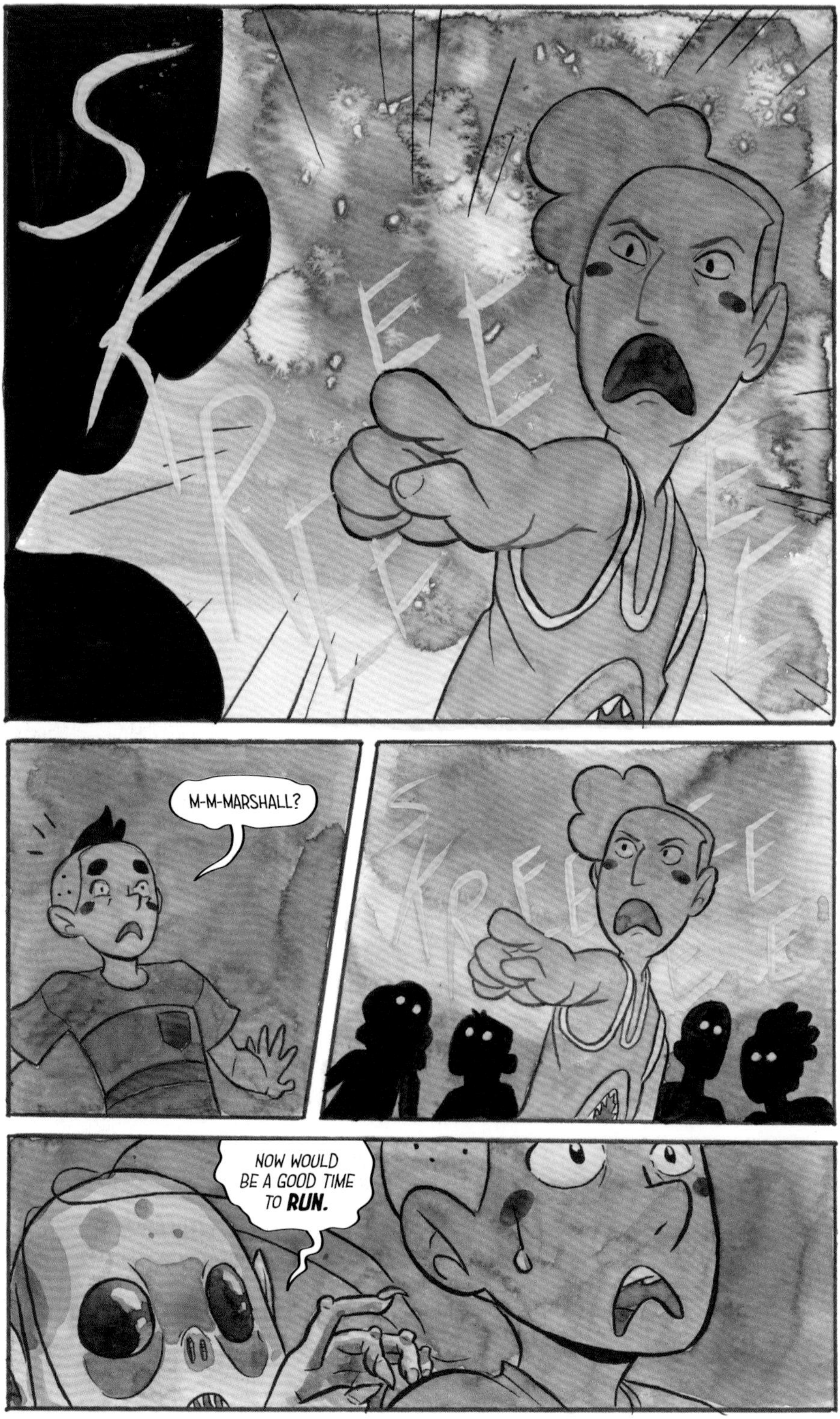
M-M-MARSHALL?
NOW WOULD BE A GOOD TIME TO **RUN.**

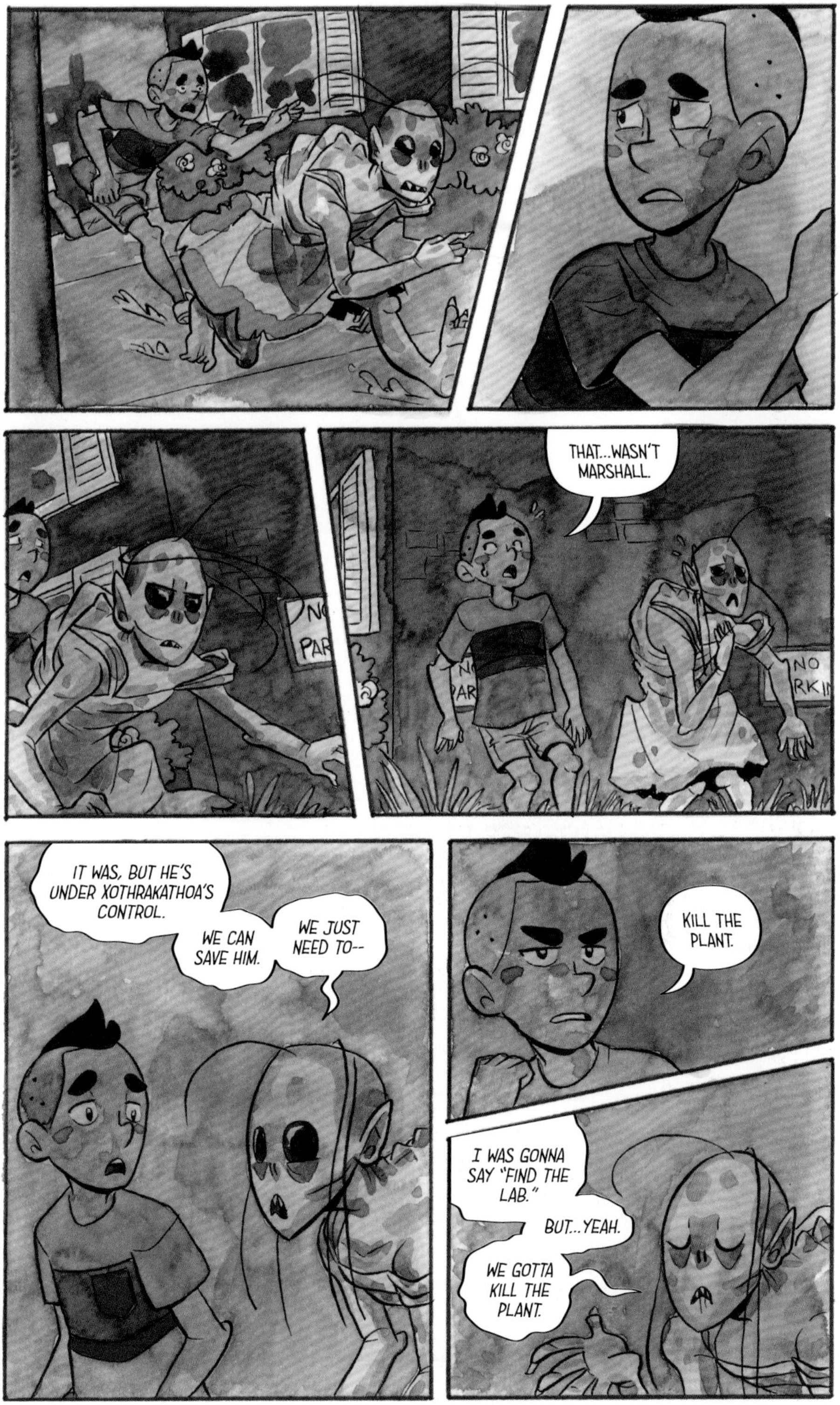
NO PAR
THAT...WASN'T MARSHALL.
NO PAR
NO RKIN
IT WAS, BUT HE'S UNDER XOTHRAKATHOA'S CONTROL.
WE CAN SAVE HIM.
WE JUST NEED TO--
KILL THE PLANT.
I WAS GONNA SAY "FIND THE LAB."
BUT...YEAH.
WE GOTTA KILL THE PLANT.

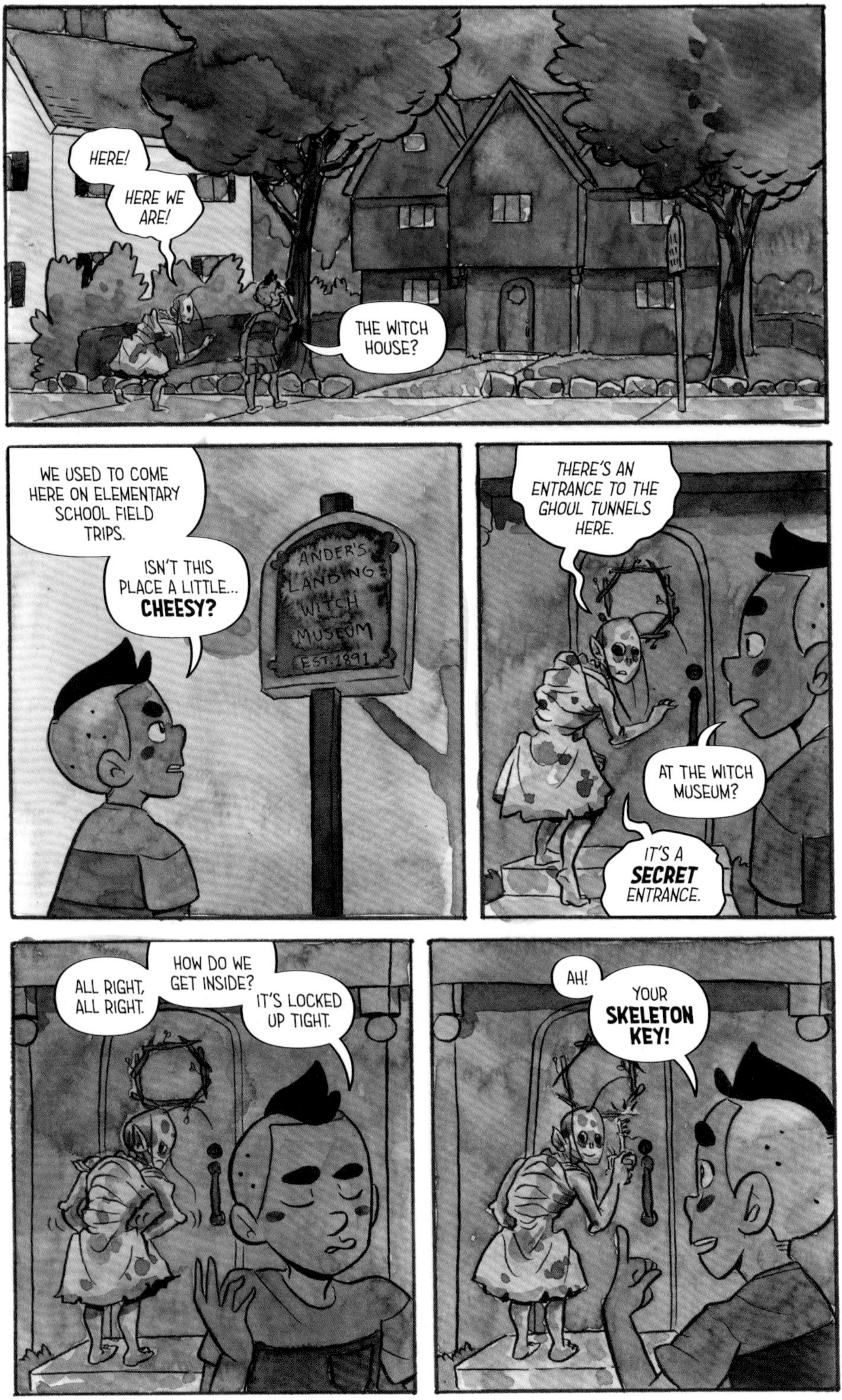
HERE!
HERE WE ARE!
THE WITCH HOUSE?
WE USED TO COME HERE ON ELEMENTARY SCHOOL FIELD TRIPS.
ISN'T THIS PLACE A LITTLE... **CHEESY?**
ANDER'S LANDING WITCH MUSEUM EST. 1891
THERE'S AN ENTRANCE TO THE GHOUL TUNNELS HERE.
AT THE WITCH MUSEUM?
IT'S A **SECRET** ENTRANCE.
ALL RIGHT, ALL RIGHT.
HOW DO WE GET INSIDE?
IT'S LOCKED UP TIGHT.
AH!
YOUR **SKELETON KEY!**

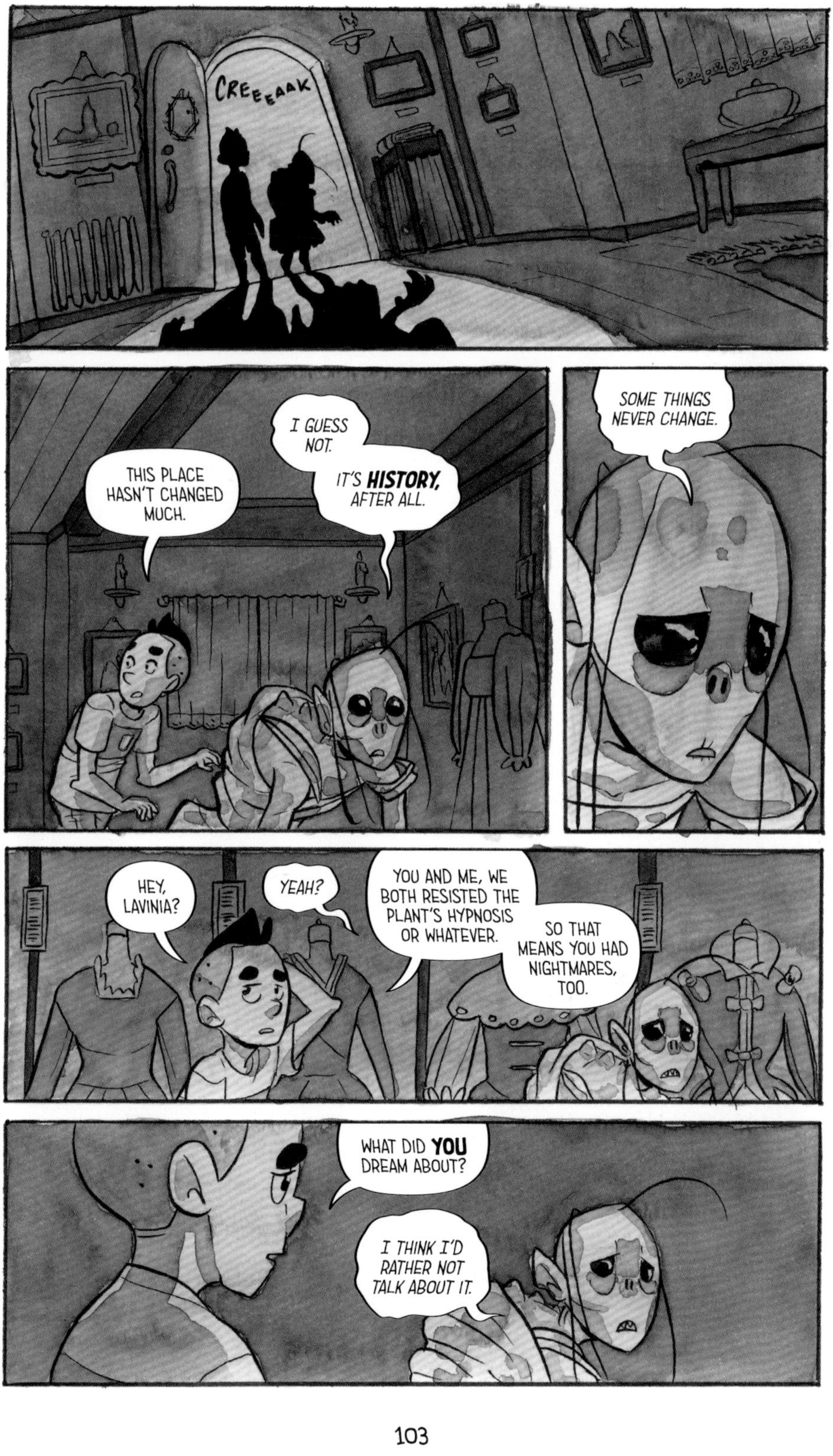
CREEEAAK
THIS PLACE HASN'T CHANGED MUCH.
I GUESS NOT.
IT'S **HISTORY,** AFTER ALL.
SOME THINGS NEVER CHANGE.
HEY, LAVINIA?
YEAH?
YOU AND ME, WE BOTH RESISTED THE PLANT'S HYPNOSIS OR WHATEVER.
SO THAT MEANS YOU HAD NIGHTMARES, TOO.
WHAT DID **YOU** DREAM ABOUT?
I THINK I'D RATHER NOT TALK ABOUT IT.

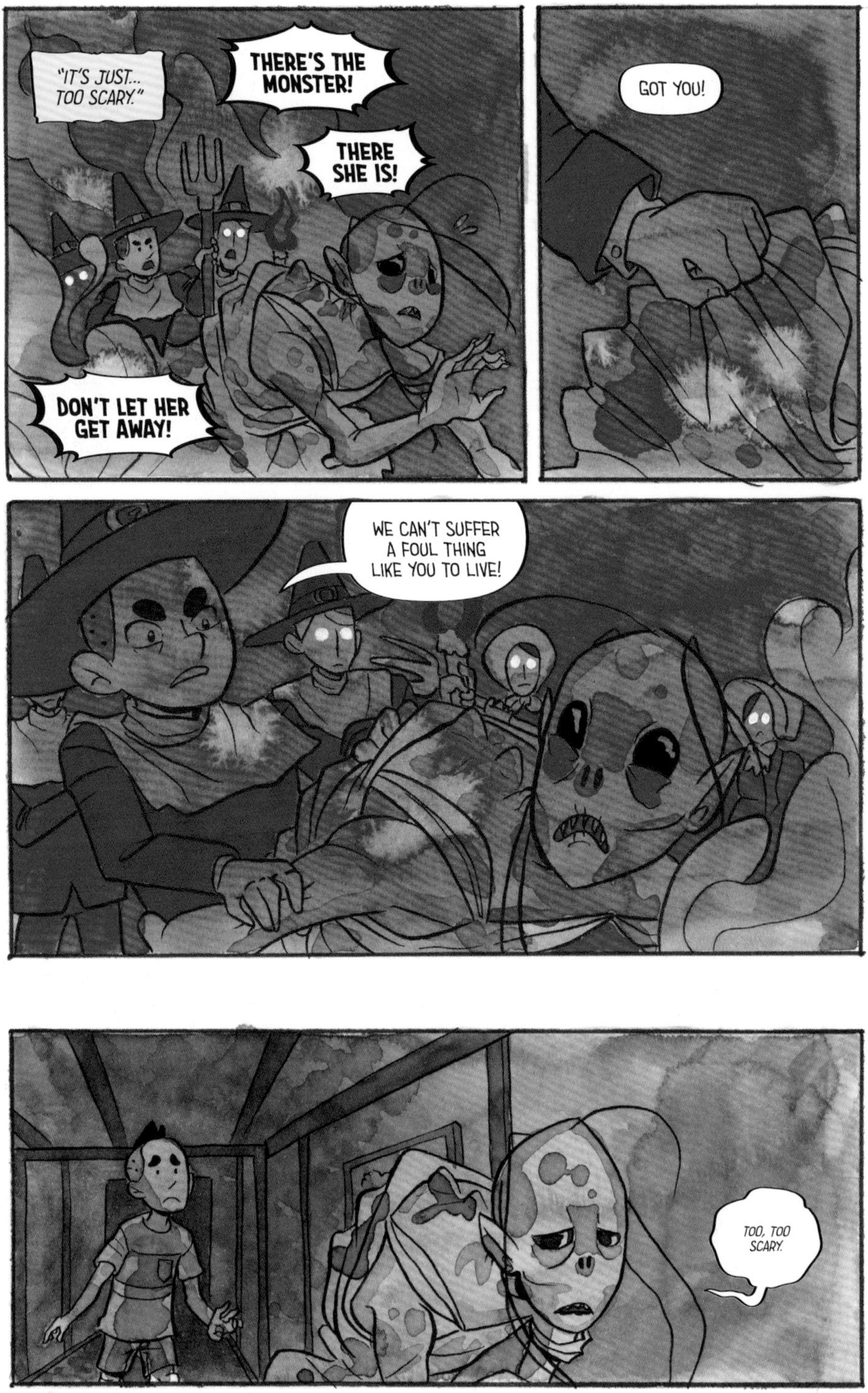
"IT'S JUST... TOO SCARY."
THERE'S THE MONSTER!
THERE SHE IS!
DON'T LET HER GET AWAY!
GOT YOU!
WE CAN'T SUFFER A FOUL THING LIKE YOU TO LIVE!
TOO, TOO SCARY.

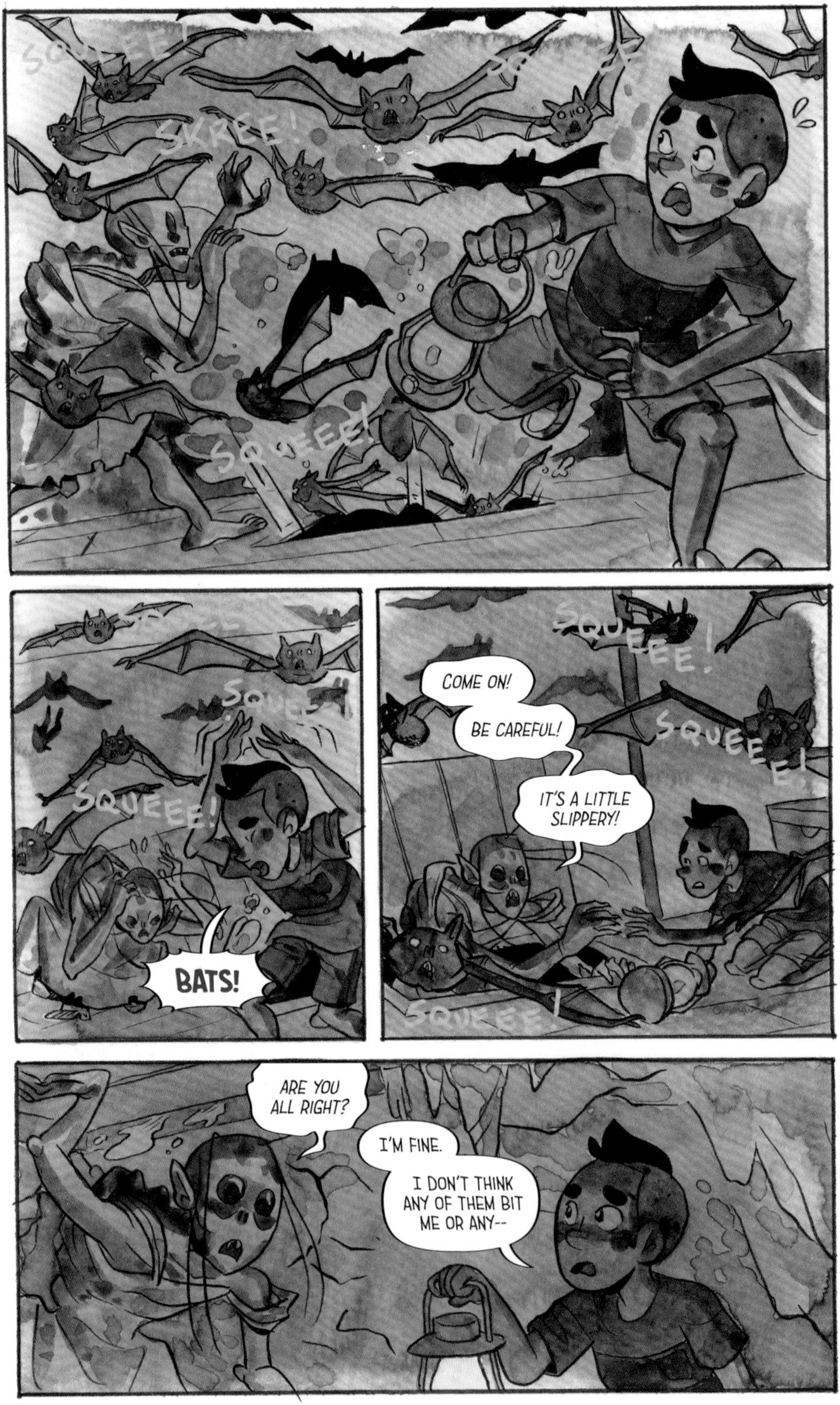
SKREE!
SQUEEE!
SQUEEE!
BATS!
SQUEEE!
COME ON!
BE CAREFUL!
IT'S A LITTLE SLIPPERY!
SQUEEEE!
SQUEEE!
ARE YOU ALL RIGHT?
I'M FINE.
I DON'T THINK ANY OF THEM BIT ME OR ANY--

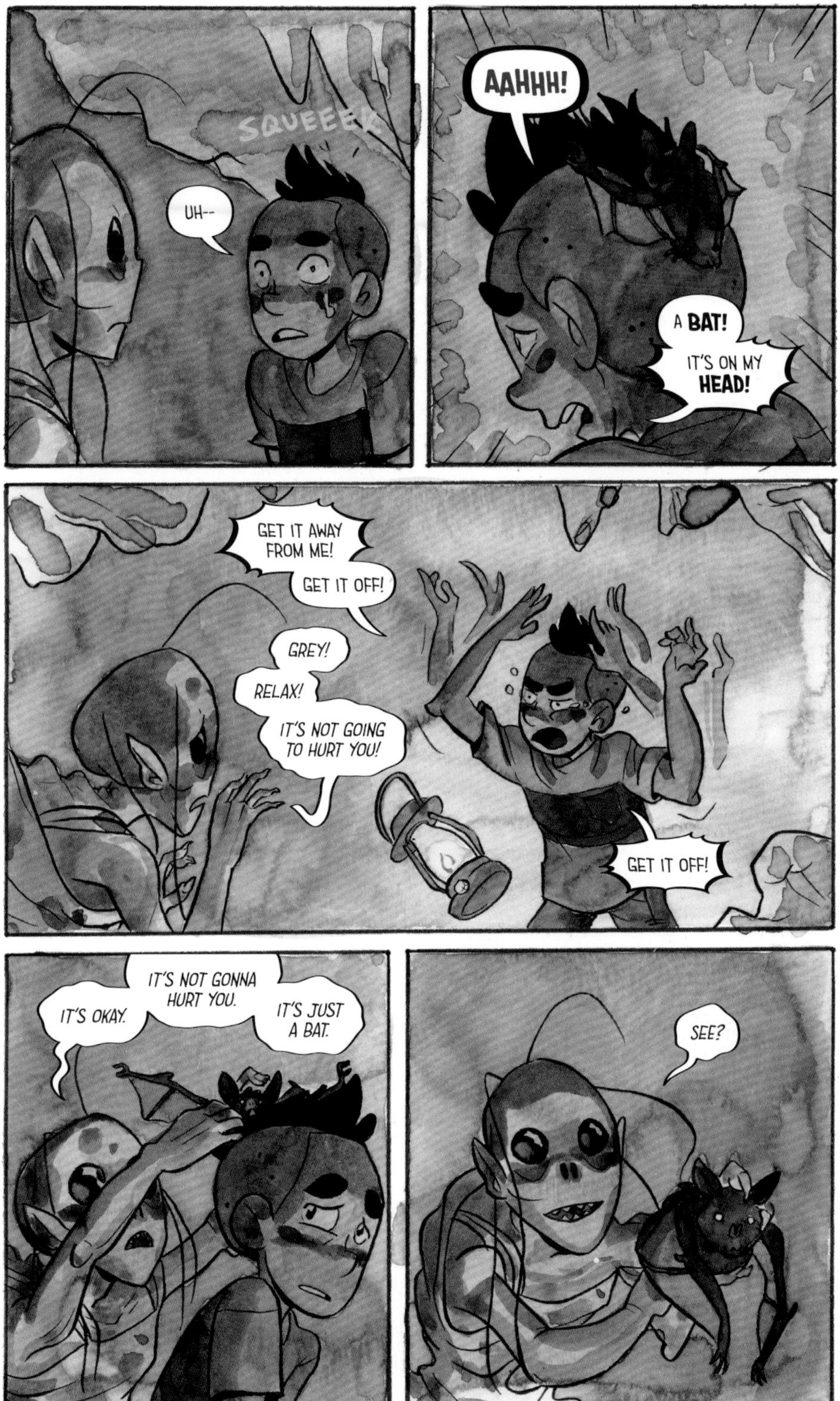
SQUEEEK
UH--
AAHHH!
A BAT!
IT'S ON MY HEAD!
GET IT AWAY FROM ME!
GET IT OFF!
GREY!
RELAX!
IT'S NOT GOING TO HURT YOU!
GET IT OFF!
IT'S OKAY.
IT'S NOT GONNA HURT YOU.
IT'S JUST A BAT.
SEE?

108

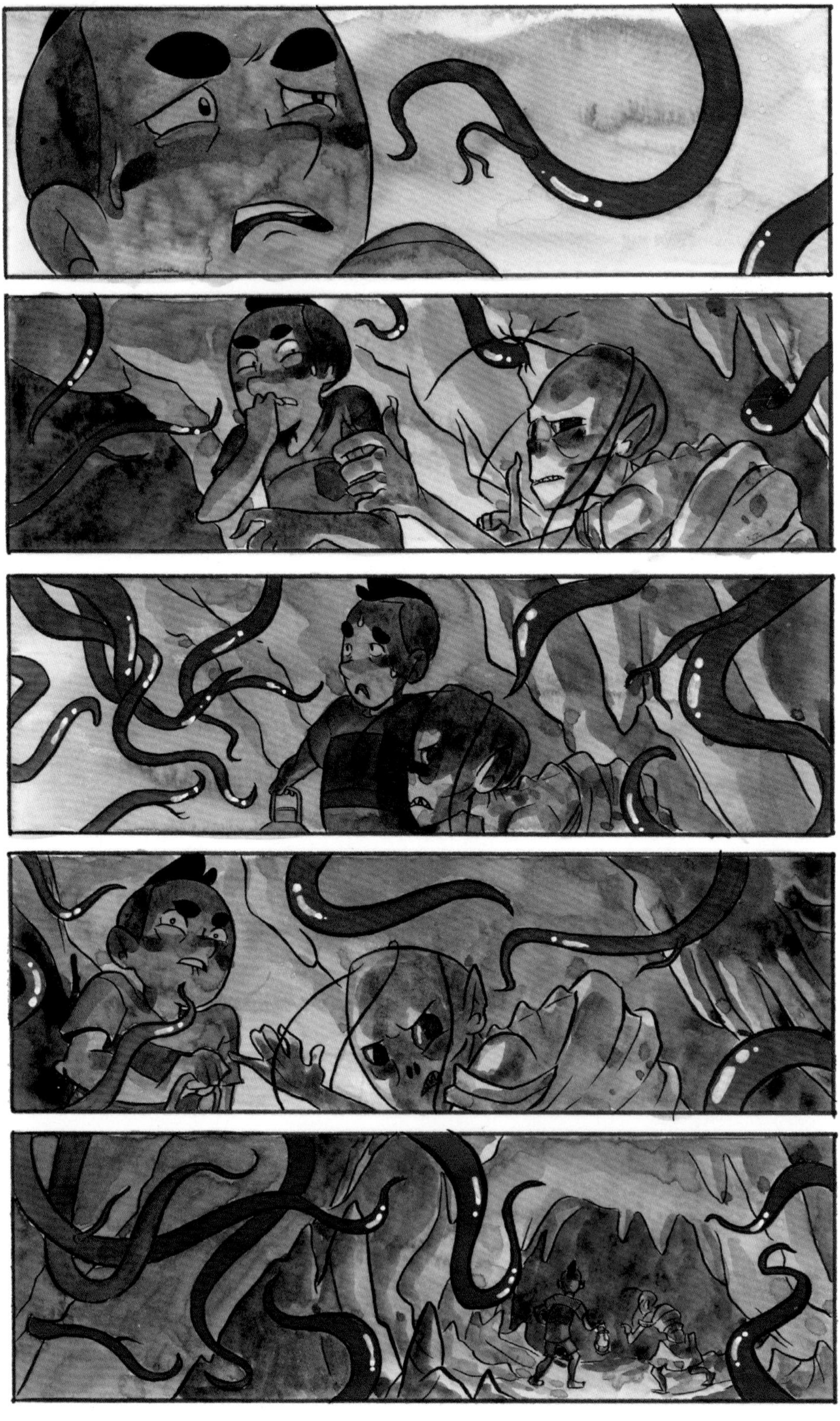

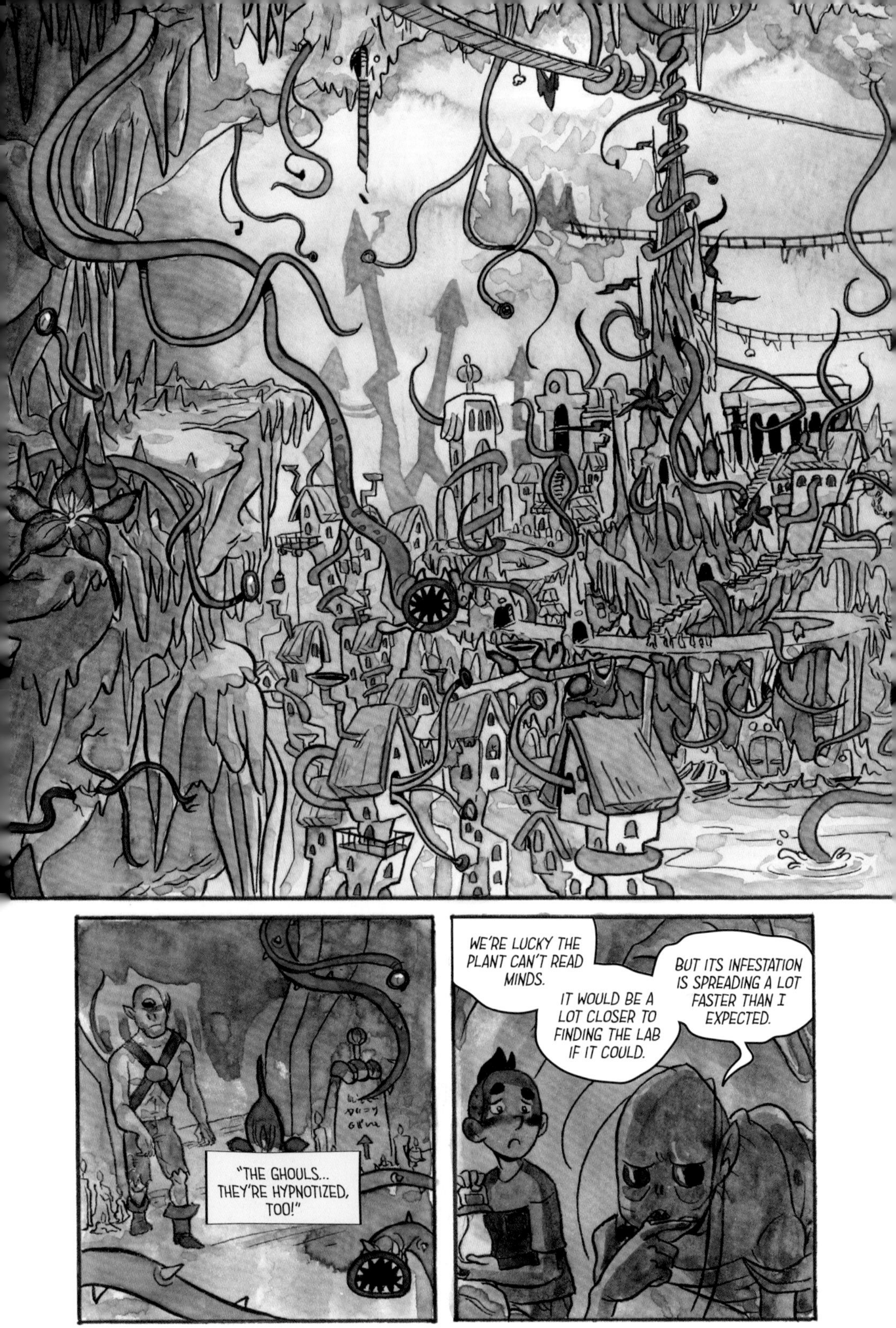
"THE GHOULS... THEY'RE HYPNOTIZED, TOO!"
WE'RE LUCKY THE PLANT CAN'T READ MINDS.
IT WOULD BE A LOT CLOSER TO FINDING THE LAB IF IT COULD.
BUT ITS INFESTATION IS SPREADING A LOT FASTER THAN I EXPECTED.

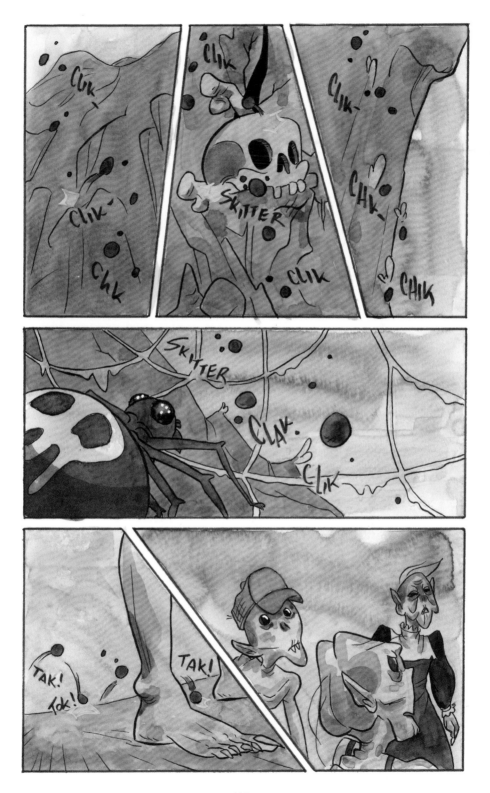

116

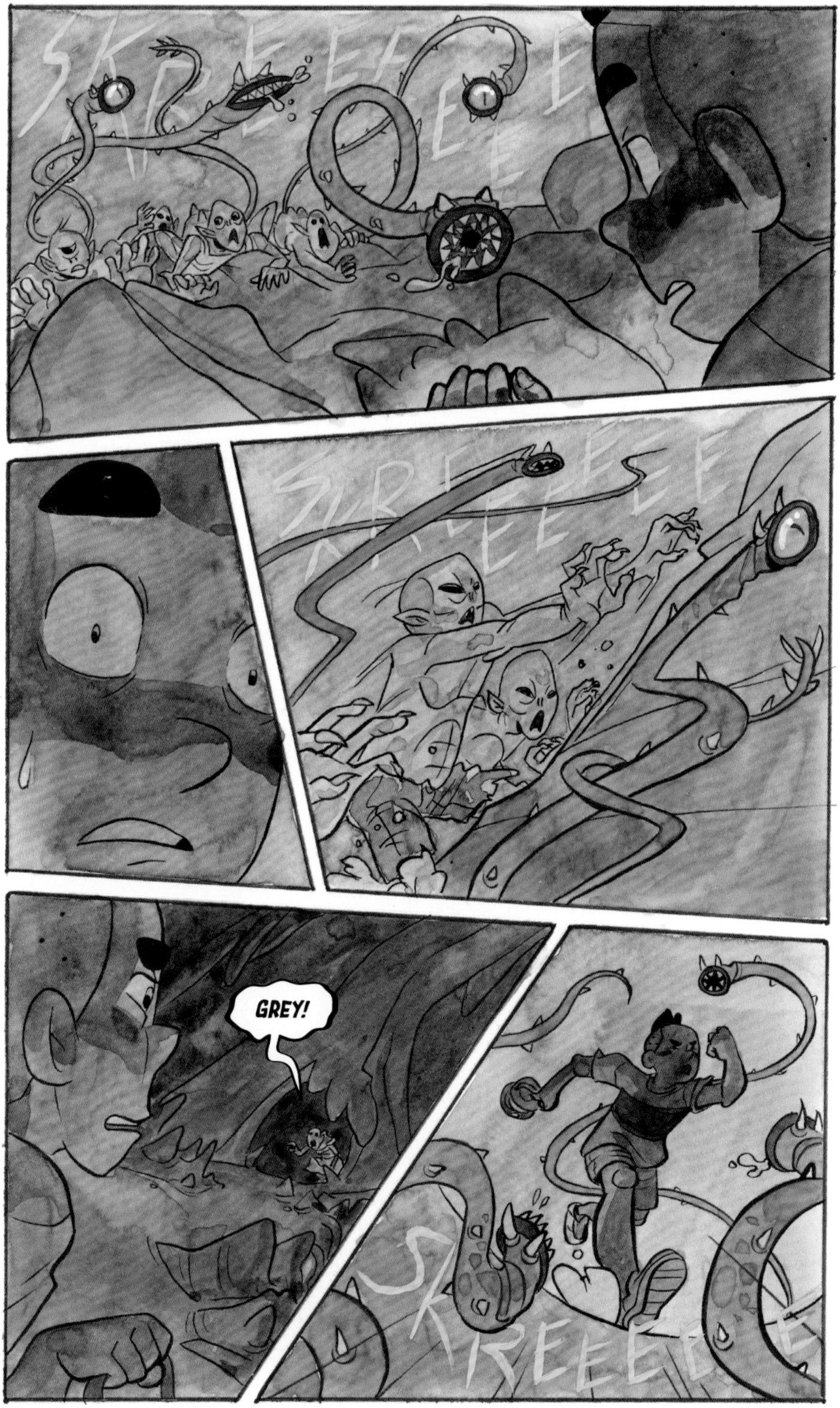
GREY!

118

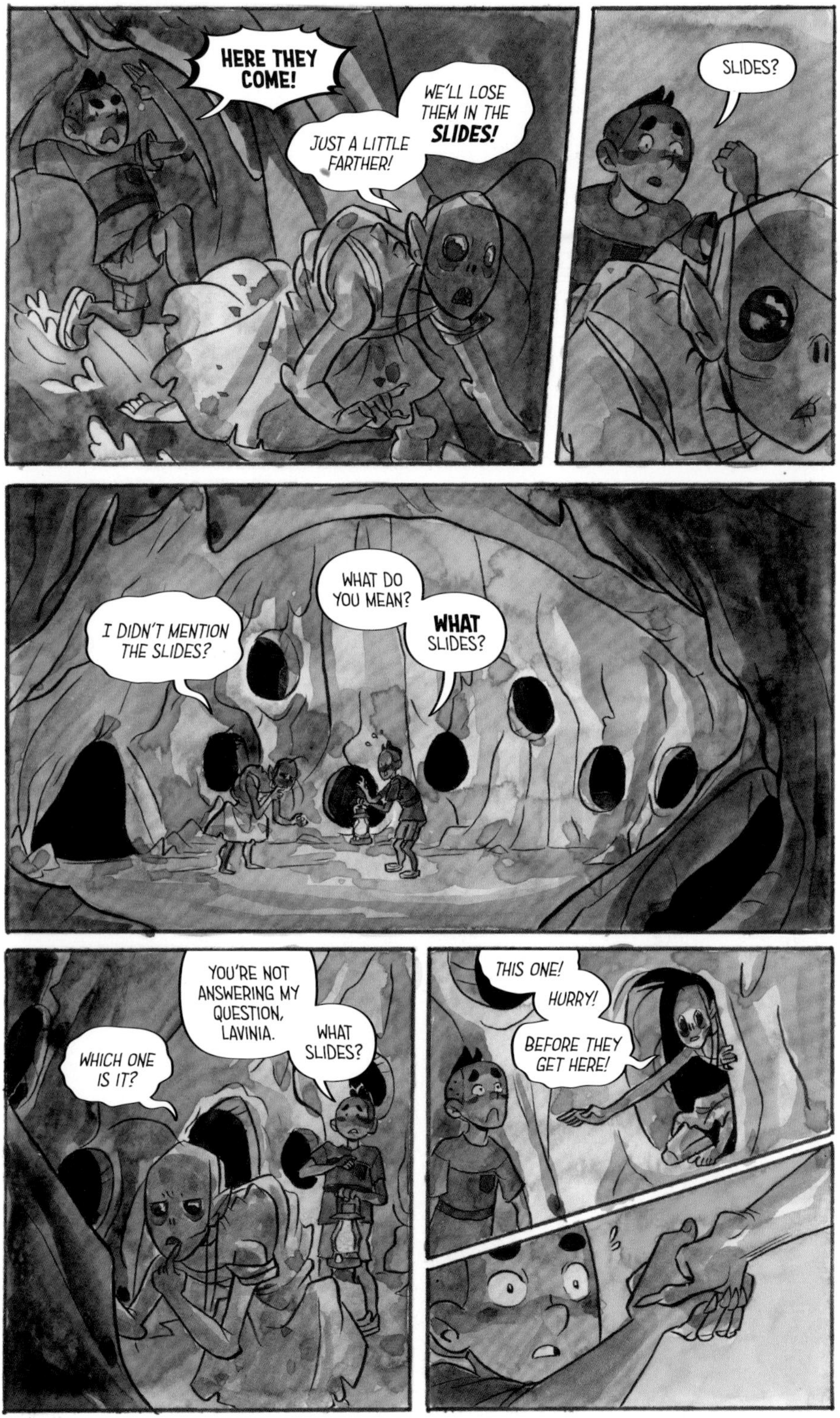
HERE THEY COME!
JUST A LITTLE FARTHER!
WE'LL LOSE THEM IN THE SLIDES!
SLIDES?
I DIDN'T MENTION THE SLIDES?
WHAT DO YOU MEAN?
WHAT SLIDES?
WHICH ONE IS IT?
YOU'RE NOT ANSWERING MY QUESTION, LAVINIA.
WHAT SLIDES?
THIS ONE!
HURRY!
BEFORE THEY GET HERE!

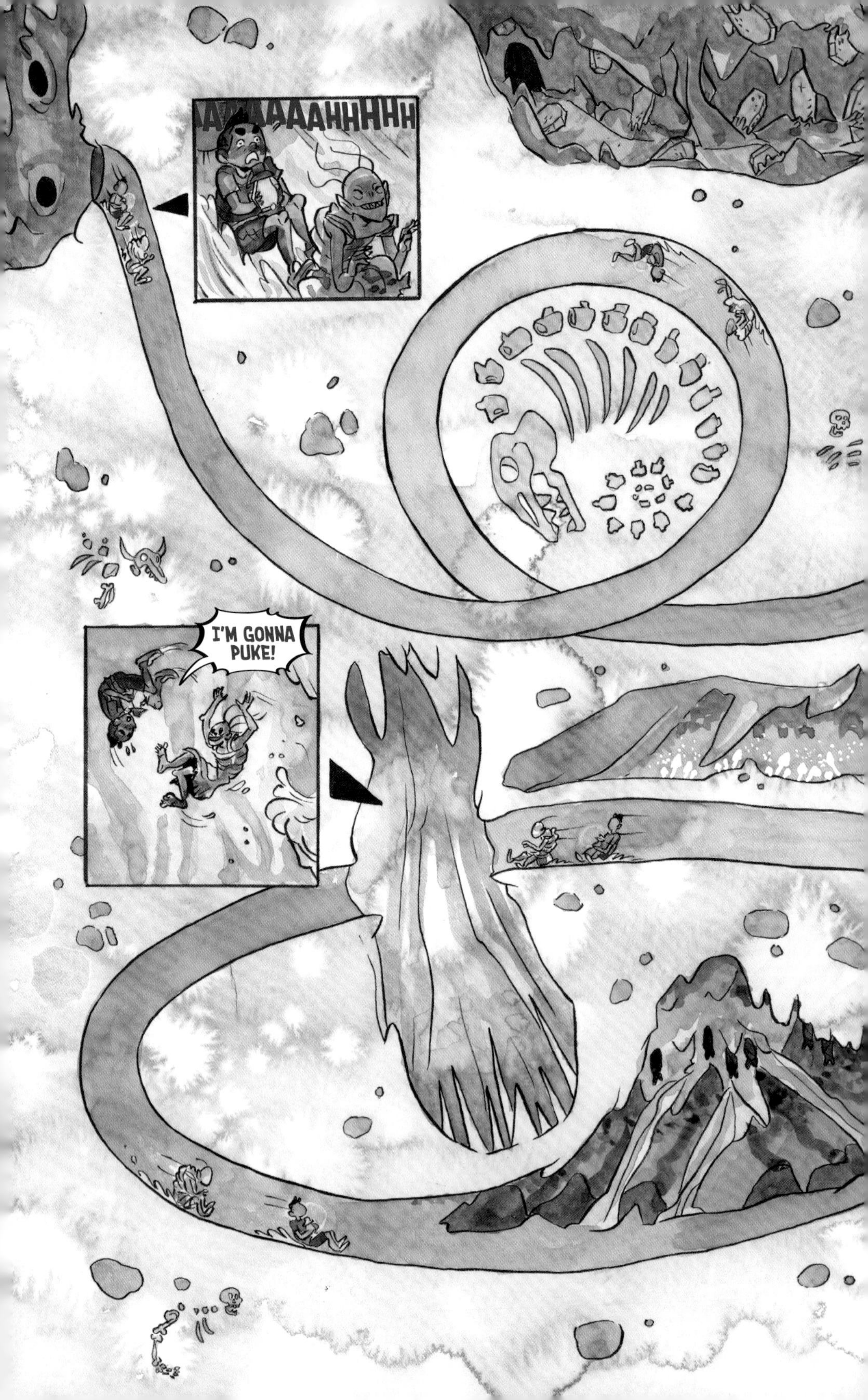
AAAAAAAHHHHH
I'M GONNA PUKE!

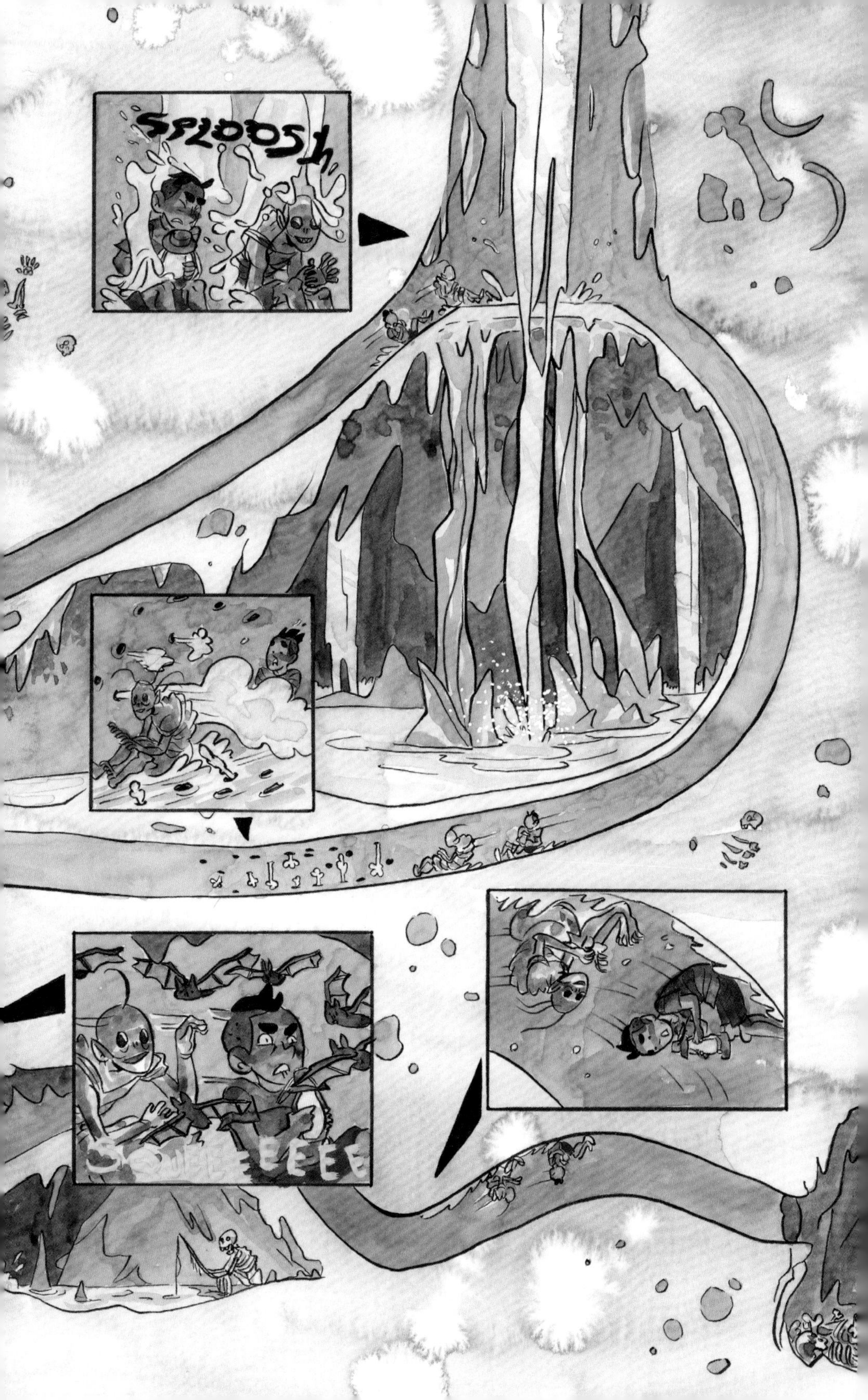
SPLOOSH
SQUEEEEEEE

123

128

129

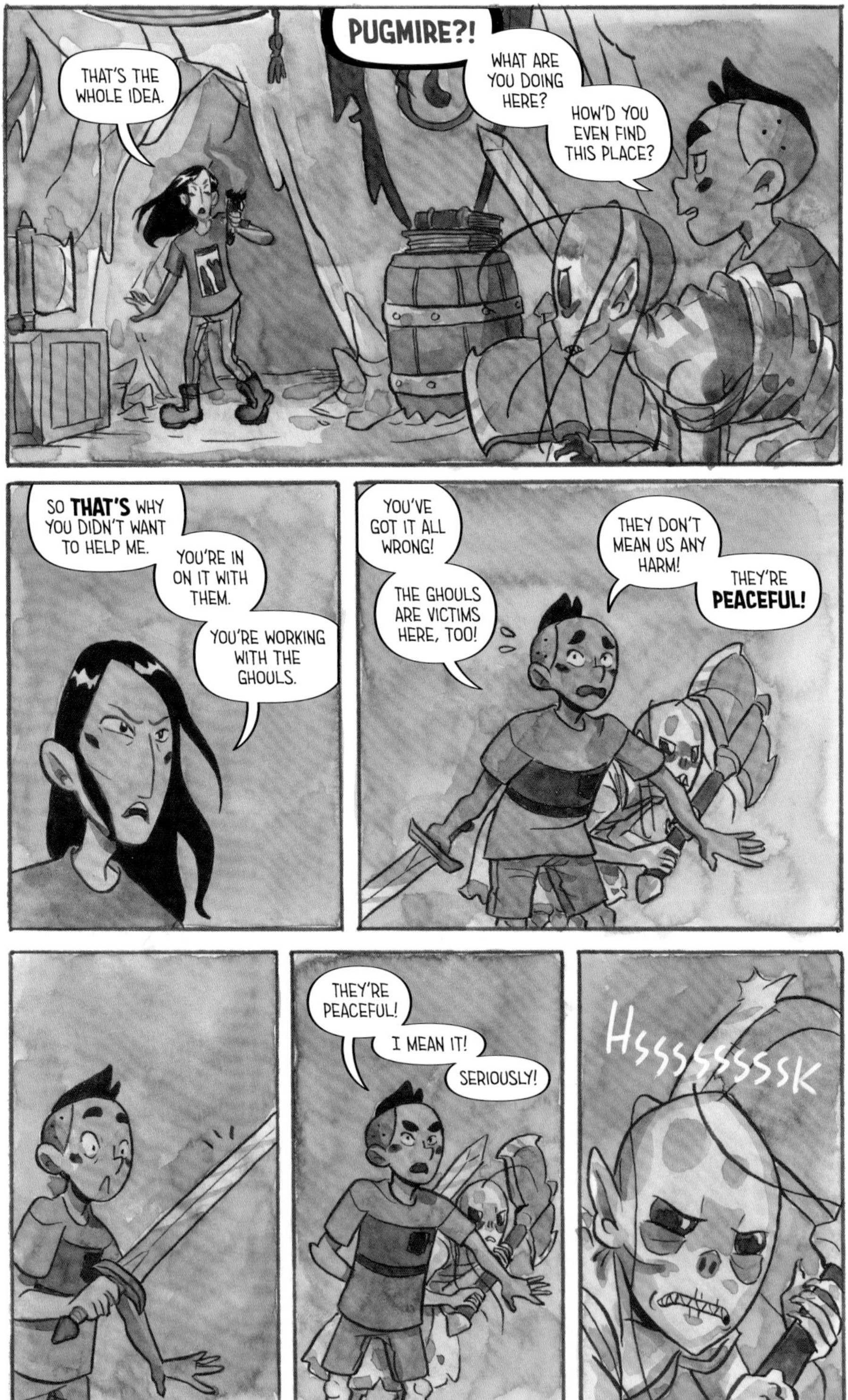

THAT'S THE WHOLE IDEA.
PUGMIRE?!
WHAT ARE YOU DOING HERE?
HOW'D YOU EVEN FIND THIS PLACE?
SO **THAT'S** WHY YOU DIDN'T WANT TO HELP ME.
YOU'RE IN ON IT WITH THEM.
YOU'RE WORKING WITH THE GHOULS.
YOU'VE GOT IT ALL WRONG!
THE GHOULS ARE VICTIMS HERE, TOO!
THEY DON'T MEAN US ANY HARM!
THEY'RE **PEACEFUL!**
THEY'RE PEACEFUL!
I MEAN IT!
SERIOUSLY!
Hssssssssk

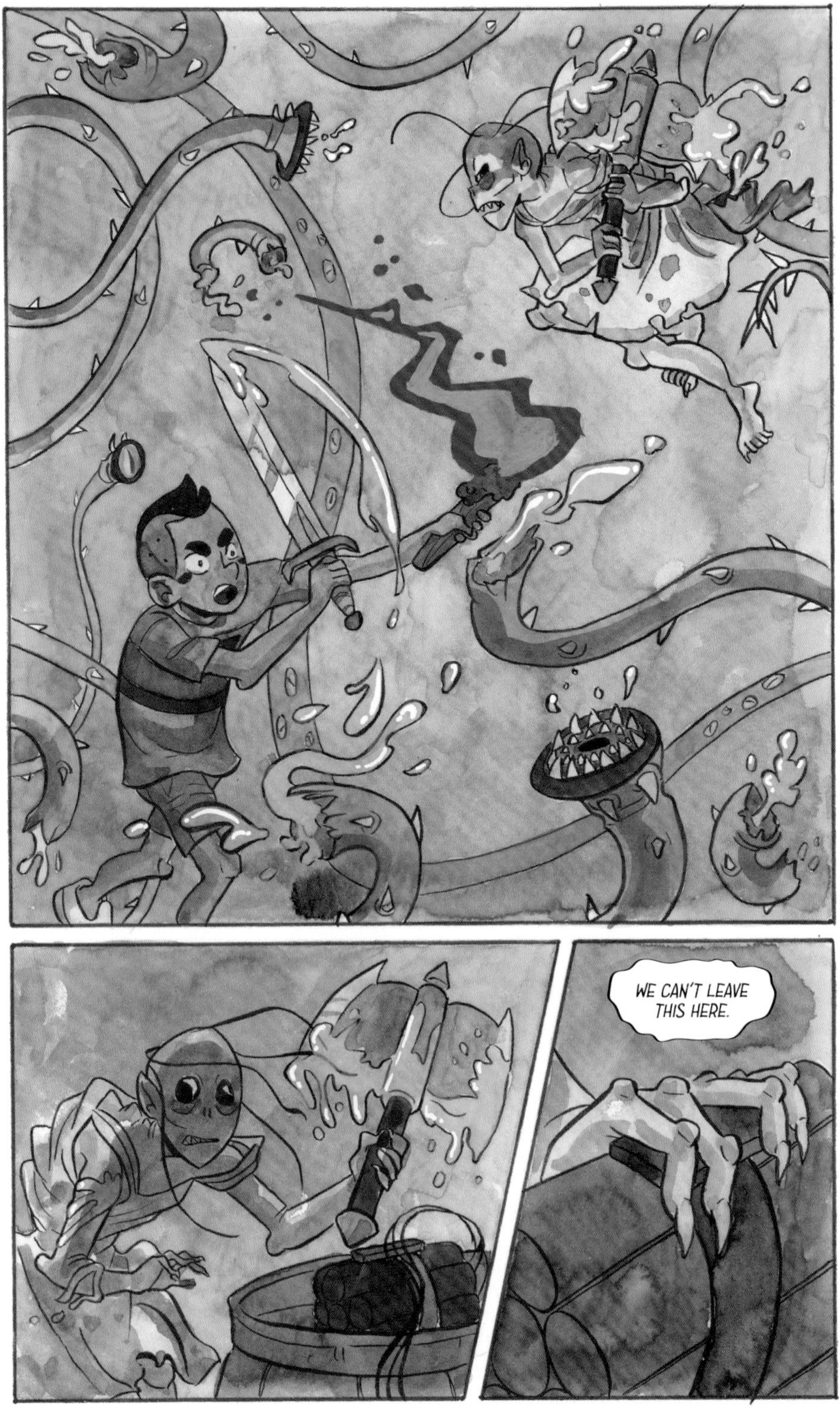
WE CAN'T LEAVE
THIS HERE.

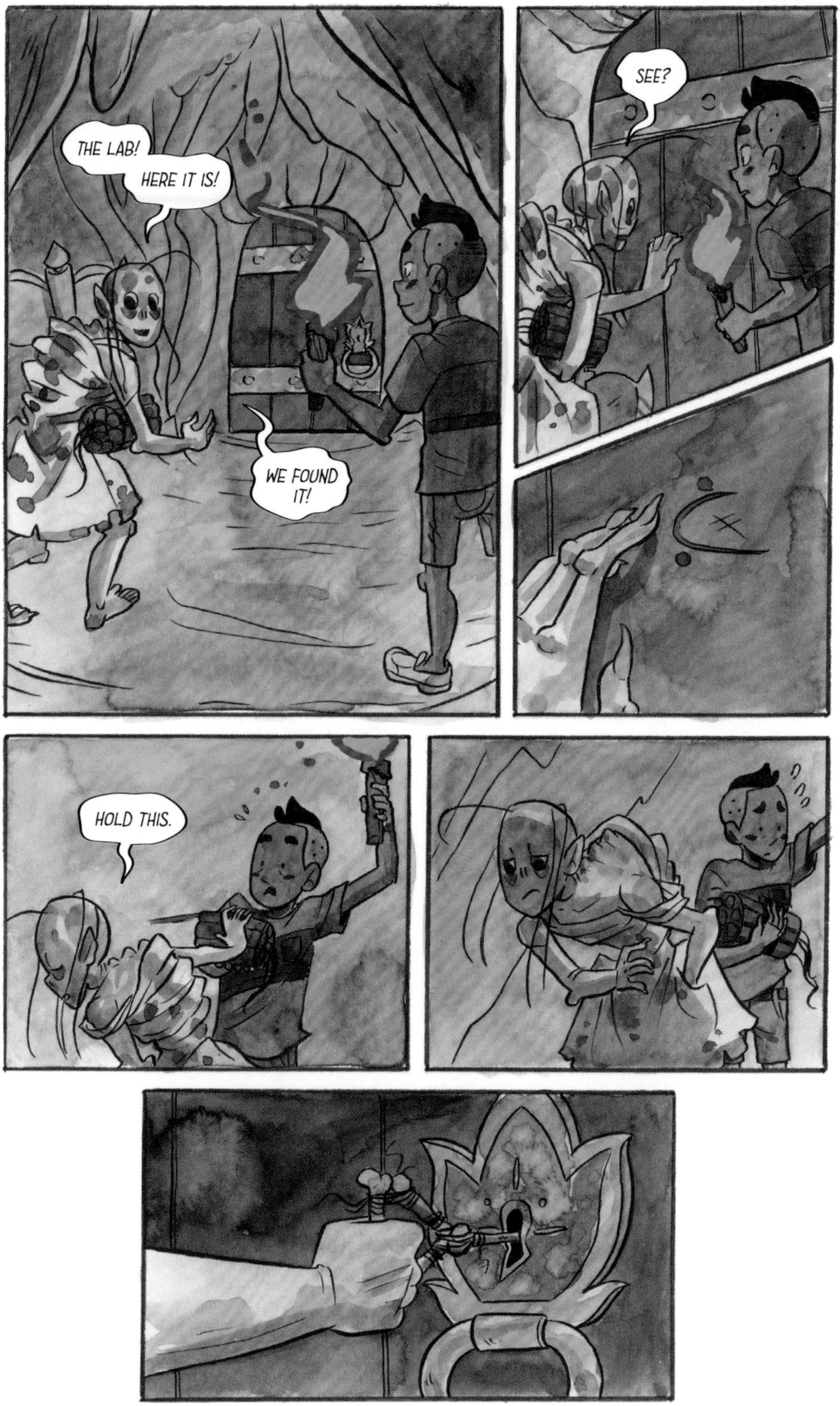
THE LAB!
HERE IT IS!
WE FOUND IT!
SEE?
HOLD THIS.

140

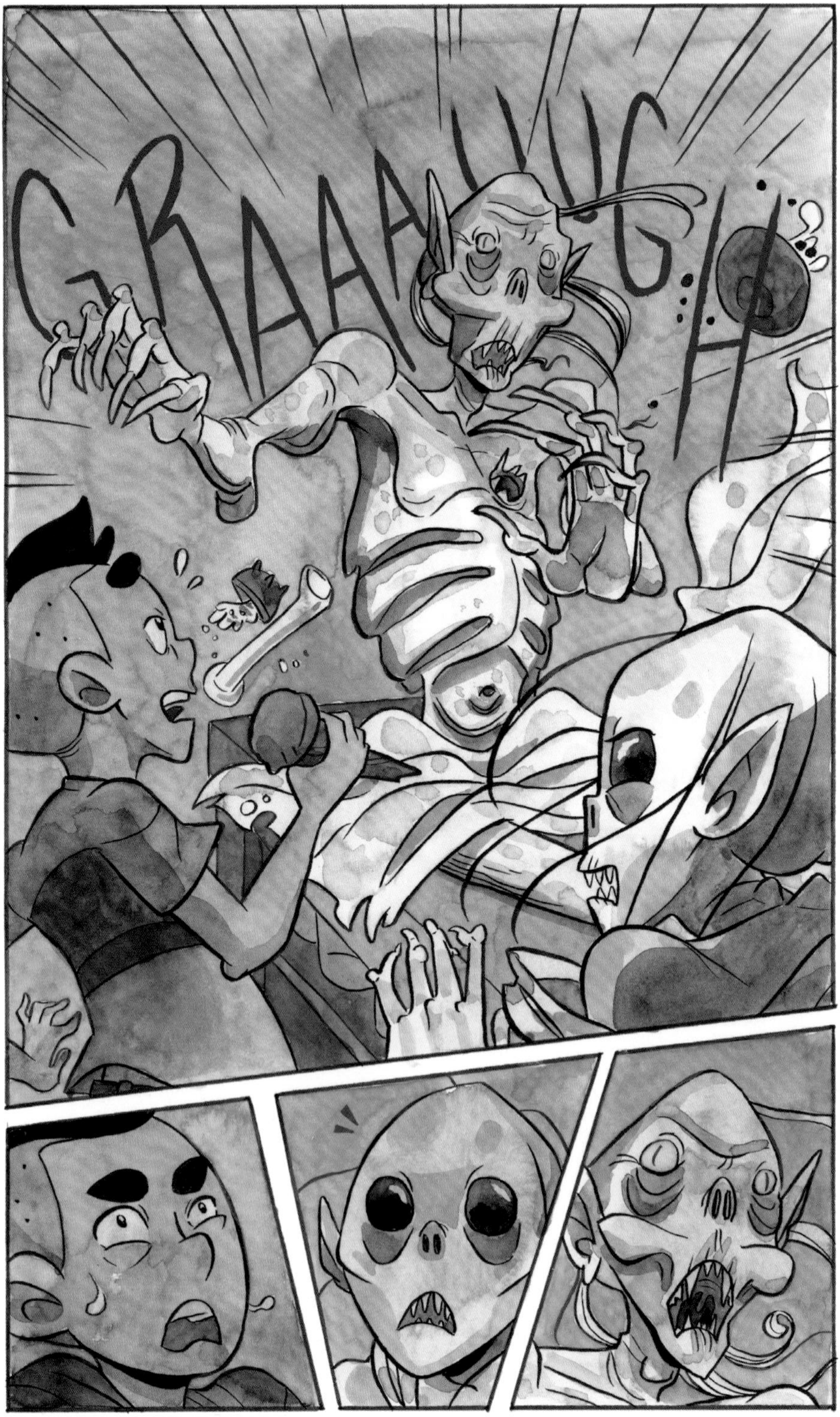
GRAAAUUGH

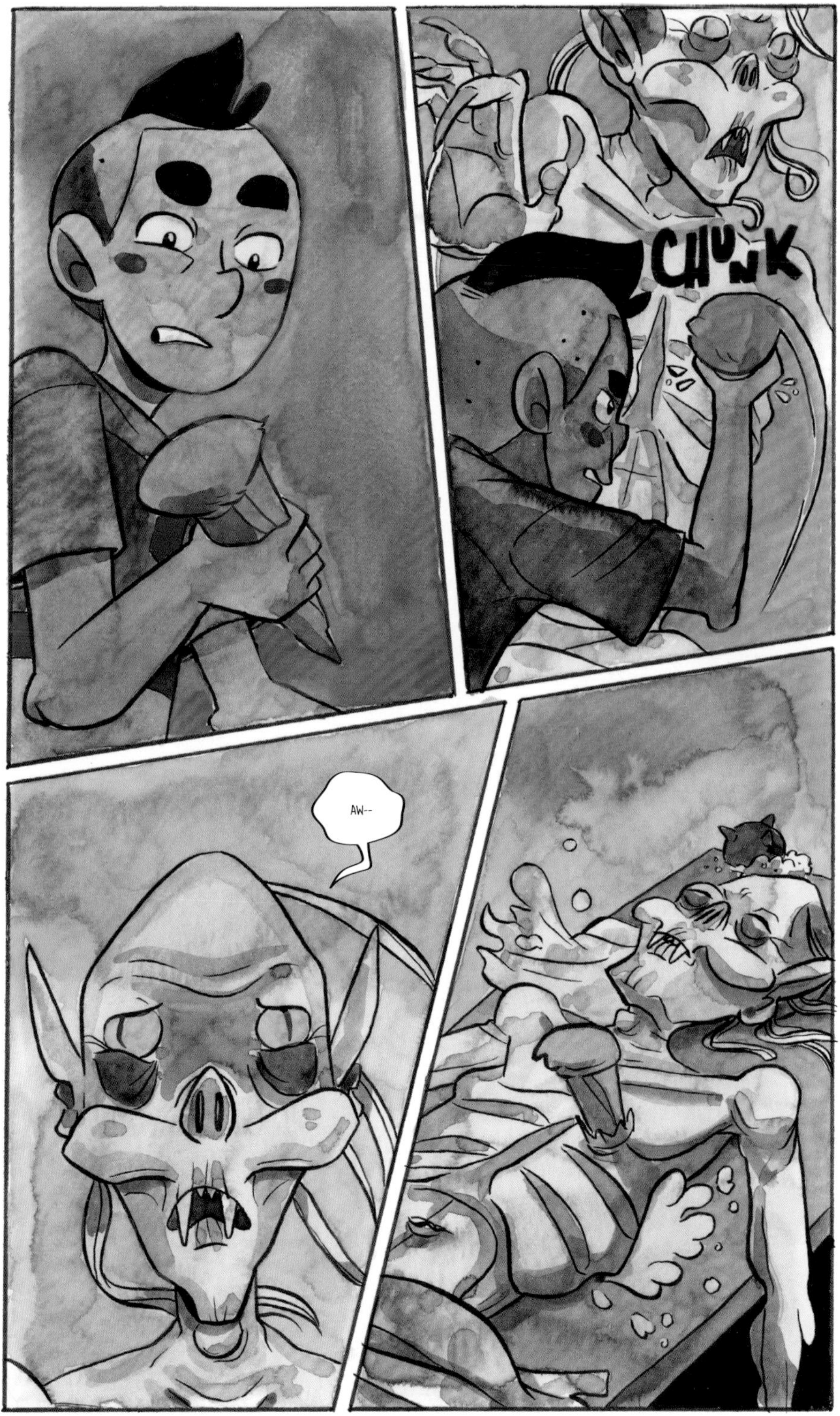
CHUNK
AW--

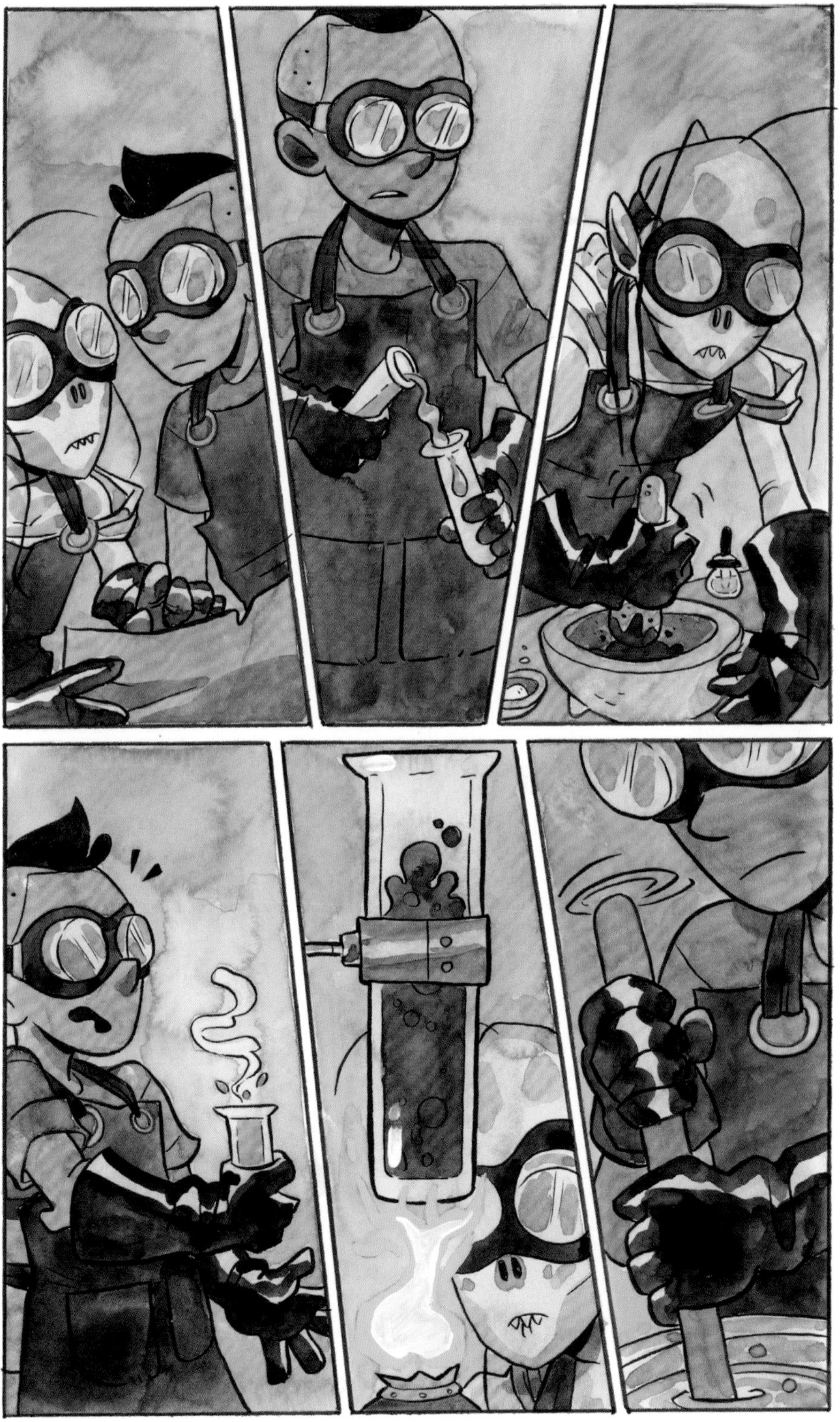

146

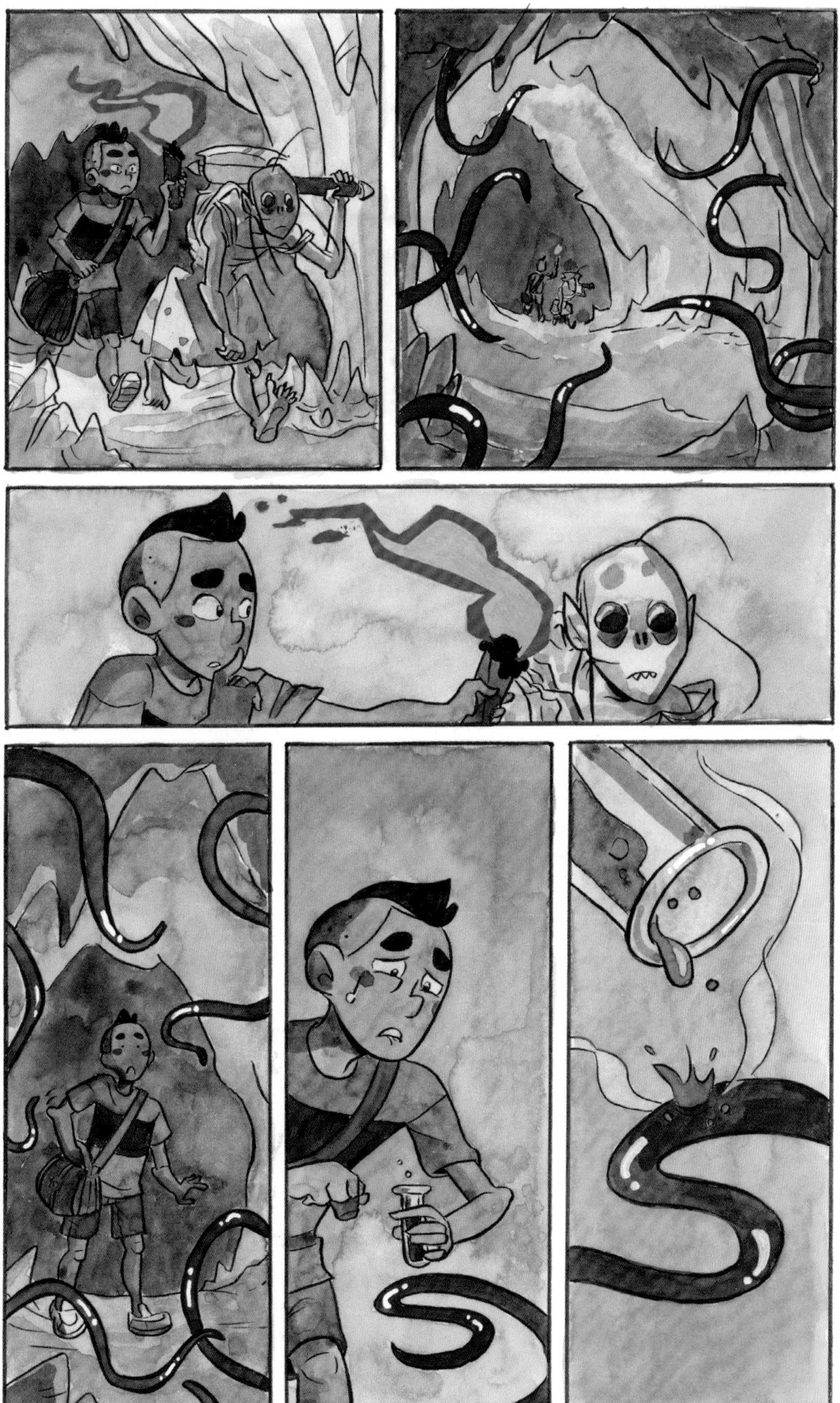

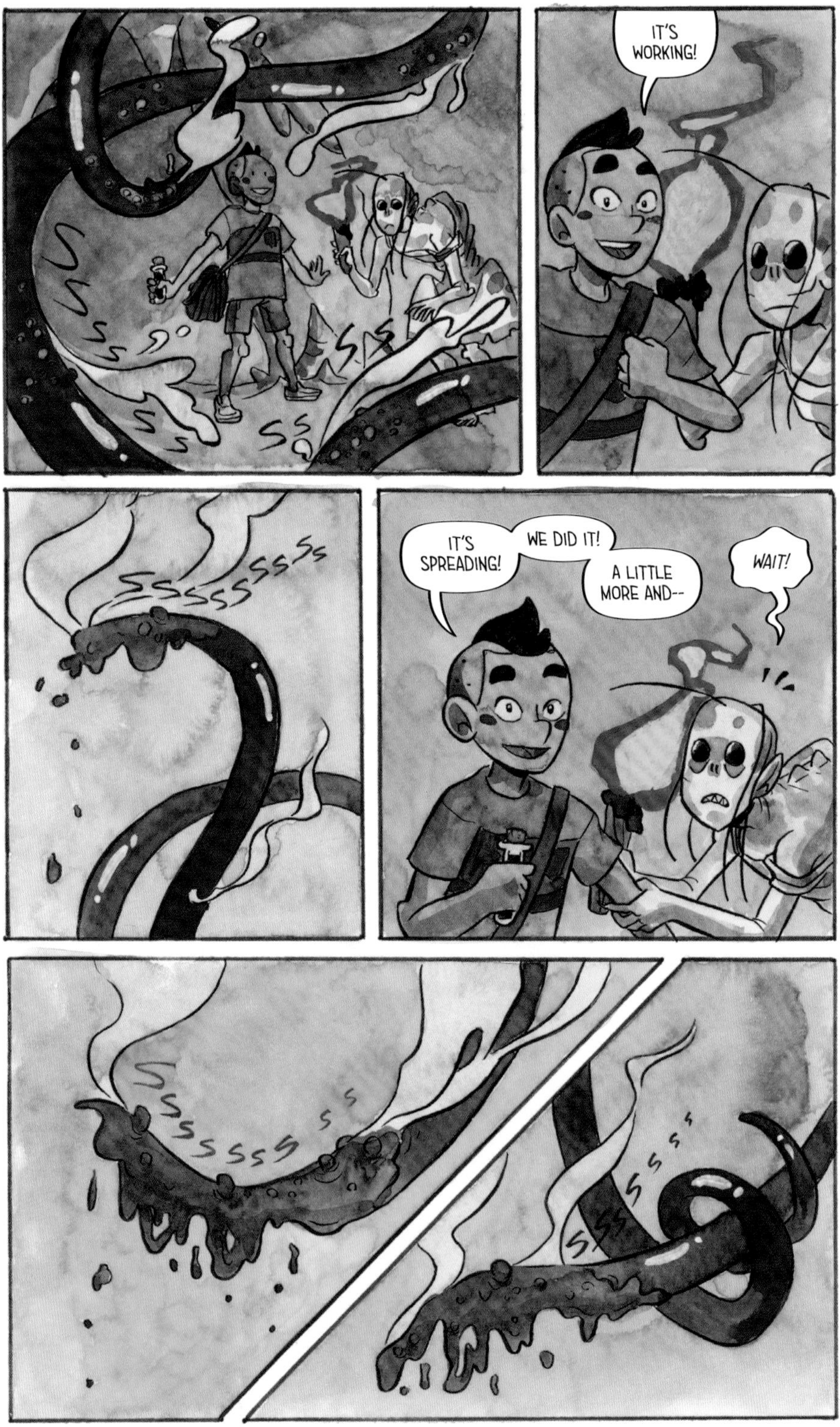
IT'S WORKING!
SSSSSSSSSS
IT'S SPREADING!
WE DID IT!
A LITTLE MORE AND--
WAIT!
SSSSSSSSS
SSSSSS

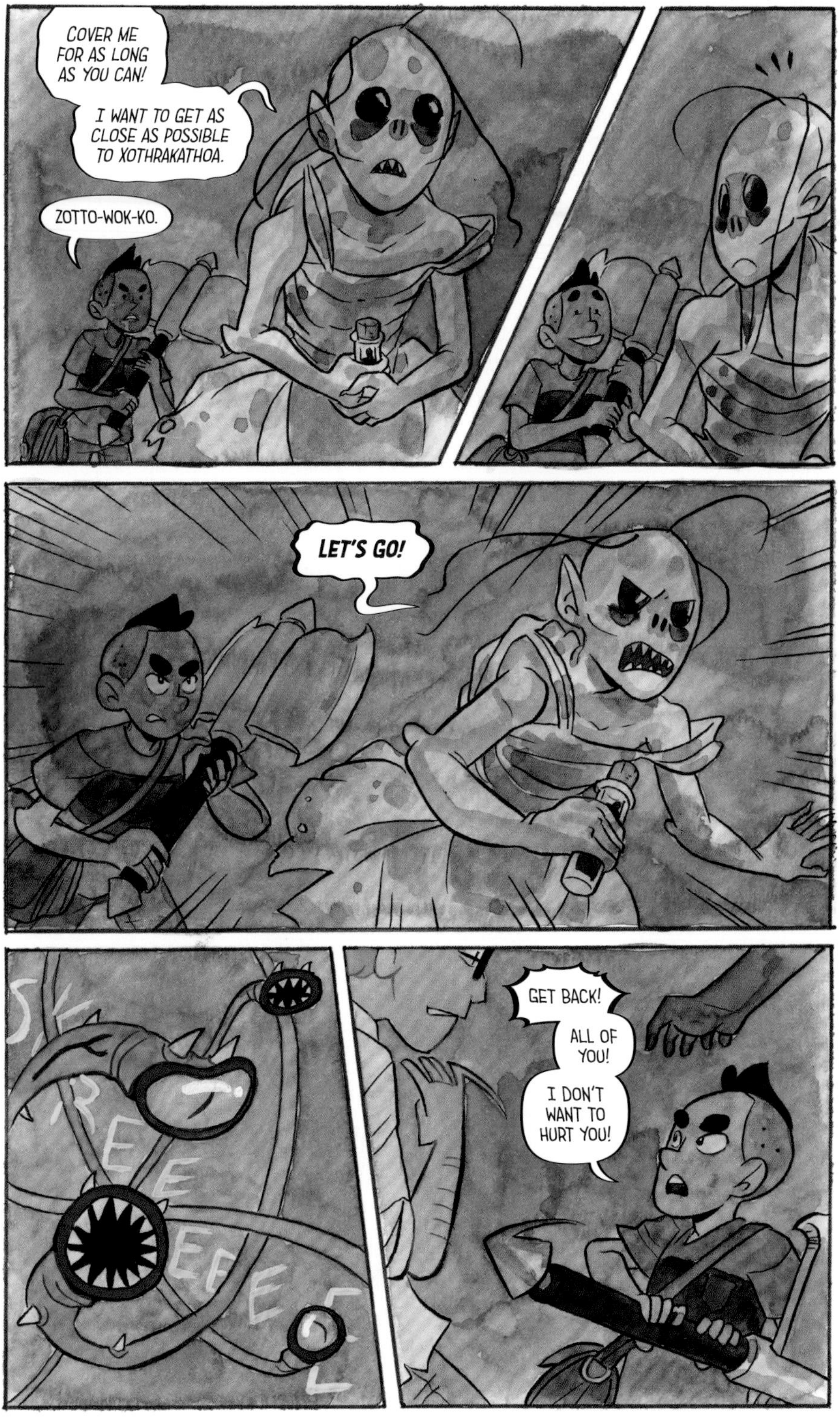
COVER ME FOR AS LONG AS YOU CAN!
I WANT TO GET AS CLOSE AS POSSIBLE TO XOTHRAKATHOA.
ZOTTO-WOK-KO.
LET'S GO!
GET BACK!
ALL OF YOU!
I DON'T WANT TO HURT YOU!

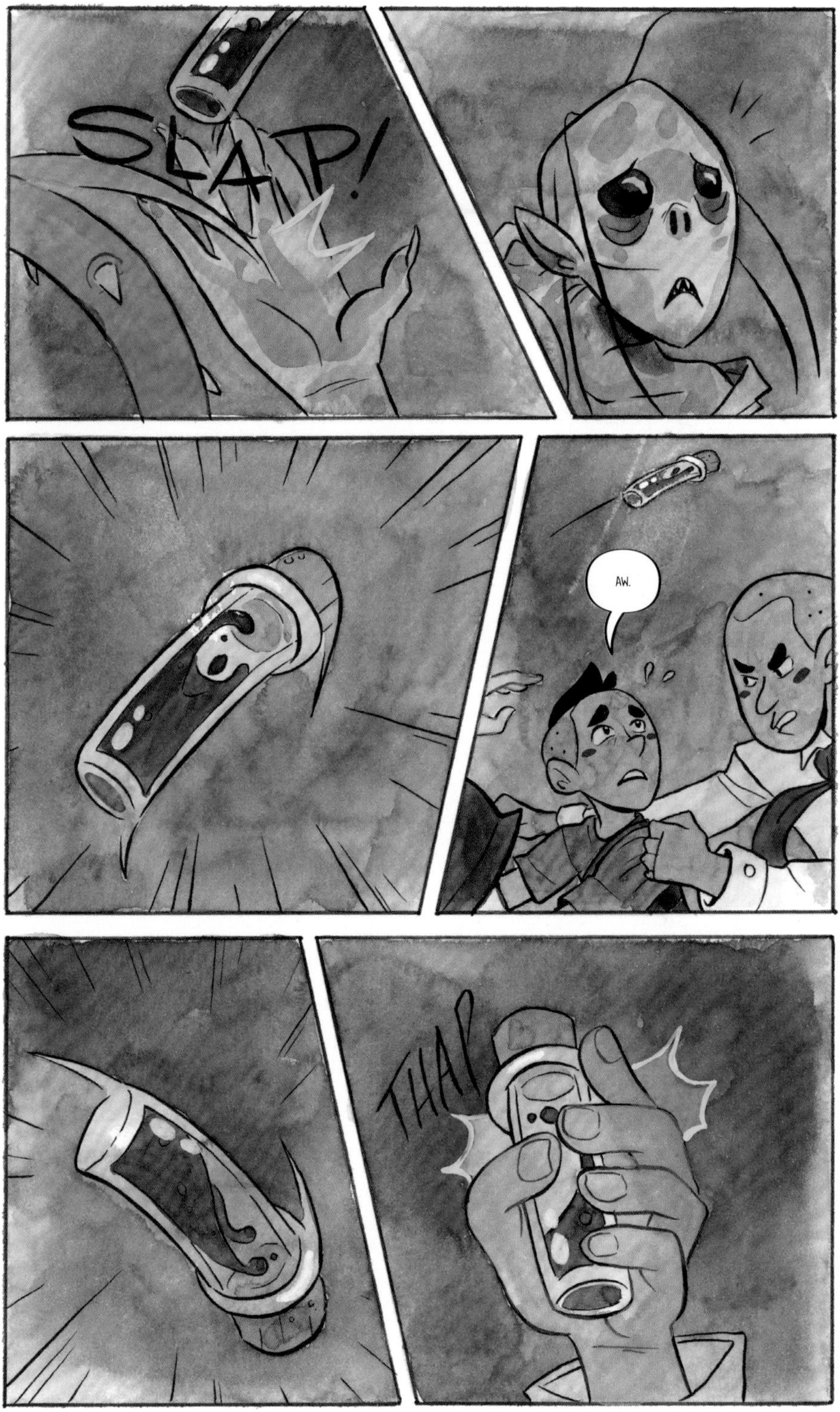
SLAP!
AW.
THAP

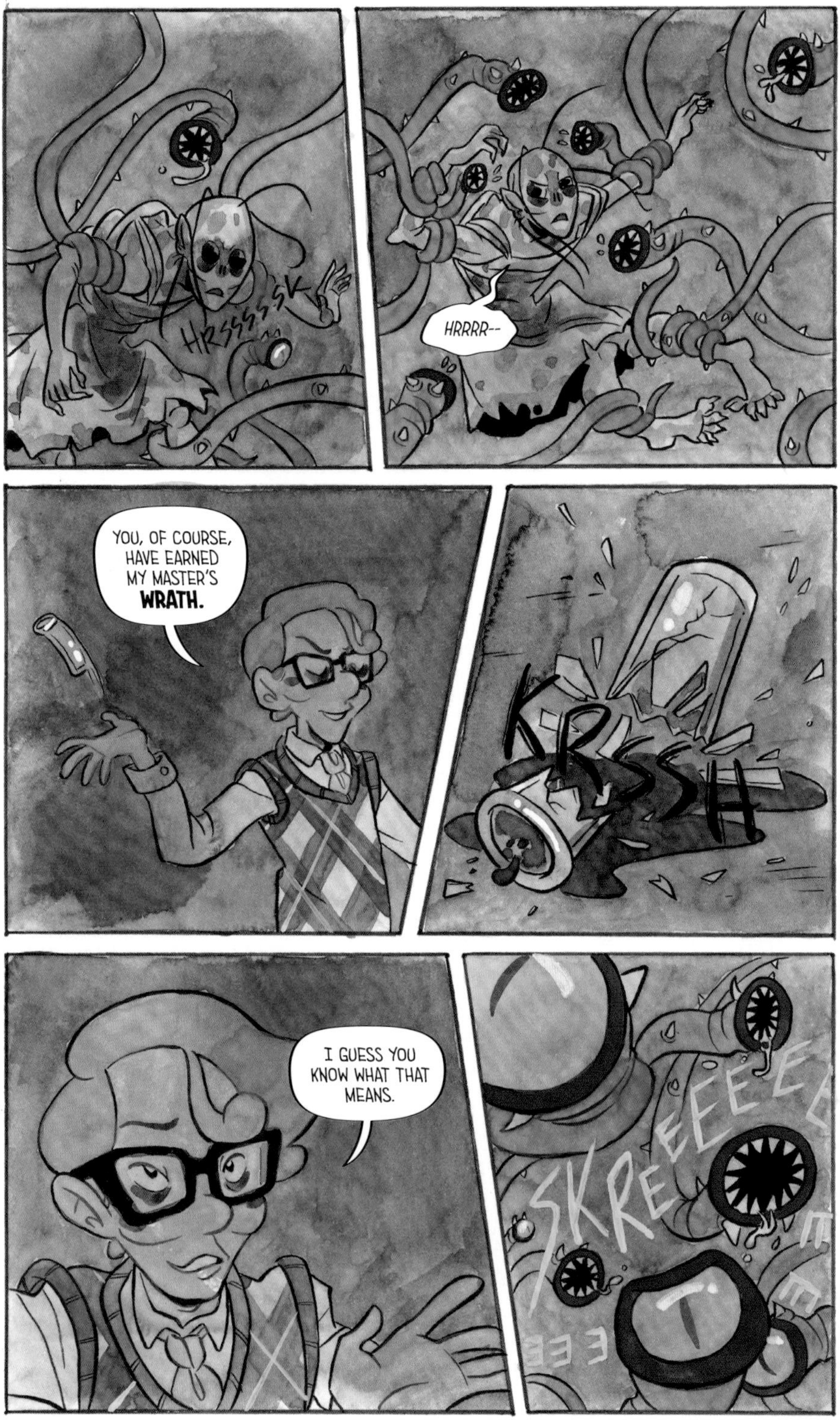
HRSSSSSSK
HRRRR--
YOU, OF COURSE, HAVE EARNED MY MASTER'S **WRATH.**
KRSSH
I GUESS YOU KNOW WHAT THAT MEANS.
SKREEEEEEEEEEE

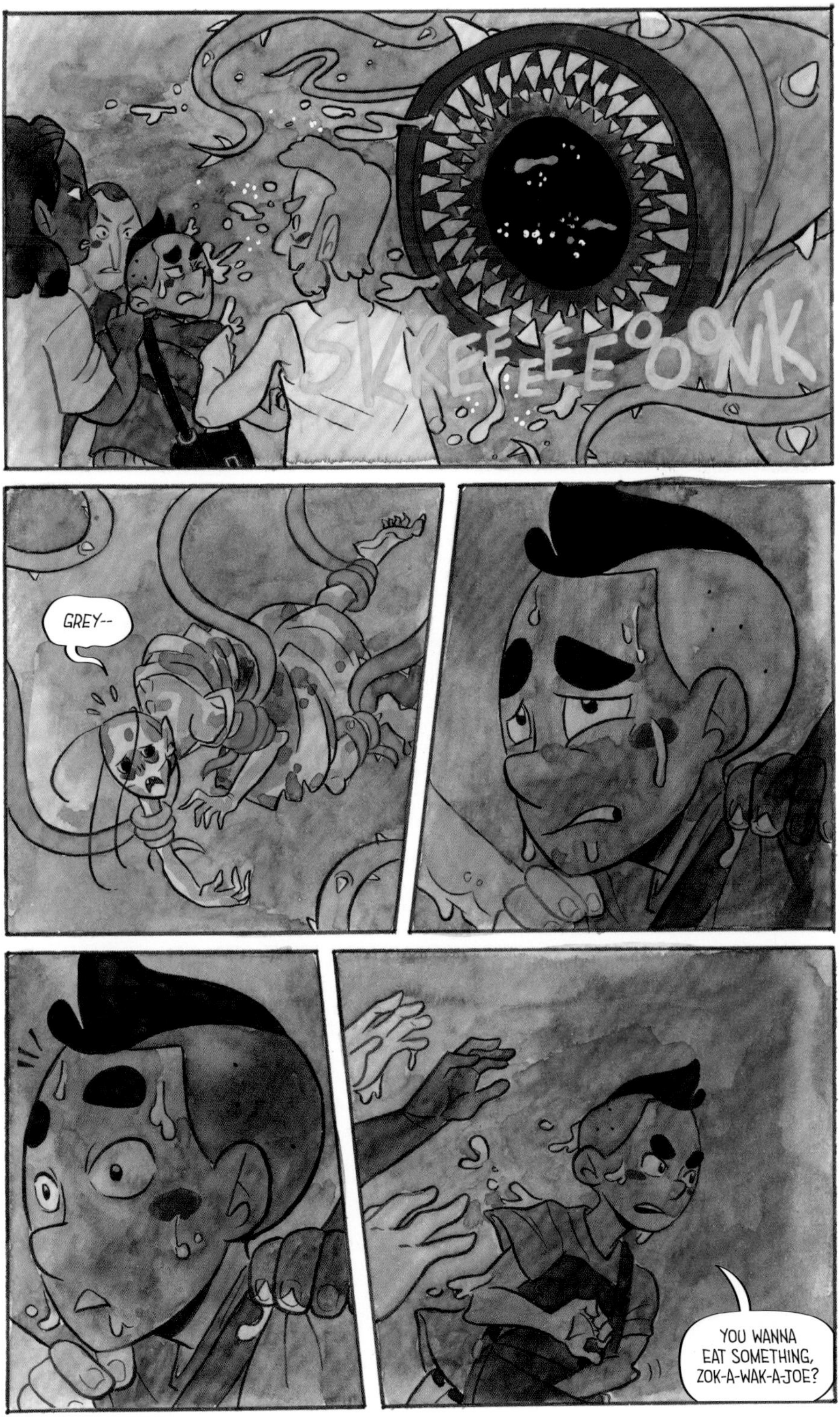
SKREEEEEOONK
GREY--
YOU WANNA EAT SOMETHING, ZOK-A-WAK-A-JOE?

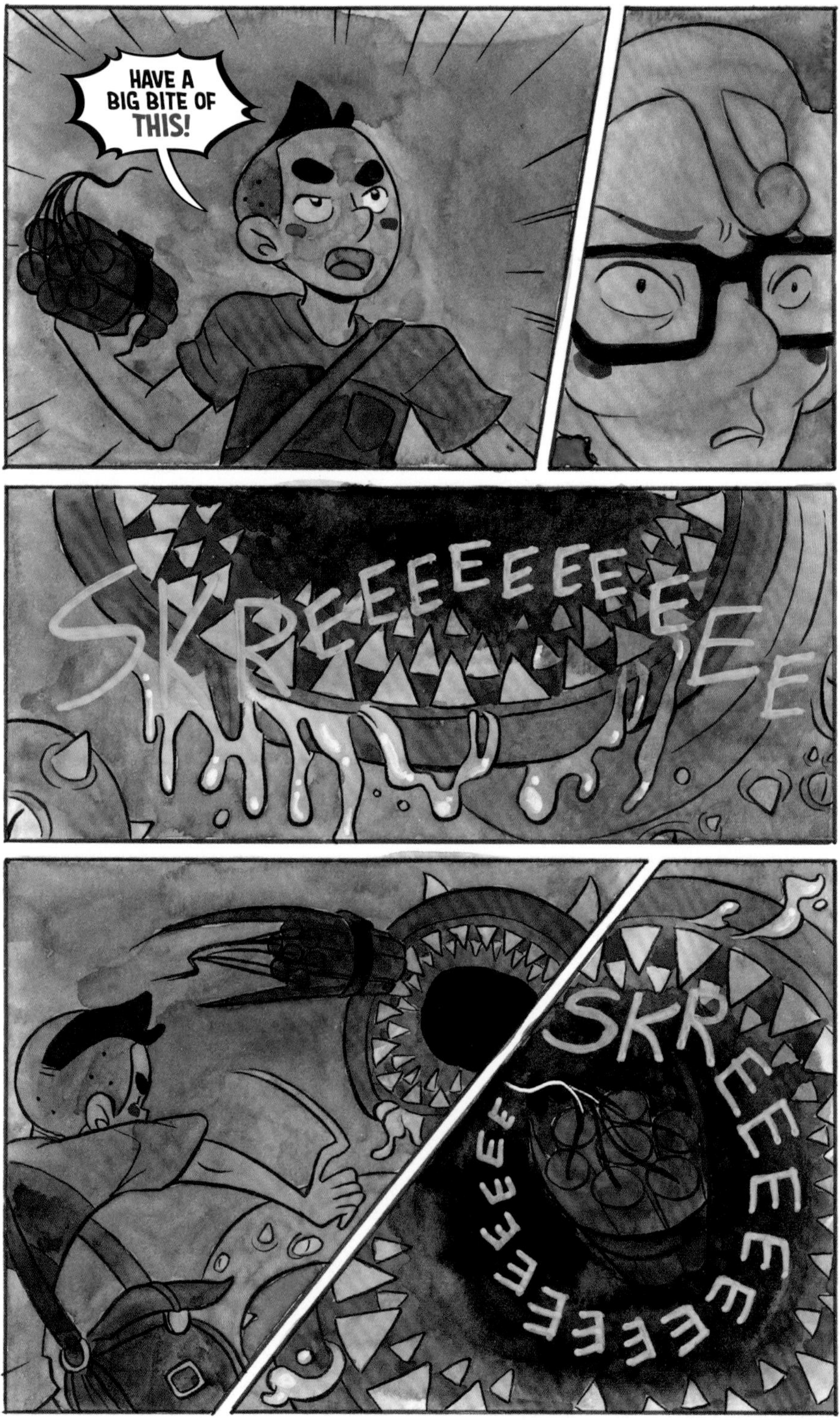
HAVE A BIG BITE OF THIS!
SKREEEEEEEEEEE
SKREEEEEEEEEEEEEE

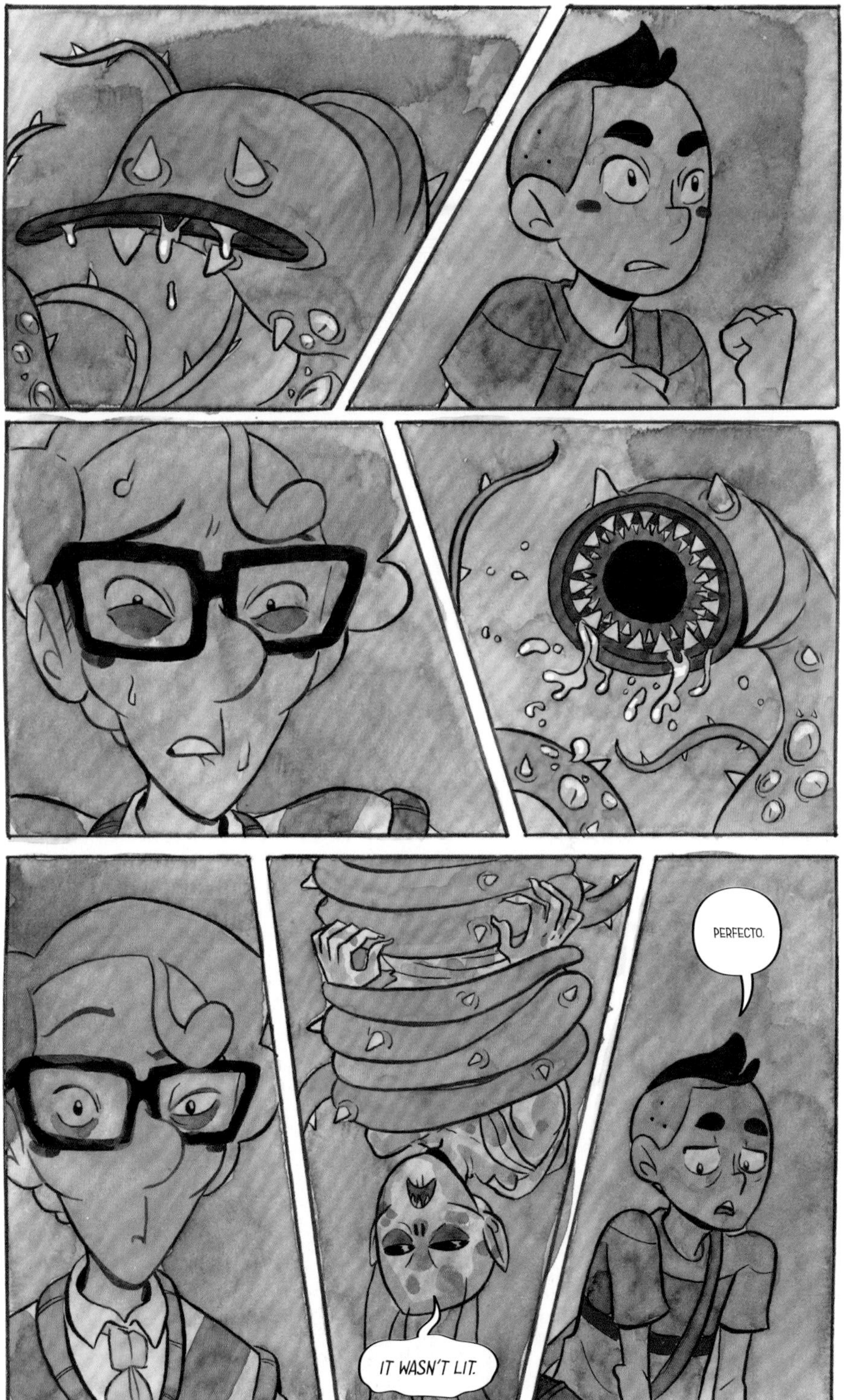
IT WASN'T LIT.
PERFECTO.

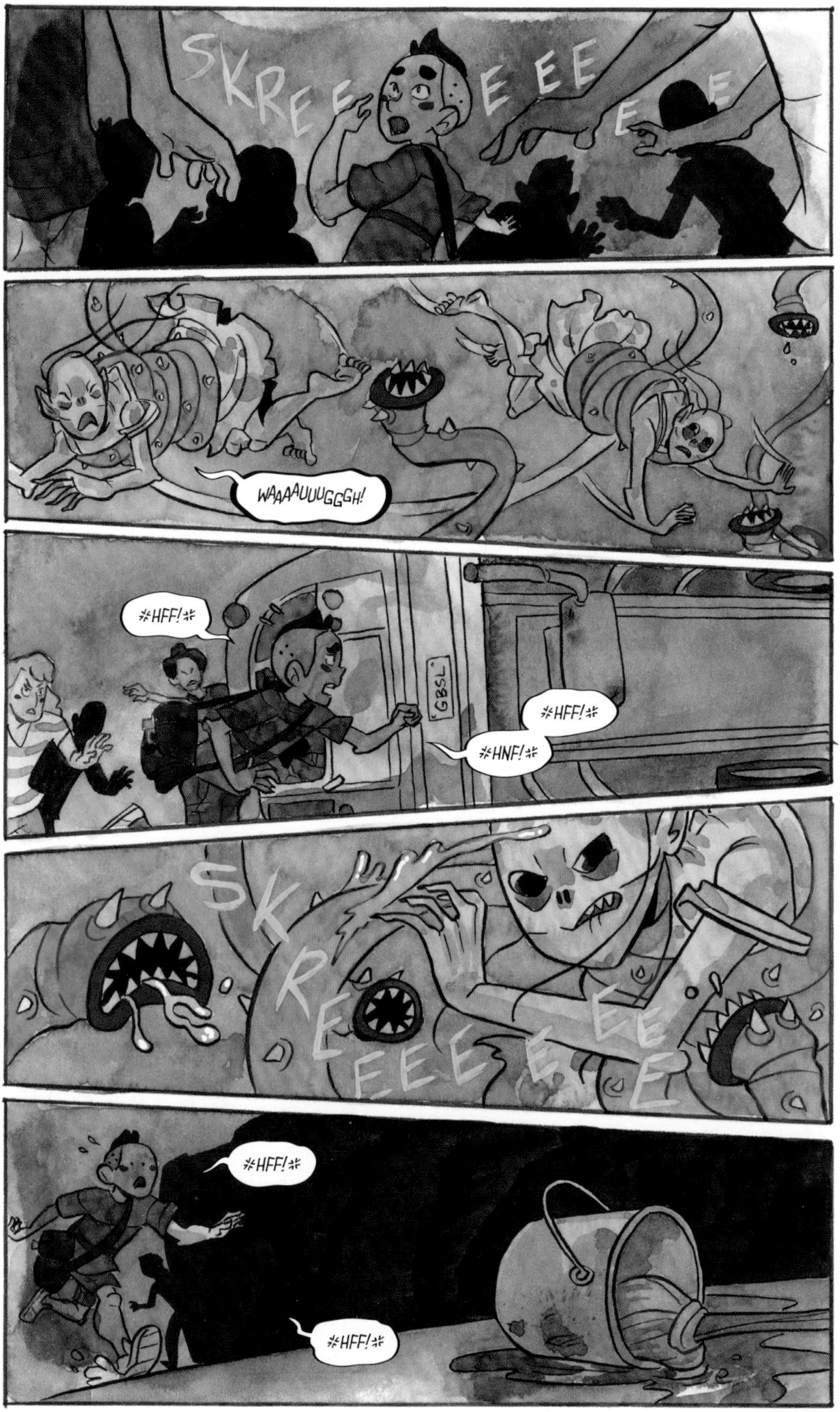

SKREEEEEEE
WAAAAUUUGGGH!
#HFF!#
#HFF!#
#HNF!#
SKREEEEEEEEE
#HFF!#
#HFF!#

165

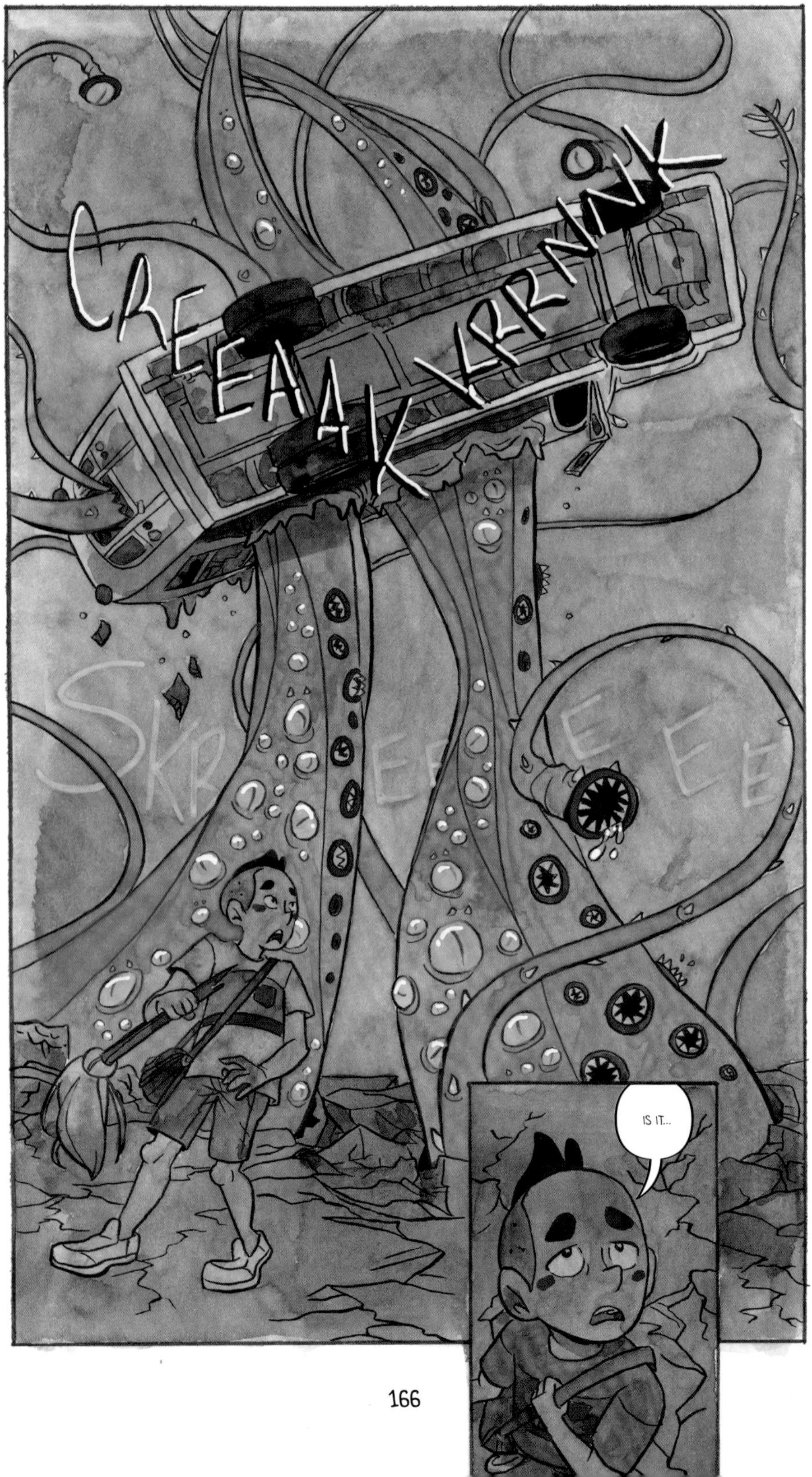
CREEAAAK
KRRNNK
SKREEEEE
IS IT...

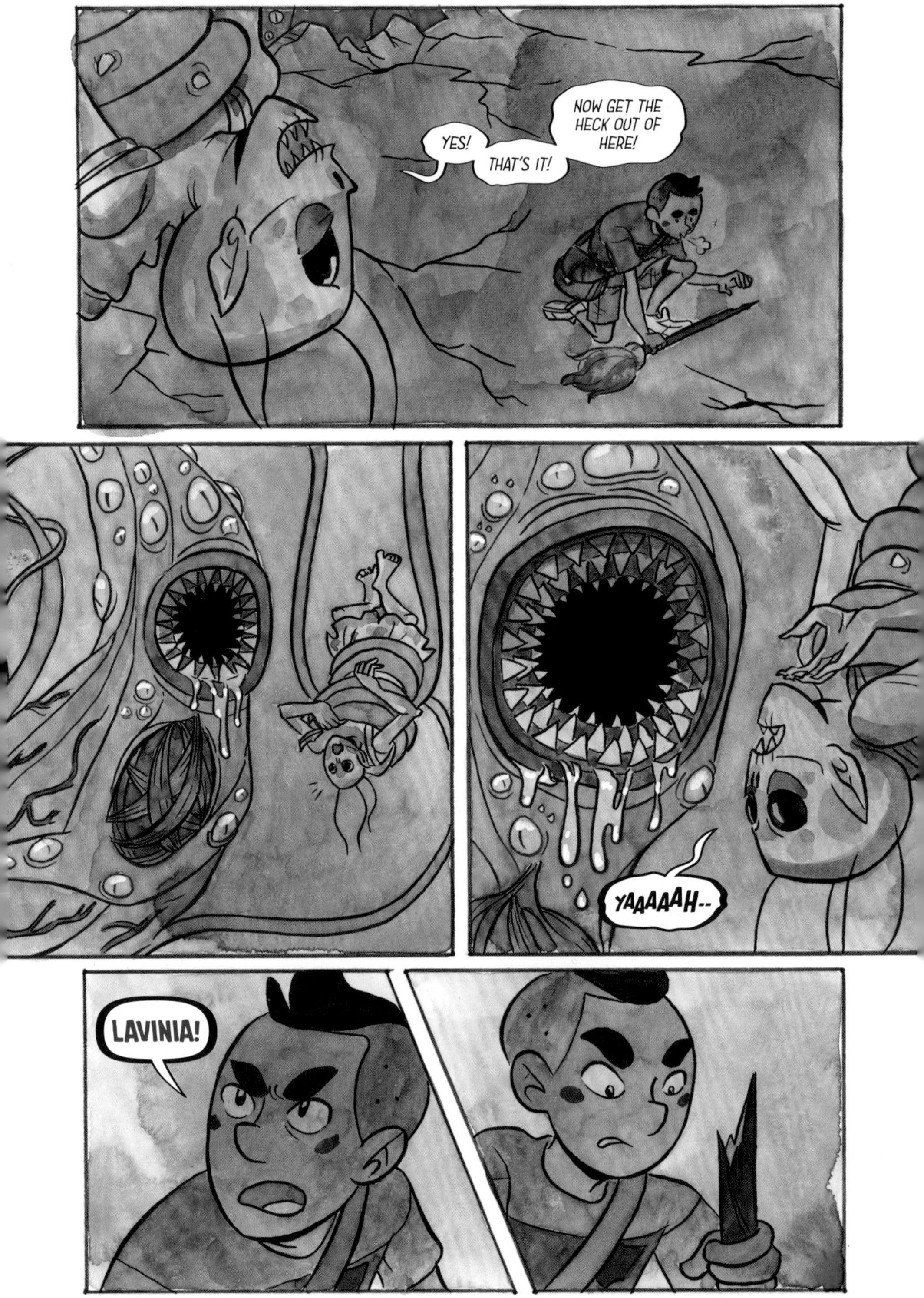
YES!
THAT'S IT!
NOW GET THE HECK OUT OF HERE!
YAAAAAH--
LAVINIA!

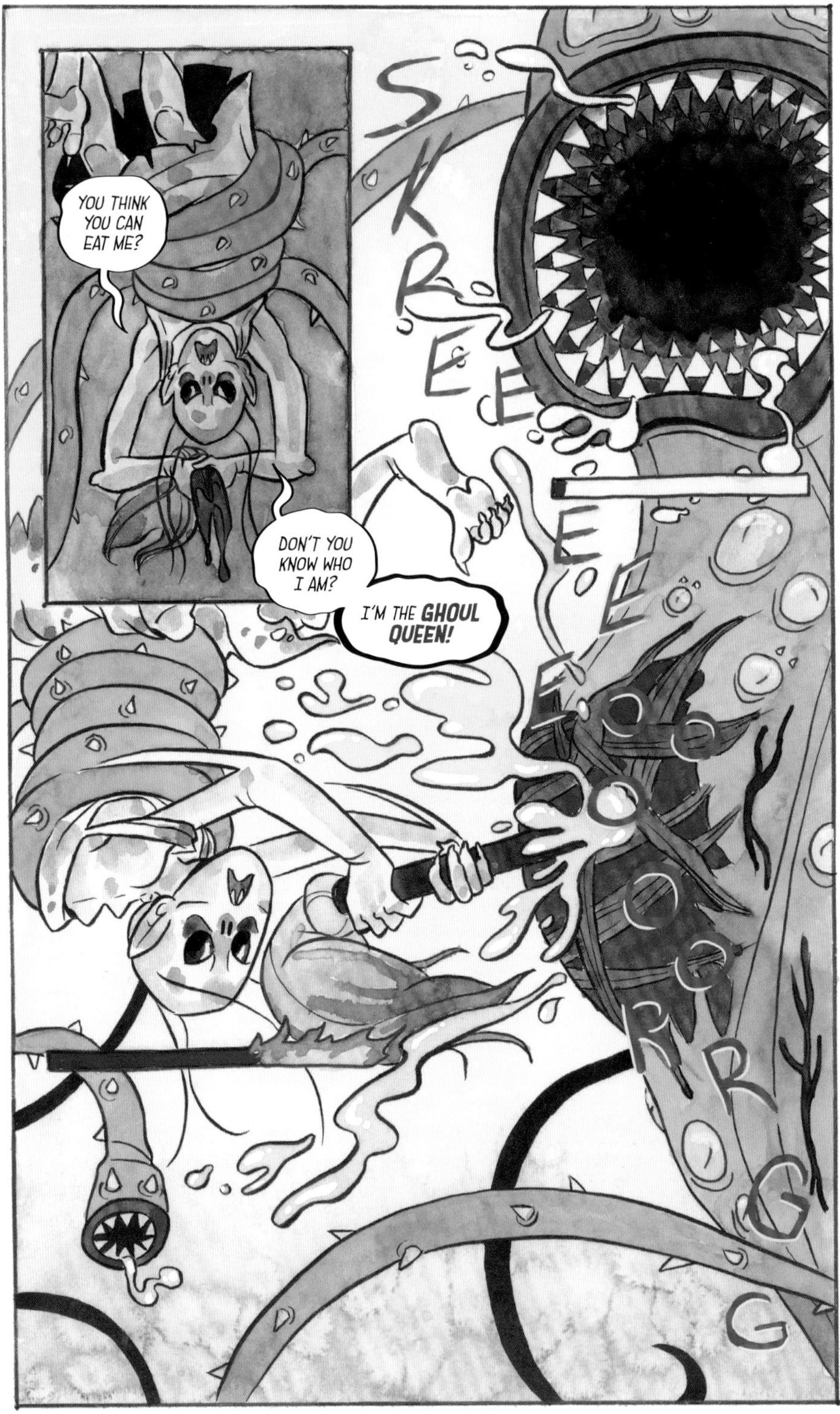
YOU THINK YOU CAN EAT ME?
SKREEEEE
DON'T YOU KNOW WHO I AM?
I'M THE **GHOUL QUEEN!**
OOOOOORRGG

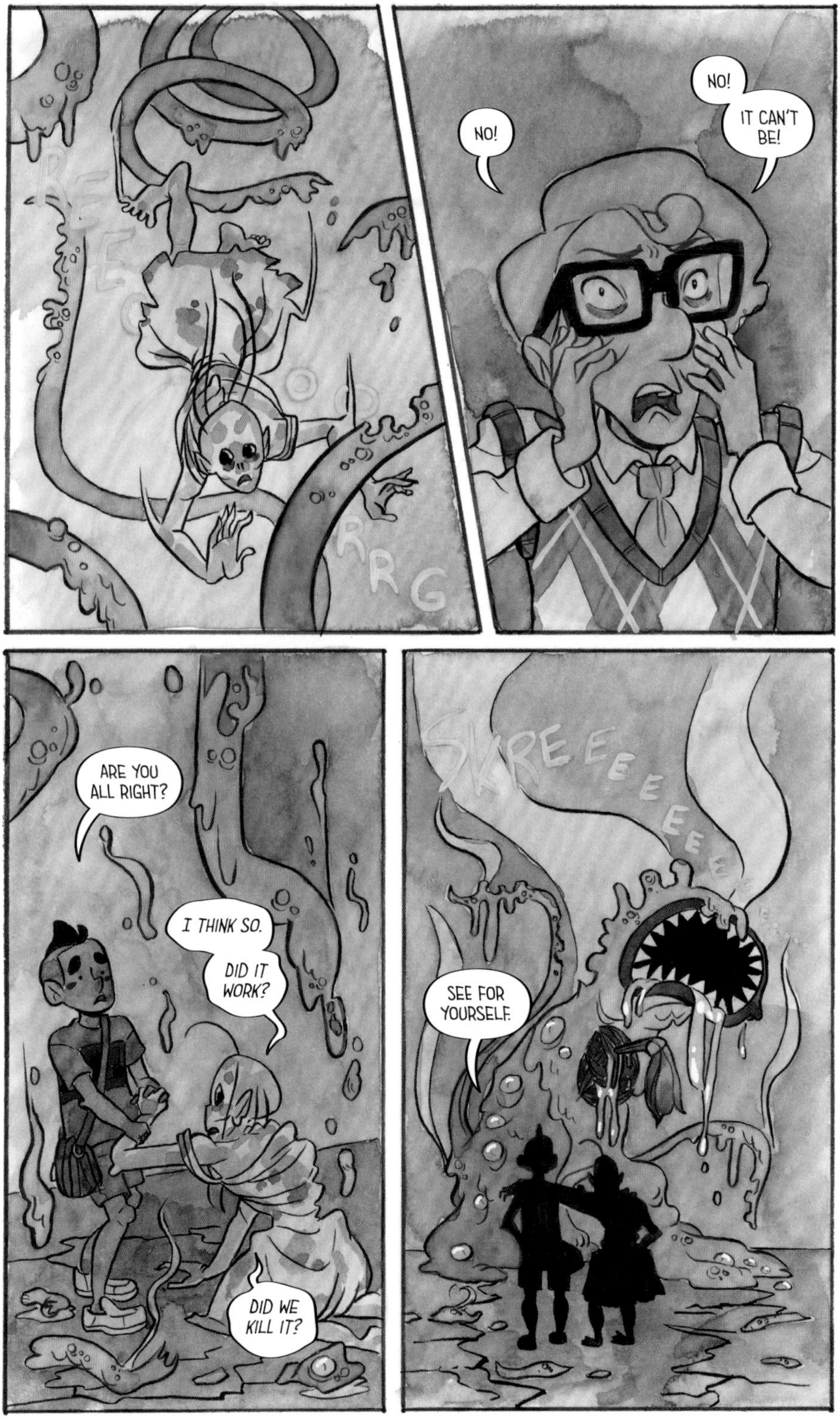
REEEOOO
RRG
NO!
NO!
IT CAN'T BE!
ARE YOU ALL RIGHT?
I THINK SO.
DID IT WORK?
DID WE KILL IT?
SKREEEEEEEE...
SEE FOR YOURSELF.

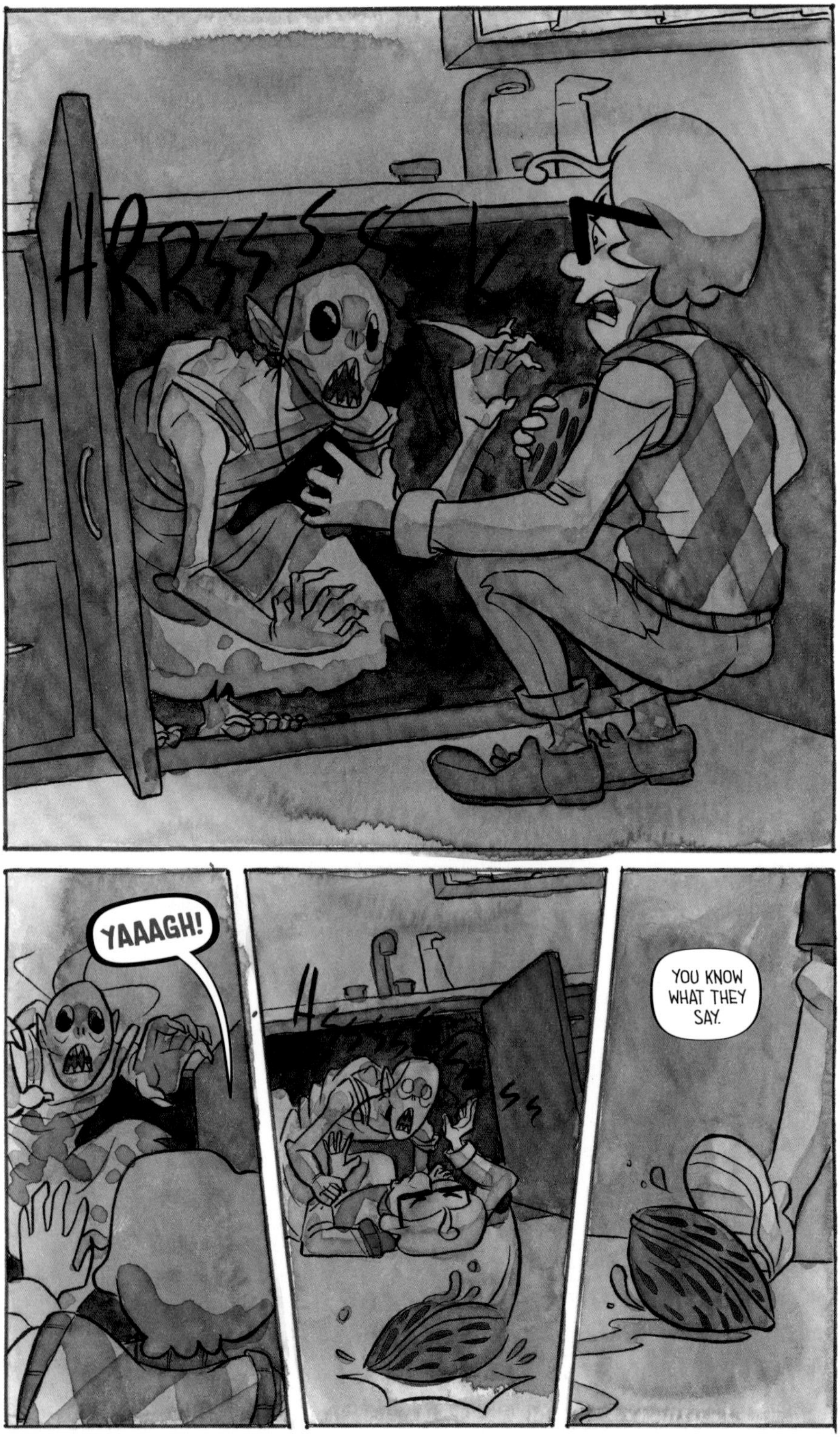
YAAAGH!
YOU KNOW WHAT THEY SAY.

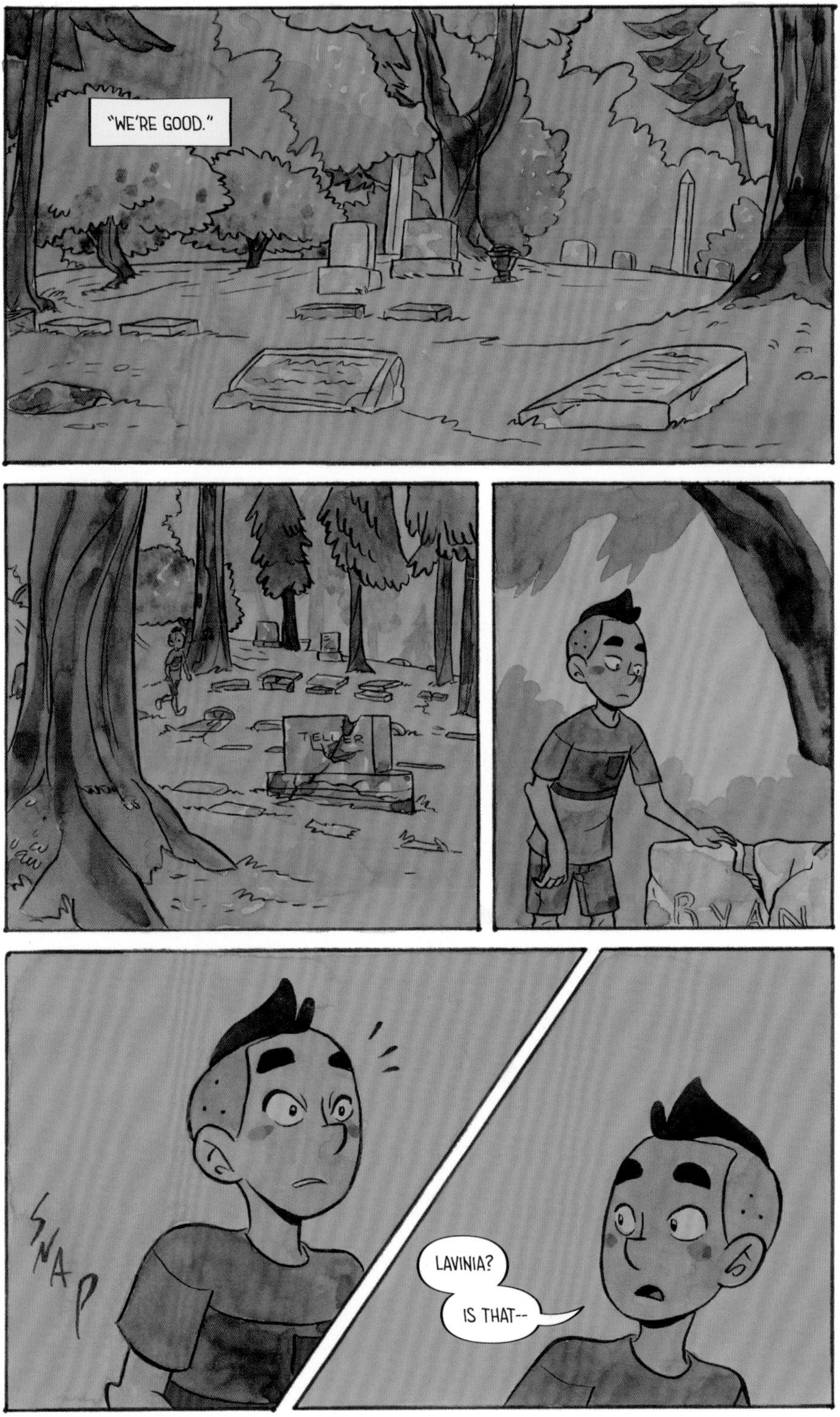
"WE'RE GOOD."
TELLER
RYAN
SNAP
LAVINIA?
IS THAT--

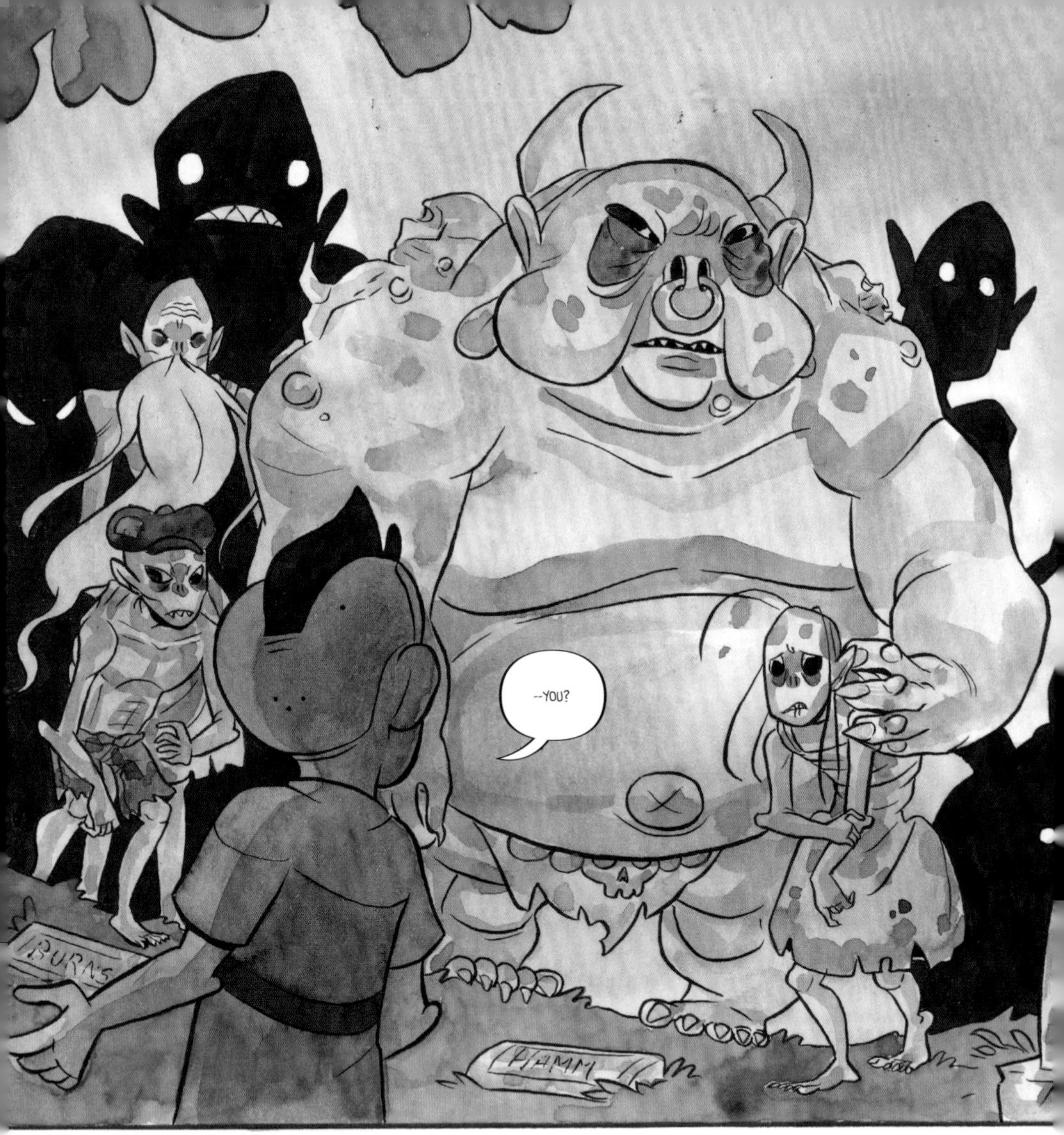
BURNS
--YOU?
HAMM

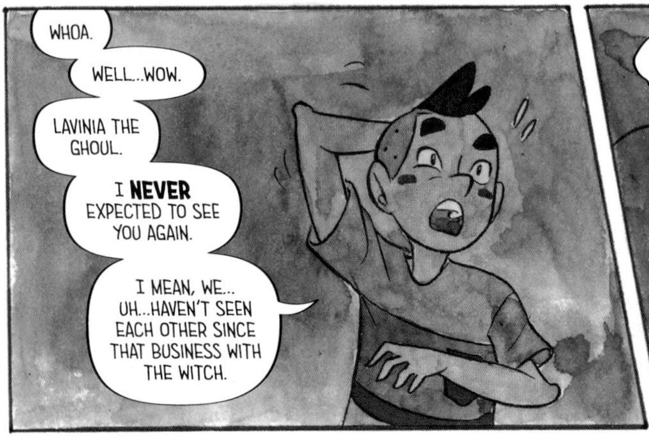
WHOA.
WELL...WOW.
LAVINIA THE GHOUL.
I **NEVER** EXPECTED TO SEE YOU AGAIN.
I MEAN, WE... UH...HAVEN'T SEEN EACH OTHER SINCE THAT BUSINESS WITH THE WITCH.

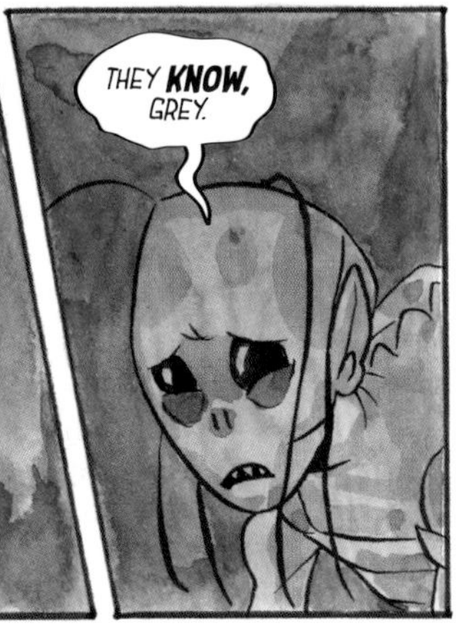
THEY **KNOW,** GREY.

ACKNOWLEDGMENTS

As always, I want to thank Cat Farris and Melanie Ujimori for all the amazing work on this book, Clarissa Wong for editing this monster and Megan Ilnitzki for shepherding it to publication, Rick Farley for the incredible design work, and Charlie Olsen for helping to make it happen. My wife, Cindy, and son, Jackson, need some thanks, too, because without their support I couldn't do this kind of work. Heck! Without their support, the work wouldn't matter in the first place. And I wanted to give a special shout-out to the Dangerous Dilettantes (you know who you are) for always having my back.

—Cullen Bunn

A huge thank-you to Melanie Ujimori. Without your lettering, this comic wouldn't be readable! Thank you to former editor, Clarissa Wong, and to new editor, Megan Ilnitzki, for shepherding this book across the finish line. Thanks once again to Cullen for always writing me fun things to draw and giving me a few puzzles to solve along the way. Thank you especially to Sally, who was a good dog and kept me company (and sane) through this entire process, and my husband, Ron Chan, for believing in me when I couldn't believe in myself.

—Cat Farris